Withdrawn

Sweet dreams aren't made of this . . .

Vivian was going to have to sleep soon, and she knew it, but she feared her dreams and where they might take her. Forty-eight hours and counting since she'd last slept. Deprivation hallucinations could be right at hand, or maybe they'd already happened and none of what she remembered from last night was real. The other alternative, the one that said schizophrenia was hereditary and maybe this was a psychotic break— that was a thought she refused to entertain.

BETWEEN

Kerry Schafer

ACE BOOKS, NEW YORK

THE BERKLEY PUBLISHING GROUP
Published by the Penguin Group
Penguin Group (USA) Inc.
375 Hudson Street, New York, New York 10014, USA

Penguin Group (Canada), 90 Eglinton Avenue East, Suite 700, Toronto, Ontario M4P 2Y3, Canada
(a division of Pearson Penguin Canada Inc.) • Penguin Books Ltd., 80 Strand, London WC2R 0RL,
England • Penguin Ireland, 25 St. Stephen's Green, Dublin 2, Ireland (a division of Penguin
Books Ltd.) • Penguin Group (Australia), 707 Collins Street, Melbourne, Victoria 3008, Australia
(a division of Pearson Australia Group Pty. Ltd.) • Penguin Books India Pvt. Ltd., 11 Community
Centre, Panchsheel Park, New Delhi—110 017, India • Penguin Group (NZ), 67 Apollo Drive,
Rosedale, Auckland 0632, New Zealand (a division of Pearson New Zealand Ltd.) • Penguin Books
(South Africa), Rosebank Office Park, 181 Jan Smuts Avenue, Parktown North 2193, South Africa •
Penguin China, B7 Jiaming Center, 27 East Third Ring Road North,
Chaoyang District, Beijing 100020, China

Penguin Books Ltd., Registered Offices: 80 Strand, London WC2R 0RL, England

This is a work of fiction. Names, characters, places, and incidents either are the product of the author's
imagination or are used fictitiously, and any resemblance to actual persons, living or dead, business
establishments, events, or locales is entirely coincidental. The publisher does not have any control over
and does not assume any responsibility for author or third-party websites or their content.

BETWEEN

An Ace Book / published by arrangement with the author

PUBLISHING HISTORY
Ace mass-market edition / February 2013

Copyright © 2013 by Kerry Schafer.
Cover art by Larry Rostant.
Cover design by Judith Lagerman.
Interior text design by Tiffany Estreicher.

ISBN: 978-0-425-26114-9

ACE
Ace Books are published by The Berkley Publishing Group,
a division of Penguin Group (USA) Inc.,
375 Hudson Street, New York, New York 10014.
ACE and the "A" design are trademarks of Penguin Group (USA) Inc.

PRINTED IN THE UNITED STATES OF AMERICA

10 9 8 7 6 5 4 3 2 1

ALWAYS LEARNING   **PEARSON**

To David, for all the reasons

ACKNOWLEDGMENTS

I owe so much to my mother, who taught me to read and imparted her love of books; to my wonderful and creative sons for tolerating my writing habit; and especially to David, who always believed I would finally succeed and had no patience with my doubts.

Jamie and Wes—thanks for inspiring this story before moving on to explore the next great reality. I hope you've found cheesy guitars and fast cars and an abundance of beverages with the word *Glen* in their names.

Deep and abiding thanks to all of the people who have read for me, especially: Trudy, who was my first reader ever; Tasha, who read literally every single draft with unquenchable enthusiasm; Adrien, who had the guts to point out the fatal flaw and helped me see the book as it needed to be (I'm sorry for the names I called you); Julie, who not only read but induced her agent to read; and Jeffe, who inspired me to do one more revision. Also, I want to thank Jo Taylor, who read the medical bits and provided her expertise.

Thank you to the wonderful folks at Book Country, in particular Danielle Poiesz and Colleen Lindsay, for their part in creating the supportive environment at Book Country and providing the opportunity for me to post my work.

And to my publishing team—editor Susan Allison for loving the book enough to sign me, editor Danielle Stockley for her wonderful vision and keen eye, and last, but certainly not least, Deidre Knight, the best agent a writer could ever dream of—from the bottom of my heart, I thank you.

Prologue

❖

Later she will remember him so: impatient with the waiting, restless feet carrying him back and forth in the grassy space in front of the fountain. She will remember the murmur and splash of falling water, the fragrance of roses, her own heart fluttering against the wall of her chest.

If only there were time, more time, enough time, she could spend an hour loving him from this distance: his chestnut hair silvered by moonlight, the lithe flow of muscle across his shoulders, the easy, swinging step. But time is something she has little of and so she steps out into the open and he turns to her in midstride, although she has made no sound, done nothing to betray her presence.

"Isobel." Only the one word, but his heart's blood is in it, and she sees by his face that he knows what she has come to say.

"When?" he asks, and she answers him, "Tonight; soon."

She crosses the dew-damp grass and they stand, not quite touching, feeling in that space between them the form and shape of a long good-bye.

"Must you go?"

Later, she will remember her own laughter, cool as the water, falling, always falling. So young, she was, her head full of widening horizons. "Silly boy, it's not forever. My father has come, as I told you. I am to become a Dream-shifter, as he is. I've so many things to learn."

All of the blue gone from his eyes, behind them the water falling, always falling like rain or tears. "I have a gift for you," he murmurs against her hair. "Come and sit."

She lets him seat her on the stone bench beside the fountain, where the breeze blows a spray of mist onto her face and hair. He drops to his knees before her and pulls a velvet box out of his pocket. Inside nestle two circles of gold. He lifts the smaller and she sees three drops of crimson set into the band.

"My heart's blood," he says, in a voice scraped raw with loss and hope. "If you wear it, it will bring you back to me."

"And the other?" she whispers, no longer laughing as the ring encircles her finger.

"Blood calls to blood." He holds out his hand and she slips the ring onto his finger.

"One thing more," she whispers, "just to be sure." She holds out to him a crystal sphere, a precious thing, and rare. Even in the moonlight it shines, and she knows if she looks into it she will see a miniature of this place: a tiny fountain, a space of grass, the bench where she is sitting. "Keep it safe," she says, curling his fingers around it.

"A dreamsphere," he says, eyes wide with wonder. "I've never seen one. Is it permitted? Where did you get it?"

"I was summoned, last night, to the Cave of Dreams, and given this. Our secret, yours and mine. Nobody else need ever know."

This she believes, as she kisses him good-bye, for she is very young and knows so little of what lies in the worlds beyond.

This, too, she will remember with regret.

One

✣

Quiet.

The curse word of the emergency room, and Vivian had been careful not to say it aloud. Still, it wandered through her head and lodged there.

Too quiet. The waiting room was empty, as were all seven treatment bays at Krebston Memorial Hospital. Staff puttered in silence, cleaning and restocking with the watchful air of coast dwellers preparing for hurricane season.

Knowing the inevitable storm could manifest in any number of forms, Vivian took the opportunity to slip into the staff lounge and dial a number on her cell. Eight rings before a drowsy voice answered.

"How is she?"

"She, who? Who is this?"

"Sorry—this is Vivian Maylor."

Silence.

"Checking in on Isobel."

"Your mother is sleeping."

Vivian suspected the speaker had also been sleeping. *At River Valley Family Home we care for your loved ones every hour of every day,* the brochure claimed. Comforting to families, but much more likely that the night worker was settled into a reclining chair with a blanket and a pillow, just resting her eyes.

"Are you sure?"

"Dr. Maylor." Thinly veiled annoyance now. "It's one-oh-five A.M. She was in bed and asleep by eleven."

"Humor me. Check on her. Please."

A heavy sigh. The sound of breathing and feet tapping on tile.

Vivian fidgeted, sank into a chair, and drummed her fingers on the table. Sticky. She withdrew her hand and wiped it on a napkin from the ragged pile next to the box of stale Walmart doughnuts.

"I'm standing in the bedroom doorway. Your mother is in bed. Snoring. Is there anything else I can do for you?"

The words offered no relief for the unease itching beneath the surface of Vivian's skin. So many years of watching out for Isobel, so many near disasters. It was hard to delegate all that to a casual stranger. "She took all of her meds?"

"Yes."

"Are you sure? She sometimes cheeks them. Or stockpiles them in her drawer for—"

"Dr. Maylor—we are taking good care of her. Isobel is fine."

"She's breathing, right? Is—"

Click.

Roxie stuck her head through the door before Vivian could succumb to the temptation to call back. "Hey, Doc—burned teenager in five—walked in, no parental units in sight. Weird one—definite screws loose. All vitals copacetic except he's running a temp—one-oh-two."

Vivian sighed and pocketed her cell. Roxie cocked her head on one side, sharp nose twitching like an inquisitive rodent. "You look wasted. Big party on your night off?"

"Funny. My life is a little tamer than yours."

"So, what then?"

"Not sleeping." Understatement of the year. Over the last few weeks her dreams, always vivid, had taken on a new intensity that carried her into waking with a pervading sense that she had traveled endless miles through a twisting maze where dragons lurked, an armed warrior at her side. Today she'd wakened aching with exhaustion and found a blister on her heel that had no rational explanation. If this trend continued she'd be joining her mother at River Valley Family Home.

"Vivian?"

"Sorry." She sagged in exaggerated weariness and held up her hands. "Too tired to move. Help me up."

"Buck up, Doc, we've got miles to go."

"Don't I know it."

The little nurse gripped her wrists and heaved her to her feet. "Go see crazy boy in five and then you can sneak a nap."

Vivian followed Roxie out of the lounge, the door falling shut behind her with a small thud. Max, all three hundred tattooed pounds of him, sat at the desk paging through an edition of what looked like *Oprah* magazine. Shelly, the tech, intent on texting, didn't bother to look up.

Everything was clean, quiet. Again, Vivian winced as that word passed through her brain, and involuntarily she reached up and touched the pendant she wore beneath her clothing, a dream catcher with a rough stone carving of a penguin woven into its center.

Her sneakers made sucking noises on the linoleum, all the way down the hall to bay five—*squeak, squeak*. She definitely needed to rethink her footwear. Outside the drawn curtain she paused, a cold finger of apprehension running the length of her spine. Dizziness rocked her as reality collided with dream. She stood still, listening to the rapid thudding of her own heart, until she was able to pull herself together, knock, and enter.

Arden Douglas, sixteen, location of parents unknown, resident of the small town of Krebston. Also a nameless player in one of Vivian's dreams. This much she remembered, along with a general sense of cold dread. But the details floated around the edge of her brain, elusive as mist when she tried to capture them.

He lay unmoving on the exam table, shirtless and barefoot, his faded jeans torn and grass stained at both knees. Chest, right arm, and face were reddened, as if from a long day at the beach, and beginning to blister. A blood pressure cuff on his left arm automatically tightened and released, one hundred over sixty. A little low, nothing to worry about. Pulse at one hundred. O_2 sats good at ninety-eight percent.

But something was off; there was a subtle wrongness in the air that set her skin to crawling.

"What happened?" She gloved and masked, then squeaked over to examine the damage. First-degree burn; a couple of areas maybe second. It was going to hurt like hell but should heal up okay. No scars for the kid to worry about.

He spoke through a jaw clenched around pain. "I already told the nurse. She thinks I'm fucking crazy."

"So tell me again."

Tell me you got too close to a fire—a campfire, a grease fire, a blowtorch. Got dunked in a cauldron of boiling water. Something explainable. Not—

"Dragon."

She shivered, but kept her tone light. "A dragon? In Krebston? Now there's one I haven't heard. Open your mouth. Say ah."

His brown eyes were opaque, almost black, the pupils dilated with pain and fear.

"Ahhhh. Like I said. Nobody believes me."

Airway clear, no signs of inflammation or swelling.

"Okay. So you saw a dragon—"

"I'm telling you, it was a dragon. Breathing fire." He sat up and swung his legs over the edge of the gurney. "You know, fuck this shit. I'm leaving. You all think I'm crazy—"

Vivian put a gloved hand on his shoulder, gently pressed him back. "Look, I'm sorry. It's not a tale you hear every day. Lie down, and tell me. Please."

He hesitated, his breathing a little too rapid and shallow. A burn could do that, but she'd seen that look on other faces;

it was the look of a survivor waking up to the reality that he was still alive, that someone else had not been so lucky. Her guess was that Arden hadn't been alone, but there was time yet to ask that question.

"You hurt anywhere else?"

"Shoulder. Thing spiked me." He indicated a smear of blood in the flesh just below his right clavicle.

"Lie back, let me look."

With a sigh, he complied. She wiped the blood away with a piece of gauze, revealing a puncture wound the diameter of a large nail. "When was your last tetanus shot?"

"I don't remember. Man—we knew better than to go down to the Finger. Stupid—"

"We, who?"

He didn't answer. He had begun to shiver. Sweat slicked his face; his breath rasped in his throat. The oximeter alarm went off—his oxygen level had dropped to eighty-five.

When Vivian put her hand to his forehead, his skin burned through the glove. She frowned. Felt a damned bit hotter than 102.

She turned on the oxygen with one hand, pushed the call button with the other. Roxie popped in. "Get an IV started, stat. And check his temp again, would you? He's burning up."

"Got it." Roxie skittered off to follow orders, but before she hit the door Arden gasped, one long indrawing of breath. His eyes rolled back in his head, his spine arched like a bow, and he began to convulse in great wrenching spasms that threatened to throw him off the table. Vivian flung her body over him, anchoring him. Heat flowed into her, uncomfortable even through several layers of clothing.

Roxie yanked the cord from the wall and the emergency alarm went off.

Max appeared in the doorway, took one look, and headed for the crash cart.

As suddenly as it began, the seizure stopped. Arden lay twisted, knees drawn up a little and to the side, head corkscrewed at an odd angle, eyes wide open and staring. His mouth gaped, a string of bloody drool festooned over his lip and down his chin.

The oximeter alarm continued to bleat. He wasn't breathing—no rise and fall of the chest, no air on her cheek when Vivian put her face close to his. She checked the carotid—no pulse.

Shelly stood in the doorway, mouth fallen slightly open, eyes wide.

"Code," Vivian said through clenched teeth. Shelly ran.

Vivian began chest compressions, aware through her peripheral vision of Max pulling out equipment and Roxie prepping an IV. A disembodied voice floated out of the loud-speaker: "Code blue, ER. Code blue, to the emergency room."

Max slapped pads on the boy's bare chest and hooked up the EKG. Vivian stopped compressions and they all stared at the monitor, waiting for some kind of a rhythm.

Flatline.

"Damn it," Vivian ground out. She'd been hoping for something that could be shocked, a convertible rhythm. Asystole was ominous. She resumed compressions, the heat radiating through her hands and body. Sweat trickled down between her shoulder blades, itching.

"Get some fluids in him."

"I can't find a decent vein," Roxie said. "Going for an IO line."

The respiratory tech arrived and stepped up beside Vivian, breathing hard. She knew him slightly, a stocky Hispanic guy named Tony. Quiet, competent.

"I'll tube him."

Vivian nodded consent, keeping up the chest compressions while Tony inserted an airway. Shaking the sweat out of her eyes, she saw Roxie cut off the blue jeans and toss them aside, then deftly insert an IO line into the right tibia. "Got it," she said, hooking up a bag.

"Tube in," Tony said. Vivian paused compressions while he checked placement. Her hands smarted and stung; she turned her palms up to see that the latex had melted away over her palms, which were an angry red. *This can't be happening, it's not possible . . .*

"Epinephrine, one milligram," Max said, injecting it into the IO line.

A lab tech trotted in with a tray of supplies.

"You'll have to draw from the line," Vivian said.

She stepped away to grab a new pair of gloves while Tony hooked up the ambu bag and began squeezing air into the lungs. He frowned. "Too much resistance; something's not right."

"Are you sure the tube is in the right place?"

"Positive."

"Keep going."

Alarms continued to blare. Max checked the leads. Still flatline.

Vivian positioned her hands to resume compressions and hesitated. During the time taken to pull on new gloves, the skin on the kid's chest had turned brown. As she stared, it cracked in a dozen places and began to ooze a pinkish fluid.

Roxie wrinkled her nose. "What is that smell?"

Hamburger. The skin on his cheeks looked like his chest—for all the world like well barbecued chicken, crispy skin and all.

Vivian began compressions again, but the skin and flesh slid away beneath her hands, revealing the ivory curve of ribs.

Max stepped back, making the sign of the cross. "We've lost him, Viv. You need to stop."

Brown eyes stared sightless up at the ceiling out of a face stiff and masklike. The flesh had sloughed off his ribs and his right arm. Bare feet splayed to the sides.

All eyes in the room were fixed on her, with the exception of the one pair that would never see anything ever again.

Vivian stopped. She drew an arm across her forehead to wipe away the sweat. "Fuck. Time of death—one forty-five A.M."

She swallowed, hard. Twenty minutes ago the boy had been moving, speaking, fully conscious. Now his body looked like something out of a horror show. Behind the fragile barrier in her brain, Dreamworld surged. As always, she fought it with logic.

"What the hell happened? Ideas?"

"Spontaneous combustion."

"Be serious, Rox—"

"I am serious. What if he goes up in flames or something? Tony, you should turn the oxygen off."

Tony snorted but complied.

"There has to be a scientific explanation."

"Up to the M.E. now. Weirdest damned thing I've ever seen." Max drew a sheet up over the wreck of flesh and bone that had been a sixteen-year-old boy.

"We've got this, Viv," Roxie said. "Go do your report or whatever."

"It was a good code," Max said.

Vivian nodded, not trusting her voice. She shed her gown and gloves and exited the scene of carnage. Once in motion, her body wanted to keep moving. Down the hall, out the door, into the clear sweet Krebston air.

But she was still on duty, and Deputy Flynne stood propped against the nurse's desk. He was not smiling.

"Not a social call, I gather." She lifted her hair from the back of her neck to feel the cool air, took a deep breath. Waited.

"Something ugly went down at Finger Beach. Heard you had a burned kid up here."

She just looked at him.

"Small town. News travels quick."

"He's dead, Brett."

He ran one hand over his buzz-cut hair. "Shit. What happened?"

"He—burned. From the inside out. Came in walking and talking and then, just—" She choked on the words. *Come on, Vivian. It's not the first patient you've lost.* "Your turn."

"Someone reported seeing a fire down there. Kids drinking, we figured. Me and Brody swung by, just to check it out. Found a body, charred down to the bones."

"God." Vivian closed her eyes.

A shimmer in the air, nothing you'd notice while distracted by a campfire and a pretty girl. A creature, squeezing, unfolding through an invisible doorway . . .

Her hand reached for the pendant. "Campfire got out of control? Accelerant, maybe?"

Flynne shook his head. "Don't think so. Well away from the fire. Also found a pelvis and a pair of legs. Female, we think. The rest was—missing."

Vivian pressed the back of her hand against her mouth, her heart beating against her ribs with such force that surely he could see it, could hear it . . .

"No ID on the ah, body. Nothing survived whatever burned the other one. It'll be a while before we know anything."

Arden, laughter on a face bright with life and adventure, his arm around a plump brunette . . .

"Dr. Maylor!"

"Sorry. I was just—processing."

"If you've got an ID, anything, on this kid, it might help."

"Arden Douglas."

Brett's face creased. "Knew him. Good kid. Any idea what killed him?"

"Honestly, no. Autopsy magic all happens in Spokane."

"Right. At the speed of a handicapped turtle. Wish we could block that damned beach off for good and all."

In the small town of Krebston, population around five thousand, give or take a birth or a death, the Finger was a legend. Strange things happened on that beach, so rumor said. A giant red stone dominated the spot, thrusting up out of the sand like a warning finger. Teenage boys called it other, more vulgar names, and if they were bold or stupid or very drunk they covered it with graffiti. Or claimed they did. The stone was always smooth and unmarred by light of day.

Sensible people avoided the place or ventured to the beach only at high noon in large, noisy groups, equipped with plenty of beer. Tourists cruised by, craning their necks to look. Sometimes they parked and ventured out of their cars to snap photos, but they never stayed long. Some said the pictures they took never came out.

Local legend had it that years ago a group of boys, led by a rebel who proclaimed to fear nothing and nobody, built a fire pit and lingered long past sunset. They straggled home just before dawn, blistered and footsore, scratched by thorns and snowberry bushes. Not one of them would say what happened. They slept for days, waking at night from nightmares that made them cry out in their sleep. The ringleader stayed missing for a week. When he reappeared he was changed: thin, silent, staring for hours at a corner or a ceiling where there was nothing other eyes could see. Those who told the story said he'd been sent to an asylum in the end.

"Dr. Maylor?"

Catching the look in the deputy's eyes, she pulled herself together. "So what now?"

"We investigate." He offered her a mock salute and walked away. She watched him go, down the wide, brightly lit hallway, and overlaid like a double exposure saw a corridor running as far as the eye could see. On either side, doors, green doors with brass handles. All of them locked. And unseen but always prowling, always searching, the dragons.

Two

✣

V ivian was going to have to sleep soon, and she knew
it, but she feared her dreams and where they might take
her. Forty-eight hours and counting since she'd last slept.
Deprivation hallucinations could be right at hand, or maybe
they'd already happened and none of what she remembered
from last night was real. The other alternative, the one that
said schizophrenia was hereditary and maybe this was a psychotic break—that was a thought she refused to entertain.

Her body felt heavy, every movement an effort, like walking through knee-deep snow. The muscles in her shoulders
and back ached from the physical exertion of chest compressions and CPR. Her eyes gritted and burned, blurring the
world around her. But her brain refused to stop, running
over the same problem like a frenzied hamster in a wheel.

Dragons. Mythological beasts, no matter what she might
dream about them. It was impossible for a creature to follow
her out of her dreams and into reality. Equally impossible that
a sixteen-year-old boy could incinerate from the inside out
while she stood by and watched it happen.

Again her hand went to the pendant, her talisman. Still there.
Superstitious, yes—but it was always missing in her dreams,

and there when she awoke. It reassured her that she could always tell the difference. Science, her goddess of choice, had failed her. The pendant? Never yet.

Pushing away dream fragments and the memories of last night, she forced herself to focus on tasks at hand. Watering plants. Straightening, sweeping, dusting. All dishes washed and put away, the stainless sink shined. Order and structure to keep chaos at bay.

It was a small apartment, kitchen and living area in one room, with doors leading off to the bathroom and bedroom. The furniture was all secondhand store specials, although she'd only bought things that appealed to her and so the mismatched array had a comfortable, cozy aspect that she was coming to love. A battered old sofa, sage green and heavy but soft and comfy and perfect for lying back with her feet up to read. An antique coffee table, scuffed and chipped, with lines that she liked. Kitchen table and chairs, also solid wood, scarred with years of use.

On one wall hung her framed poster print of Escher's *Hand with Reflecting Sphere*, the only artwork she possessed. As a child she had spent hours getting lost in the curves and strange realities of that drawing, and still it hung as a reminder to her of the fragile nature of reality, the need to guard carefully the borders of what Isobel had taught her as a child to call Wakeworld.

In front of the one window and above the front door hung dream catchers, gifts Isobel had given her. "Always guard against the Dreamworld, darling," her mother had whispered. "You never know what might come through."

All these years later the dream catchers went everywhere Vivian went, the only gift her mother had ever given her.

Memories were nearly as dangerous as dreams, and she pushed them away. If she wasn't going to be sleeping, she needed to be doing. There were a couple of boxes still to unpack, and she moved on to that task. One was a box of books, all of her old favorites. She had an e-reader now and little room for a library, but there were some books she couldn't part with. The dog-eared covers reminded her of long blissful hours curled up in various corners of her life, traveling with beloved characters to far distant worlds. Most were fantasies—Tolkien, C. S. Lewis, Kay, Davidson. A few were remnants of her childhood—*Little Women*, *National Velvet*, *Anne of Green Gables*. So many more that she'd had to give away, each with a wrenching sense of loss.

Someday she would own a big house with all of the bookcases she needed. In the meantime, she had only one, doubling as storage for paper goods and a landing point for her landline phone. As she lined the books up on the shelf, she realized that the answering machine was blinking. For a minute she stood staring at it, blankly. Almost all calls went to her cell. When her finger pushed play, she half-expected a sales pitch and a pre-recorded message. Instead, Jared's voice came on, smooth as silk, but with an undertone of little-boy-lost that tugged at her heart.

"Vivian—please. I miss you. Let me talk to you—you owe me that much. Tomorrow, all right? I'll drive up. We can have lunch. I have something for you."

In the silence after his voice clicked off she stood, feeling alone and small and suddenly unsure. It had made sense to end things with him, to take the job up here in this little town away from his offers of financial help and support. Away from Isobel.

All her life Vivian had been responsible for somebody else—her mother first, followed by a string of loser boyfriends and then finally Jared.

Jared was not a loser. In fact, if there was a definition of driven overachiever, he was it. At twenty-seven he had passed his bar exam and been recruited by an old-money law firm in his hometown of Spokane. "It's a place to start," he'd told her, eyes glowing with the thrill of the hunt. "You wait—I'll get a job in L.A. or New York. Give me five years. We'll be rich, Viv. You won't have to work and you can shop at all of the best stores and dress to the nines . . ."

But she wanted to work. And she was quite comfortable in blue jeans and tennis shoes and abhorred the parties he dragged her to. On the other hand, nobody had ever tried to take care of her before, and it had felt safe and comforting to have someone else concerned about her well-being.

She was too tired to think about this. Too tired to think about anything, but the message had buzzed her body with adrenaline and pushed the possibility of sleep even further away. Without an awareness of ever making the decision, she slipped into her shoes and a sweater. There was a single bookstore in Krebston. She'd been planning to check it out, and now seemed as good a time as any. It would be good to buy a new book, something solid and real that she could hold in her hands and put on the shelf when she was through. Maybe a walk would put her thoughts in order and bring her to the place where she could sleep.

The sign on the door said *A to Zee Books*. In the glass a dual image: a reflection of Vivian's own windblown self, and the inside of the store where a man sat on a stool behind the cash register. His head was bent over a book open on the counter, a fall of dark hair screening his face. All around him, books, stacked on the counter, in boxes on the floor, shelved in neat and orderly rows, spilling into towering stacks where there was no more room.

Something about the man's hand, poised to turn the page, struck her as familiar. Standing on the other side of the glass, Vivian had a sense of déjà vu but could come to no true memory. The sensation unnerved her, and she might have bolted if he hadn't looked up then. His eyes widened. His hand froze in the act of turning the page. She stared back through layers of reflection and unreality, as though both of them were caught out of time.

A slow smile spread over his face, crooked, forming a dimple in his right cheek. He slid off his stool and moved toward her.

Vivian opened the door. A gust of wind pushed her through and into the store, dry leaves scuttling around her feet.

"North wind," the man said. "Trying to make itself at home."

"The sun looked warm."

"It's October. In Krebston. You look half frozen."

"I walked fast. It's not that cold." But she shivered as she spoke, wrapping her arms around herself for warmth.

"Sit for a minute; I'll bring you a coffee." He nodded toward the back corner of the store, where deep armchairs squared a low table holding a chess board. "It's warmer back there."

She hesitated, and again he flashed her a crooked grin that decided everything.

Breathing in the smell of books, Vivian walked past the loaded shelves and sank into one of the chairs, noticing for the first time an array of wind chimes and hanging sculptures suspended from the ceiling. They were made of wood and glass, ceramic and bone, an endless variety of weird and wonderful. Some were beautiful, others strange, and a few dark and almost forbidding. Above her head a flight of dragons soared, outspread wings in jeweled colors, each one set with a prism that caught the light and broke it up into rainbows. On the walls, hung above the book shelves, were paintings that rivaled her Escher in strangeness.

The man reappeared with two ceramic mugs. He set one down on the table and handed her the other. His hand brushed hers, the touch sending a flood of warmth up her arm, and she found herself gazing directly into his eyes. They were dangerous eyes, translucent amber agate, light filled. Grateful for an excuse to look away, Vivian bent her head over the steaming cup of coffee, no sugar, and with the perfect amount of cream.

"I'm Zee," he said, folding his long body into the chair across from her and picking up his own mug. "Haven't seen you in before—are you from around here?"

Again his hands caught at a forgotten memory, like an elusive word on the tip of the tongue. Big hands, built for strength, but they held the mug with a surprising delicacy.

His voice, strange and familiar all at once, pulled her back to the moment, and she risked a glance at his face. Those eyes were watching her with an intensity that made her cheeks flame. She took a long swallow of scalding coffee and promptly choked, coughing and spilling a wave of coffee over her hand and into her lap.

He took the cup from her and set it down, waiting without comment until the paroxysm eased and then handing her a stack of napkins. Having something to do, a real embarrassment to deal with, eased her nerves a little and gave her time to lecture herself into a state of semicalm.

Neither of them spoke.

Somewhere a clock ticked off seconds in the silent room. No other sound but Vivian's breathing, and Zee's.

"That's a fascinating pendant," he said at last. "I've never seen anything quite like it. Do you mind if I have a closer look?"

Wordless, she held the pendant out and leaned toward him. Zee bent his head down to look. His breath was warm on her cheek. The scent of him—clean soap and wood, and a tang of turpentine—filled her nostrils.

She felt her breath quicken, hoped he couldn't hear the rapid beating of her heart.

"A penguin in a dream web," he said. "Where did you get it?"

"My grandfather gave it to me."

Vivian, her senses flooded with his nearness, with the memory of dream, found herself blurting out whatever came first to her less-than-functional brain. "He said it was my totem animal."

"You don't sound exactly happy about that."

"A totem indicating OCD and conformity? Possibly accurate, but not how I'd like to think of myself."

"A penguin doesn't have to mean conformity."

"The only other thing to think is cute and cuddly. Also not traits I aspire to."

"Penguins are actually rather fierce. And then there's the way they fly in water. Unique. I've also heard of a penguin or two that swam north while all the rest were heading south. Kinda blows the whole conform-and-follow-the-leader image."

"You're scrambling," Vivian said, laughing a little. It felt good, small and dry as the laugh was, and a little of the tension drained out of her.

"I'm not. Here, just a minute . . ." He got up and wandered around the shelves, then came back with a small book, old, the cover water stained, the pages dog-eared. *Spirit Guides and Totems.* He flipped through the pages. "All right. Listen."

PENGUIN TOTEM—THE SIGN OF THE DREAMER AND THE MYSTIC

If the penguin is your totem, you are most likely a vivid dreamer and may receive messages while in the dream state. The penguin can lead you from one reality to another, just as he is able to shift smoothly from the world of air to the world of water and back again. Water symbolizes astral consciousness and is an important symbol of the dream dimension.

Silence. "Oh, come on. You can't really believe that stuff."

"Actually, I do." His eyes challenged her, and again she looked away, finding a new topic of conversation in the gallery lining the walls. Strange and surreal, those paintings. A flavor of Escher about them, and something else, an unsettling echo of something known but forgotten.

"Are the paintings yours?"

"How did you know?"

"You have paint on your cuticles and you smell a little like oil paint and cleaner. It's a good smell," she added quickly, lest he take offense, and then wished she hadn't. "Where did you get the ideas?"

"Dreams. Ever had the feeling that dreams might be real? Or that we might be dreaming when we think we're awake?"

This struck too close to home. "Dreams are chemical reactions in our brains. No more, no less."

"You don't believe that."

"It's what the textbooks say."

"And what do you say?"

Something about him challenged her for the truth. She hesitated, played with the coffee mug. "I—yes—maybe. But science says—"

"Once we all believed the world was flat. I've had dreams I certainly can't explain. Are you telling me you haven't?"

She flushed, and then admitted, "All right, yes. I've dreamed things before they happened. Dreamed people before I met them. And I've felt, sometimes, like what happens in a dream feels more real than what happens when I'm awake. But this makes no sense."

None of it made sense. Dragons. Agate-eyed warriors who turned out to be bookstore-owning painters.

"Science isn't right about everything," Zee went on. We want it to be—everything cut and dried and logical. But think about this—for the entire history of this planet, until the last few years, really—people have believed in dreams. Portents and omens and oracles. The aboriginal peoples and Dreamtime. Even in our culture, people buy dream catchers—"

"Those are decorative."

"Sure they are. And you really think that's the only reason? I think underneath all of our carefully acquired logic and rationality, we are afraid that dreams might cause us harm. We fear them. And so even symbolically we like to surround ourselves with things that keep them out."

He was speaking to the heart of her now, the dilemma that had been with her since childhood. Wakeworld and Dreamworld and Between—worlds her mother talked about incessantly as though they were real. Isobel was crazy, Vivian knew this now, but as a child she had believed and feared. The fear was still with her, bone deep, and at the depths of her psyche it lay side by side with a long-buried belief that dreams were indeed as real as waking, and maybe even more so.

"But they can't hurt us, the dreams. It all happens in our heads. I believe they affect us—how could they not? Such an emotional impact might change our decisions or our actions. But to reach out into the real world and touch us . . ."

Vivian shivered. A deep cold enveloped her. Her mouth had gone so dry that she could hardly swallow, and the room and the man across the table seemed suddenly far away, as though she were looking at them through the wrong end of a pair of binoculars.

"I've always remembered something my grandmother told me when I was a little kid. I'd had some nightmare or other, and I was sure the monster had followed me into waking and was hiding under my bed. No way I'd have ever told my parents I was scared of a dream, but Grandmother happened to be visiting. It was like she sensed it. She came into my room where I was hiding under the covers. She said . . ." He furrowed his brow, remembering. "She said, 'Don't be frightened, little one. The Dreamshifter guards the portals of the dreams. The monster can't get through, as long as he is watching.'"

"Dreamshifter." The word buzzed around in her head, meaningless but full of import.

Zee touched the back of her hand, his fingers warm against cold skin. "Are you okay? You look pale all of a sudden."

"Very tired," she managed. Her lips were numb. "I didn't sleep last night."

"Well, you should sleep. You want a ride home?"

She did. With dismay, she discovered that what she wanted was for him to drive her home, and then come into the apartment, make love to her, and hold her while she fell asleep. She shook her head, then levered herself to her feet. "I need the exercise."

Zee also got to his feet. Taller than she was by a good foot, an intoxicating mix of muscle and gentleness and quiet strength.

Breathing, that was important. That, and getting away, getting home, before she betrayed any more of herself to a man who was a total stranger, no matter how attractive or how often dreamed of.

"Let me lend you some books, before you go. I have some good ones on dreams."

"I thought this was a store. Where people buy things."

He laughed. "Well, it is that. But I have a collection of older books that nobody in Krebston is ever going to buy. There is one, at least, on lucid dreaming."

"I couldn't—"

"It will give me a reason to see you again. You know—you never even told me your name."

Her heart was racing beyond all reason; her knees were weak. She fought back a ridiculous urge to push a stray lock of hair back from his face, to run her hand along the strong line of his jaw, touch the hint of a cleft in his chin.

"I'm Vivian," she heard herself say. "And I'd love to see the books—"

A smile lit up his face, and there was that dimple again. "Maybe we can talk about them when you've read them. Hang on a minute; they're in the back."

He vanished through a door into the back of the store, returning a moment later with a small stack of books—a large, slim volume, and three that were smaller and fatter. Pulling out a bag from under the counter, he slid the books into it and handed it to her.

There was something new in his eyes, a thing she couldn't read, as she took the bag from him. "I'll bring them back soon," she said.

"I'll be waiting."

Three

✢

Zee held his breath as he watched her walk away. Night after night, year after year, he had dreamed of this woman and had loved her in those dreams beyond all measure. All of his life, it seemed, he had been waiting for this day. It took the discipline of years not to follow her, to remain standing in the doorway and watch her cross the street with that quick light step. When the cascade of auburn hair vanished around a corner, the world, light-filled an instant ago, seemed to go dark.

Unwilling to deal with customers now, Zee locked the door and put up the *Closed* sign. He needed time to process this event, to think about what to do next. To wonder how she was going to react to one of the books he had given her and to think that perhaps he shouldn't have followed the old man's directions quite so precisely.

Ten years ago, almost to the day, Zee had been doing time in county jail on a set of assault charges, stuck with a court-appointed attorney who advocated the guilty plea and a deal for every one of his clients. Which meant no way out of doing time. He was coming to terms with this reality when one of the guards came back to his cell and turned the key in the lock.

"Good news, Arbogast, you made bail."

"No shit!" his cellmate said. "What about me, Sarge?"

The officer snorted. "Come on—who would bail you out, Nelson?"

"Fuck, man, that's cold."

Nelson probably did have somebody somewhere who might bail him out. But the probability of anybody springing Zee? That was as far off the charts as winning the lottery. Even if his parents had any extra money, which they didn't, they certainly wouldn't have wasted it on their wayward son. His grandmother was long dead. There was nobody else.

Keeping the questions out of his face and off his lips, he followed the officer out of the cell, down the hall, and into processing in silence. When he walked out the door half an hour later, a free man with an empty wallet in the pocket of his jeans, he looked around for a familiar face.

There wasn't one.

The only person in sight was a wizened old man—no more than five foot six, and that was stretching it—leaning against a bona fide, sixties-era hippie van. He smiled. "Warlord—I have work for you."

The words nailed Zee's feet to the pavement. He knew the shock registered clearly on his face, felt the cracks in his meticulously constructed façade. "Where the hell did you come up with that name?"

"Are you denying it belongs to you?"

In dream, only in dream. Where he carried a sword and killed men and beasts with an abandon of violence that sometimes made him afraid to sleep, and sometimes fueled the brawls that landed him in jail.

"Who are you, and what do you want?"

"Several things. For starters—I want to commission a painting."

No question of it, the façade had crumbled. Zee gaped stupidly, speechless.

"Oh, come now. I know you are an artist. So—do we have a deal?"

The hot blood rose to his face; desire tingled in his hands.

It had been months since he'd had access to brushes and paints and canvas. He had no idea who this strange little man was or how he knew so many secrets. It didn't matter. "I haven't heard any deal yet," he said, but his throat was dry and tight, and the words were barely more than a whisper. He'd do just about anything for the opportunity to paint.

"I set you up with an apartment and whatever art supplies you need. You get a stipend for clothes and food. You stay out of fights. And you paint."

"What's the catch?" There had to be one. Life didn't hand out freebies. Ever.

"You will paint your dreams for me. I will buy the ones that I want from you."

A devil's bargain. Most of his dreams ought not to see the light of day. But Zee felt himself nodding assent. The old man held out his hand and the deal was sealed with a shake.

For the course of an entire year, Zee splashed his dreams onto canvas for the old man. In the beginning he maintained some control, choosing what to paint and what to hold back, but he soon lost himself in the work. Sometimes an entire day would vanish in what seemed minutes, and he would emerge from a fog to look at what he had produced with shock and a touch of awe.

One thing, though, he held back. Night after night he dreamed the same dream; day after day he painted other things. On a dark, cold November morning it broke through his defenses, and he slapped it onto a life-size canvas in brilliant colors.

The old man came to visit at the end of that day and stood looking at the painting for a long time. "I thought so," he said at last. "Though I hardly dared to hope. I will buy this one."

"No," Zee said. "Any one but this."

"This one. It is the one I was waiting for." He named a price. Zee blinked, not quite comprehending, and for the first time in that year the old man laughed.

"I have another bargain," he said. "It, too, comes with a

cost. I'm going to buy you a store. A bookstore, maybe. You like books, yes? There will be money in the bank for you and lots of time to learn the business. In your free time you will paint." He held up his hand to silence questions. "You will, of course, stay out of jail. And if this woman"— he pointed to one of many paintings of a gray-eyed girl with a thick mane of auburn hair—"walks into your store, you will befriend her and give her a book that I will leave with you. Agreed?"

Zee nodded, not trusting his brain or his voice to produce anything short of gibberish.

"One more thing." The old man produced a package, addressed to Miss Vivian Maylor in a spiky black hand. "There may come a time when you will need to give her this."

"How will I know?"

"You will give it to her on the day that you hear of my death." Intense blue eyes held his, and he remembered the chill that shook him in that moment.

In the years that followed, Zee tried to become a better man. He channeled his impulse for aggression into martial arts for a few years, and then tried to subdue it with yoga and meditation. He studied the religions of many cultures. He painted. Bit by bit the bookstore filled up with titles of interest: an eclectic mix of classic literature, genre novels, old and rare texts, things mystical and weird. His art extended from the canvas to hanging sculptures. Some things he sold in the store. But he had developed the habit of painting from dream, and some of these he kept in his apartment upstairs, off-limits to customers and friends alike.

The old man had begun, in the last few years, to seem unreal, despite the regularity of bank deposits showing up in Zee's account. The woman continued to make regular dream appearances, but he had begun to doubt she would ever materialize, and now, at last, here she was.

Climbing the stairs to his apartment, Zee paced the length of the wall where his dream paintings hung. So many years, so many dreams. Vivian figured in most of them. There were also dragons.

The doorbell rang.

Not the dinger that went off when someone entered the store, but the doorbell to the back door of his apartment, the one accessed by climbing the narrow fire escape stairs. In the entire time Zee had lived here, nobody had ever rung that doorbell because nobody ever climbed those stairs. He'd always considered the buzzer as a practical joke from a builder with too much time on his hands.

It rang again, and he felt a hiss and slither of time, a sense that this was not the first time he had stood at this juncture, with an abyss of darkness opening in front of his feet.

The feeling passed. Only a doorbell, not a call to arms, but still his body felt changed when he crossed the studio into the living area and opened the door—subtly charged, all of his senses expanded.

A strange woman balanced easily on the narrow steps. She was tall, with striking hazel eyes under delicate brows. Trying to categorize her, he ran up against the word *alien*. The eyes a little too widely spaced, the nose too perfect, something vaguely wrong about the mouth. No makeup or jewelry, and the long black gown she wore was out of place in Krebston.

The hair on the back of his neck stood on end; he felt the once-familiar rush of adrenaline.

She looked up at him through thick lashes, hesitant, insecure. "Hello—you would be a friend of Vivian, yes?" Her voice was lightly accented, and he ran the gamut of known languages through his brain and failed to find a match.

His own hand was already in motion before she struck with the knife. He blocked the thrust, grabbed her wrist, twisted the knife away from her. Before she had time to scream, he had wrenched her into the room and slammed the door behind both of them. He pinned her against the wall with her own blade at her throat. It was carved from stone, slightly curved, and stained with blood.

The sight of it moved him.

He leaned his weight into her, pressing the flat of the blade against her white throat so that the skin puckered along the sharp edge but didn't quite break. "If you scream, I'll kill you," he said.

It was intended as a threat, but he realized with a shock that he meant it.

The knife felt alive in his hand. An infinitesimal amount of pressure and beads of crimson appeared on the pale skin. He swallowed, tasting desire.

"Warlord," she said, almost purring. "We meet at last. Step back. You're not going to kill me."

His hand withdrew of its own volition. His right foot stepped back and the left followed, even though his intent was to stand and fight.

Delicate as a cat, she stepped past him and he followed her down the hall, into the studio. "What the hell do you think you're doing?"

Looking back over her shoulder she smiled. A lover's smile, intimate, pupils dilated black. "You want to cut me, Warlord? Kill me? You would like that, I know."

All the nights of his life he had dreamed of violence. Swords, knives, the dull thud of flesh beneath his fists. Bones cracking, lips splitting. Always it was there, an undercurrent that would not be quelled, but never before had he thought about harming a woman.

The impulse appalled him, but his body persisted in sending messages to his brain. How much pressure it would take to clamp the windpipe below that white skin, how wide the spray of blood if he drew the edge of the blade across her throat. He knew exactly where to thrust between the ribs to pierce her heart or her lungs, how to make a slower death with a gut wound.

And he stood, hands at his side, watching as she moved among his pictures, reading his dreams.

"Would you really rather paint than kill?" she asked him.

"I don't know what you're talking about." The lie felt rough on a tongue taught a rigorous discipline of truth.

"Come—I know what you are."

He managed a step toward her, but it took everything he had. His knuckles whitened on the hilt of the knife, and he raised his arm to throw. She held up a hand and shook her head. "No, no, Warlord. Me you cannot kill."

A wall of resistance held him back. Invisible. Impassable. Mustering all the strength of his body and his will, he forced himself against it, gained another six inches of ground, and could go no farther. He stood there, breathing hard, sweat soaking his body. What manner of woman was this? All the old mythologies and fairy tales converged on a single word.

Witch.

"What exactly do you want?" he asked.

"You, Warlord. I require your service."

He laughed, a harsh sound that grated on his own ears. "No."

"Do not be so hasty. You have not yet heard what I offer to you." His vision hazed as she moved toward him, rounded hips swaying, lips parted. She wore no bra beneath the bodice of her gown, and he jerked his eyes away from her breasts with a physical jolt, not that it did him any good. She pressed her body against his, smiled up into his face.

When he took a step back, she murmured, "Stand still," and he felt that same resistance in the air around him, holding him trapped and quivering.

The woman ran a long-fingered hand along his cheek, down his neck, and over his chest. "You waste yourself. This is not the body of an artist; it is the body of a warrior, and a lover. I offer you both of these things—the opportunity to kill, the luxury of my bed. What say you?"

Desire shook him to the marrow of his bones. His body responded to her. Images played unbidden through his brain—perfect breasts beneath his hands, his lips. The flat expanse of her belly, the smoothness of her hips.

He wrenched his gaze away. Over her head hung a portrait of Vivian, gray eyes staring into his.

"No," he said. His lips felt stiff and numb; the word was an effort.

"Your body says otherwise." She grabbed his hips, pulled them hard against hers. He closed his eyes so as not to look at her, knowing she felt his arousal.

"My body doesn't rule me," he managed to say over the thundering of his heart. "Tell me what it is that you want."

She kissed him, a long, lingering kiss, and when he did not respond, she stepped back. "She will not be able to satisfy you; a warrior needs a woman of power. A pity."

"What do you want?"

"So direct. All right, I will tell you. I know all about you, Ezekiel. And I know about the Old One, and the promises he has made. You think he has the woman's best interest in mind. You think you are going to help her. But if you give to her what he left with you, it will lead her into grave danger."

"Why should I believe you?"

"I applaud your caution. You should trust no one. Him least of all." She moved to stand before one of the portraits of Vivian. "Do you love her so much, then? No, don't answer. I see it in the way you paint her. I hope you realize that even should she come to you from Dreamworld she will certainly be changed . . ." She stopped, her eyes narrowing.

"You've seen her in Wakeworld. Where is she, Warlord? Tell me."

He didn't answer.

She took the knife from a hand unable to resist her, held it so the tip pressed just into his bottom lip. A warm thread of blood ran down his chin. He did not flinch.

"Tell me where she is."

"I can't tell you what I don't know."

"What about the Key? Did the Old One give you that for safekeeping?"

He felt a pressure on his mind, a compulsion to answer, and was grateful suddenly for all that he didn't know. "He never gave me a key."

"I see that you will answer only as you are compelled. Time-consuming, to think of all the right questions. It is for her own good, Warlord, that you should tell me all you know. You will be saving her life."

"I find it difficult to trust a woman who holds me at knifepoint."

"How else should I persuade a Warlord to hear me? Violence speaks to violence, does it not?"

The truth of that was more than he wanted to admit. He repeated, "I don't know anything about a key. I don't know where she is." His thoughts churned. What if the witch was right about the old man? If his intentions were dark, then following his instructions further was the last thing Zee wanted to do.

The woman leaned forward, licked the blood from his chin, kissed his lips; her eyes were deep pools of hunger and promise. "I will find her without your help. But I ask you this—if you love her as you say, then help her. If she should find the key, you must bring it to me."

"If I were to do this, how would I find you?"

"Ah, details." She held the blade to her wrist and cut. Blood welled against the pale skin. Wetting her fingers, she lifted them, dripping, to his lips, his tongue. The salty tang of blood flooded his mouth with saliva. Reflex took over and he swallowed.

"Blood calls to blood. If you want me, bleed yourself and call my name. Jehenna. Here—keep this as a gesture of good faith." She wrapped his fingers around the hilt of the knife. "Stand still, now. Don't move."

And he stood, bound by her voice, as she walked out of his field of vision. Heard her footsteps cross the room, heard the door slam. The sound freed him from immobility. Impossible, what had just happened here. Except that blood flowed from a cut in his lip. In his hand he held a knife with a curved stone blade.

Shaking himself out of a stupor, he crossed to the door and locked it, then went into his bedroom. Shoving aside a stack of boxes in the closet, he exposed a locked metal gun safe bolted to the wall and opened it with the key he kept hidden under a loose corner of the carpet. Inside lay his M1911 handgun and his throwing knives.

He picked up the gun, slammed a magazine into it,

imagined firing a shot. Once a week, on Sunday mornings, he did target practice at Benny's Range. Sunday afternoons he cleaned the gun, polished it, then tucked it back into the box. Also on Sundays, he practiced with the knives. He was good with a gun, but the blades had always felt like an extension of his own fists. Now he fastened the sheaths around waist and ankle, made sure everything was concealed beneath his clothing.

Two other items remained in the box: a spherical object in a velvet bag, another obligation left him by George Maylor. What it was, he had no idea. The instructions were clear: *Open only at the end*. What this meant, Zee had no idea. The other thing was a manila envelope, business sized. Written on it in a distinctive, bold black hand were the words *Vivian Maylor, c/o Ezekiel Arbogast*. Zee lifted it, hefted it in his hand, probed it with his fingers. Only paper, no hint of an object, large or small. No key.

Time enough to decide what to do; it need not be now. He laid the envelope back in the box. Then he wrapped the stone knife in a T-shirt and laid it on top, before turning the key in the lock and piling boxes in front of it once more.

He stared at the closet from the middle of his room, wondering how it was possible that everything should look the same when everything that mattered had changed.

Four

✣

Vivian scrubbed her hands at the sink, lingering, extending the ritual longer than necessary to buy herself a moment of time. Although she'd managed to catch a few hours of sleep after her walk to the bookstore, she'd wakened feeling like someone had pounded every inch of her body with a baseball bat. Questions to which there were no answers swirled in her head.

Work was a welcome relief, normal, something that helped her focus on reality.

Normal, but far from easy. On the examining table behind her, a woman was slowly suffocating from the secretions in her own lungs, cumulative damage of thirty years of tobacco. She'd never taken a puff in her life—all of the smoking had been done by the man who sat in the chair beside her, holding her hand, looking a good ten years younger than his age and in perfect health.

No rhyme nor reason to anything in this world.

"Dr. Maylor—"

Roxie stood in the doorway, lower lip trapped between her teeth. Vivian jerked paper towels out of the holder and used them to turn off the faucet. "What is it?"

"We've got a bit of a situation; you'd better come out, if you can."

A bit of a situation could mean anything from a difficult patient to a staff dispute about what toppings should go on a pizza. Not an emergency per se. Although if it was the question of pizza, that sometimes came damned close.

"One minute," Vivian said. She turned back to the couple behind her. "Now, Mr. and Mrs. Anderson, you both understand there must be absolutely no more smoke in the house, yes?"

"I'll quit," Carl said. "It's time."

Alexis patted his hand. She pulled aside the oxygen mask to speak, but before she could get a word out a paroxysm of coughing shook her. Carl supported her thin shoulders, his face marked with helplessness and the sure and certain knowledge of loss.

"I'd like to admit you to the unit," Vivian said, when the coughing had eased. "We can treat the pneumonia better here—"

The woman shook her head, looking to her husband to speak for her.

"Stubborn. Says she's spent enough time in the hospital and she's not staying," Carl said. "There's no point wasting your breath."

No one spoke for a minute, the significance of the cliché punctuated by the labored breathing of the woman on the bed.

"Keep the oxygen on," Vivian said, finally. "Use the inhalers the way I showed you. A nurse will be coming out to check on you and give you IV antibiotics. I'll send a referral to hospice."

She slipped out of the room, away from the love and loss and guilt that filled it so thickly it stifled her own breath. Staff had gathered in a little clump behind the desk, their voices subdued for confidentiality, but hands were emphatically waving and nobody looked happy.

Not a pizza problem this time.

"What's up?"

They turned to face her, all of them, huddled into a flock. Max licked his lips, his eyes feverish. "Brett's in six," he said.

Vivian stared at them, absorbing.

Six was a code of sorts. It was the bay at the end of the hall, the place they put patients who might disturb the rest of the public. Psychiatric emergencies, the loud and intoxicated.

"Brett who?"

They stared back, eyes wide, faces tense and pale.

"Flynne." Shelly looked ready to cry. Her hands trembled visibly and Vivian understood. Deputy Brett Flynne, who was on duty the night Arden died. Who had been investigating things down at the Finger. He'd been a deputy when most of the staff were still in high school. Dependable, reliable, a community fixture. And now they'd put him in six.

"What's going on?"

"Raving," Roxie said. "And cold. Brody's in there with him."

"Explain."

"Hypothermic. Temp is ninety-five. And—he's talking about penguins. I already put warm blankets on him and ordered the IV warmer from central."

Vivian bit back a surge of panic. Her job, somehow, to calm and organize, to appear sane and together even when she felt like she was flying apart. "Look, guys—something caused this, something will fix it. We deal with it like we always do. Follow the protocols. The second the warmer gets here, start a bag of normal saline. Shelly, call the lab and get them to draw blood stat. Max, get Mrs. Anderson discharged, will you? She doesn't need to be here for this."

Everybody scattered to assigned tasks, and Vivian let her feet carry her down the hall. *Squeak, squeak.* Damn it, she'd totally forgotten to get different shoes. She paused for a moment outside the door, half-expecting another dream fragment.

But there was no flash of dream, no déjà vu. When she entered, Brett was huddled under a pile of blankets, shivering hard enough to shake the examination table. The skin of his hands and face looked dead white; his lips, blue tinged, moved in an endless recitation she couldn't quite hear.

Deputy Brody stood at a small distance, eyes averted, face flushed, shoulders rounded with embarrassment. His hands made a gesture of invocation when he saw her, then returned to the security of his belt and the array of defensive tools he carried. Pepper spray, Taser, sidearm, handcuffs.

Brett didn't react to her entrance; his eyes remained focused on a far corner of the room.

"What happened?" She crossed the room, put her hand on his forehead. So cold. She picked up one of his hands and pressed the nail bed, checking for circulation. Not good. Respirations shallow and slow.

"We were down at the Finger—he wanted to go over the evidence for the murders again. So he's over there by the stone looking at bloodstains, and all of a sudden he shouts, 'Look out! Penguins!' And then he starts shaking like he's got the plague. That's not it, is it? The plague? Some sort of chemical weapon or whatever?"

"I very much doubt that, but we can check you over if you want."

Brett's hand clenched hers, squeezing her fingers to the point of pain. His eyes focused on hers, staring, intent. "The penguins are coming," he whispered, as though it were the most important message in the world.

She kept her voice low, as calm as she could make it. "I don't understand, Brett. We're not seeing any penguins, Brody and I."

He released her, his hands fumbling aimlessly at his breast. His muttering grew louder; she could understand the words, meaningless. "The penguins are coming, full of grease. Lord, deliver us from ice. The penguins are coming, full of grease, Lord deliver us from ice. The penguins are coming . . ."

She couldn't find a pulse in his wrist. Placing the stethoscope on his chest she heard his heart, slow and weak. An oral temperature read ninety-three degrees. Roxie's initial reading had been ninety-five. He was getting colder.

Hypothermia.

It made no sense. At today's temperature you'd have to

be outside for hours without a coat to get this cold. Still searching for the rational explanation, she asked Brody, "Was he wearing a coat? How did he get so cold?"

"Regular uniform, same as me. There was a wind off the river, but nothing extreme, you know? Sun was shining. He was fine, and then he wasn't. That's all I can tell you."

Goddamn it. She'd had one patient burn up on her table. She wasn't about to let another one freeze to death. Hypothermia should be easy enough to treat, but he was getting worse, not better, and she had absolutely no idea what was causing the problem. This time she wasn't going to mess around. She'd get him stabilized as much as possible and airlift him to Spokane. Maybe the doctors at Sacred Heart could see what she was missing.

Roxie half-ran through the door with an IV, the warmer, and another armful of warm blankets. Working together without a word, they laid him back and wrapped the warmed blankets around him. Brett lay as they'd placed him, drowsy now, his eyes closed, fingers twitching. His lips still moved, fitfully, but Vivian couldn't make out any words.

"Max called for airlift," Roxie said. She'd managed, somehow, to find a vein, and was filling tubes for the lab before hooking up the warmed IV. Vivian moved the blankets long enough to slap pads on his chest and hook up the EKG, wrapping him up again at once.

Vivian looked up at Brody. "You could track down his wife and ask her some questions—any history of mental illness? Any drug use? That sort of thing."

"Look, I've been his partner for five years. If you're suggesting—"

"I'm not suggesting anything. We just don't want to neglect any possible leads. Okay?"

"All right. It's just—"

Vivian gentled her voice. "I know. We're doing everything we can for him. Okay?"

Brody nodded and stalked out. She'd given him something comprehensible to do and hoped it would help him. There wasn't much chance he would turn up anything of use.

At least Brett's temperature had stopped dropping, but he wasn't warming. And he should be. He was a healthy man with no history of serious disease. Frankly, she couldn't think of a disease or a drug that would cause what she was seeing here.

Which forced her, at last, to confront what she'd been avoiding. Arden, and the way her dreams lingered long after waking. The strange conversation she'd had today with a man she had dreamed before she met him.

Her hand went to the pendant, seeking comfort from the cool stone that had been with her for years. She had almost managed to erase her memory of the day it was given to her, could go days and months with it buried deep in her subconscious. It was a day that didn't fit with the rest of her life, didn't fit with anything. She had almost persuaded herself over the years that the events of that day never really happened, were only dream.

But there was the pendant, and she had no other story to explain its existence.

She'd been seven years old that summer. Old enough to begin to question Isobel's version of reality and struggle with her own. Other kids were amazingly casual about dreams. Sometimes they were frightened by nightmares, but they laughed away their fear. Their dreams seemed to fit in the same category as Santa Claus and the tooth fairy, beings Vivian had always known did not exist.

They talked about all of these things in a casual banter that astonished Vivian, whose experience was so far different, and so she kept her own vivid dreams to herself.

As she did her home life.

Her classmates, for the most part, had two parents, brothers and sisters, maybe even aunts and uncles and grandparents. Sometimes they all lived together; sometimes they didn't. They talked about these people in terms that had no connection to anything Vivian knew. Parents cooked, cleaned, and bought groceries. Had jobs. Watched over homework. Read bedtime stories.

Vivian's mother did none of these things. She had no father. She'd asked about him once.

"He's a prince," Isobel said, her voice far away and her eyes looking into Dreamworld.

"That's not true," Vivian said, bossy. "I'm too old for fairy stories."

"Who says fairy stories aren't true? We fell in love long, long ago—"

Vivian knew all about where babies came from and was having none of this. "Isobel. I am seven. If you were with some fairy-tale prince that many years ago, then where did I come from?"

Her mother's eyes focused, just for a minute, and Vivian shivered a little with happiness and a touch of fear, to have her mother look at her and really see her. "I found him in a dream. At least I think it was a dream. So real, darling." All at once Isobel began to weep, wrenching sobs that frightened Vivian more than the cutting and the blood. She knew what to do about blood; tears were something else altogether. You couldn't call an ambulance for tears.

Almost two years before, when she was five, a neighbor showed her how to dial 911. Gave her instructions for when it was okay to call: If your mother isn't talking or eating and can't get out of bed. If she has an accident with something sharp and is bleeding. If she takes too many pills. There were no instructions about tears.

Knives and scissors were a problem. And razor blades. Vivian did her best to keep them away from her mother, but she was little and had to go to school. Things happened. Sometimes this meant trips to the emergency room and stitches. Sometimes it meant the 911 number and an ambulance, all sirens and flashing lights.

Once, her mother stayed at some mysterious hospital for days, and then weeks. Vivian was not allowed to visit and was made to stay with an aunt and uncle in a house full of stray kids. Only they weren't her aunt and uncle—they knew it and she knew it—but they made her play that strange game of pretend.

Ever since Isobel had come home, a social worker, Beth, came in regularly to check on things. She was easily lied to. Isobel hated the hospital; Vivian hated the uncle and aunt. Together they colluded to pretend things were okay.

Mostly, they managed.

On this particular morning, Vivian had fixed herself cereal and was eating it alone at the table when Isobel entered the kitchen. She was dressed to go out, in a fitted black suit jacket and skirt. Her lips were red and she smelled of perfume and hair spray.

"Get dressed," she said.

"I *am* dressed."

"Something nicer."

Vivian shook her head. Dresses hindered her, kept her from climbing trees and rolling in the grass. They were also hard to wash. Recently she had learned to operate the washing machine and did both her own laundry and her mother's when Isobel was too busy with imaginary friends.

"I suppose I'll have to take you like that. Put your shoes on."

"Where are we going?"

"To visit your grandfather."

"I have a grandfather? Where does he live? How come I haven't met him?"

The rest of her questions were met with silence. By the time she located her sneakers and buckled herself into the car, Isobel was off in a world of her own.

Isobel Maylor often talked to herself. Today was no exception, and the words spilled out rapid-fire as she drove, her hands waving a graceful and expressive counterpoint. Vivian guessed that this grandfather might be one of her mother's imaginary friends and began watching for a phone booth from which she might dial the magical 911 if they happened to get lost or stranded.

Several hours later, the car stopped in a patch of gravel

at the end of a tree-lined lane. A wizened old man popped out onto the porch before the dust had time to settle.

Vivian stared at him. He was real, all right, even though he did look like a gnome out of a picture book. He stood there, the door open behind him, while Isobel stepped out of the car, her shiny black heels sinking into the dust. Vivian followed.

"Isobel," the old man said. He stood perfectly still. "And Vivian. At last. It's about time we met."

Isobel walked past him without a hug or even a touch on the arm, into an open area with a kitchen and sitting room, Vivian trailing behind. "Go in the other room and stay until I call you," Isobel ordered, gesturing toward a closed door.

Vivian's eyes turned to the old man, and he nodded. "Do as your mother says, child. Only the next room, mind. Do not go through the green door."

She complied at once, more than happy to escape; the tension between the two sizzled and popped with a complex vibration that trembled her insides.

An ordinary wooden door opened to her shove, admitting her to a small room with a couch and a stack of books piled unevenly on a rickety coffee table. At the far side of this room was the forbidden green door. Vivian, having been warned about the door, found herself immediately drawn to it, but she only gave it a long look before plunking down on the couch. She sorted through the pile of books and picked up a fat paperback. The cover attracted her, a picture of a knight on horseback, waving a bright sword. But flipping through the pages she found only unfamiliar words, without even a sprinkling of *was*, *and*, or *the*. She was proud of her newfound ability to read, and angry that this book shut her out.

The voices from the other room grew loud and distracting.

"Take me back," her mother said.

And her grandfather's voice, sad now, she thought. "No, Izzie, I can't."

"Yes, you can! You took me away, all those long years ago, and everything's been wrong since then."

"You don't understand the danger, child."

"Give me the globes then, and I'll find my own way. You said they would be mine, and then you took them away, too."

"I had to. I regret it deeply. They gave you the dream sickness, Isobel. It isn't safe."

"If you loved me at all, you would give them back to me!" Vivian knew all too well the rising of her mother's voice. It meant blood. There would be another trip to the mysterious hospital for Isobel, and the aunts and uncles for Vivian. Whatever it was her mother wanted, Vivian wished the grandfather would just give it to her.

Her eyes kept turning to the green door, only a few steps away from where she sat. On the other side of the door she wouldn't be able to hear them shouting.

Her grandfather had told her not to.

Loud sobs decided her. She hated listening to her mother cry.

Still, one hand on the doorknob, she paused, knowing disobedience had consequences.

Her grandfather's voice again. "The reason I did what I did is because I love you, Izzie. You must understand. I was wrong to go against the rules—"

"I hate you! My life is a gaping hole, and it's your fault. I loved him, and you dragged me away. You gave me the globes, and then you took them from me. Let me go back. I was whole there . . ."

Vivian slid through the green door and shut out the voices behind her.

Standing with her back to the closed door, she looked around the room. An odd assortment of objects spilled off shelves and onto the floor. Kind of like the Goodwill store, but not as neat.

A gray cat emerged from behind a shelf and wound around her ankles. Squatting on the floor, she rubbed its soft fur and it purred, butting its head against her hands. When the cat got up and stalked off with its tail in the air, she followed. Down a narrow aisle, careful not to touch anything. Past shelves full of books with cracked leather bindings. They smelled old and interesting, and she felt that they wanted her to open them. It frightened her to think that the books might want something, and she left them very much alone.

Farther in, she found a whirling creation of balls and wire that stood as tall as she. Here she stopped, mesmerized. Watching carefully, for a long time, she thought she could see how to move things to change the pattern. But once again, she moved on without touching.

She found weird cuckoo clocks and other things that ticked and whirred; sand glasses with different colors of sand streaming at varying speeds through the glass; a collection of carved wooden masks. She walked by all of them, stopping to look but not ever truly tempted to touch, still following the cat.

And then, at the far end of the room, sitting alone on a rough wooden shelf beneath the only window, she found the wooden box. It glowed in a ray of sunlight, satin smooth, worn with age. There were carvings on the lid—two dragons, their necks intertwined, wings widespread.

Vivian instantly coveted the box. It was made for secrets: small enough for her hands to carry, big enough to hold treasures. A tiny brass key was set in the lock.

Her mother's voice was louder now, shrieking, the words muffled by walls.

One quick peek inside the box. Nobody would ever know.

The cat sat down by her feet and licked a paw as her fingers turned the key and opened the lid.

Little balls of clear glass nestled into a crimson velvet lining, all different sizes, like marbles but without the swirl of color at the center. Vivian ran her fingers through them, watching reflected colors shift and change, feeling the energy around her shift as well. A chiming sound, like a bell only different, filled the air. She paused, alarmed, certain the adults would come running, both of them angry, but their voices continued in the other room.

Picking up one of the little balls between thumb and forefinger, she held it up to the light. Suspended in the center was a tiny, perfect tree; a tire swing dangled from a long branch.

Such a peaceful world, so quiet, so safe.

A breeze brushed against her cheek, and she looked up, startled, to find herself standing in a field of grass and flowers, wind blowing her hair into her eyes. She pushed the bothersome strands behind her ears and saw the tree towering above her, with the tire swing turning gently, invitingly, in front of her. No sign of a house or people anywhere. Nothing but the tree and this wide, green field all dotted with yellow and blue, stretching away as far as she could see.

At first, it was sheer delight—her favorite daydream come true. Sunlight warmed her hair, the wind sang to her, and the marble clasped in her hand sang with it. Nobody came by with sharp words to call her inside and lecture her about bugged telephones and listening ears. No razors and blood and ambulance sirens.

But by the time the sun hung like a ball of fire on the western horizon she shivered in an unrelenting breeze, her belly tight with hunger. The swinging had long since lost its charm and she sat with her back to the trunk of the tree, knees drawn up against her body for comfort and warmth.

Her grandfather was still a long way off when she saw him coming through the field toward her, looking more like a gnome than ever, his wizened face sharp in the waning light.

"Well," he said, sinking down into the grass beside her. "I suppose they were meant for you. But not yet, child, not yet."

"The box wanted to be opened," she said.

"There were other things that wanted you—why this one?"

She met his eyes then, so dangerously bright and blue, and said, "Because I wanted to."

"You were fortunate, child. If I had not come for you, you would have been lost here, forever; do you understand?"

She shook her head, defiant. "I would have walked somewhere. I would have telephoned for help. Somebody would have found me."

"Now you are being foolish. This is an entire reality—you must understand that. There is nobody else in this world but you and me."

Nobody else. The words rang true. She held up the marble in her hand, studying the tiny tree, the swing. A tricksy wish, like all storybook magic turned out to be. Fairy wishes always turned into a curse of some kind, no matter how hard someone tried to get it right.

"I see you believe me. So I will also tell you this. The globes can take you to many wonderful places, but many dark and dangerous places as well. You were lucky."

She was fascinated now. "What kind of places?"

"All are within the Dreamworld. Each of those globes contains somebody's dream."

Confused, and remembering some of her own dreams, she felt her stomach clench with sudden fear. "But I'm awake. How can we be in a dream if I'm awake?"

"Because you are who you are."

"And I can be awake in someone else's dream?"

"Yes. And some of them are beautiful and peaceful, like this one. But some are full of monsters and evil things."

"Dragons," she whispered.

"Yes, dragons."

She squeezed her hands together until the bones hurt, pressed them between her knees.

A warm arm wrapped around her shoulder, pulling her against him so that her cheek rested on his chest. A steady heartbeat, even breath. His lack of fear comforted her, and in a moment she was able to whisper, "The dragons. I think they're looking for me."

A moment of silence, long enough for her to wonder whether he was going to lie to her. She'd learned that grown-ups often lied. The social worker, the aunt and uncle, her teacher at school. She pulled away and looked for the this-is-for-your-own-good expression on his face. Instead, his blue eyes looked straight into hers, and he half smiled.

"I imagine they are."

She hadn't expected that.

"They scare me."

"As they should."

He fell silent and stared at the sinking sun. The look on his face reminded her of Isobel's when she was in one of her moods, and she shook his arm to bring him back to her.

"So what do I do? About the dragons?"

"Oh, that's easy, for now. Stay out of the Between. Later—well, there's time enough to talk about later."

"What's Between?" She waited, her lip caught between her teeth, scarcely daring to breathe.

"Listen carefully. This is important."

She nodded. If he was going to tell her how to be safe from the dragons, she didn't plan to miss a word.

"There's Dreamworld, right? Your dreams and everybody else's. This, for example, is somebody else's dream, but it's still a dream."

"Okay." This was good. Confirmation of what she'd already known.

"And there's Wakeworld. Where all the stuff the idiots call reality happens. Like school, and chores, and spinach for dinner."

"And Isobel."

A deep sigh at that. "Well—your mother kind of breaks the rules. Part of her is in Wakeworld. But mostly she's stuck in the Between." He brushed his fingers across the back of her hand. "You know when you're not really awake and not really asleep? That place?"

She did. Everything was all mixed up there—you couldn't tell what was Dreamworld and what was Wakeworld.

"Well, that's where the dragons lurk. And other things, too. Stay out of the Between and you'll be all right."

"But I can't—I have to go through it when I go to sleep."

"Yes, and when you wake up."

"So, what then?"

"Be quick about falling asleep and waking."

"Are we stuck here then, in this dream place?"

"No. You're never stuck anywhere unless you want to be."

"That doesn't make sense!"

"True, nonetheless. Look—if you wish it strongly enough, there will always be a door to take you home. This doesn't work for everybody, mind. You have certain—gifts."

Vivian sat still and thought about things. About Dreamworld and Wakeworld and the hunting dragons. About her mother and that lost look in her eyes, the look of the Between.

"How did you get here?" she demanded in a sudden flurry of temper. "There's a trick. You're not telling me."

He smiled. "You're smart, that's a good thing. Look—there are the globes, that's one door. But for those who have the touch and know where to look, the doors are everywhere."

"For me?"

"Not yet—but maybe someday."

"What about Isobel?"

"Ah, yes." His eyes were sad. "Your mother has just enough ability with doors to get herself stuck."

"Can't you get her out?"

He shook his head. "Not until she wants to come. She's trying to get somewhere else."

"But won't the dragons get her?"

"Not the dragons, no—those are for you to worry about. We've left her alone long enough, though—are you ready to go home?"

Vivian nodded. "Can I come back here?"

He shook his head. "Not soon. All of the dreamspheres will be yours someday."

"Truly?"

"Truly." He pulled a chain from his pocket and hung it around her neck. A strange pendant hung from it, and she lifted it with both hands to see better.

A circle, with a web woven into the center out of some iridescent string. A stone creature at the center, wearing a tiny brass key around its neck on a collar. Vivian squealed—the creature was a penguin, and she adored penguins. She wanted to keep looking, to take it off and play with it, but her grandfather's voice stopped her.

"Wear this always. Never take it off—water won't hurt it; neither will the sun. It will help keep the dragons away. Can you keep it secret from your mother?"

"Of course." Keeping real things secret from Isobel was easy. She wrinkled her nose. "The chain isn't very pretty."

"No, but it's strong."

"Silver is prettier."

"Hmm. Trust me on this—silver isn't for you."

She shrugged. The pendant was perfect, and a shiny chain would just draw attention to something she wanted to hide. Just to be sure, she tucked the pendant under her shirt.

Grandfather nodded approvingly. "There you go. Are you ready now?"

"Yes. Let's go home," she said.

"See if you can make the door."

She closed her eyes and thought hard about her room at home—the bed with the blue blanket, the bookshelf with the books she was just learning to read, the stuffed penguin that slept beside her at night. She thought about school and chocolate and ice cream. She thought about her mother and how she needed to be taken care of.

"Open your eyes," her grandfather said.

There, right in front of them, a door hung in the air. For a long minute she sat and stared at it, frightened. But Grandfather was not alarmed at all. He gave her that half smile again, but she thought he looked tired all at once.

"Well, open it, then."

She did so.

Behind her were the big tree and the wide green field; through the door, her grandfather's strange room with the window and the shelf where the marble box had stood.

The shelf was empty now, a dark rectangle marking the

spot in the surrounding dust. Her grandfather stood beside her, and she only now noticed that he held the box in his hands. Isobel, still in Grandfather's room, half ran toward them. The sense of strangeness grew, Vivian on one side of this door, her mother on the other.

As hard as she tried, Isobel could not come through that opening between the Wakeworld and Dreamworld.

"Give them to me," she said.

Grandfather's face looked more wizard than gnome, Vivian thought. Stern, that was the word. "Go home, Isobel. I won't let you touch them." It was not the sort of voice one dared to disobey, but Isobel did, still trying to reach through the door, her hands bouncing back from an invisible barrier.

"Give them to me. They should be mine." Tears tracked mascara down both cheeks.

"Put the marble in the box, please, Vivian," Grandfather said, and she placed it carefully with the others. He smiled at her, then turned to Isobel again.

"Go home. Take the child with you. She's created enough mischief for one day."

Vivian opened her mouth to object, but he winked at her and nodded, and she smiled back, a little warm glow at her heart. Through the door with a skip and a jump, she tugged at Isobel's hand. "Come on, let's go home."

For a brief instant hazel eyes looked at her and the penciled eyebrows rose.

"Take her home, Isobel," Grandfather said. "Don't bring her here again."

One more smile for Vivian, to show that he wasn't angry, and then he closed the door.

It vanished in the blink of an eye, and she stood beside Isobel, staring at a wall where only a moment ago there had been a door.

"Vivian!"

She startled, guilty. "What, Rox?"

"Helicopter's landing—"

A huge breath of relief escaped her. They'd managed to keep Brett stable—he wasn't warming up at all, but his heart was still beating, he was breathing, his urine output was adequate. In Spokane they could warm his blood on a dialysis machine, maybe figure out what it was that she was missing.

Unless what she was missing had something to do with Dreamworld and the Between, in which case there wasn't anything the medical profession could do to make things right.

But maybe her grandfather could. First thing when she got home, she was going to track him down. The old man had some explaining to do.

Five

✢

The apartment door looked different somehow, but Vivian couldn't think of any reason why. Same old chipped enamel paint in a dull greenish brown. The number 27 in cheap stick-on letters, with the 7 tilted at a drunken angle, caught in the act of falling over backward by badly timed adhesive. A fist-sized dent at eye level, reminder of the previous tenant's boyfriend, who rumor said was doing time in county jail on domestic violence charges.

Behind the door waited the possibility of a hot breakfast and a comfortable chair. After a drive home through the cold night air, her plan to call her grandfather seemed less reasonable, but it was still on the agenda. In order to get to any or all of these things and the warm bed waiting when they had been done, she would have to open the door.

And she found, for the first time in her life, that she was afraid of this simple and common act.

Fear was irrational.

With quickened breath, she put her hand to the knob. It was unlocked. Every horror movie she'd ever seen flashed through her memory, and like every heroine doomed to death she talked herself out of the impulse to flee. She'd been tired and in a hurry when she left for work, had probably forgotten to lock it. How stupid would she feel if she called the cops out to show her an empty and perfectly normal apartment? There was no evidence of breaking and entering.

She shoved open the door.

A woman sat at her kitchen table.

Tall, willowy build. Wide hazel eyes under uptilted brows, a delicate nose, a face beautiful but wrong in a way Vivian felt but couldn't explain.

"Miss Maylor, don't be frightened, please. We must have conversation, you and I."

The accent was foreign, the voice pitched low, rich as dark coffee with cream. There was something familiar about the eyes. Vivian felt a slight pressure on her mind, a suggestion that she allow her thinking to be done for her. It was an offer of comfort, of ease. *Let me worry about your officer, and your mother. Be at rest.*

She felt herself take a step into the room, heard something crunch beneath her foot, and looked down to see one of the dream catchers broken on the floor.

"What are you doing in my apartment? What do you want?"

"Miss Maylor, please. You have no cause to be alarmed. I come on behalf of your grandfather."

"My grandfather?" She felt slow and stupid. Her free hand found its way to the pendant, smooth and familiar to her touch.

"I am his representative. His—attorney, if you will. And you are his executrix. So, as you see, we have much in common, and much to discuss."

"I don't understand." The bottom dropped out of her stomach, leaving a dizzying emptiness. Her vision warped and tunneled, everything fuzzy and out of focus except for the woman who sat at her kitchen table. The woman herself was extraordinarily vivid, as if she were the only three-dimensional thing in the room. Her delicate eyebrows rose in a question mark.

"I'm sorry, did nobody tell you?"

"Tell me what?"

"Your grandfather met his end early this morning. I see this is a shock to you. Come, sit. Surely you have many questions."

"He's dead? When? How?"

"I'm sorry, I don't have the details. Perhaps you can speak with the coroner later."

Vivian's mouth felt like the Sahara. She was dimly aware of closing the door behind her, stumbling across the room to the table. "Why? Why me, I mean?"

"Your mother is not fit. There is no one else."

Vivian's head cleared. She was sitting at her kitchen table across from a strange woman who had entered her apartment without permission. A woman who was telling her that her grandfather had died, now, just when she needed him to be there. She reached into her pocket and clutched the cell phone. It would take only a moment to dial 911.

"What are you doing in my apartment?"

"I apologize for that. It is cold outside—I asked your landlord to unlock for me."

"And she did it, just like that."

"Of course, once I explained who I am, and why I am here. She said to tell you she is very sorry for your loss."

Vivian rubbed at the kink in her neck. "Why exactly are you here, Ms.—?"

"Call me Jehenna."

"Jehenna, then. It's not exactly the usual practice for an attorney to personally break the news."

The woman reached into a shapeless leather bag, her eyes never leaving Vivian's, and drew out a set of papers, which she laid on the table between them. "You will find here your grandfather's will. You inherit everything. His home, his possessions."

Vivian set the phone on the table and scanned the document. It seemed authentic. The language was right— difficult, obscure legalese; all of the signatures were there, including George Maylor, her grandfather, and a scrawl that might say *Jehenna* if you looked at it with your eyes crossed. But this was uncharted territory and she was definitely not thinking clearly. She needed Jared. "I'd like to call someone—"

"Why would you do this?"

"He's an attorney. I'd like to have his advice—"

"What is his name? Perhaps we have met."

"Jared Michaelson. He's with Baskin and Clarke—"

Jehenna waved a dismissive white hand. "I am sure he is occupied now with other things. You have plenty of time to contact him. He can probate the will, if you wish. I am here only to explain some things and to bring to you some bequests."

Jehenna reached again into the bag and pulled out an envelope, laying it on the table on top of the will. It had been sealed and then neatly sliced open. Vivian's name was written in a spiky black hand.

"You've opened it," Vivian said, taking the envelope and drawing out a single sheet of loose-leaf paper.

"It was left with Mr. Smoot with instructions for him to get it to you at once should Mr. Maylor pass on. Mr. Smoot thought it best he should understand any bequests so he can offer you his best assistance."

The note was written in the same bold, black hand as her name on the envelope:

Dear Vivian:

You are young yet, and I had hoped to save you this moment for reasons beyond the scope of this note. If you are reading this now, it is because I am dead. You are my only heir, which makes you a Dreamshifter, and sadly, the last of them. I have done what I can to help you, little as it is. Unfortunately, it is not safe to write more, lest it fall into the wrong hands. Be careful of doors, they can lead to unexpected places. Edwin Smoot, my attorney, will explain more to you. TRUST NO ONE until you have time to talk with him.

George Maylor

Vivian reread this missive twice, then folded it and put it back inside the envelope.

"He says his attorney is Mr. Smoot."

"Mr. Smoot was unavailable," the smooth voice answered. "Your grandfather's death was sudden. Mr. Smoot believed it would be best for you to know at once."

"He might have called."

"He felt a face to face would be more productive and has scheduled you in for Tuesday next, if you will be available then? In the meantime we had promised to deliver the bequests immediately upon Mr. Maylor's death."

"I really think I'd rather wait and talk with Mr. Smoot."

"Ms. Maylor, you are being stubborn. Mr. Maylor was getting old—he had a hard time accepting that times change. When he was young, Mr. Smoot would have been available to personally deal with all of his needs. Now Mr. Smoot himself is aging. He also runs a busy and successful law firm. He must use his staff, or he cannot get his work done. Mr. Maylor did not understand this, but I'm sure that you will."

The wide eyes were serene and steady, but Vivian felt a growing unease. Memory ghosts swept her mind with cobwebby fingers. She had seen this face before, feared it, somewhere, in Wakeworld or Dreamworld.

Jehenna set a package on the table. It was wrapped neatly and precisely in brown paper, corners creased and symmetrical and secured with clear packing tape. Vivian's name was written in the same black hand as the envelope and the letter.

Time slowed as she put her hands to the paper—smooth beneath her fingers, except for the places where it had once been folded; here there were little ridges, the edges of the tape snagging on the skin of her fingertips. When she tore the paper away, everything in her world came to a sharp focus.

This moment.

This act.

In the middle of the torn paper sat a wooden box with

dragons carved into the top, dark with age. A box big enough for secrets, small enough to carry with you. A box she had seen once before.

"Open it. Are you not curious?"

"It's locked." The lid refused to yield to her fingers.

"Perhaps the key is yet in the envelope. It would be a small key."

Vivian peered into the smaller envelope, and then the larger one. She picked up the brown paper wrapping and shook it over the table. Nothing.

Memory stirred.

Blue eyes, alarming in their intensity, looked directly into hers as her grandfather hung the chain around her neck.

"Keep it a secret. Do not lose it." He'd frightened her a little, with his sharp face and his knowing eyes, and she had kept her promise, never revealing it even to her mother.

"You must have the key somewhere," Jehenna said. "Bring it here."

Vivian hesitated. She didn't quite trust this woman, but the box called to her as it had when she was a child. In this moment she wanted nothing more than to see those globes again, to hear the sound of crystal on crystal.

And surely she was being paranoid. It made perfect sense for Mr. Smoot to send a junior partner on this errand. Feeling strangely detached, almost as though she were watching herself on a screen, she drew the pendant out from under her shirt. The penguin still held in its beak a tiny brass key.

Bending down to the table, Vivian fitted the key into the lock. It turned with a little click. Jehenna lifted the lid and there they were, just as Vivian remembered them, small glass spheres in varying sizes, hints of movement flickering across their surfaces.

"Do you know what these are, then?" Jehenna asked. She leaned forward over the table; her eyes glowed.

A cold chill settled at the base of Vivian's spine. She shivered. "I have some idea." She closed the box and pulled it closer to her.

"I find I am very curious about these little globes—they are lovely, aren't they?"

Their eyes met, and Vivian's unease deepened. She should do something, but her tongue seemed glued in place; her body refused to move. Her brain calculated the time it would take to snatch up the box and run for the door, how much of a lead she might have if she made the break. But she sat still and watched as Jehenna opened the box again.

The woman lifted one of the globes to the light, looked through it, then returned it, drawing out another. Vivian saw naked hunger in her face, even as she said, lightly, "As I thought—only a bauble, a toy. He mentioned them to me once as though they had some magical power. Your grandfather was, I fear, a little crazy at the end. It runs in the family, I understand. A very sad thing. Now, my dear. There should be, somewhere, another key."

Vivian blinked. "I don't know anything about another key."

"It should have been with the bequests he left for you, but it isn't. I thought perhaps he had already given it to you."

Vivian's hand tightened on the pendant. "This is the only thing he ever gave me."

"That can't be right. In all the times you saw him, surely—"

"I only saw him once."

For an instant, so brief Vivian wondered if she'd imagined the expression, the smooth face revealed utter malice, then shifted back to a serene sympathy. "Well. No matter then. I am sorry to be the bearer of such sad news. He was old; I suppose that's some consolation." Jehenna stretched her arm across the table and gestured at the web-and-penguin pendant. "That's lovely. Quite unusual. And that's all you have from him, you say? Perhaps he gave the other key to your mother to keep?"

"No. If he did, I would know. I packed all her belongings myself."

"We all have secrets. Packed to go where?"

"She's—not well. We're trying a home in Spokane for now."

"Perhaps I could speak with her myself, if you would give me the address."

"She's not good with visitors. But when I see her, I could ask about a key."

"That would be lovely." Jehenna pushed her chair back from the table. "I should be going. No, don't get up—I'll show myself out."

The box was in her hands.

Vivian fought the inertia that bound her, managed to struggle to her own feet. "Wait—those are mine."

Jehenna looked at her, a smile flickering at the corners of her lips. "You have no need of them. I do. Good-bye, Vivian."

And the door swung shut behind her with a soft, final click.

Not ten minutes later the doorbell rang. Vivian felt an unexpected rush of relief and gratitude to see Jared standing in the doorway. He carried a bouquet of roses. Long stemmed. Red.

The color of blood. For an instant her vision swirled and there was blood on the floor, blood on Jared's hands.

It passed, and despite her resolution to the contrary, she found herself wanting to fling herself into his arms, to be held and comforted and made love to. But when she looked into his green eyes she remembered a clear agate gaze, a crooked grin, and she stood quietly to the side, holding the door so he could come in.

"You've been working too hard; you look exhausted." Jared crossed the room and rummaged in the cupboard.

"There's a vase under the sink."

She sank down on the couch to watch him fill the vase with water and arrange the flowers. Tall, dark, and improbably handsome, the sort of man who turned female heads wherever he went, the man every fortune-teller predicted to every love-hungry girl who crossed her palm with silver. Her friends had told her she was crazy to break things off with him, that she would regret it, but all she felt was a quiet regret that she had been unable to love him.

The litter of paper on the table caught her eye. The will. Things she would rather not have to explain, but it was too late now to clean up; he was already crossing the room to set down the flowers. His brow furrowed as he picked up the will and scanned it over. "Were you going to tell me about this?"

"Yes. Of course. I only just found out a few minutes ago."

But he'd sensed her hesitation. His eyes hardened; his eyebrows drew together. She recognized with a weary inevitability the way he stood, legs braced, hands lightly curled. Primed for a fight.

He crushed the brown paper wrapping in his hand. "What was in here?"

Cornered, she got to her feet and faced him, feeling a surge of answering anger. There was nothing she wanted to tell him. Not a single, solitary thing. And if she spat out the comments that were swirling around inside her head, she could never take them back.

Once more, she tried. "Let's not do this. It was a particularly difficult night at work, and my grandfather's death was a shock. I haven't slept—"

"I told you I was coming—"

And that was the tipping point. "Right—you told me. You didn't ask. You didn't wait for confirmation. You left a message on my fucking phone and take that as a binding contract—"

"I was planning to take you somewhere special."

"Then you should have asked. And I would have told you that another day would be better."

For a long moment he stood, fists clenched, glaring, and then he deflated as if she'd stuck him with a pin. His shoulders sagged; his eyes were bleak. "No, you would have told me not to come at all."

He was right; she couldn't argue that.

"Look, Vivian, I don't understand what you're doing."

"I'm experiencing independence."

"But you could do that in Spokane. You could work at Sacred Heart or Holy Family—a real hospital, not in this podunk little town. It hurts me to see you living like this. So unnecessary—"

His hand described a broad sweep around the apartment.

"I like it," she said. "Please don't condescend."

"Vivian—"

"Jared. I explained it once; I'll explain it again. I've never had a chance to be on my own, to do my own thing. Spokane is too close to you, and to Isobel."

"Fine, then. Live here if it makes you happy. I'll come up and visit on the weekends. In a year or so, when you're tired of it, we can be together again." His voice almost broke, and her heart softened.

But there were no words, nothing to offer, no action she could take.

"Jared—"

He strode across the room to her and knelt at her feet, turning his face up to hers. His eyes were glassy with unshed tears, and she realized she had never, in the year that she'd known him, seen him cry.

He pulled a little velvet box out of his pocket and opened it. Inside, a gold ring with a diamond that had to have cost him a fortune. Pressure built behind her eyes. "Oh, Jared," she whispered, feeling loss as a hollow ache within her breast.

He took her hands in both of his. Kissed them. "Vivian, please. I need you."

"I can't."

"There's someone else. There must be."

Again an image of the bookstore flamed across her mind's eye, Zee's hands and the contradiction they implied, strength and tenderness, the warrior and the artist. But she'd only just met him; one encounter meant nothing. "I'm not seeing anyone, Jared."

"I don't believe you." He was back on his feet, face flushed, his body taut.

He startled when the phone rang. Not her cell phone, the house phone. She ignored it.

"Answer it," he said, his voice harsh.

"It can wait."

"It's him, isn't it? Answer it!"

"No—"

He stalked across the floor and snatched up the receiver. "Who is this?"

Her heart pounded as she watched him go still with listening, and then he turned and handed her the phone, his face a mixture of fury and shame.

Vivian turned away from him to answer.

"Vivian? It's Melody at River Valley. We've got a problem—"

"What happened?"

"Your mother—well, she's gone."

"What do you mean she's gone?"

"Gone. Vanished. She isn't anywhere in the house."

Vivian closed her eyes, clutched the receiver until her fingers ached. "When did you see her?"

"Half an hour ago. She went into the bathroom for a shower. The door was locked. I swear to God she can't have come out into the house. We were watching—"

"That's not possible—" *None of this is possible.*

The voice on the other end dissolved into tears. "I know. I'm so sorry, but I swear on all things holy we were watching . . ."

"The police?"

"They're looking for her."

"Call me if you hear anything. Anything at all."

Vivian's body felt boneless, everything spinning away into madness and confusion. *Breathe, Vivian. In, out, feel the floor under your feet, find the center. What if there is no center?* She pulled the pendant into her hand, felt its warmth, thought about what Zee had said about the penguin moving in and out of realities with ease.

"What is it?" Jared's voice had softened.

"My mother's gone missing."

"I told you she needed a higher level of care."

"You wanted her locked up."

"She needs to be locked up. She's crazy, Viv, you know—"

"Something happened, something's wrong—"

"You wouldn't listen to me—"

She shook her head, held up her hand to gesture him off. "Go home, Jared. And don't call me."

"Don't be stupid. You need me to look over the will—"

"Smoot can do it."

Jared snorted, an ugly little laugh born of anger and hurt. "Good luck with that. Smoot's dead."

"What?"

"Smoot's dead."

Vivian stared at him blankly.

"Murdered, early this morning. And robbed, apparently."

"Oh, my God!"

"Try watching the morning news sometime; you'll hear these things."

All she could do was stare at him, feeling the cold shock run through her. The only person she had felt she could still go to, the only person she could trust, dead. Murdered. Jared continued to grin; she knew he was humiliated and angry, but still the gap between them had grown immense, an uncrossable chasm.

Jared took a step toward her. Held out his hand. "Come on, Viv. You need me."

She forced herself to meet his gaze, willed her voice steady. "It's over, Jared. I don't want to see you again."

His face paled, then flushed. A muscle twitched in his jaw. "We can talk about this—"

"No. No point in talking. Please. Take the ring and go."

A long moment he glared at her. Long enough for her belly to twist and her knees to go weak. To watch the hurt in his face transform to a rage that set her teeth against each other, drove her heart into a quick and erratic rhythm of fear.

At last, he picked up the box with the ring and shoved it into his pocket. "You know what? Fuck you." He swept the vase off the table and it hit the floor with a crash, glass exploding everywhere, the flowers crimson splotches amid the mess.

When the door slammed behind him she stood gasping, arms clutched around her belly to hold herself together in a world that no longer made any sense at all.

Six

✣

Vivian was mopping up water and picking up broken glass and flowers when the full implications of Mr. Smoot's murder finally reached her. On her knees in the middle of the wreckage, the fragrance of the bruised roses filling her senses, it occurred to her that the woman who had so easily walked out of her apartment carrying the box of crystal globes was very likely the same woman who had murdered Mr. Smoot.

Hands shaking so that it was hard to press the buttons, she dialed the phone number listed on the letterhead of her grandfather's will and was not at all surprised when the secretary denied any knowledge of a Jehenna working for the firm. She called River Valley Family Home and was told there was no news to report. After a long hesitation, she looked up the number for the Spokane Police Department and told a bored-sounding receptionist that she might have information in the Smoot case. The receptionist thanked her for the call, took her number, and said a detective would be calling her back.

Vivian very much doubted this call would be happening anytime soon.

Her insides were shaking, an intolerable sensation that drove her to pacing the apartment, aimlessly picking things up and putting them down. She considered trying to repair the broken dream catcher, but the hoop was crushed and fractured in a number of places and she set it aside. She turned on the TV and turned it off again. Sat down at her computer and opened Facebook and then closed it. There was nothing she could say and she was not interested in anybody else's news at the moment.

She found herself wondering how her grandfather had died, and the thought that perhaps he also had been murdered threatened to push her over the edge and into hysterics.

"Get a grip," she muttered to herself. "Do something useful."

Her life with Isobel had provided plenty of practice at calming herself during anxiety-provoking moments, and she forced herself to run through the list of the tried-and-true. A few deep breaths. Some intentional muscle relaxation. Intellectual exercise to move her brain away from emotion and worry into the arena of logic and reason. There were new books to be read.

Wrapping a blanket around her shoulders to counteract the chills, she brewed a cup of tea and settled down to leaf through the volumes Zee had insisted on lending her. *A Practical Guide to Lucid Dreaming* was the first. The first few chapters described the practice; the rest of the book offered instructions on how to begin and develop the ability. This one she set aside—the idea of exercising some control was attractive, but her dreams were all too real already. The second was a scholarly tome, *A History of Dreaming*, with articles by psychologists from a variety of different approaches. Opinions ranged from Freud's belief that all dreams were sexual in nature, to Jung's theories of the collective unconscious, to the modern belief that dreams were meaningless artifacts of memory and experience. Book number three, *The Door*, was written by a psychic. Precognition, dream interpretation, all appealing topics but not something she could settle into. Not now.

The fourth book set her heart to racing. *The Dragon*

Princess. At first glance it looked like a picture-book fairy tale.

Another look made it clear this book was not for children.

The cover art was a strange and beautiful painting of a creature half woman, half dragon. The wings and tail and sinuous body, twined around the letters that made up the title of the book, were all dragon. The upper body—naked breasts and all—was pure woman, and the face and body were Vivian's own.

The image jolted something loose that had been locked away deep inside her, a dream that she kept even from herself. No clear memory, only flashes of flight, wings, flames, and danger. A very strong compulsion urged her to get up and toss the book out a window. Instead, she exhaled between her teeth and opened it, to find that the whole book was written in a script now familiar, a spiky black hand that matched a certain note in her pocket.

THE DRAGON PRINCESS

In all the worlds, the Wanderer was alone.

Once there had been others, but one by one they had grown old, or fallen prey to monsters. Some had suffered the failing of the mind that came sometimes from walking through too many dreams. Others grew weary and returned to their homes to die.

His body didn't change. As long as he kept moving, from dream to dream, the curse of age would not catch up with him. Half a century of adventure, and still he passed for a young man.

A responsibility came to him, now that the others were gone: to choose a mate, to make an heir to carry on. It had been impressed upon him, generation after generation, that he must choose wisely. Perhaps because of this, in one world after another, Dreamworld and Wakeworld and in Between, he had failed to find a woman he could love. Through one door after another he passed, closing each one behind him with care, until he was drawn at last into Surmise.

Exactly what Surmise was he didn't know, not then. When he walked through the door on that fateful day, he knew only that he stood upon mountains at sunset. Against a sky ablaze with crimson, the dragons were flying. Something about them spoke to the ache in his heart—the fierce, wild glide, the way each held itself apart, even while flying in formation. Tears glittered cold on his cheeks and he spread his arms wide, as though he, too, could fly.

A voice startled him.

"Good evening, Dreamshifter."

She sat on a rock in the shadows. Little more than a child, he thought, seeing the thick cloud of auburn hair falling all the way to her waist, a face as open as a flower. Her eyebrows, uptilted slightly over hazel eyes, gave her a quizzical expression at odds with her air of assurance.

"I don't know what you mean by that," he'd said, as he was bound to do. There were secrets to be kept.

Sliding off the rock, she glided over to stand beside him and without hesitation slipped her hand into his. It was slightly cold and felt small and defenseless. He tucked both her hand and his into his pocket, wanting to warm it.

"Tell me," she commanded, tilting her oval chin up to look into his eyes. Hers were extraordinarily clear, seemed to look directly into him and read what was so carefully hidden.

When he didn't answer, she pulled her hand away. "You mustn't lie to me. I am a princess." It felt a loss to him, weary and heartsore as he was, as though her hand had already become a part of his, belonged here, curved inside his fingers.

"I can't tell you," he said. "Not now."

The princess smiled for him, returning her hand to the warmth of his pocket. "You love the dragons, I can see," she said, and he nodded. Words seemed distant and unreal, in another world, through an endless series of doors that he could not begin to hope to reach. The dragons blurred before his eyes, doubling, trailing sparks.

After a lapse of time he became aware of her tugging at his arm. "This way. I know a place where you can rest."

He followed her into a shallow cave. A nest of dry grasses provided a warm soft bed, and at her urging he lay down, allowing her to play with his hair and sing him off to sleep. A dream, it seemed to him, a matter he had not the power to resist. In the middle of the night, with sleep weighing him down, he woke to soft hands caressing his body, and without ever fully waking or opening his eyes he made love to the princess there in the cave.

A dream within a dream, he thought, waking much later to a dim gray light. A dangerous matter, but he had walked through many dreams and his mind had always brought him back, at last, to Wakeworld. Turning to his side, his hand fell onto her tumbled hair, along a rounded arm and onto her naked breast. She stirred and opened her eyes, smiling a slow smile. Her hand reached for him again, stroked his thigh, and he felt his flesh stir at her touch. He had been a long time alone.

"No," he gasped, trapping the hand in his and holding it away, aghast at the thing that he had done. "I—am older than I look."

A soft laugh greeted this remark. "I, too, am older than I look. Do you want to know my true age, Wanderer, or shall we keep these things a secret between us?" Before his eyes she changed, a woman grown, young, old, and in between, laughing all the while. "Tell me, if I do this—or this—shall you really tell me no?" And all of his objections were swept away in a rush of passion the like of which he had never known or imagined.

In all the worlds.

And since she knew already what he was, and what he did, bit by bit she coaxed the truth from him. Days later, when he was so far gone his thoughts were barely his own, she murmured into his ear, "Teach me."

He laughed, and spoke the truth. "There are rules. I can teach only one person—one successor. My child, or my grandchild."

"You have children then? Where are they?"

"No. I have no child." Something stirred, a memory of why he had come, and what he was seeking. He put his arms around her and stroked her shining hair. "You might give me one, and I will teach him everything I know."

She pushed him away, pouting. "Why must it be a matter of blood? I can learn—you know I can."

It was too late to begin to resist her. He felt the danger, the coil of power she had wrapped around him. In that instant it occurred to him to wonder why she never took him down into the village, never had contact with another living soul. If she was a princess, why did she live in a cave at the top of the mountain, always within sight of the dragons? Where was her castle, her servants, where her kingdom? Dimly he recognized sorcery at work but found himself helpless before it.

"I promise to give you a child when you have taught me."

When he thought of leaving her, it seemed to him that he must die. And he must have a child. Thus it was that he took her by the hand and led her through the door by which he had come into Surmise. And after that another. And another. He taught her all the ancient secrets, so that he might keep her ever by his side.

She kept her promise. Her belly began to swell as a child grew within. There came a day when she chose not to join him in his wandering. "It is time for the baby to come. I must rest." He longed to stay with her, but she commanded him and he was not able to resist her will.

And so he went about his tasks alone—maintaining the doorways, as he had been taught, keeping them closed that the reality of one world might not flood into the reality of another.

When he returned to look for her, she was gone. The cave at the top of the mountains was empty. He asked after her in the town of Surmise but each time he asked, he saw eyes wide with fear, and each and every citizen of that land denied any knowledge of a princess.

At last, an old man, tottering on his feet and with a beard down to his knees, responded to his question. "I have no fear. Am I not about to die? What can she do to me? You speak of the Sorceress, the Dragon Queen. No princess she. Time everlasting she has come and gone, grasping ever for more power. All of Surmise is her weaving."

That was all. He would say no more.

Things began to go badly for the Wanderer. Doors would not stay closed. Madness spilled into one world after another as the doors to Dreamworld stood open, as one dream flowed into another, became a river of dream that flowed at last into Surmise. As fast as he could run he closed the doors, only to find them open again behind him.

Year followed year, a long and weary time. At long last, after traveling through door after door, always seeking, ever alone, he found her wandering in a meadow, a chain of flowers in her hair. She looked as she had when he first laid eyes on her, ever young, ever beautiful.

"Where is the child?" he asked, keeping a distance between them.

"She is safe."

"You promised—"

"And I have kept my promise. I bore you a child. One last thing I would ask of you, beloved." She crossed the distance between them and took one of his hands in hers. "I would see the key to the Forever."

He pulled away, shaking his head. "No. That is the one thing I cannot show you."

She kissed his lips, pleaded with her eyes. "You do not love me."

"I do. More than my own soul, gods help me, and I have broken all the rules for you save this. This one line I will not cross."

"Tell me then, if you cannot show me. About the key, and where it leads. And then I will take you to your daughter."

All men sin, at need. The Wanderer was no exception. He was weary and alone and desired greatly to see his child. And so, he told her the thing of which he was never to speak.

The Sorceress smiled then. "She is in Surmise, as she has always been."

"But I have looked for her there—"

She only smiled, and her smile told him how wrong he had been to tell her, and what he must do to try to set things right.

"There is something I have not yet shown you; come with me." And she followed him through one dream, and into another, until at last he opened one final door and stepped aside.

"It is empty," she said. "There is nothing there."

"Ah, but if you stand at the center, it will be full of the greatest treasure."

She laughed at his flattery and entered, always seeking to learn new secrets. Behind her back, before she could turn and lay a command on him, he closed the door behind her, and put a seal on it, meant to last for happily ever after.

He left her there and went away to do his work and to find his daughter. As for the Sorceress, she knew two things the Wanderer did not know, not then, though he learned them later to his great sorrow.

One, the blood of dragons ran through her veins, and as everybody knows, the magic of dragons can do what the magic of man does not understand.

Second, and perhaps most important of all, she knew the truth of Happily Ever After: that in all the worlds, no such thing exists, not even in a dream.

Vivian let the book fall closed in her lap, turning it upside down so the disturbing front cover was out of sight. She shivered, letting all of the implications of the story run through her. After a little while she got up and put on her coat. She put the book into the bag and carried it with her out through the door, locking it carefully behind her.

This time she wasted no time outside the bookstore. A bell jangled as she entered, and Zee appeared at once from behind a stack of books. His face lit up at first sight of her, then sobered when he saw her expression.

Vivian stalked across the floor, jerked the book from the bag, and thrust it into his hands. "Explain."

Furious and frightened as she was, still she felt her heart turn over as she watched those hands run over the outrageous cover.

"I was afraid you'd take it this way," he said after a long silence.

"How else should I take it?"

His lips twisted into a mischievous grin. "Amazement over the sheer brilliance of the art, that would be good."

Already the anger was running out of her, but she stiffened her spine and kept an edge of harshness in her voice. "I'm not hearing any explaining."

He sighed. "Sit down, why don't you? This might take a while. Let me put the *Closed* sign up."

And Vivian sat as directed, watching his smooth stride as he crossed to the door, the way he moved with incredible lightness for a man so tall, the way his hair fell over wide shoulders, the narrowness of his hips . . .

She averted her eyes as she caught herself admiring his ass, reminded herself that she was angry, had a right to be angry, and that he was not to be trusted.

"Coffee?" he asked, and she nodded, worried her voice would betray her if she spoke.

He brought two mugs and sat down across from her as he had done yesterday, only now everything was changed because the book lay on the coffee table between them. "All right—ask what you want to know."

"Who painted that cover?"

His jaw tightened and his free hand twitched. But he met her gaze when he answered, "I did."

"But how?

"It was commissioned. I was given the title, told how the image should look."

"But—you hadn't met me. My eyes, my face—" *My body*.

"I dreamed you."

The words fell like stones into a pool, and both of them sat in silence as the ripples of implication spread.

She felt the heat rise to her face at the thought of him dreaming her naked, felt her breath catch in her throat. When she was able to find words of her own again, her voice sounded like it belonged to somebody else.

"How did you get the book?"

"From him. He said you would walk into the store some-day and I should give it to you."

"My grandfather said this."

"Is that what he is to you?"

"If we are talking about George Maylor, then yes. He is my grandfather. Was." An unexpected grief washed over her. She had seen the old man only once, but always she had believed he would come back for her. The loss of all he could have taught her was enormous. Besides, he was the only family she had other than Isobel, and just knowing he was out there somewhere had made her feel a little less alone.

Averting her face to hide the tears she was unable to blink back, she missed Zee's reaction to her words, but there was a new tension in his voice when he answered her.

"Was? You speak of him as though he died."

"This morning. I just found out. His attorney came to tell me, to bring me the will." So much easier to tell the story this way, even though she had come to realize that Jehenna was far from being anybody's attorney.

"That," Zee said, "changes everything." He turned the mug between his hands, back and forth, forehead creased, eyes distant.

Thinking. Making a decision. She knew the look, had seen it on the faces of hundreds of patients making choices about life and death. This treatment, or the other one. Try chemo or accept the inevitable. Life support, or organ donation.

At last he set down the mug, very gently. "There's something else that he left for you. You'll have to wait a minute—it's upstairs." He got to his feet, paused. "You will wait, yes? I think it is important."

"I'll wait." Where else was she to go? She kicked off her shoes and curled her feet up under her, cradling the hot mug with both hands. All the world was shifting around her, but at least the coffee remained the same.

No more than a couple of moments and Zee was back with a manila envelope in hand.

"I'm sorry," he said, sitting down across from her. "About your grandfather. And—about the book. I know my painting you must seem strange—"

"Stalker strange."

"I told you, I dreamed you."

"That's really not helpful." He had dreamed her naked and half dragon, had been moved to paint her from dream. Her face flushed again at the thought of those hands painting the contours of her naked breasts. "It's not just the picture," she made herself say. "Did you read the story?"

"Yes."

"Does it make any sense to you?"

"It's meant to be more than a fairy tale."

"That's what I thought. But I don't know what."

The envelope was thoroughly sealed, wrapped in layers of packing tape that refused to give to her fingers. Vivian dug the stiletto out of her pocket, flicking open the blade with a touch of her finger on the release.

Zee whistled. "That even legal?"

"It works," she said, slicing through the tape in one smooth gesture. She didn't know about legal, but the bone-handled stiletto was comforting and familiar.

Inside the envelope lay a single sheet of paper. Vivian recognized the handwriting, her name at the top.

"How long have you been holding on to this?"

"Nine years."

She felt herself staring, pressed the palms of her hands flat against the table to steady them. At last she asked, "And the book?"

"The same."

"Just waiting for me to walk into your store one day."

He shrugged, then leaned toward her. This close she could see the fine umber lines running through the translucent agate of his eyes, noted the dilation of his pupils, felt his breath stir her hair. "Yes." His voice was husky and low. "Always waiting."

Vivian's heart was too big for her chest, thudding against her ribs. There was a real danger that she could get lost in his eyes. If he kissed her—

She tore her eyes away from his, breathing hard. Out of her peripheral vision she watched him lean back again in his chair.

Don't look at his hands, so close to your own on the table. Don't think about his lips, or try to sneak another glimpse of those eyes.

A ready distraction lay on the table in front of her, a note that had been in this man's possession, waiting for her to claim it, for so many years. George had written:

Vivian,

I swear to you, my intentions were good. How you must feel, thrust into the maelstrom without warning or preparation, I can only imagine. But the war with Jehenna is a thing of my creation, and I believed it mine to carry it through. If you are reading this then I have failed, and the burden of my sins falls on your shoulders.

Each Gatekeeper may teach only one successor, and I gave that to Jehenna. When I tried to teach your mother— well, you have seen the results of that. I dared not try again with you, lest your mind also break. You will have to learn on your own.

Beware—Jehenna's power is subtle and great and she will try to twist all those who might help you. Be careful where you place your trust. She seeks the key to the Forever—understand that you must keep it from her, even should this cost you your life. Destroy it if you can; it is not a thing that should have ever fallen into human hands.

You will have to journey to Surmise, which is as good a place as any to look for her. It's easy enough to find—all dreams lead to Surmise, soon or late, even though it lies in the Between.

You are strong—you may well succeed where I have failed.

George

P.S. Tell the Warlord—seek Excalibur.

And that was all. Somewhere a clock ticked off seconds in the silent room. No other sound but Vivian's uneven breathing, and Zee's, measured and slow.

After a moment he got up and walked away. Came back with a fresh cup of coffee, which he set on the table in front of her. "Drink," he said.

Vivian obeyed, several long swallows, feeling it burn all the way down into her belly.

"Well?" Zee said at last. "You look like I handed you a hydrogen bomb on a timer."

She managed a shaky laugh at that. "When you met him, did he seem crazy to you?"

His brow furrowed, thinking, and then he shook his head. "Crazy? No. Eccentric, I'd call him."

"Eccentric how?"

"Well, giving me these things to keep for you, when I'd never met you. Buying that painting and making it into a book. He called me Warlord all the time—Vivian, what is it? Are you all right?"

At his use of the name, the room restricted down to a small circle: the chair she was sitting on, the warmth of the ceramic mug in her hands, the fragrance of coffee, the low table with its scarred chessboard, a game half played, *across from her, half risen from his chair, frozen in time, a man with agate eyes and a face scarred beyond recognition, long hair bound back with a leather thong, callused hands bloodstained, holding a sword—*

"Vivian?"

She blinked. Managed to draw breath. Zee's hands were stretched across the table toward her, and his voice said again, insistent, "Are you all right? Do you need to lie down?"

It was possible to shake her head no, she did not need to lie down. She held up one finger to signify that he should give her a moment. Air was necessary and in short supply, and she focused on drawing it deeply into her lungs and releasing. Once, twice, three times. And then she said, in a voice that sounded distant and strange to her own ears, "He left a message for you."

Seven

✤

V ivian lay flat on her back in bed, wide awake and staring at the ceiling.

Thank God she had the night off; she was in no condition to work. Her thoughts made her dizzy, alighting on one dilemma only to flitter away to another, forming connections that logic would have considered insane.

She'd finally realized, sitting in A to Zee Books, that all of the science and logic that she'd held to be true was built on false premises. Reality was no more real than dream, perhaps less so. Nothing was as it seemed, and this knowledge had hit her like a ton of bricks. She scarcely remembered making hasty excuses, fleeing from Zee and his dangerous eyes, half-running all the way home.

Maybe she would go back, tomorrow, and apologize to Zee. Maybe she wouldn't. He was a disturbing and complicated piece of this puzzle, and she didn't know how far she could trust him. Didn't know that she could trust anybody.

It had been a restless afternoon and evening, her body at once weary and unable to rest. She'd cleaned and polished and organized, then called Isobel's family home to check in. No, they still hadn't heard anything. The police were looking. They would absolutely let her know the second they heard a word.

She called Sacred Heart to check on Brett. Still raving about penguins, still far too cold, still alive. She thought about making a call to find out how her grandfather had died and discovered that she didn't want to know. She read through the will, carefully, forcing her distracted brain to focus and make sense of the convoluted phrases.

Just in case, she pulled up Google Maps and found directions to the cabin she had inherited. Maybe she should drive up there, maybe even tonight. But cell phone service was likely to be sketchy driving through the pass, and she needed to be available if the police found Isobel. Or if a detective ever called back to talk to her about Mr. Smoot.

At last she'd climbed into bed, hoping to sleep, but her thoughts refused to stop churning.

Beneath the anxiety caused by this sudden intrusion of the ineffable on her attempts to order her life, her worry over her mother and Brett and her failure in losing the globes to Jehenna so stupidly, a secret exultation began to grow. Her childhood belief that there were realities beyond this one, whole unexplored realms of space and time, began to reassert itself, as though all the years of unbelief had been the dream.

Little by little her mind quieted. She felt her body go easy, breathing slow and regular, heart pumping blood on a journey through arteries and arterioles and capillaries, then returning through the network of veins. A constant, smoothly repeating cycle as rhythmic as the movement of stars and planets beyond.

Never had she felt more awake and aware, tuned to a precise focus of attention that included the sounds of her body, the tiny noises made by the apartment at night, the humming of a quiet town outside her windows.

She came to understand that there was another sound. Not new, although she'd never noticed it before. It had always been there, beneath all of the other noise, but she had not been tuned to it. Now it drew her, and she stepped out of bed, slipped into sweatpants and her favorite big shirt, and padded out of her bedroom to investigate.

A stone wall stretched across her living room. High as the ceiling, it reached from wall to wall, intersecting the sofa right down the middle.

Surely this was a dream.

That was her first thought, but she felt too awake for a dream. Her hand sought out the pendant and found it. As she enclosed it in a fist, it pulsed against her fingers. The sound intensified, a low vibration matching the rhythm of the pendant. A rectangular shape appeared in the wall. A door.

Vivian approached, laid her hand against it, and gave a tentative push.

The door swung open. Instead of the rest of her apartment—the other half of the sofa, the computer desk, the window—a dark cavern lay before her. The entrance was illuminated feebly by the electric lights of her apartment, the rest of it an inky blackness into which she couldn't see.

Behind her, warm light, an ordinary world. An instinct told her that if she turned away now, climbed back into bed and pulled the covers over her head, the wall and the cavern would be gone by morning. There was no need to take a single step into the unknown waiting for her.

Except for this: Isobel missing. Arden burned from the inside out. Brett freezing under the power of something unseen. These things could not be ignored, and neither could the reality of this dark chamber.

Clutching the pendant for courage and luck, Vivian entered the cavern. Her bare feet slid a little on smooth stone. The air smelled of minerals and eons of time. For an instant a whiff of something hot, there and gone. Over her shoulder she caught one more look at her apartment, neat, ordinary, familiar.

The door snapped shut.

Only then was she able to see what had not been visible before: filaments of light, winding about each other in a complex dance, chiming like rung crystal wherever they touched.

Too beautiful. Too intense. A glass must feel like this

when the high note strikes it, in the instant before it shatters. It was impossible to move, to think, to do anything other than stand there as the woven symphony of light and sound vibrated through her body.

After a time she became aware that her feet were moving, following the play of light through the darkness.

Summoned.

The thought came to her from somewhere outside herself. This was no accident. This door had always been waiting for her, waiting for the moment when she was able to hear the call. With every step the lights grew brighter and more vibrant, the sound louder. Nothing existed outside the light and sound.

Until there was also heat.

A gentle warmth at first, radiating from ceiling, walls, floor, growing in intensity. And with it, a smell of hot rock, of a clean and smokeless burning, every step hotter and hotter until the heat became as vivid as the light and sound. Her clothing scorched and smoked. Holes appeared in her sweatpants, her shirt, blackened at the edges. The fabric disintegrated and fell away. Naked, she kept moving forward, through the ever-growing light, vibration, and heat. Her skin glowed, tingled, but she felt no pain.

At last, as though she had run into an invisible wall, she stumbled to a stop, both hands pressed over her eyes to shut out the blinding light.

"Hail, Dreamshifter," a voice said. "Stand up straight. Let me have a look at you." There was none of the compulsion inherent in Jehenna's commands, but Vivian found the idea of disobeying improbable and foolhardy.

Her hands fell away from her eyes and she squared her shoulders and stood, naked, at the edge of a high-ceilinged chamber, perfectly round. Beginning at her feet, rising to a peak at the center, a heap of crystal spheres sent tendrils of light and color swirling into the room. These were also the source of the vibration, each one emitting a hum in a different key.

Curled at the top of the pile in a sinuous tangle of legs

and tail and wings, an enormous creature—the source of the heat as the globes were the source of light and sound. Crimson, carmine, vermillion, with golden-green eyes so large the pupils were taller than she.

Dragon.

Don't look at the eyes. A protective voice inside her head, memory maybe, warning.

Laughter from the dragon. "It won't make a difference, the looking or not looking. You can't escape me, Dreamshifter. I am your destiny."

Vivian braced herself against the sensory overload, aware of a mind moving within her own. A silent battle waged between them as she resisted the intrusion, struggled for a way to shield her thoughts. The dragon snorted and spoke directly into her mind, soundless. "You waste your energy. Come—there is no need for words between us. Let me read you."

"No." Her voice breathless from the effort, Vivian managed to speak out loud. Something about this small act of defiance closed a shield around her; she could feel the searching intelligence looking for a way in, skimming the surface but unable to dip deeper. Even the vibration and the heat receded, muted by an invisible barrier.

"Hmmph." The dragon's eyes narrowed a little, like an offended cat. "So ineffective, the use of words. Imperfect. Imprecise. But if you insist."

Vivian ignored the comment, ignored the weakness in her knees and the hammering of her heart. "Why have you summoned me?"

The dragon stretched out its long neck, head swinging from side to side. Again the questing mind moved against hers, but the boundary held. "You are a Dreamshifter. It is tradition that you should stand before me, once, at the beginning. How is it you do not know such a simple thing?"

"My grandfather died suddenly. He had no time—"

"Time, time. He had the time of all the worlds. What he wanted you to know, that he has told you."

This fit with the cryptic notes. What Vivian really wanted to know was why, but she didn't think that question would get her anywhere. Instead she asked, "What are you?"

Enormous wings unfurled at the question, diaphanous membrane, iridescent. They beat the air, creating a wind that threw Vivian to the floor of the cave, where she clung to the stone until it passed.

"I am the Guardian, mortal. Even this, he did not tell you?"

"I know only that I am now the Dreamshifter."

The Guardian opened her mouth, and again a gust of wind rushed over Vivian, this time scented with hot rock and steam. The exhalation pushed her backward; the inhale sucked her forward, closer than she wanted to be, scraping her bare skin on the stone floor of the cave.

"Pah. You stink of sorcery." The voice had a purring quality that sent shudders through Vivian's body.

"I'm not a sorcerer. Sorceress. Whatever—"

"You've been touched by one."

She opened her mouth to deny this when the realization struck. "Jehenna."

Again the wings beat the air. "The Dream Weaver of Surmise. What do you know of her?"

"She came to me. She stole the crystals my grandfather gave me—"

At that a spurt of bright flame jetted toward Vivian and she buried her face in her arms, pressing her body flat against the stone as the heat passed over her. The great wings clapped three times in the air, a sound like thunder rolling through the cave. When Vivian dared to look up, she saw that the Guardian's color had faded to a dark, dull brick. A tear welled up in one great eye and fell onto the heap of globes with a hiss and sizzle.

"Please—what are they?" Vivian asked. "What does it mean?"

"They are dreamspheres. Each one is the seed of a dream. If you hold the seed, you can enter the dream without passing through the Between."

"So the Sorceress can walk into dreams? What harm can that do?"

"Harm? What harm? She will weave each dream into the Between, make it part of her Kingdom of Surmise. The dreamers will all be drawn into her web. And, Dreamshifter, understand—she can change the dream and twist it. Already she has done great evil, but with these?"

"I still don't understand. If the globes are dangerous, why did my grandfather have them?"

A jet of blue flame flickered out of the enormous nostrils. "An ancient arrangement, a favor called in. Each new Dreamshifter is given one dream. As a gift, a talisman, a place in which to escape. They have held them over the years, passing them on from one to the next—you must get them back."

Vivian's stomach twisted; she tasted acid at the back of her throat. "I don't even know how to begin. There must be somebody else, someone more powerful, more wise . . ."

"No one but you." A heavy weight of finality marked the words. Vivian, always solitary, as both child and adult, had never felt so entirely alone, destined to pursue an impossible task through all the dream worlds and into the Between.

"Please—" she whispered, not even knowing what it was that she begged for.

"I will hold to the agreement—no other help will I give."

"Tell me this, at least—what key is it that Jehenna seeks? Do you know?"

All color faded from the Guardian as she asked this question, leaving her black as night. "A thing that should have been destroyed."

"What does it open? How do I stop her?"

"I have answered what I will. These things are not to be spoken."

"But—"

"Enough!" A blast of fire passed over Vivian's head.

"But I need your help."

"I can tell you only this. If you fail in your trust, Wakeworld will go mad. Dreamworld will become a place of torment. As for the Between—" The dragon paused, sucked all of the air in the cavern into her lungs and expelled it in a gust of wind that rattled the crystal globes against each other in a vast chiming.

"Listen carefully. I promised one special boon to the last Dreamshifter. You are not to choose a dream at random—he left one for you. This is all the help I am able to give. Take it and go."

The serpentine neck unwound and stretched a head the size of a small house toward Vivian, so close she could feel heat radiating from its skin. If the creature so much as snorted now, she would be incinerated. The mouth opened to reveal teeth longer than she was tall, each one glittering diamond bright. And there, lodged in a space between the front fangs, a tiny crystal sphere.

Vivian's body shook. Her knees buckled, and she almost fell. With an act of will, she caught herself, forced her body forward one step at a time. The teeth loomed, a forest of diamond-tipped spears. Unable to breathe, the darkness beginning to close in around her vision, Vivian stretched her hand out and touched the sphere, trying to grasp it between thumb and forefinger. It was wet with dragon saliva, slippery, and the palsied trembling of her hands didn't help.

She sensed impatience from the Guardian and willed more strength into her fingers. For an instant, just long enough, they steadied, and she lifted the crystal away from the sharp teeth and closed it into her fist.

"Done!" the Guardian cried out.

All the crystals chimed in one mighty chord.

As though someone had flipped a switch, the light went out. The Guardian and the cave had vanished. Silence was absolute. Stretching away in front of her, as far as her eyes could see, was a narrow high-ceilinged corridor lined with identical green doors, all closed. Behind her, the same corridor, the same doors. Backward or forward, stretching away into infinity. Only this and nothing else.

Her clothes had been incinerated and she stood, naked and shivering, not knowing what to do next. When her hand sought the pendant it was there, warm beneath her fingers. She clung to it as the only familiar thing left.

But even though it comforted her, it told her something else. This was not a dream. And if she wasn't in Wakeworld or Dreamworld, then this had to be Between.

Eight

✣

O ne foot in front of the other, her footsteps soundless on a floor of black-and-white marble, Vivian walked. Nothing else to do, that she could think of. No way to go home. One direction looked the same as the other. Eeney, meeney, miney, moe—

She knew this place, this feeling of suspended motion in the middle of endless possibilities. So many nights she had lain suspended, caught between Dreamworld and Wakeworld.

The Between. Ever shifting, ever leading somewhere and nowhere. She had traversed so many corridors over the years, made of marble, concrete, stone. Some were tunnels, some were hallways, some were open to the stars. Mazes there had been as well, winding pathways through forests or well-tended gardens. Some nights she had floated the current of winding rivers or meandering streams on a raft, in a boat.

All that remained constant was the sensation of suspension between one reality and another and the ever-present doors. Odd how reality felt less solid here than in Dreamworld, and yet this was where the danger lay.

Here the dragons lurked. Even as a child she had sensed them, always hungry, always seeking. But in the past she had been able to slip over the boundary into one world or the other, waking or dreaming. Now she was trapped.

Mindless panic seized her. She broke into a mad run down the corridor, careening into doors, tugging at the knobs. Locked, all locked. Fear ran behind her, driving away all rational thought, pushing her to the point of utter exhaustion. At last, drenched in cold sweat, her breath coming in sobbing gasps, heart laboring in her breast, she stopped running.

As her breathing eased, a strange calm came over her. This was not some random fate. She was a Dreamshifter, sent here by design. She had already faced a dragon, and it had done her no harm. In her hand she held a dreamsphere, hers, taken from the mouth of the Guardian. Holding it carefully between thumb and forefinger, she lifted it to the light. Suspended at the center was a nearly empty room, holding a tiny table. When she looked up, she stood in the doorway of a room that was an exact but larger image of the scene within the dreamsphere.

Her first impression was of dust. Inches of it, softly blanketing everything in sight. She sneezed, once, twice, thrice. A fly buzzed on the sill of a window so dirty nothing was visible through it and only a dim and dreary light was able to filter through. Inside the small room stood one small, round table. On it, an envelope, furred, like all things else, with the dust of years.

An odd dream for her grandfather to leave her, she thought at first. With all that was at stake, surely he could have given her more than a dusty and nearly empty room. She stepped across the threshold, careful to leave the door wide open. Her feet sank into the dust, sending it swirling around her. When her hand groped for the pendant, it was gone, but she had expected this. Six steps brought her to the table. She picked up the envelope and brushed it off. Her name, Vivian Maylor, was written on the front in George's spiky black hand. It was sealed, and too heavy to hold only paper. She tore it open and a crystal sphere fell into her hand, chiming against the one she already held.

The note said only: *Beyond the living rainbow the dragons guard Forever.*

A flare of anger at the old man ignited inside her. Riddles. Secrets. All of the courage it had taken for her to come this far, and this was what she had to show for it. No way forward, no way back, just a dusty dream and a meaningless message.

And another globe. Maybe this dreamsphere would take her home, or at least away somewhere safe. She looked into it and snorted in disbelief at what she saw.

A penguin. Of what use, in any world, could a penguin possibly be to her? Maybe Jehenna was right and the old man was insane.

Or maybe this was a trap.

The thought came to her unwanted. What if everything was an elaborate setup by the woman who had come to her apartment, claiming to be a friend, claiming so many things? Vivian realized that she hadn't even verified her grandfather's death.

As if on cue, she felt a low rumble, heard a heavy dragging sound in the distance. The fine hair on the back of her neck quivered and lifted, her flesh puckered into goose bumps. Whatever made that sound would have to be big. Clumsy, maybe, unless it had wings and could take to the air.

Dragon.

If the dragons were coming, she must not be trapped in this room with no way out. At least in the hallway she could run. She sprinted for the door, stirring up a cloud of dust that clogged her nostrils, coated her throat, made it difficult to breathe. The sound continued, echoing from down the hallway, still out of sight, approaching at a speed that was indecent for something that sounded so big and heavy.

A new cadence had been added to it, a rhythm she didn't recognize: faster, a counterpoint in two. *Slap slap, slap slap.* Vivian had no idea what it meant and had no desire to wait around and find out.

She pushed for speed, racing down the hallway, knowing that whatever was behind her would be faster, that there was nowhere to run, nowhere to go. Blindly, legs pumping, feet sliding a little on the marble floor, she fled the unseen menace.

A glance back over her shoulder to look for her pursuer stopped her legs in their frantic churning, momentum throwing her sideways so that she had to stumble a few steps to catch her balance.

Webbed feet awkward and slapping on the tile, wings spread for balance, beak stretched forward, agape, as though drinking in oxygen, came a small black-and-white creature. It slowed as it approached her, changed its trajectory, and came to a halt no more than a foot in front of her.

A penguin. Three-dimensional and in the flesh, the reality of a tiny image suspended in the center of a crystal globe clutched in her fist. The bird fixed her with an unblinking gaze out of black obsidian eyes, then gave a sad little squawk and pressed itself against her legs, trembling.

In the distance, the dragging sound came again, and with it a cry that chilled her blood.

Vivian tried to take a step forward, but the penguin moved with her, one flipper hugging her leg.

Another cry rent the air, and with it a clear sound of claws scrabbling and scratching on marble, the dragging scrape of a heavy body. Far away in the distance but growing ever closer, she saw an ungainly body, sinuous and lizardlike, an angular head on the end of a serpentine neck.

Beside her the penguin panted, beak open, trembling.

Damn it.

Vivian bent and grasped the feathery body around the middle, hoisting the penguin into her arms. It was an awkward shape to carry, heavier than expected. Feet and beak scratched against her bare skin.

Down the corridor came the dragon, faster now, wings unfurled. There wasn't space for them to fully extend and allow the creature to fly, but they seemed to provide balance, the ability to move with greater ease.

Vivian ran. Stumbled. The dragon was gaining.

I am the Dreamshifter, she reminded herself. *I need a*

door. Staggering with fear and exhaustion and the weight of the penguin, she approached the nearest door, put her hand on the knob.

It was locked.

"Open," she murmured, "please open."

Flame burst from the dragon's open mouth, rushed down the hallway in a fireball that was going to incinerate her. She was going to die in the Between, naked, carrying a penguin.

"Open!" she said, a command now, a necessity.

A small click. The knob turned, and Vivian dove through the door and slammed and bolted it behind her.

Nine

⁜

Zee twisted sideways on the seat to stretch his cramped legs and ease the kink in his back. Nearly midnight, which meant he'd been sitting here in the cab of his pickup for going on eight hours, watching the apartment building across the street, number twenty-seven in particular.

An hour ago the bedroom light had gone out. No movement, no lights, anywhere in the apartment or the street, which left him nothing to do but think. He would have given a great deal to avoid this. His thoughts were conflicted and clashing, all sharp angles and opposing beliefs, and he could find no way to reconcile them.

George's only message to him had been bizarre and meaningless: *Seek Excalibur.*

After ten years of patient waiting, this was the sole explanation he was to receive—a cryptic reference to a mythical sword. And with that, any hope he'd ever had of a relationship with his dream girl blown out the window by that scandalous book cover. Zee could only imagine what she was thinking, to have had a stranger paint her so.

He found himself considering the possibility that Jehenna's accusation was true, that George Maylor had used him all these years as part of a dark and malevolent scheme. Whatever words had been written in that note had driven the blood from Vivian's face, made the gray eyes wide with dread. Zee had wanted to take it from her shaking hands and read it for himself, had hoped she might be moved to trust him enough to confide. Maybe he would have done better to read it himself and see what it contained before deciding to put it in her hands. But he had promised the old man. Promises meant something; breaking faith was not a thing to be lightly done.

And it was still possible that the old man had been acting in good faith. Jehenna was a dangerous woman who would lie as casually as she pushed back that dazzling cloud of hair. Zee had absolutely no doubts about that.

All of the years of discipline and peace had not turned him into a virtuous man. The sight of blood welling along the edge of a hungry blade had waked a hunger he had only suppressed. If he joined Jehenna in the offer she made him, she would give him this in abundance. An adventure, an adrenaline rush, as long as he served her purposes and her needs; no illusions on this point—if he joined her, eventually she would kill him.

He thought he understood her, and George as well. What was unclear was how Vivian played in this twisted game of power the two of them had manufactured between them. Both of them wanted something from her, each claiming that the other was dangerous and of evil intent. He didn't know which of them he should trust.

The solution, when it came to him, was simple.

It didn't matter. Whether Jehenna spoke truth, or George, the outcome remained the same. Zee owed no loyalty to either of them. He had made Jehenna no promises, and his commitment to George was over. He had delivered the message and the book, done what he had said he would do. Fuck both of them. Vivian was in trouble and must be protected.

Acting on instinct, he had followed her earlier when she walked out of the store, had walked her safely home and watched her go into her apartment. She'd made it easy for him, walking fast, head down, hands stuffed into her pockets, not paying attention to her surroundings. Which was also a confirmation of his fears: She was no match for a creature like Jehenna.

He hadn't wanted to leave her unguarded for a minute, but loitering for hours on the street corner in a town like this was not really an option. People would notice. Some busybody would call the cops. And so he had retraced his steps back to the store and prepared for a lengthy surveillance.

The knives were already in their holsters, the M1911 at his hip, extra ammo in his coat pocket. A thermos of coffee, a couple of sandwiches, and he was set. Walking out the back door, locking it carefully, he felt a tug of regret for the life he had lived here, a presentiment that he would not be back. He loved the profusion of books, had painted his soul into the pictures upstairs. Still, he strode out to his decrepit old Ford without a backward look.

He'd been watching ever since. People had come and gone, in and out of the other apartments. A dog had chased a cat up a tree and set up vigil beneath, until a child came and coaxed it away.

Nothing remotely out of the ordinary. Nothing to fear. In the last hour, nothing had moved. Not so much as a random car driving by. All of the lights were out. It was cold. It was tempting to run the truck for a while, create some heat, listen to the radio, but the street was too quiet for that; he couldn't risk drawing attention.

He could find no reason for the unease that intensified as the clock ticked closer to midnight. Reason or not, he felt his body changing, the adrenaline surge creating a heat that drove off the chill, a new wakefulness sharpening his vision.

Not that there was anything to see.

Another hour he watched, two. His windows fogged with his breath, and he rolled down the passenger side so he could see.

At last he could bear it no longer. Knowing he was most likely jeopardizing the last tiny shred of hope that she would ever willingly speak to him again, he got out of the truck, careful not to slam the door, and crossed the street to her apartment.

His foot kicked a loose stone, and it skittered off across the pavement. Then he was on grass, crisp with frost, crunching under his feet. He paused on her porch, all senses on high alert. The fist-sized dent in the battered green door looked old. There were no other signs of violence or trouble.

He knocked, a thundering intrusion into silence, and waited for what seemed an eternity, but there was no answer. No sound of television or music. No footsteps. She'd been tired, he told himself. She must be sleeping.

Again he knocked, louder this time. Only a vast and enduring silence in response.

Walk away, he told himself. *There is no evidence here of anything out of line.*

He'd never been good at caution. It was an easy lock. Old skills came back to him, and with the aid of his credit card he had the door open as quickly as if he'd had a key, and he stood staring at another thing that was simply not possible.

No one had gone in or come out in the time he'd been watching. And there had been enough daylight left for him to see Vivian moving about her apartment.

And yet he stood looking at a scene of disaster. In the kitchen, drawers lay smashed and splintered on the floor amid their contents. The refrigerator door hung open. A broken plastic jug lay in a pool of milk. Flattened yogurt containers. Sandwich meat, bread. Fragments of dishes shattered on top of the mess. In the living area, couch cushions littered the floor, slashed, stuffing extruding from gaping holes. Books lay bent and broken, spines split, covers twisted.

Zee drew his handgun, jacked a round into the chamber, and pulled the door closed behind him. He crossed the room, avoiding stepping on books, picking his way through the rubble.

The bedroom was empty, bedding dumped on the floor,

the mattress slashed open. Dresser drawers were staggered across the floor, clothing draped over them in clumps. The bathroom, also empty, more drawers pulled over and smashed on the floor with their contents.

Vivian was nowhere to be seen.

The one thing left intact in the apartment was her computer, and he wondered at this, but it made a kind of sense. The destruction was excessive but indicated a search. Somebody had been looking for something.

And he had recently met somebody who was looking for something directly connected to Vivian. If anybody could get in without being seen, Jehenna was the one who could do it. *Not human,* he thought with a shiver. Who knew what she was capable of? And a not-human might not even know what a computer was, might not know that it could hold valuable information.

He wiggled the mouse. The screen saver cleared and he was looking at Google Maps and an address across the mountains into Idaho. No way to be sure, but he had a pretty good idea who used to live at that address.

Sitting on the chair, he began a hasty search. E-mails first.

The door opened.

Zee was already on his feet, pistol up and aimed, before he saw the uniforms and realized he'd just drawn on two officers of the Krebston PD. Half an instant, and both of their service weapons were trained on his heart.

"Drop the weapon!"

Zee hesitated. *I could take them both.*

"Now!" There was an edge of fear to the voice, and he realized he'd already missed his chance. He bent and dropped his gun to the floor.

"Hands on the wall, and spread your legs."

He complied. The older cop frisked him, confiscating the knives and snapping cuffs onto his wrists. "What are you doing here, son?"

"I found it like this—was checking to make sure nobody was hurt."

"Yeah? Why didn't you call it in?" The short cop looked like he'd woken up on the wrong side of his life and was pissed about the injustice. Zee stared him down, kept his voice calm and matter-of-fact.

"Don't carry a cell phone, couldn't find the landline in this mess. Look—I'm worried about Vivian—"

"You just let us do our job." The older cop had a steady face, deeply lined. His eyes were intelligent. Looked like he'd been in the business for a while, and Zee figured he would like the guy, given half a chance. "Neighbors called, said they heard loud crashing over here. We show up, and here you are."

No good answer for that one. Zee held his tongue.

An exchange of glances, a hand signal, and the pissed-off cop moved into the apartment, weapon drawn.

"What's your name, son?"

"Ezekiel Arbogast." No point lying. Everybody in town knew him.

"Am I going to find any warrants for you?"

"I've lived in this town for ten years, Officer. If I'd been in trouble, you'd know." As long as they didn't start digging. As long as they didn't pull up his record. "Look—I can understand how it looks to find me here, but I'm worried about Vivian . . ."

"Tell me again, Mr. Arbogast, what exactly are you doing here?"

"I told you I was worried about her—"

"And why was that?"

Because she's the new Dreamshifter, doesn't have a clue what she's doing, and there's some sort of Superwitch out to get her already. Right. Silence was better than any lie he could come up with, so he held his tongue.

"And the gun?"

"It's registered. I have a permit to carry."

"Well, we'll just check on that."

"I wouldn't have drawn on you, sir. Things were out of order. I thought maybe the bad guys were coming back in."

"All clear." The bitter cop was back.

"We'll need you to come to the station—give a statement."

"I have no problem doing that, as long as you dispatch somebody to look for her. Seriously—"

"Let's go now, Mr. Arbogast. We'll give you a ride."

"Look, are you charging me with something? Because I'd much rather drive my own vehicle—"

"Book him now. Save time later," the bitter cop said.

"Cool your jets, Sparky. We did startle him. Go to the car and radio in his name. See if he's got a permit like he says, any warrants."

"Fine. Waste of time," Sparky muttered, stalking off. Every muscle in his body radiated disapproval.

"Now then, Mr. Arbogast. Tell me again why you are here."

"We're friends. I own the bookshop—she comes in to talk. Her grandfather died today and she was—distressed. I tried to call and she didn't answer. So I came over—found this."

"How did you get in?"

When you lie, make it simple. Keep the eyes steady, but not too intense. Don't look away. "It was unlocked. Another reason I was worried."

The officer had pulled out a small notebook and begun jotting notes. "Anywhere you know of that she might be?"

"You could try her boyfriend. Jared Michaelson. He's with Baskin and Clarke, in Spokane." That one was a guess—he'd seen an exchange of e-mails. It didn't matter, really—all he needed was to talk his way out of this room.

"Anywhere else?"

"She works at the hospital."

Feet stomped up the stairs. "He's clean." Sparky bristled with frustration. "No warrants. The gun is registered to him; got a permit like he says."

"Any priors?"

"Not in Washington. Take a bit to run the other states."

"All right, Mr. Arbogast. Turn around, I'll get those cuffs off."

Once free, Zee massaged his wrists, trying to rub away the all-too-familiar sensation. His heart pounded. This was going to get unpleasant. They'd dig up his past, sure as death and taxes. He thought uneasily about the knife locked in his strongbox. The blood on the blade. If they got a warrant and searched his place, he was going to be in a whole lot of trouble.

"Can I have my gun back? The knives?"

"They will be returned to you at the station." The decent officer nodded at him. Sparky scowled.

Feeling their eyes on his back, Zee walked out the door, keeping his pace easy and unhurried, although he wanted nothing more than to break into a run. Outside, two more men in uniform stood discussing the situation. Zee moved past them, dipping his head in recognition. "Hey."

They returned the nod without interrupting their conversation.

He crossed the lawn, got into his Ford. The thing was old—he'd owned it before George Maylor appeared with his unconventional offer, and kept it just to have something of his own, not paid for under the bargain. At the time it had seemed like a good idea—now not so much. The damned thing didn't want to start. By the time it had turned over three times, only to splutter and die, the cops on the porch had turned to watch him.

On the fifth try, it decided to run. One of the cops gave him a small salute, laughing, and he waved back, driving carefully and well under the speed limit. He took a right and headed for the police station as promised. It was on Fourth and Guildford, a one-story brick building that could use a face-lift. An unmarked and a couple of panda cars sat out in front. One available parking space between a rusty Subaru and an SUV.

He slowed, then kept on driving, straight down Fourth to where it ran up the hill and headed out of town, watching for lights in his rearview all the way.

As soon as he hit the town limits, Zee kept his eyes out for a side road heading in more or less the right direction.

The first choice turned into gravel, then a dirt track, until it ran out in a dead end. He backtracked and took the first turnoff that headed in the right general direction, a gravel road that wound through forest. Every mile or so, a barely passable drive led off the road to a trailer or a cabin. No visible people. No other traffic.

An hour later, he rolled into Metalline Falls. A small community, nicely isolated, but it had taken way too long for him to get here. By now they'd be looking for him. How hard depended on what they'd turned up with the background check.

He figured they were definitely looking for him.

Reviewing maps in his head, the Google Map in particular, Zee drove through the small town and turned off on a known but little-used route—a steep pass, narrow, and gravel all the way. Nobody would be out here this time of year except for the hardiest sportsmen, and most of them weren't going to be bothered with hunting down an escaped criminal.

Ten years of good behavior wiped out in one morning. Part of him wanted to regret this; part of him felt an odd relief. No matter how hard he'd tried to channel the energy of his dreams into the actions of a peaceful and law-abiding citizen, somewhere deep inside he'd known that he was destined for another fate.

Nature or nurture? He'd spent a good bit of time debating this question in the light of his own development. When he was a child his parents moved constantly, always looking for a place where life was easier. This involved evading the wrath of local churches who had given handouts according to the dictates of charity only to encounter increasingly pressing demands without any of the expected gratitude or sanctity in return. Which meant, for Zee, every year a new school and a new band of small-town kids to whom he had to prove himself. Not easy for a dreamy kid who preferred books and pencils to sports.

The name didn't help. Ezekiel Maccabeus Arbogast. Every year, he told the teacher his name was Zee. Every year, in front of the entire class, he was badgered to produce his given name. The church-educated kids were the worst, the ones who inevitably began singing "Dem bones, dem bones, dem dry bones" whenever he walked into the room.

And yes, his parents had named him after Ezekiel, the prophet who had the weird visions about the bones coming to life, and also after Judah Maccabeus, the warrior hero. God alone knew what they'd been thinking, but he guessed that reading through the Bible while smoking weed might have played into the decision. None of the kids seemed to know about Judah, but they sure did get the Ezekiel part.

At least once a year, somebody beat him up when they caught him alone. Walking home from school, out behind the church. Adults somehow never noticed when the beatings were going down, and his parents paid no attention to the black eyes and bloody noses, other than to tell him it was time he became a man and learned to fight back.

On his thirteenth birthday he took their advice.

Over strenuous objections on his part, his mother planned and executed a birthday party, inviting the entire seventh-grade class. Not in the cluttered single-wide, of course, but to a bonfire out in the field.

As soon as the cars and pickups started dropping off kids, Zee knew he was in trouble. All day he'd hoped against hope that nobody would show up. Instead there were fifteen kids. They smiled at his mother and called her ma'am; hummed *dry bones* under their breath as they greeted Zee and trooped out to the isolated fire pit.

Dem bones dem bones

"You kids have fun, now."

Dem dry bones

His mother sashayed out of the firelight toward the trailer, limbs loosened by the six-pack she'd shared with his dad, hippie skirt swishing around her legs, long hair trailing in waves over her shoulders.

Toe bone connected to the foot bone

One of the boys wolf-whistled at her back.

Something inside Zee twisted. Careless and self-centered

as she was, she was the only mother he had. One of the few decent things he'd learned from his father was to treat her with respect.

Foot bone connected to the ankle bone

"Nice ass," another boy chimed in, insolent, his eyes pinning Zee in the shadows.

His name was Carl; he was on the football team and swaggered around school bullying the smaller kids. Worked in the bush with his dad summers, logging. He'd been the first to start the inevitable song. Not the kid you wanted to mess with.

"Shut up," Zee said.

Ankle bone connected to the shin bone

"She's hot for a mom," Carl said.

"I said shut up."

"Oooh, you gonna make me? Hey everybody, the prophet wants to pick a fight. Think God is on your side, prophet?"

Shin bone connected to the knee bone

A setup. Already they'd formed a ring around the campfire, with him and Carl closed in. The song was no longer only in his head; all of the voices took it up as a chant.

"I don't want to fight," Zee said, eyeing the circle. "I just want you to shut up about my mom."

Carl stepped forward, put a hand at the center of his chest, shoved him. Zee tripped over a branch, stumbled backward and almost into the fire.

The chanters picked up the intensity.

Knee bone connected to the thigh bone
Thigh bone connected to the hip bone

Above, a sky crusted with stars, lancets of cold and distant light. The chanting ring of kids around the fire, faces flickering in and out of shadow. The smell of smoke. Fear. Humiliation.

Trapped, he ran at his tormenter, fists clenched, and sprawled flat on his face as Carl stuck out a foot and tripped him. Face pressed into the dirt, he struggled to draw breath into lungs emptied by the force of the fall.

Hip bone connected to the back bone

Back bone connected to the neck bone

Something broke inside him in that moment. He got to his feet another person. Cool, clearheaded, with an understanding of his opponent and his own body that he hadn't possessed a minute ago.

Neck bone connected to the head bone

"Fist bone connected to the jawbone," Zee said, and swung.

When they pulled him off his foe a couple of minutes later, his knuckles were bloodied but he was otherwise unmarked. Carl was not so lucky. His nose twisted off to the right and spouted gouts of blood over his face. His front teeth were missing. Both eyes were already swelling. He lay sobbing, only half conscious, his breath burbling over the blood in his throat.

One of the girls, more sensible than the rest, had run to the house for Zee's parents, and his father staggered out to the fire, drunk and shouting imprecations at his son. The rest of the night was a blur. Subdued kids. Angry parents. And in the end the cops and his first trip to juvenile hall.

More important, that was the night the dreams began. Vivian. Himself as Warlord. It was the night he first began to hunt the dragons.

Ten

⚜

Something struck the outside of the door with the force of a battering ram. A tremor ran through the wood, and Vivian backed away, expecting the door to crack beneath the assault. The penguin slipped out of her arms and belly flopped onto black-and-white marble, letting the momentum carry him forward where he vanished beneath a leather recliner.

Another blow sent Vivian across the room to crouch behind the chair where the penguin had taken refuge. The tiny part of her brain that was still rational commented that this was an act of futility. If the predator made it into the room, there would be no place to hide and the chair would certainly not offer any meaningful protection.

A totally different part of her brain pointed out that she was naked in a dream that did not belong to her, accompanied by a penguin.

Silence, just long enough to acknowledge the thunder of her pulse, her ragged breathing, to notice that this dream she'd blundered into was an elegant apartment with a hint of familiarity about it. And then came the horrific sound of something sharp and vicious rending the door, top to bottom.

Vivian cowered, waiting for flames and claws and teeth, but once again the door held.

A bloodcurdling cry of rage and loss, followed by the rumbling, dragging sound of something heavy moving away from the door.

Clasping her knees against her chest, Vivian closed her eyes and rocked, trying to release the chemicals of fight-or-flight, to stop the shaking and calm down so she could think.

A rustling sound, a slight vibration of the chair she leaned against, startled her onto her feet, heart pounding all over again. It was only the penguin, which stood staring at her, black eyes bright and unblinking. It was the most penguiny-looking penguin she had ever seen. Too big for an Adélie, too small for a King, with a breast a little too white and a beak a little too yellow and obsidian eyes that glittered with un-natural intelligence. White patches marked each cheek. There was something unsettling about the way he looked at her that made her think of Poe's eternally silent raven.

"Quoth the penguin, nevermore," she muttered, fumbling for the pendant and finding it missing. Still in Dreamworld then. This did nothing to make her feel better. Once there had been a sense of safety in the words *only a dream*, but she knew better now. The dragon was gone, but there was no guarantee it wouldn't be back, maybe with reinforce-ments. Besides, this was somebody else's dream, which meant she and the penguin were not alone here. The dreamer might not appreciate a dream invasion by a freakish penguin and a naked woman.

Somehow she needed to get from this dream and into Surmise, but walking back through that door and into the Between was not an action she was prepared to take, not with the dragon nearby.

An inventory of her resources was not helpful: two dreamspheres, one that would take her to a small and dusty room, and one that had brought her the company of an un-settling and completely useless penguin.

It occurred to her that maybe she could use something from this dream, and she began to pay closer attention to her surroundings. The room was luxurious, but cold and sterile. Thick, woven rugs softened the marble floor. She and the penguin had taken refuge on a little island of furniture. Pristine, sculptured, uninviting furniture, upholstered in bold geometric patterns of black and white. The recliner was leather, brand-new, not softened or worn with use. The sofa was meant for cocktail dresses and fancy drinks and was not at all friendly to a naked, dusty woman and an inquisitive penguin.

An island separated the living area from the kitchen, which was also stark and cold. Black marble countertops, sleek black inset appliances. Above, a cathedral ceiling with a skylight, dark now. A scratching sound brought her eyes back to see the penguin setting out across the floor, wings spread a little, his body swaying from side to side with every step.

"Hey, you! Poe! Come back here!"

He ignored her, and she pursued him across the open space and down a hallway. More doors. Vivian cringed a little, but they looked like normal, ordinary doors painted spotless white. All were open, revealing a bathroom, a study, and a master bedroom.

The penguin waddled into the bedroom, Vivian following. This room, too, was done in black and white, even the wood of the dressers aged to a dark brown that was nearly ebony. A king-sized four-poster bed was spread with a black coverlet.

Cold. Vivian clenched her teeth to keep them from chattering, and when the penguin vanished into the walk-in closet she followed, determined to find something warm— even if it was just a blanket. The bed was too pristine to think of stealing the comforter. What she found in the closet was better than a blanket—a long, terry cloth robe, black like everything else in this place. She wrapped herself in the robe with a little hum of pleasure. It was warm and soft and fitted her perfectly. She slid her feet into a pair of slippers—heeled, which was not exactly comfortable but certainly warmer, surprised to discover them an exact fit. Something about the rest of the clothing—business suits, evening gowns, designer jeans and silk shirts, nudged at her like something familiar, and yet they were totally foreign to her usual comfortable attire of faded denim, T-shirts, and sneakers.

The other side of the closet was masculine: a row of tailored suits, shoes polished to a mirror gloss. These clothes she knew for certain she had seen before. Somebody wore these suits, somebody she knew.

A whiff of cologne drifted into her nostrils, a musky scent she also knew. *Jared. Jared wears that cologne. He also wears suits like these . . .*

Even as she recognized this thought and her heart convulsed with understanding, she heard familiar footsteps in the hall. She looked up to see Jared standing in the bedroom doorway. "Vivian—you're not ready for dinner."

Words failed her. What she guessed could be a good dream for Jared was fated to become a nightmare for her. Clenching the crystals into a fist, she rubbed her naked ring finger with her thumb, remembering roses on the floor, a splash of crimson.

There was a feeling of inevitability as he approached, as though she lacked will and substance, a flimsy creature without a life of her own. Which made a rudimentary kind of sense. This was Jared's dream, after all; this cold, stark reality was the creation of his subconscious.

"Where have you been?" he demanded.

"I—nowhere."

"You're lying. What do you have in your hand?"

Vivian put her hands behind her back, took a step away from him. "Nothing. Please—let me get dressed, we'll go for dinner. Where did you want to go?"

But he refused to be sidetracked, continued to advance. His face was all hard angles, no warmth, no softness anywhere. Jared could get angry, had an undercurrent of potential violence, but underneath there had always been a softness, missing now. She had hurt and rejected him, and now she had intruded on a dream driven by primal emotional constructs.

"Let me see."

"No, Jared, please."

Another step back. She tripped over the hem of the robe, twisted her ankle, and almost fell. He caught her, turned her, grabbed the hand that clutched the dreamspheres, and pulled it up behind her back, pinning her.

She wanted to kick, to scream, but the pervading feeling of unreality stopped her. Just another nightmare. Unable to run, unable to scream, powerless to change the course of events. This was the nature of dreams. No point in fighting. Sooner or later, you always woke up.

But this wasn't just any dream. All the rules had changed, and there was no guarantee that she would ever wake up. She remembered with an unexpected flash the book on lucid dreaming that Zee had lent to her, wished she'd done more than skim through it. People modified their dreams all the time, and she was a Dreamshifter. That had to mean something.

And so she searched for the words that seemed so far away, and gasped, "Jared, you're hurting me—"

He ignored her, pried her fingers open one at a time, took the globes from her. She heard him draw in his breath in a long inhalation of surprise, felt her arm released. Vivian almost expected him to vanish into some other dream. But after a short moment he brushed by her and began shifting hangers, looking at dresses, as though he hadn't just wrested the crystals from her by force.

"This one, I think, with the Jimmy Choos." He handed her a flimsy bit of fabric in stop sign red.

Over my dead body. Out loud she said, "Yes, of course."

And as he stood waiting, watching, she slipped out of the warm comfort of the robe, letting it fall to the floor at her feet. His gaze burned her naked skin, and when she took the dress from his hands she turned her back to pull it over her head. She smoothed it over her breasts and hips with dismay. Not much dress to start with, and she had nothing on underneath.

When she turned back to him, Jared held the robe in one

hand, digging in the pockets with the other. Finding nothing, he turned it upside down and shook it. "You have something else. You're hiding something from me."

"No, the globes, that's all. Please give them back. You don't understand what you're doing . . ."

His only answer was to grab her arm and drag her out into the bedroom. Without transition he held a small velvet box in his hand. For just a split second his eyes flickered from green to hazel; the shape of his face wavered. She blinked and his eyes were green again, his face familiar.

A dream, she reminded herself.

Over his shoulder she caught a glimpse of Poe, exploring, climbing with great determination up onto the high bed. Jared turned to see what she was looking at. "What—the hell—is that?"

"Penguin," she gasped, surprisingly close to laughter. Her breath came more easily; she felt more real.

"I can see that. What is it doing *here*?"

"I believe it's making a nest on your bed," she said, reveling in the grace of speaking words of her own.

Jared's brows drew together, his hands fisted. "Is it yours?"

"Maybe. Or maybe the other way around."

Jared's face flushed crimson; a vein pulsed in his forehead.

"Get rid of it."

"I can't."

"Fine. I'll get rid of it myself. Later. Right now I have something for you." His voice was too soft, his eyes like green glass.

He opened the box.

Vivian backed away. The ring was wrong. In Wakeworld the ring he'd offered her was gold, the stone diamond. This was a silver ring, with a black stone such as she had never seen. Black wasn't the right word; it was beyond black, beyond the absence of light. Vivian shook her head and put her hands behind her.

"Put it on," he said, and there was a threat in his voice.

It's only a dream, she tried to tell herself, but that logic didn't work. Not anymore. Jared was all about gold, about diamonds. He loved expensive things, expensive symbols even more. Pure gold, that's what she would expect in his dream. A diamond the size of his fist, maybe.

A door. She needed to make a door, to get away before he forced that ring onto her finger. Remembering how she had done this as a child, she closed her eyes and thought about home. Her apartment, cozy and organized. The dream catcher still hanging over the window, her favorite chair. Unbidden, Zee's hands and eyes came into her mind and she pictured him sitting in her chair, a mug of coffee in his hands.

When she opened her eyes the green door was there, right beside her. Her heart lifted as she reached for the knob. Jared twisted her arm behind her back and held her.

"Where does the door go, Vivian? The house of your lover?"

She braced her feet, tried to twist away. He had the ring in one hand, only had one free to hold her. If she could just get the door open, surely she could somehow get through it. But he got both arms around her and pulled her body hard against his. "Too good for my ring, is that it?"

"Stop it, you're hurting me."

He tangled a fist in her hair and wrenched her head back, forcing her face up to his. "Put the ring on."

"I can't—" She didn't recognize her own voice in the croak that escaped between her lips.

He tightened his grip, the tension between hair and scalp an exquisite pain that made her gasp for breath.

"You are mine, do you understand? Mine. To do with as I please."

"No—"

"No? I'll show you." He dragged her toward the bed by her hair. It was all she could do to remain on her feet; no way she could fight or get away. Poe met them halfway across the room, hissing and pecking at Jared's shins. Jared kicked hard with his foot. A dull thunk, a black-and-white form tumbling across the room.

"You bastard!" Despite the pain, Vivian kicked hard, felt her toes connect with his shin.

A backhand blow to her cheek, a flash of stars. Her legs turned to rubber; her body became a distant thing, held upright only by the agony of his fist in her hair.

From a great distance, she watched as he dragged her body to the bed and threw it down. It sprawled loosely on its back, the red dress creeping up over vulnerable thighs. Watched as he unzipped his trousers.

Floating above the bed, she felt a dim sympathy for the body below. It must hurt, that violent pounding, so far from an act of love.

At first she floated light and easy, but she began to feel heavier, to drift lower and lower, closer to the animal coupling. She resisted the pull, but it was stronger than she was; the bodies grew closer, closer, until she could feel hot breath hissing across her cheek, hands pinning her to the bed,

the thrust, the pain
his bed
his dream
his woman
trapped
NO.

Through the sensory assault she tried again to summon the door. Green. Cool green, the color of spring, of tamaracks when their leaves first emerge. An ordinary knob, cool to the hand, open this time. A door not vertical but horizontal, open not closed. A door beneath her on the bed.

And then she was falling. Her eyes flew open. Watched Jared's mouth gape in shock as her body slipped from his hands. She tried to call out to Poe but had no voice. She crashed, her teeth snapping together. Every bone in her body jarred, her skull bouncing once, twice, with an explosion of light behind her eyes before the darkness came.

Eleven

✣

For Isobel, all times, all places are as one.

That she should be engaged one moment in a fruitless search for razor blades in the bathroom and the next moment find herself in this blood-spattered kitchen with no chain of events, no passing of time in between does not seem strange. Both are prisons of a sort, outside either her desire or her control.

She remembers continuity, long stretches of it, days, maybe even years, where events seemed to follow one another in a logical sort of way. But mostly there is no narrative to tie it all together, and she knows, besides, that nothing is ever what it seems. Everything in this room, all that she can see and touch and smell, is nothing more than a collection of particles. If she believes *here is floor, here is chair*, the particles will hold together so she can stand, or sit, but floors and chairs come and go without reason.

At this time, in this kitchen, she is fastened to a chair by rope so solid she doesn't have to work to believe that it will hold her. A woman stands over her, a woman both familiar and strange, who runs through many fragments of existence. Something in the woman's laughter excites her and she laughs, too, although nothing here is funny and her hands, bound behind her back, ache with their position and the tightness of the rope.

Although she is here in the kitchen she is also standing on a stone platform in a dark cave that stinks of dragon and of blood. In both places the woman is with her, holding the knife, and something is going to happen, does happen, a monstrous thing, she knows, but she can't remember, won't remember.

She is sitting on a bench in a garden where a fountain plays, and the man she loves with every atom of her body puts a ring on her finger, a small gold ring set with rubies red as blood. It is the blood of his heart, he tells her, for her to keep with her always, and she slides an identical ring onto his finger, a promise.

She is sitting in a rocking chair and she holds a baby in her arms and she is the mother now. The baby cries and she rocks and soothes, because that is what mothers do. There is another chair in the hospital where she finds herself, again and again, oh so tired, pretending to swallow the pills they give her. Risperdal, Desyrel, Seroquel. She knows their names, knows they will seem to stop this shift of realities, but fears this more than anything. If she ever fully believes there is only one world, one time, that everything around her is real, then she will truly be insane.

This chair in this now is all of these things and none of these things. Her head is full of voices, all with different stories to tell, and it is hard, so hard, to hear the voice of the woman with the hazel eyes and the long dark hair, who very much wants her to answer a question.

Over and over the woman says one word—*key*. Isobel hears the shape of it, knows it is the name for an object meant to open doors. Vivian has a tiny key on a chain around her neck that she thinks Isobel does not see, but she will not speak of her daughter in this now. She lets herself slip away from the woman and her demanding voice, following the trail of other voices that leads nowhere and everywhere other than here.

When she again surfaces, the chair is gone and Isobel finds herself in a place both new and old. Here there is a fountain, mesmerizing and perfect. Water droplets rise and fall, fragmenting ordinary light into colors, bending reality.

She knows this fountain, this space of grass, the stone bench where she sits and has sat a hundred times before.

She also knows the castle towering black in the not very far away, all sharp turrets and twisting towers.

Her mind grapples with what she sees. The fountain belongs in Dreamworld. This she knows because it was her dream, her very own, even though she chose to give it away. As for the castle, she lived there for eighteen years. It belongs to Surmise, and the two—the fountain and the castle—should not come together in this way.

Even with this disconnect, time holds steady between the fracture lines. She looks past the falling water to watch a man pacing a well-worn path along the far edge of the pool. Logic, surfacing from a long imprisonment, tells her that this cannot possibly be *him*, not after all these years. See— this man's clothing is ragged. There are holes in his elbows and one knee. His hair is gray; there is a stiffness in his steps, as though his knees hurt him; and above all, he does not look up with eyes alert and wide, blue as the sky above them, does not sense her here and run to fling his arms around her, is so intent on this pacing, forth and back, and back and forth, that he is unaware of her presence, he whose heart beats faster whenever she is close by.

And so she knows that it cannot be him, and yet her heart refuses to accept this and beats an erratic and rapid rhythm and her knees begin to tremble. She presses her hands flat against the cold stone bench, grateful that it clings together, remains solid, does not become another chair in another place and time.

As she sits, she becomes aware of the sound of the fountain, the plink and splatter of water drops, the susurration, the flow. A bird trills and is answered by another. Near her feet a grasshopper explodes into the air with a crackle of wings. A low buzzing, the sound of bees, is all around her. Even the sound of the pacer's footsteps on grass, the rhythmic pad, pad, pad of his feet reaches her and she realizes that the clamor in her head is still and silent.

It is a luxury to sit in silence without the constant voices in her head, asking, demanding, instructing, so many of them and all at once so that she can't possibly ever get it straight what it is that they want. She has taken endless notes over the years, has tried writing color-coded shorthand, what this voice says in red, and that in green, and another in blue, but there are too many and they all talk at once and she can decode only bits and pieces. This has, for uncounted years, seemed so important that she feels she is neglecting a duty on the days when she gives up and sits silent and overwhelmed, or when she takes the pills that mute them.

At times the only thing she can think to do is to lay a sharp edge against her skin, to release the blood that powers her brain, hoping to break free. Always they find her—her daughter or her jailers—always there are sirens and bandages and the spell once more of medications.

But now, in this moment, the voices are silent and she watches the man, pacing, and it occurs to her, at last, that he is sad, with his bowed head, and his hands clasped behind him, that perhaps he wears away the hours and the grass like this because it is the only thing that eases some ache in his heart. She feels that ache herself, and so, even though it isn't, cannot possibly be him, she gets up and walks around the pond toward him, intercepting him by standing directly in his path as he paces in her direction.

He stops in his trajectory, staring at her feet. She is barefoot, she realizes, feeling for the first time the dust between her toes, slightly cool, and looking down she sees also that her legs are bare and that she is wearing only a nightgown. But then she looks up and sees him raise his head. His eyes, so wide, so blue even after all these years, reach hers.

There is a sunrise on his face. He whispers in a voice on the edge of breaking, "Isobel?" And then she is in his arms and he holds on to her as though she is life itself, crying, "Tell me it is really you, I cannot believe."

She is laughing and crying all at once, trying to tell him, "Yes, Landon, it is me," and he is kissing the tears from her cheeks, her eyes, and then his lips find hers and the kiss is the end of all the insanity, a perfect moment of rejoining something that should never have been sundered and nothing else matters, nothing, except that the two of them are together.

"I couldn't find you," she says, "except for that one dream." Sees his face change as she says the words and begins to understand what has happened here, why the fountain and her prince are in Surmise, a thing that should not be.

It takes a moment, over the beating of her heart and his, before she hears the laughter, and another moment beyond that before he hears it also and they pull away from the kiss, still clinging to each other, and turn toward the sound.

The woman of the hazel eyes stands in the water under the fountain, but her hair is not wet. Neither is the gown she wears and she is laughing and clapping her hands. "You should never have given him the dreamsphere, child." She holds something out on the palm of her hand, round and shining. Tosses it in the air and catches it in her hand. Again she laughs.

"You should see yourselves. If you were young yet, it would be beautiful—true love, here by the fountain. But you are old, or worse yet, middle-aged, and look like fools."

"Have you not done enough?" Landon says, and there is bitterness in his voice.

"Oh, I've hardly begun."

Isobel feels his arms tighten around her, pulling her harder against him. She recognizes this gesture as a signal for something bad about to happen, and her heart begins to hammer in fear.

"Let us be," Landon says. "There must be more important things you could do with your power. You've been gone a long time."

"One hundred years the old bastard locked me up. Do not underestimate yourself—you are an important piece on my chessboard, if it makes you feel any better. I play to win. There must be sacrifices."

"No," Isobel murmurs through flashes of dream, shards of memory.

"Come here, Isobel," the woman says, no longer laughing.

Isobel clings to her prince. She knows she cannot resist the Voice and the way it phrases commands. Still, Landon's arms are warm around her, and her mind is clear for the first time in so many years and she feels that this is the only solid ground. If she takes one step away from him, it will all fall apart around her; nothing will be solid, ever again, even her own body will disintegrate, and there will be nothing ever after but the voices and the noise.

Her body tenses, but she stays where she is, her hands twisting into the worn fabric of Landon's tunic. She wonders, just for an instant, why he wears these threadbare clothes, but then Jehenna is speaking again.

"Isobel, come to me at once. Leave him; he is nothing but a dream."

Isobel presses her lips against Landon's, knows he is the only real thing she has ever known. Everything she ever wanted is right here, holding her in the circle of his arms; this is her sanity, and she is not going to step away from it, not for all of the magic in the world.

But before she can stop them her feet are moving without her consent; she is stepping away, breaking the safe circle of the arms that hold her. Her hands are still clenched in the fabric of his tunic and she will not open them as the Voice pulls her away. The fabric tears in her hands, and she is walking backward, empty hands stretched out to Landon.

His hands clasp hers, holding on, tight, tight.

"Let her go," Jehenna says, and his hands loosen and allow Isobel's to slide away. Their eyes hold as the current of the command pulls her away from him, saying all that needs to be said.

Isobel's feet are in the water. It is cold, but she cannot stop to shiver, cannot slow her pace, until she bumps up against the rocks, feeling the spray of the fountain falling over her like tears, as though the pond itself is weeping for the pain that wrenches her heart.

"I will come for you," Isobel hears Landon say as she closes her eyes, knowing she will open them somewhere else. She tries to hold on to this clarity, the look in his eyes, the promise that he will find her.

The ring still circles her finger, and that is her only hope.

Twelve

❖

The truck had been running on fumes for miles. When it hiccupped, jerked, and sputtered to a stop in the middle of the narrow track, Zee was only grateful to have made it so far. None of his plans extended to finding a way back; there was no point. Whatever happened next, there would be no return to his old life.

His best guesses and calculations, based on his glimpse of the Google Map in Vivian's apartment and what the old man had told him, indicated that the cabin shouldn't be much farther on. He looked around to make sure he wasn't being pursued and then struck out on foot.

No ncighbors anywhere in sight. The last he'd seen was about half a mile back—a single-wide trailer, the yard a morass of discarded furniture and rusting appliances. The place had been disturbingly evocative of his own childhood, enough so that if he hadn't been looking for Vivian he might have turned in to investigate.

But time pressed, and with every minute, every hour, more of his dreams surfaced to conscious memory and his apprehension grew. Jehenna figured in some of them, powerful, ruthless. Battles, wars, hand-to-hand combat. And always the dragons. He shifted from a fast walk to a jog, resisting the urge to break into a full-on dash. He had a distance to go; pacing mattered.

When at last he reached a driveway leading off to the right, he was breathing hard and having doubts that he was in the right place. The mailbox, hand-lettered *MAYLOR* in permanent marker, gave him his second wind, and he picked up speed. The driveway was nothing more than two rough tracks made by tires, with grass growing between. A windbreak of poplars screened him from the main road.

Half a mile, maybe, and he came out into an open graveled yard, hemmed in by a grove of evergreen trees. A raven flew up at his approach, cronking loudly as it passed overhead, wings audibly whistling through the air. A car was parked in the yard. Not George's car, Zee was pretty sure. Not a cop car, either. This was a shark-gray Lexus, still screaming showroom despite the fresh layer of dust.

Nobody in the vehicle. Nobody in sight anywhere on the property. Which meant that whoever belonged to the car was in the cabin, despite the yellow crime-scene tape draped across the steps to the deck, undisturbed.

Zee wished for his gun and his knives. Stupid to head unarmed into a situation like this. The witch could be in there, or somebody equally unpleasant. He picked up a branch from the yard, hefted it, chose one that was stouter.

The door was unlocked, although it stuck and he had to yank hard, stumbling off balance when the friction released and it swung open. An invasive, heavy stench of iron and rot struck his nostrils. Blood. A pool of it congealed on the kitchen floor, busy with flies. A kitchen chair lay overturned beside it. Blood splattered the walls, the ceiling.

There were footprints in the blood, two sets. Both small, women or children. One person, wearing shoes, had walked around the kitchen, careless of either blood or footprints. Another person, barefoot, had walked into the middle of the largest pool of blood and had not walked out. Four small, perfectly square marks right next to these footprints. Chair legs.

Zee's eyes narrowed. The feet with the shoes had been

everywhere. If Vivian was here somewhere, she had company. He stood still, listening, looking.

A sitting room shared the same space as the kitchen. A reclining chair, a television and stereo. The floor was split wood, polished smooth by years of scrubbing rather than any particular process of sanding and sealing. An open door across the sitting room revealed a bedroom. Drawers pulled out and dumped on the floor. Mattress and pillows slashed. Same story in the bathroom. Another door opened into a small room that held a couple of chairs, a sagging sofa, a coffee table with a stack of books and magazines. It looked more like a waiting room than anything else.

This room was intact. And sitting on the old sofa, his startled gaze registering Zee's appearance, sat a man who matched the Lexus in the yard. Tall and dark, with eyes of an unusual shade of green. Impeccably groomed hair and a tailored suit that hadn't come off any rack. A suit like that should fit smoothly without wrinkle or bulge; the slight unevenness on the left meant a concealed weapon in a shoulder holster. Zee's hand tightened a little on the stick.

"Where is she?"

"She who?" Cool insolence in the eyes, one leg crossed over the other.

"Vivian. Where is she?"

"I have no idea what you're talking about."

Zee held himself in the doorway while his senses registered all of the details. The open door at his back. Another door across the small chamber, green with a brass knob. Long, deep scars marring the paint. A dark brown area rug on the floor, concealing the possibility of bloody footprints.

The man got to his feet. Zee stood poised, watching the hands. He would have to be quick if the stranger went for a gun. But the hands went into the pants pockets instead, casual, lord of the manor. "Supposing you tell me who you are and what the hell you are talking about?"

Zee took a deep breath, expelled it slowly through his teeth, and took a guess. "I'm a friend of Vivian's. You must be Jared."

Bingo. A tightening of the jaw, a shift in posture from lordly to defensive. Zee pushed on. "Look, I don't know if you're aware of this, but her apartment has been totally torn apart. She's not answering her cell. Is she with you?"

"I certainly don't see her here anywhere. Do you?" The tone, still insolent, held an undertone of fury. Good. He could use that.

"What about in there?" Zee nodded at the green door.

"Locked. Look—I appreciate your concern, but if she was going to turn to anybody, it would be me and not some casual acquaintance. Why don't you just head back home—"

"What are you doing here?" Zee's sharp eyes had caught sight of an edge of white paper protruding from beneath a magazine. Jared's right hand had rested protectively on top of this. The left was loosely curled into a fist, concealing something.

"Not that I have to answer to you—but as her attorney, I sort of have a right to be here—"

"Nobody has a right to be here besides the cops. Crime scene. We're both out of line on that. I don't suppose you noticed the footprints in the kitchen?"

Jared's nose wrinkled. "I spent as little time as possible in there."

"And here you calmly sit. Maybe you did something to her. Trashed her apartment looking for something. Came here and repeated the search."

"That's insane."

"Is it? Show me what you have in your hand."

Zee was primed and ready. Jared went for his gun but never got close before the stick struck him across the knuckles, sending the gun skittering across the floor. In a heartbeat Zee had a strangle lock around his throat. "Both hands, out where I can see them."

Jared raised his hands, the left still clenched.

"Now, open your fist."

"Fuck off. It's none of your business."

Zee tightened his grip, shifting pressure to the carotids, blocking off blood from the brain.

Jared's arms and legs flailed in an uncoordinated, frantic attempt at escape before his face slackened and his muscles went loose. Zee released the pressure. He wasn't going to take the chance of killing somebody Vivian might love.

Easy enough now to open the fingers. A small crystal globe rolled and hit the floor with a chiming sound.

Zee stood long, looking at the man, and then the globe. Thinking, drawing conclusions.

Under the concealing magazine he found a copy of George Maylor's last will and testament. It was possible that Vivian had given Jared a copy to look over. He couldn't have been the one to ransack the apartment, because Zee would have seen him come and go. But Jehenna could have given it to him. That and the crystal. Which meant he was working with her and treacherous.

Half-expecting to find some mysterious key, Zee rifled through the unconscious man's pockets. Then his socks, his shoes. He found a ring of very ordinary keys—car, house, maybe office. A wallet with credit cards, money, ID. A small velvet box containing a diamond ring.

The ring made his heart skip a beat, but he told himself there was hope as long as the ring was in the box and not on Vivian's finger.

Jared moaned and stirred, his eyes flickering open. It took a moment for the fear to register. Zee did nothing to put him at ease. He picked Jared's gun up off the floor. Removed the cartridge to check the ammo, slammed it back into place.

"Taurus .22," he said. "Tends to jam. Hard to aim. Effective enough at close range."

"Vivian won't thank you for killing me," Jared managed. His voice cracked a little, and he swallowed hard.

Zee allowed himself a grin. "She might, once she finds out you've taken a bribe from Jehenna." He realized, all at once, that he had come to some conclusions about things.

"I don't know what you're talking about."

But Jared's eyes shifted away as he spoke. His left hand clenched convulsively, and when he found it empty his eyes narrowed into hate. He sat up. "Give it back."

"Hey, I don't have it. Wouldn't touch it with a ten-foot pole. I would suggest to you that you let it be."

"She gave it to me. It's mine."

"Look, buddy, you're in trouble you haven't begun to comprehend. So is Vivian. If you love her at all, you will let the shiny thing go, get out of here, and call the cops." He paused for a minute to think, then added, "Forget the 'if you love her' part. There is no *if*. No choice involved."

"I want what's mine."

"No, you don't. You really don't." Zee gestured with the pistol. "Out the door and into your car. Go call the cops."

"And if I don't?"

Zee clicked off the safety.

Jared's eyes had been darting around the room. They locked on something in the corner, a small round object that shone with refracted colors, and he flung himself down onto hands and knees in that direction. Zee clocked him at the base of the skull with the barrel of the gun, and he slumped forward on his face, unconscious.

Thirteen

❖

The green door was impervious to violence. After several
full-body blows that nearly dislocated his shoulder, Zee
tried kicks at the level of the lock set, but this also accom-
plished nothing. The credit card trick not only failed, but
something sizzled and popped when he made the attempt,
and the card broke into three jagged pieces.

He forced himself to stop, think, breathe. The gashes in
the door were evidence enough, without his own frenzied
efforts, that it wouldn't open to force. Someone else had
tried and failed. He didn't have lock picks and doubted that
they would work if he did. George had done something to
seal it.

Maybe there was a window he could get through. He
made his way back through the cabin, past the blood in the
kitchen, and paused on the porch, wary. The Lexus was
gone.

Zee had dragged Jared's unconscious body outside,
shoved it into the car, put the keys in the ignition, and then
locked the front door of the cabin to keep him out. It appeared the idiot had come to his senses. Which meant there
would be police heading this way as soon as he could find
cell phone service.

As Zee made a circuit all around the cabin, looking for

windows, a logic problem presented itself. Not only were there no windows, there simply wasn't space for anything more than the rooms he'd already seen. Logically, there could be nothing behind the green door.

A shed out back turned up a sledgehammer. Zee packed it back into the cabin and swung it at the recalcitrant door with all of his strength. The shock reverberated through his body, clattering his teeth together. The hammer left a mark in the green paint, but not so much as a dent in the door. Again and again he struck: until his body was soaked with sweat, until his breath came harsh and difficult in his throat, until his arms quivered and refused to strike another blow.

He leaned his forehead against the closed door between his hands, palms open against the unyielding wood.

"Vivian!"

Silence, except for the sound of his own heart beating to the rhythm of defeat.

Exhausted, he slumped onto the couch and reviewed the events of the last twenty-four hours. *Warlord—seek Excalibur.* Riddles and games, games and riddles, like some sort of carnival show. The age-old myth of the magic sword.

Idly, he rifled through the stack of books, hoping the distraction might jar something loose from his subconscious. The old man had eclectic tastes—*The Fellowship of the Ring*, *The Girl with the Dragon Tattoo*, *The Fugitive*—one by one he sorted through the books, then stopped with a crumbling paperback in his hands. It was old, the edges of the pages yellowed and brittle, the binding broken. A picture of a knight on horseback adorned the cover. *Les Légendes Arthuriennes.*

Zee vaguely remembered reading this years ago, but his memory was fuzzy about where the stories fit into the grand scheme of Arthurian legends. He flipped through the pages, looking for bits about Excalibur. His French was rusty; the book was thick. The clock ticked the seconds of his freedom away. Once the cops showed up, there was no chance of solving the puzzle, no hope of helping Vivian. He had no doubt there would be sufficient evidence to arrest him, and with the old man dead and Vivian missing, there would be nobody to bail him out. Not this time.

Zee set to work methodically. Where would an old man hide a clue in a book? He checked for dog-ears, scanning all of the loose pages for any sort of markings. Nothing. He held the book by the disintegrating spine and shook it. No bits of paper drifted out.

He got up and paced, thoughts churning. Somewhere in the book there must be a clue. A code, maybe, something unforgettable about the plot that should trigger an association.

A subtle vibration stopped his feet, made him hold his breath to listen. At first there was nothing, no indication of danger. And then, just when he thought perhaps he was manufacturing nonexistent terrors out of adrenaline and frustration, he heard the sound of something large and heavy dragging over gravel. Then again, nothing. The minutes ticked by. He heard, felt, breathed nothing but quiet.

Adrenaline still humming through his nervous system, he sank back into contemplation of Arthur and his legendary sword. Excalibur. Symbol of the knight errant, the holy quest, magic. Wielded by the Once and Future King, returned to the Lady of the Lake at his death. Every language gave it a different name: Excalibur, Caliburn, Caladvwlch, Escalibor.

A new sound jolted his head upright. A heavy beating, like wings, only too loud, too big—as though a jet had mutated into a living creature. He looked out across the sitting room, through the picture window. Tree branches tossed in a gust of wind that rattled and creaked the old cabin. A dark shadow fell over the grass.

Silence.

When the front door exploded, his hand was already on the trigger of Jared's gun, firing at a gigantic horned head thrusting through the splintered wood. Unbothered by the shots, the head lunged farther into the room, propelled by a serpentine neck. An enormous golden eye took Zee's measure.

The shock was less than it would have been twenty-four hours ago. Zee's brain made short work of registering the relevant facts—*dragon, real, danger*—and suggested he take immediate action for survival.

He fired off another volley of shots, aiming for the eye, but the head whipped upward at unbelievable speed, bullets ricocheting off scales in a whining frenzy that slammed into the floor and walls. A thin line of heat creased Zee's cheek, and he felt the wetness of blood.

A flesh wound, nothing serious. He backed against the green door, holding fire, searching for a place he could shelter but coming up empty. There was nothing to prevent the rest of the creature from crashing through the wall if it chose, in which case it could pick him off at its leisure. On the other hand, if it decided to flame from its current position, he was charcoal. Shooting was dangerous unless he had a clear shot at the belly or the eye, and the dragon was apparently smart enough to figure this out. It kept its ugly forehead directed straight toward him, nothing but bone and horn and scales to target.

The only option was to get through the green door and away.

Think, Zee. George meant for you to get through that door.

The old man had been anything but random, had planned meticulously for years. Every book sitting on that table was there for a reason. Wizards and dragons, real-life assassins, mythological kings. *Seek Excalibur. In the old French,* Escalibor.

Sirens sounded in the distance, getting louder. Heading this way.

The dragon rumbled, ears swiveling to listen. It snorted and withdrew its head. Again the sound of giant wings. The shattered door framed nothing but blue sky and a bit of green tree, suddenly blotted out by shadow.

A passage from *The Lord of the Rings* drifted into Zee's head—Gandalf standing beside a lake seeking entrance to another recalcitrant door. He thought about the message left him by the old man, about the book of legends written in the old French. And he thought maybe he knew the answer to the puzzle.

Outside, the sirens reached a climax and stopped. A crunch of tires on gravel. Doors slamming. Air thrumming with the beating of the dragon's wings.

A voice shouted. "Get down!"

Zee's first thought was relief. They could distract each other, the dragon and the police. A fortunate diversion, allowing him to get where he needed to be without being eaten or barbecued or arrested. A perfect plan, except for the part where the cops were just men trying to do their jobs. Men who wouldn't have a clue how to deal with an airborne, fire-breathing monster.

Keeping low, he crossed the room, flattened himself against the wall, and peered out through the doorway. Three black-and-whites. Six uniforms, all crouched behind the cars for shelter, service weapons ready, looking not at him but up.

Following the trajectory of their collective eyes, Zee caught a glimpse of the dragon before it flew out of his narrow visual range. No longer clumsy and heavy, in the air it was a sinuous flying machine, scales rainbow bright and glittering in the sunlight.

He hadn't expected it to be beautiful; not that this recognition changed what needed to be done.

The initial shock had settled and allowed him to collect his thoughts. Stupid to fire at random as he'd done. A waste of ammo that had almost gotten him killed with his own bullets. He released the clip to see what he had left. One shot.

One. In a gun accurate only at close range.

Meanwhile, the cops were repeating his mistake in a flurry of gunfire. At least they had reloads, and the chances of getting killed by a ricochet outdoors were less. Maybe someone would fire a lucky shot. Or maybe the dragon would get spooked by the noise and fly off elsewhere.

To pluck some unsuspecting person off a street corner. No, the dragon must be killed.

Again the shadow, rolling in fast, darkening grass and gravel. The air thudded with the cadence of giant wings. Wind bent the trees, rolled small stones across the yard. And then the dragon itself, unspeakably big, blindingly bright, flew into his line of sight. Most of the cops cowered down, arms over their heads. Two continued to fire, ducking at the last possible second as talons struck one of the squad cars with a crunch of glass and metal. The car rocked up onto two wheels, teetered, and crashed upside down.

One of the men was trapped beneath it, his legs crushed, his mouth screaming wordless agony. Again the dragon swooped down out of the sky, this time shooting flames that engulfed the car. A horrible shriek echoed through the clearing, followed by shouts from the other men as they struggled to pull their fallen comrade free.

And then the dragon once more, in a low pass right in front of the cabin.

Zee was ready this time. He aimed, calculating the creature's velocity, the wind, the angle of his shot. Maybe if he'd had a rifle, all of that would have counted for something, but he knew he was at the mercy of pure dumb luck.

He pulled the trigger.

The dragon kept moving, and Zee's heart sank. But then the huge wings stuttered and drooped. Instead of rising back up in a graceful arc, the creature continued a forward trajectory, losing altitude as it went, cutting a furrow through gravel and grass until at last it shuddered to a stop in a twisted heap.

Two of the cops approached the unmoving mound of wings and scales, cautious, weapons extended, keeping their distance. Two stayed on their knees beside the blackened form of their comrade. They'd managed to get him free and away before the car blew up, the three of them at a distance from the flaming wreckage. He wasn't screaming anymore, but he must still be alive. One was rolling up a jacket to put under his feet; another leaned over him, saying something in a low voice. Encouragement.

Which left one officer free. One man who had kept his

calm throughout the onslaught, who held his gun like an extension of his own body. He looked from the dragon to the other men, then back to the cabin. Zee could almost read his thoughts—something was bothering him about the shot that killed the dragon. He was putting together the trajectory, the timing of the shot, and was going to come and investigate.

Avoiding the direct line back to the green door, faster but visible to curious eyes, Zee circled around the living area, keeping to the perimeter. He paused to reconnoiter before making a dash across the line of fire. Framed against the sunlight in the broken doorway, he made out the silhouette of a man with a gun.

"Drop your weapon!" The gun aimed directly at his heart.

With a feeling of déjà vu, Zee did so. The .22 was empty, anyway. He slid it across the floor with his foot, watched the cop bend to pick it up, toss it away behind him.

"On the floor, hands behind your head."

This he wasn't prepared to do. The two of them stood, eyes locked. "Nice shot," the cop said. "You saved us from whatever that thing was. But I'll still shoot if you don't get down."

"Can't," Zee said. "With all due respect."

Without looking away, he measured with mind and body the distance from where he stood to the green door. Ran over again in his mind the words he thought would open it. The cop didn't want to shoot him. There would be a hesitation, a belief that there was nowhere for him to go if he ran deeper into the house.

Maybe long enough to get through the door. Maybe not.

Zee lowered his body toward the floor, as if about to comply, watching for the moment when the other man's gaze relaxed, when he took an incautious step forward.

At that precise instant Zee flung himself behind the big recliner, shoved it across the floor so that it would lie between him and the green door. Keeping low, he zigzagged toward his goal.

"Stop or I'll shoot!"

A voice that meant what it said, but Zee kept moving. Into the little room, pulling the first door closed behind him. Down on the floor behind the coffee table, half-skidding to a stop with one hand against the green door.

"Search Escalibor," he murmured, wrenching at the doorknob.

Still locked. Nothing happened.

Shit.

The door behind him burst open, the business end of the .38 aimed right between his eyes. "Give it up," the cop said. "Nowhere to run." Footsteps ran through the house toward them. Backup.

Zee closed his eyes. Words, ideas, stories swirled through his brain.

And then he smiled.

"*Cherche* Escalibor," he said.

With a little click the green door cracked open.

Zee rolled through the open door and slammed it shut with his foot.

He heard a thud as something hit the door, followed by a grunt of pain. His lips twisted in a grin of commiseration. Somebody's shoulder was aching from that blow. His own was bruised enough to make lifting his arm a difficult proposition.

Confident that the door was going to hold, he got to his feet and looked around. Vivian wasn't here. The room had a sense of untouched emptiness. Nobody home.

Still, he called her name. "Vivian! Are you here?"

No answer.

No sound save for an erratic clicking, ticking, and hissing, not unpleasant but two degrees off normal.

The room was the size of a warehouse and crammed with strange and wonderful objects. He traced the ticking sound to a long row of time devices. A clock face with thirteen hours, one with twelve but each hour divided into forty-five minutes instead of sixty. They ticked in an odd counterpoint.

Sand glasses, identical in size but flowing at different rates, made the hissing. And a complicated structure of steel wire and copper balls, spinning in a way that suggested the possibility of extra dimensions, accounted for the clicks. For longer than he intended, he found himself watching this, trying to follow the path of the little copper balls and regularly losing track as they seemed to vanish and reappear. At length he shook himself and moved on, with an uneasy sense of uncounted time having passed.

Making his way through narrow aisles that wound between shelves and tables, he almost tripped over a wooden box with the word *Schrödinger* painted on the lid in capital letters. His foot knocked the lid loose, revealing a pink towel covered in cat hair. Otherwise the box was empty.

Zee replaced the lid, moving on between shelves of books, masks, statues, and images. A picture caught his attention. A castle—something out of a fairy tale, with dragons flying around turrets and pinnacles. Technique drew him first, the artist in him admiring detail so fine it seemed photographic, wondering how it had been done and what made it appear so nearly three-dimensional.

He leaned closer to see better. No artist in the world could paint a scene with such perfection. And yet it could not be photography, because such a place could not exist outside of dream.

It seemed to him, in that moment, that time stopped. The ticking and whirring of the clocks, the slow hiss of running sand all faded. In the glass of the picture, superimposed over the lifelike castle, he saw a reflection of his own face, a face that shifted and altered before his eyes: by turns bearded and unshaven, thin and haggard, desolate, laughing, and then finally a face so deeply scarred that its identity was unrecognizable, except for the eyes, which were always and ever the same. This face, these eyes, were his and not his. They moved independently of him, blinked when he had not blinked, leaned closer to see him better. The vision cleared, as suddenly as it had begun, and he saw again his own face, strange and familiar, with a bloody furrow on the right cheek carved moments ago by a stray bullet.

Zee's eyes shifted to a shelf below the painting. He had a vague impression that before it had held books, but now a single object lay there, long and narrow, half obscured by a thick layer of dust.

It was a sword in a worn leather scabbard. The hilt was plain and serviceable with a single black stone set into the pommel. Zee put his hand to the grip and drew back, startled, as impossible memories flooded his mind: battles he had never fought, dragons he had never slain. A moment of hesitation, and again he reached out for the sword, noticing this time how each finger fit to familiar patterns of wear.

With a hiss of leather on steel he drew the blade and flourished it experimentally. Keen and well balanced, it moved in his hand like memory. Dreams, he thought. He had carried this sword through all the nights of his life, and now here it was in his flesh-and-blood hand.

A distant, plaintive meowing roused him from his reverie. Fastening the scabbard around his waist, he sheathed the sword and followed the sound through the narrow aisles to the Schrödinger box. More meowing, faint at first, growing louder and more demanding. Bumping sounds came from inside the box. Zee lifted the lid. A large gray cat bounded out and coiled itself around his ankles, purring.

"Where did you come from?"

He bent to look in the box, which appeared quite ordinary inside. Nothing but the old pink towel, liberally covered in cat hair. No special door, no way in or out other than the lid. Zee set this aside, rather than replace it on the box.

The cat meowed again and padded off, the tip of her tail twitching, to vanish between winding stacks of books. Surely the books had been over there, and the timepieces here. The wire sculpture with the copper balls had held a different shape; the tempo and rhythm of it had been subtly different.

A shiver ran up and down Zee's spine, but the cat meowed again, imperious, and he turned and wended his way through the maze of shelves until he found her sitting in the middle of an empty space of floor. Just visible through the dust he could see cracks in the form of a rectangle. Green cat eyes gazed at him, intent, expectant, and Zee knelt, thrust his fingers into a gap, and opened the trap door.

Fourteen

❦

Cold. So very, very cold. Head pounding, scalp stinging. A dull ache, low in her belly and between her legs. The sour taste of fear in her mouth.

Vivian reached for the pendant, found it, but the little penguin was no longer comforting.

Only a dream. If this was Wakeworld, she shouldn't be feeling physical pain from acts that had occurred in a dream. But then, she also shouldn't be seeing a penguin, and the unmistakable form of Poe stood beside her, white breast and cheek patches glowing in the dim light, eyes glittering.

Moaning softly, she levered herself up to sitting.

Her stomach heaved.

She would not vomit, would not cry, only a dream, only a dream, only—

In the nick of time she leaned forward and spewed a thin, sour stream of bile between her spread legs, befouling the skirt of the red dress. Tears of weakness and misery slid down her cheeks and dripped off her chin.

Poe pushed his beak against her shoulder, a gentle nudge, and she ran her hand down his back, the feathers soft and faintly oily. Taking comfort from the companionship, no matter how unlikely, she blinked back the rest of her tears and looked around her.

She'd fallen into the entryway of her own apartment, and here, too, everything was wrong.

A wasteland of broken and savaged furniture and belongings spread out around her. Someone or something had raged through here, trampling and destroying everything indiscriminately.

For a minute she considered calling the police. When in trouble, dial 911. This time, though, there was nothing they could do to protect her, them or anybody else. Her eyes went over the slashed couch cushions, the upended drawers. Someone had been looking for something.

Again her hand went to the chain, reassuring herself that the penguin talisman still hung there.

The phone rang.

Vivian stayed where she was, the sodden red gown clinging to her thighs. Talking to somebody, anybody, was out of the question. Each ring jolted through her like a shock of electricity. She thought about searching for the phone and hanging it up, but it was buried beneath a pile of debris and moving was just too hard. The voice mail kicked in.

Jared's voice.

"Viv—I'm worried. I know you're probably not there—why would you be, after what happened to the place—but if you come back, call me. Please. We need to talk. Let me help you." Silence, only his breathing through the machine, and her own—too loud, too fast. "Well, okay. I know you're not there. Just—I don't know what else to do . . ."

A click of disconnect.

Her brain spun, trying to reconcile the concern in his voice with what he had done to her in Dreamworld. She put her face in her hands, winced away from pressure on the cheek where he had struck her.

Too much. Her stomach heaved and her body came unfrozen in a mad dash for the bathroom, where she vomited again, this time mercifully into the toilet. When the paroxysms ended, she stripped out of the gown. It smelled of sex and vomit and Jared's cologne, and her belly twisted again.

Wadding the accursed thing up into a ball she stuffed it into the trash can, then stepped into the shower.

Standing under a flow of water as hot as she could stand it, she scrubbed all traces of Jared from her skin and hair, letting her mind drift where it would. The Guardian, the key, the advent of Poe, the book—

Oh, God. The book. It had been here in the apartment somewhere. In a few minutes, when the water ran cold and she was forced from the shower, she would look for it in the rubble. She was pretty sure she wouldn't find it.

And then, at last, the other thing came to her.

The dreamspheres. Jared had taken them. Which meant what? That he had in his possession access to a small and dusty room with nothing in it. She still didn't like the idea of the dreamspheres in Jared's hands.

She slammed the water off and climbed out of the shower.

All of the towels had been dragged onto the floor and trampled. Shivering until her teeth chattered, she let her skin air-dry while she dug through the jumbled mess of clothing strewn around her bedroom. She found a pair of jeans and a sweatshirt that were a little rumpled, but clean. A pair of underwear. Socks.

Poe appeared in the bedroom doorway, a slice of bread impaled on his beak. He looked both ridiculous and adorable, and she found herself laughing. It was laughter on the edge of hysteria perhaps, but still she felt the weight of guilt and fear and despair lifting a little.

The penguin waddled across to her, poking at her hand with the breaded beak, and she took it from him, realizing as she did so that it had been long since she had eaten. The nausea had receded, leaving in its place pangs of hunger. Poe cocked his head to one side and peered up at her.

"All right, you're hungry," she said.

In answer, he turned around and waddled back toward the kitchen. Vivian followed.

Most of her food had been ground into a broken mess of pottery and glass, but she found a can of tuna, which she opened for Poe, and another slice of bread and some turkey slices to make herself a dry but edible sandwich.

By the time she got down to the last bite, exhaustion had set in. Even chewing seemed like too much effort, and she knew she wasn't going to accomplish anything without sleep. The door was locked, for all the good that had done her. She inspected all of the windows: locked, nothing unusual visible outside.

Of course, if a dragon wanted in, or a sorceress, all the locks in the world would make no difference.

With the last of her strength she turned her mattress slashed side down. Sliding her hand down between the head of the bed frame and the wall, she felt for her stiletto. It was gone. She felt a pang of loss. The knife had been with her since she was sixteen, had protected her more than once. The handle was bone, worn smooth with use before it came to her, comfortable and familiar.

Isobel spent six months in the state hospital the year Vivian turned sixteen. Once again she'd been dragged into a foster home for her own good. The parents were kind but clueless, elderly church types who lacked the most basic understanding of the forces shaping the kids under their roof, two girls and a boy. The girls were seeking a fragile sanity in drugs and boys. Their arms were scarred with razor blade cuttings aimed at dulling emotions they couldn't handle. The boy, Jake, was fifteen, and nothing but rage.

He'd already savaged the other girls, and when he focused his burning gaze on her that very first night at dinner, Vivian thought about a gun. But guns were hard to conceal, especially sharing a room, and the trouble would be endless if she got caught. A knife, on the other hand, an object that could ride easily in her pocket, was another story. She had an uneasy fascination for sharp blades, maybe born of the years of vigilance in which she'd kept all sharp-edged objects away from her mother.

The fascination led her beyond the basic pocketknife she could have secured at the Walmart to an underground transaction that yielded a stiletto. It cost her the stash of money she'd been stowing away for years, but it paid for itself within the very first week. Jake would bear scars for the rest of his life, but he might think twice before assaulting another woman.

Ah, well. The stiletto wouldn't be much use against a dragon. Or Jehenna, for that matter. Still, she would have felt safer if it were in its usual place under her pillow. Too tired to stay awake, safe or not, Vivian wrapped herself in a blanket and lay down on the naked mattress, the pendant clutched in one hand. As she fell directly into the sleep of exhaustion, she was wondering how she would begin to look for the key.

Fifteen

✤

D reamworld.
　　　Vivian was clear on this. She stood at the center of
a garden, bounded on all four sides by an overgrown hedge,
ten feet tall and impenetrable. An old maple, scarlet and
gold, draped its branches over a wooden bench, half buried
in a drift of leaves. Dead, dry flower stalks poked up out of
the grass, brown and skeletal. A ray of sun broke through a
mass of clouds and warmed her skin and hair, an intense
physical pleasure that felt too real for dream. She raised her
face to the sky, breathing in the scent of fallen leaves and
earth. Poe waddled about, poking his beak into the leaves,
exploring.

When the fear came, she felt it as a gradually expanding
fracture line, slight at first, but growing. Light and shadow
flickered on the hedge, artifacts of a breeze moving the
branches of the sheltering tree. A leaf drifted down and
landed at her feet. All peaceful, all serene.

But her heart thudded against her ribs with a logic of its
own. The penguin stopped exploring and pressed against
her leg, feathers puffed and ruffled. Vivian dug in her pockets for the stiletto, then remembered that it was lost.

Something white caught her eye, half-buried in a pile of
crimson leaves. Flies buzzed around it; a sweet, cloying

stink filled her nostrils. Reluctant, but compelled, she knelt and uncovered the thing. A hand, dead white, bloodless. It lay palm up, the fingers slightly curved, a delicate woman's hand. On the fourth finger a familiar diamond ring.

Paralyzed, she knelt there in a heap of bloodred leaves, trying to scream and unable to make a sound.

A rustling in the hedge drew her eyes. Branches shivered and shook.

With a supreme effort of will she staggered up onto her feet. A wooden gate, braced with black iron, appeared in the hedge at the far side of the clearing. She tried to run toward it, but her legs felt weighted and the earth softened beneath her, sucking her down. Her right foot sank into deep mud, throwing her forward on her hands and knees. Clammy cold seeped through her jeans into her knees; her fingers scrabbled in loose, wet earth, unable to find purchase.

All the while the thing behind the hedge tried to force its way into the courtyard. She could hear it breathing now, caught a whiff of hot rock and mineral over the odor of leaves and dirt and corruption. Pulling, kicking, digging her fingernails into the sod, she dragged herself forward inch by inch, until her foot pulled free at last with a sucking sound. Half-running, half-crawling, she made it to the gate, curled her fingers around the cold iron, and pulled herself back to her feet.

The iron shifted and changed beneath her fingers, became a wooden door. It was locked.

Overcome by panic, she rattled the knob and beat on it with her fists. She tried again to scream, but still no voice would come. Poe pressed up against her leg. Warmth flowed out of him and into her, and she remembered.

I am the Dreamshifter.

"Open," she said, trying to infuse some authority into a voice that came out as a barely audible croak. But the lock clicked at the command. She turned the knob and the door swung open.

Behind her the pursuing fear, before her a small clearing, surrounded by old-growth forest, dense and grim. Sun slanted across the tops of the trees, but the ground was all in shadow. She stood there, hesitating, fearing to flee from one danger into another.

Poe darted past her, through the doorway and into the clearing, and that decided it. Vivian followed. When she turned to look behind her, there was no sign of either door or hedge.

Between. She could feel the winding threads of dream and waking even before her hand reached for and found the pendant. Her eyes searched out the pathway that would lead into the inevitable maze and found it on the far side of the clearing.

There would be dragons. Even if she had managed to leave behind the creature that had pursued her through the dream, there would be others. Her back itched, as though eyes were staring from out of the undergrowth, but when she looked she saw nothing more than the trees, dense and old, branches bearded with gray moss. Thorn bushes and foreign plants filled the space between their trunks.

She knelt in the cool grass beside Poe and stroked his feathers. His black eyes fixed on hers. "I don't suppose you know what we're meant to do next." She spoke aloud to bolster her own courage, but her voice sounded very small and vulnerable, and it seemed that the trees were listening.

He cocked his head to one side, staring in silence as he always did.

Vivian sighed. "Great help you are. Well, come on then. Since we're here, let's see if we can find Surmise."

The path was little more than a game trail, rough and narrow. Brambles tore at her jeans, branches slapped at her face, and fallen logs blocked the way, forcing her at times to work her way around through nearly impassable undergrowth. As she'd anticipated, it wound around and twisted in on itself, spinning side trails off into different directions. By the time the sun had traveled across the sky, darkening the forest to a twilight gloom, she knew she would never be able to find her way back to the clearing where she had started.

Once or twice she heard branches cracking in the distance and stopped with her heart in her throat to listen. Nothing but birds, a chirping that must be crickets or frogs, the sound of wind in the treetops. They had moved deeper into the forest, and she began to feel that they would be trapped at the center, imprisoned. The air grew increasingly more oppressive; the trees looked older and stranger. Poe waddled along behind her, ever silent, ever present.

There was no way of judging time or distance, but she guessed they'd been walking for a couple of hours before they came across the stream. Poe flung himself into the water in a belly flop that sent water spraying in all directions. Vivian knelt and splashed cool water over her face. She was thirsty. Her memory insisted on supplying images of bacteria and amoebae as seen through a microscope. Teeny little creatures lurking in the water, just waiting to cause diarrhea and vomiting to anybody stupid enough to drink. Not quite that thirsty yet, although soon she would be.

Leaving Poe to play, and hopefully find himself a frog or a minnow, she sat down on a fallen log to rest. She was bone weary, and it was so quiet. Undisturbed by people, unbothered by time, her mind drifted a little, from trees to birds to fairy tales.

When the first branch cracked in the distance, she thought it just another forest sound. A bird squawked. And then the woods went silent. Poe bellied out of the water, shook himself, and stared off into the trees.

Vivian found she was holding her breath and had risen to her feet without thought or intent.

In the forest, something lurked. Something she could feel in her blood, in the rapid beating of her heart, in every fluttering breath. *This is how the mouse feels when the cat is hunting.*

Without ever making the decision she found herself running, half blind, crazed with an unreasoning terror. The path became a tunnel, roofed by low-hanging branches; then the tunnel became a funnel, one of those pens built to drive cattle into a pen, to meet the branding iron or the butcher.

She tried to stop her legs, to think, to plan, but she kept running, despite the pain in her chest and her side, the gasping agony of her breath, the aching heaviness of legs pushed past endurance.

Poe.

She looked back over her shoulder. No penguin.

Damn it.

Her legs stopped their frenetic pumping. She turned full around and retraced her steps, hands pressed to her aching sides, sucking in air in great burning gulps. Poe came around a corner at full speed, short legs churning, neck stretched forward, useless wings outspread. When he saw her, he emitted a pitiful little *quawrk* and ran full tilt into her legs, quivering, feathers ruffled, beak open and gasping.

A new sound now, in the distance. No mere breaking of twigs, but a cracking of branches. Treetops swayed, but there was no wind.

Vivian's feet were glued to the path, bones turned to jelly. She was doomed to cower here like a frightened rabbit and let the thing get her.

No, you're not.

Scooping the penguin up into her arms, she got herself moving again. This time she pushed her way off the path, forcing her way through a wall of undergrowth that scratched and tore and resisted her. She came to a barrier that wouldn't let her through, solid interlaced thorns. Behind her a swath of swaying and falling treetops moved in her direction, a crashing and dragging growing ever closer.

Poe struggled in her arms, pecking at her hand. She released him and he dove forward onto his belly, wriggling through a gap, low in the tangle of thorns. Clumps of feathers caught on the branches, but he vanished from her sight and she flung herself down and followed.

Barbs tore at her shirt and into her back; she felt the sting, the wetness of blood, but she was moving through the barrier, grass and dirt cool beneath her hands, fingers digging down into the soil for traction, elbows pressed close to her sides. It seemed to last forever; wriggle forward, dig with her fingers, pull, push with her toes. Again and again, until her fingernails were bleeding and her back burned and bled.

When she broke through the other side, the wood had changed.

Here the trees were even taller. The tops of them formed a canopy that shut out the sky. As compensation for the gloom, the forest floor was relatively clear. No more thorn bushes, no brambles.

No more maze.

Something was wrong about this. All of her experiences with the Between had involved some sort of winding pathway or tunnel or corridor. But the pendant still hung around her neck, assurance that they hadn't passed back into a dream, and this sure as hell wasn't Wakeworld. Uneasy, she turned in a full circle, looking for any signs of danger. So far, there was no sign of a pursuit, nothing visible that was cause for alarm.

Poe huddled at her feet, running his beak through his feathers, nuzzling, preening. A smear of red marked his breast. Vivian knelt beside him. "Let me look," she said, and he stood still and let her examine the gash in his chest. It was jagged but shallow. Should heal up all right, although she wished she had something to use as a disinfectant.

With no path to follow, Vivian struck out in the direction she hoped led away from their pursuer. The greater the distance they could put between themselves and the dragon, the better. It would have a hard time here, if it was of the size she thought it. Most of the trees were too big to push over, close enough together to hamper its progress. Birds twittered and chirped. A woodpecker pounded away at a nearby tree. Peaceful as it seemed, Vivian kept walking, still driven by a sense of ever-present danger.

At last she felt she couldn't take another step. Exhausted, she sank down to the earth with her back against a sturdy tree trunk. The scratches ached and throbbed, but she couldn't reach them, could only tolerate the pain and be grateful she lived to feel it. Poe settled down beside her.

Bees buzzed around a flowering bush. A squirrel scolded off in the distance. Vivian's nostrils filled with the scent of moss and earth, the bark of the tree. Under these calming influences her breathing slowed and deepened, her mind drifting close to the edges of sleep.

A sound startled her awake.

Not a dragon this time. Male voices, the creak of leather, the cracking of twigs. A horse whickered. Perhaps the voices meant rescue. Or not. It didn't really matter—there was nowhere left to run.

Sixteen

⚜

"Get up."

The voice is relentless. Isobel touches the ring for courage. They have not gone so very far, not this time. Landon will find her, surely, and Jehenna will grow tired of tormenting them, soon or late.

They stand together in a circular, cavernous space, lit by a ring of flaming torches. The ceiling is high and lost in shadows. A stone, bloodred in the flickering light, thrusts upward through the darkness—

through this cavern and into the dungeons above
through the dungeons and into the field where the maidens and the dragon meet—

Time slips, and she is a small child here. A dragon looms but she is not afraid of her, not of Mellisande. The creature is sad and angry, but not at Isobel. Fear beats at them both, child and dragon, bonded by mutual captivity. Something evil happens here, something dark. Isobel is a part of it, but again time fractures and she doesn't know if it is happening, has happened, or is yet to come. A thousand warnings clamoring inside her head and no way to silence them, no way to shut them out. No way to change what will have always been . . .

Isobel shudders and closes that door in her mind, tries to focus on the now and not the then. Her bare feet and legs are cold. The power from the stone thrums through her body in a constant vibration. If she listens to it, tunes herself to its rhythm, the voices fade and the fear ebbs.

Power.

A man comes running, tripping over the hem of his long scarlet robes and almost falling. He smells of fear and his face is the color of curdled milk as he throws himself onto his knees, forehead pressed against the black stone.

"My Queen."

"You know me, then."

"We have waited your return, My Queen." His hands are shaking, and he twists them in the robe. "Gant always said you would someday return."

"And where is Gant?"

"He died, My Queen."

"You arc High Priest, then?"

"Yes, My Queen."

"Has he passed on to you what must be done?"

"Yes, My Queen. Every word of the ritual has been preserved."

"Bring her."

"Yes, My Queen. At once, My Queen—"

He scurries off through a stone door.

A shuffling, scraping sound vibrates through the soles of Isobel's feet. Metal screeches against stone and the dragon is coming and this has happened before, and before, and before, only this time something is different.

Mellisande is old. Always there has been a smothered rage, a longing for the sky, but now Isobel feels a deathly weariness when the dragon enters the chamber. A web of silver mesh wraps the girth of the great belly and traps the folded wings against the creature's back. The once-fiery eyes are faded to dark amber; the heavy head hangs low.

Jehenna staggers as though she has been struck, her face bloodless. "What have you done to her?" she gasps.

The priest cowers, looking from the Sorceress to the dragon in confusion. "Idiot!" Jehenna shrieks, slapping him on one cheek and then the other. "You have let her grow old!"

He cowers onto his knees, his voice shaking. "My Queen. She is fed daily, exercised regularly. She is bathed and polished and bedded in fresh stone. She has been pining for you, so Gant said."

"She wants to go back to her mountain." Isobel is surprised to hear her own voice break in; she has not planned to speak, but the dragon's misery can hardly be borne.

"What would you know about what she wants or does not want?"

Isobel knows this is a time to close her mouth and claim ignorance. An unexpected courage stiffens her spine. "I've always been able to read her."

"You? You are insane. You think you hear voices everywhere—"

"Hers is louder. Can you not hear her? The silver pains her; she longs for the sky and the light, to hunt and catch her own food rather than eat the human cattle—"

"Enough of this. Be silent."

Isobel holds her tongue while slow tears trace a path down her cheeks.

"Ah well," Jehenna says at last. "Her blood is weakened, but it must suffice. Soon, very soon, I will have no more need of her."

"My Queen, it will take time to contain a younger dragon—"

"I'm not talking about a dragon, fool. For now"—her voice rises into command—"I require blood."

The dragon breathes out a flameless blast stinking of carrion and brimstone, whirling Jehenna's hair and gown in a gust of dragon wind. But she is bound by the silver and Jehenna's will, and she turns and lumbers away to stand broadside along the raised dais at the center of the chamber.

The priest follows, carrying a stone knife as long as his

arm. His hands are shaking; he looks as though he might fall.

"Give it to me." Jehenna snatches the knife from him. "I'll perform the rite myself."

This is it, now, the dark and evil thing, and Isobel is powerless as the woman—her mother—takes her hand and leads her up the steps and onto the dais. Here the stink of rot and decay spins in her head. A basin, carved from dragon bone, sits next to the towering stone, stained black with the blood of countless years.

Isobel feels herself begin to wail, a child again. She stands where she is placed, her body shaking with cold and fear, that endless sound flowing from her throat unbidden. Jehenna presses the tip of the knife against the scar at the base of Mellisande's throat. Leans her weight against the toughness of the dragon skin. A small pop as the blade enters, a hiss as it withdraws. Blood splashes smoking into the basin. Where it strikes the stone it sizzles; puffs of steam go up with a smell of brimstone.

"Isobel, hold out your arm," Jehenna commands, and Isobel obeys. A web of scars mars the whiteness of her skin, drawn there by blades of her own choosing over the years. The stone knife slashes across her flesh once, twice, bright blood spurting and falling into the basin, swirling into the black. Jehenna cuts her own wrist and adds her blood to the mixture.

Hope leaps in Isobel's breast as she watches her bright blood flow into the basin. Perhaps she will be permitted to die at last. But then she remembers Landon, and she doesn't want to die, doesn't want to be part of the dragon's pain or Jehenna's power, but she cannot move until the command is lifted.

Time blurs. Crimson and black swirl before her eyes, the smell of hot iron and stone fills her nostrils, the voices clamor and shout.

When she comes clear again the priest is wrapping her bleeding wrist with a bandage, stanching the flow.

Jehenna's hands, smeared with crimson, are already raised in invocation. "Blood of my blood, heart of my heart. As you live, I live. With my death, yours." She dips a smaller stone cup into the basin, swirls it, and drinks.

The effect is immediate. Lines on her face smooth away; her hair thickens, brightens. She smiles and turns to Isobel, holding out the cup. "Drink and say the invocation."

As a child, a small child, before her father locked her mother away, Isobel stood here in this place. She drank the blood then, felt it burn in her throat and bind her to the dragon. But she is not a child now; she is grown and has returned to Surmise. The stone speaks to her, vibrates through her; the stone is power and strength and an unexpected sanity.

"Why?"

"How dare you question? Drink."

"I don't understand why you want to prolong my life. You've never wanted any good thing for me."

Hatred distorts the beautiful face, burns in the hazel eyes. "He cast me aside because of you. His precious heir. You are my revenge, and so you suffer. It gives me pleasure to prolong your pain."

Isobel shakes her head, realizing that something has shifted. The voice does not compel her to drink. She has power of her own, has finally tapped into it after so many weary years. She walks across the dais to the dragon and presses her bare hand over the still-bleeding wound, crooning softly to the dragon's pain. The blood, hot and caustic enough to etch stone, does not burn her, and the flesh begins to knit itself together beneath her touch.

I owe you a gift, Mellisande says into her mind. *What would you have?*

It is a voice she knows, one of the many that has filled her head with a torrent of sound for so many years. There is no relief in this recognition, only a responsibility she cannot answer. *I am beyond your help,* she returns, *nor do I have the power to release you.*

Let me ease your suffering, at least.

And with these words the voices go silent one by one by one until in Isobel's mind nothing remains but her own thoughts, orderly and clean.

Behind her, Jehenna begins to murmur a spell. The air thickens with webs of realities, and Isobel knows that even with this unexpected gift of silence her mind has been broken for too long; she lacks the strength to save herself. She feels the door open behind her but does not turn, keeps her focus on the dragon.

My thanks for this. I wish—

"Nahl! Put her through the door."

Strong hands grab her and pinion her arms behind her back. Isobel twists, kicks, manages to turn and spit into the priest's face. Something needs to be done, something she so nearly has the understanding to do, and she will no longer submit passively to her fate. But the priest is stronger and drags her away from Mellisande, across the stone.

A door stands open and she knows what lies inside, increases her struggle. She clings to the door frame, plants her feet, throws all of her weight backward to put the priest off balance. *Keep faith,* she hears the dragon say, *the New One is coming, she may free us yet.* And then a blow to the back of her head and the world goes dark.

Seventeen

✣

The men were on horseback. Six of them, all clad in rough leather from head to toe: tunics, chaps, knee-high lace-up boots. Even leather hoods, with openings for the eyes and slits at the sides of the nose. Gloved hands holding drawn swords, sharp and lethal, meant for the shedding of blood.

They formed a circle with Vivian at the center, Poe flattened against her legs, hissing. Not one of the men spoke— there was only the creaking of saddles, the stomping of hooves, and the huffing sound of a reined-in horse fighting the bit. Vivian made herself keep breathing, tried to focus on a spot just in front of her feet instead of on swords and horses and hooded men.

At last, one of them sheathed his sword and bared his head. He grinned, a sudden flash of white teeth in a tanned face. Long blond hair, sweat darkened, hung over his shoulders. "Not quite the quarry we had in mind, but much more pleasing to the eyes. What do you here in Surmise, My Lady? And what, pray tell, is that creature you have with you?"

As if on signal, the other riders, save one, also removed their hoods. Two were scarcely out of their teens, dark haired, identical faces, both sets of eyes looking her over in a way that made the hot blood pulse in her throat and rush up over her face. The fourth was also dark, wiry, with a face serious and intent. The fifth swept his sword up in the air and swung it in the sort of arc that would have separated a head from its shoulders if it happened to come in contact. His black brows formed an unbroken line across a high and craggy forehead, and a burn scar distorted one side of his face. "Commoners aren't allowed in the forest," he said. "You are in violation."

The final rider, taller than the others, lean but powerful, remained hooded and silent.

Cornered, Vivian looked around at the rough, bearded faces, searching for some indication of help or mercy. "I'm not from here. I didn't know. Just point me in the right direction and I'll go. I promise."

The silent one dismounted and strode the few paces toward her. She backed away. Stumbled over a stone and staggered right into the shoulder of a horse. She careened forward again, which brought her up against what she'd been trying to avoid in the first place.

She could feel the heat of his body, could smell the sweat and dust. And saw, through the holes cut in the hood, eyes of clear agate, traced in umber. Eyes seen not so long ago in a bookstore, and long before that in dream. Her heart leaped with joy and relief. "Zee!" she said, reaching out her hands to him.

No recognition sparked in his eyes. "Who are you? What are you doing here?" he demanded.

The familiar voice, but different. Harsh. A voice accustomed to shouting orders, not talking about books and penguin totems and alternate realities.

"But you know me! You lent me books. You said . . ." Her voice trailed off into silence.

"My Lady—I don't play games. Tell me your name and your purpose."

She tried one more time. "But you know my name—"

"Let me have her," the dark-browed man said. "I'll make her talk sense."

"Nobody touches her, Barson." The hooded man didn't move, kept his eyes locked on hers. Her heart thudded, ungainly and loud. Voices went on around her, only half-heard.

"And if she should want to be touched?"

"Kill her and be done, I say. Her and that monstrous bird. That pest of a dragon is still about here somewhere. She'll slow us down."

"Pest? Bit more than a pest, I'd say. Big old bastard is what it is. Took a whole cow from the Flynt place."

"Try not to frighten the lady."

"Gonna be a lot more than talk to frighten her before she's done."

A sound in the distance. *Crack.*

All eyes turned toward it. Nobody spoke.

And then controlled chaos. The horses shied, bucked, swirled in a trampling of hooves. Men fought the reins to bring them back under control. The hooded man turned away from Vivian to seize the reins of his black horse, murmuring calming words.

Crack.

The hooded man sprang up into the saddle. "Duncan—stay with the girl." His horse reared and fought, but he mastered it with words and hands and rode away directly toward the thrashing treetops, followed by all but the blond man, who reined in his mount and came back.

Swinging down to the ground, he tethered his horse to a sturdy branch and turned to face her.

Vivian tried to speak, but her throat was dry and tight and no sound came out. She tried again. "What is it?" No need to ask, though; she already knew.

"Nothing much. One of the dragons has been getting friendly with the villagers."

Only a dragon.

"Sounds like they could use you—you should go."

A spark of amusement flashed in his blue eyes. "The dragons are partial to young ladies. You've been taken into protective custody, so to speak."

A flicker of hope sparked into life. "So they're going to kill the dragon, then?"

His eyes widened. "Kill it? You're really not from around here, are you? Dragons are sacred and can't be killed. They're hoping to drive it off, before . . ."

"Before what?"

"I wonder what they're doing over there." He shaded his eyes with his hand, following the sounds of voices and breaking branches. "The beast should have taken flight by now."

"Before what?" Vivian said again.

Duncan turned his eyes back to her. "If the dragon keeps to this territory, eventually there will be a sacrifice."

"A sacrifice. Chickens? A cow?"

His eyes shifted away from hers.

Cold sweat trickled down her back.

"The dragon and the maiden," she managed. "How positively mythical. And of course we would never sacrifice useful, local, residential maidens. Such a waste. A stranger now, fortuitously arriving just as the dragon begins to be a marauding problem. Convenient, isn't it?"

A flush of color stained his cheeks, making him look young and unexpectedly vulnerable. "Look," he said. "Go if you want. Chances are the dragon was already hunting you. Night is coming. The best you can hope for is to starve to death, lost in the woods. The worst—death by dragon. Or one of the other creatures out there. Or, you can come back to the castle with us and take your chances." Once again, the impish grin. "If you come back all meek and mild, I promise you can do whatever you like with me later."

In spite of herself, Vivian smiled back.

A warning shout went up from the men away in the forest. Treetops thrashed in a path headed in their direction. Duncan's face hardened. He pulled the hood down over his face. Drew his sword.

"Get down low, under a bush—no, that fallen log is better. Lie flat, and be still." His voice was pitched low, urgent. Vivian obeyed without question, crawling on her belly toward a tree that had fallen but hung up on a rock, leaving a space just big enough for a slender woman to squeeze under.

A slender woman and a penguin.

Poe flung himself down on his belly and wriggled in under the shelter. For Vivian it was not so easy. Clawing her fingers into the earth, she wriggled and twisted her body under the log. A broken branch raked down her back with searing heat. Her forehead and nose pressed into the mud. She couldn't fully expand her rib cage and she couldn't seem to get enough air. Turning her head a little to the side, she caught a narrow window of daylight—a visual strip revealing earth, restless hooves, a pair of booted feet.

Then a shadow. A rushing sound, like wind. Leaves flurried and spun, branches cracked and fell. The horse bugled in panic, hooves trampling the grass. A grunt from Duncan, a horrible scream from the horse, a wet and tearing sound.

Vivian wanted to block her ears, to dig herself farther into the earth, but her arms were pinned beneath her.

The dragon shrieked, a wordless cry like nothing in all the worlds. The shadow lifted with a rush of wind, a heavy beating of wings.

Hooves thundered toward them then, and there were other hooves and other booted feet. Voices.

"Gods, Duncan—what have you done?"

"I had no choice."

"You know what this means."

"I know."

She felt the shadow as a pair of boots appeared in her window of vision.

"Get up." It was a tone that meant nothing good for her, and she didn't move until inexorable hands gripped her arm and dragged her out and onto her feet.

Vivian stood where the hooded man put her, shivering, trying not to look at great gouts of thick black liquid that bubbled and steamed on the grass. An overpowering stench twisted her stomach and she swallowed hard, determined not to shame herself by vomiting in front of this hard-handed man who was and was not Zee.

Duncan's horse, at least part of it, lay in a spreading pool of crimson. The hindquarters were missing. Guts spilled out onto the grass, gleaming wetly in the last of the light. Beside the mess Duncan knelt, clothing splattered with blood and the black liquid, and where it touched his clothes the fabric had disintegrated, leaving smoking holes. A raw burn covered the right side of his face. Sweat glistened on his forehead and the pinched skin around his eyes spoke of pain. A sword lay on the ground beside him, the blade clotted black.

The man with the black eyebrows, Barson, dismounted and began binding Duncan's hands together at the wrists.

"What on earth are you doing?" Vivian demanded.

"He broke the law."

"But he protected me," she said, hearing the disbelief in her own voice. "The dragon came for me and he saved me. He's burned. He needs a doctor. What the hell is wrong with you?"

In her memory she saw Arden's body convulse, the eyes roll back in his head. He'd been burned. Clawed. Poisoned, maybe.

Ignoring the savaged half body of the horse, picking her way around the pools of sizzling dragon blood, Vivian crossed the clearing and knelt at Duncan's side.

Splotches of black still clung to his face, sizzling, burning deeper into the flesh. She had sense enough not to touch it with her bare hands, had nothing to use to wipe it away. "Doesn't anybody have medical supplies? Bandages? Anything?" She looked around the circle of men. They all looked back at her. Nobody moved.

She tore off her T-shirt then, aware of eyes on her bare skin, ignoring them. Balling the fabric up to protect her hands, she gently dabbed at the still-sizzling skin, blotting up the blood. Breath hissed out between Duncan's teeth as he strangled a groan.

"I'm sorry," she said, "we need to get this shit off you before it burns to the bone. Are you hurt anywhere else?"

"No, My Lady."

"Enough." The black-browed man grabbed her from behind and dragged her upright and away. The twins picked up Duncan between them and thrust him up behind the saddle of one of the horses. For a minute she thought he'd topple off, but he shook his head as though to clear dizziness and gripped the horse with his knees.

Barson swung up in front of him.

A new hand on her shoulder, restraining her. "He must answer to the crime of shedding dragon blood," Zee's voice said, implacable.

Something inside Vivian broke from control. She turned and beat against his chest with her fists. "This is wrong. Let him go!"

When he pinioned her wrists she bit at his hands and took advantage of his distraction to kick at his shins, a useless gesture. The leather boots were heavy and hard, and she battered her own toes against them in futility.

"Stop this." His hands were like iron.

Tears rolled down her cheeks. She needed to wipe her nose. "The dragon is a monster—it tore that horse in half, would have killed Duncan. And me. He *saved* me. What kind of man are you? Too scared to even show your face."

At her words, she felt him go very still. He released her.

And then he reached up and removed the hood.

Vivian gasped. The beautiful agate eyes were set in a mass of scars, old and new—thin white lines, garish red welts, fresh cuts still healing. They twisted his face, pulled his mouth into an uneven grimace. It gave him a sinister, lethal look.

"What's the matter—not what you were expecting?" His voice was hard.

She couldn't find words.

"Be careful what you ask for." He turned away. "Erhard, Varlon, track the dragon. See if it lives or dies."

Without a nod or a word, the twins rode off, bent low

over the necks of their horses, reading signs in the earth that Vivian couldn't see.

"Liam—take the bird. The lady will ride behind me. We'll barely reach the castle before dark."

"I'm not going anywhere with you," Vivian said.

"Warlord—allow me." Barson's eyes raked over her half-naked body. She crossed her arms over her breasts and turned away from him.

The Warlord was also looking her over, but with a different expression. "You're bleeding."

"Scraped my back on a branch. Nothing serious."

"They'll smell you. Between you and Duncan, they'll be flying in from the four winds." He picked up her T-shirt from the dirt. It fell apart in his hands, disintegrating where the dragon blood had touched it. Tossing the rags aside with a grimace of distaste, he turned and dug in his saddlebags. "Here, put this on."

She stood unmoving, stubborn and defiant.

The Warlord pulled a rough woolen tunic over her head, dressing her as though she were a child. It hung to her knees and was wide enough for two of her. Then he picked her up and placed her bodily behind the saddle, swinging up in front.

"We go now, and we ride fast."

He kicked his horse into a gallop. Her arms were still trapped inside the tunic and she clutched hard with her knees, struggling to keep her balance until she could get her arms free, clinging to him for balance.

She'd been on a horse once, as a child, sitting tamely in the saddle while somebody else led her around the yard. This was another matter entirely, bouncing up and down, sliding from side to side, trying to get a grip on the stiff leather that denied her grasping fingers purchase. In the end, she was forced to wrap both arms around him and hold on.

The path fell into darkness. Her back hurt, her heart ached, fear ran behind her and above her. She felt like prey, hunted, harried. When they burst out of the woods and into a wide field, the sun hung low on the horizon but the sky was still blue.

Above, three winged creatures soared in high, lazy circles. Vultures, she thought. Vultures with serpentine tails and four legs apiece.

No vulture known to man had ever been that size.

The Warlord spurred the horse to a faster pace, leaning forward over its neck. Vivian clung to him, watching the sky. It faded from blue to gray, with rose at the horizon. The winged creatures grew larger, circling ever closer in a downward spiral.

Across the plain, over the leather-clad shoulder that half-obstructed her view, a castle came into sight—a fortress of spires and turrets, a black silhouette against the sunset.

The horses stretched low over the ground, hooves flashing, necks white with foam. The men urged them on with shouts and curses.

Closer and closer circled the dragons.

Vivian could hear wings now, a great rhythmic beating. The castle was too far away; they would never make it in time. Men were visible on the watchtower and at the drawbridge, but they still looked small, improbable. A foul wind swirled around her. She was aware of a rushing sound above her head, felt something rake across her shoulders with a blow that threw her off balance. She caught a glimpse of a pale belly, a spiked tail, and sharp talons red with blood as she slid to one side.

Her hands slipped and clawed at Zee's leather tunic. She was half on, half off the horse, a rag doll bouncing awkwardly at odds with the rhythm of the pounding hooves, and then she was falling, the ground coming up to meet her with a jarring force.

She tried to get up, to run or at least to crawl, but the breath had been driven from her lungs and she couldn't move. Her shoulders were on fire. Lying there, looking straight up, the monstrous belly and bloody talons filled her vision. The dragon circled. The wings drew in as it began an earthward dive and then the Warlord's face came between her and the monster. His strong arms were beneath her and she was lifted, clasped against his broad breast, clinging desperately as he raced toward the castle.

A giant shadow followed them with a thunder of wings; they would never make it, never, and then it was cooler and dark and they were no longer moving. Men's voices around her, the clatter of hooves on cobblestone. She tried to look around, but darkness veiled her eyes. She fought it. She would not go gently, damn it, would not—

would not—

Eighteen

❖

Suspended in an easy darkness, Vivian took care to remain perfectly still. If she moved—so much as the blink of an eye, the twitch of a finger—she would wake, and this above all things was to be avoided. A spark deep in her brain sputtered about danger and responsibility, but she held it at bay. In this state of semiconsciousness, she could believe that she was in her own bed, that when she opened her eyes she would see a familiar world—two square feet of kitchen counter, the stainless sink, the bookcase holding beloved and well-worn volumes, the spider plant hanging by the window, the computer whirring its predictable colored screen saver, the dream catcher hanging intact over the door.

Her old world, her old life.

A finger twitched despite her best effort and with that one tiny movement full sensation came crashing in. Red-hot spikes of pain drove into both shoulders. Her head pulsed with every beat of her heart. A line of fire traced itself down her back. Worse even than the pain was the sensation that she was spinning out of control without gravity or direction. She heard a muffled, murmuring sound, as of voices in the distance, and opened her eyes to see who was talking.

Swallowing back a wave of nausea, she squinted against too-bright light. The first thing she saw was Poe, standing at attention, his black eyes fixed unwavering on her. He had the determined look of a penguin who has been standing still for quite some time and can continue to do so indefinitely.

"Still here, I see." Her throat felt like sandpaper, her voice too loud in her own ears.

She lifted a hand to her throat. The pendant was there. So she was somewhere in Between—Surmise, most likely. That's where the scarred man who was and was not Zee had been taking her.

Keeping her breaths shallow so as to move as little as possible, feeling the cold sweat slick on her forehead, she lay perfectly still, listening.

No sign of anyone about, but still she heard the sound of distant voices. Without moving her head, she shifted her eyes from side to side to take stock of the place where she found herself.

She was lying on a four-poster bed at the center of a round chamber. The walls were stone, hung with hand-woven tapestries. Heavy wooden chairs, piled with silken cushions in shades of indigo and scarlet, were set about the room in groups of twos and threes. Overhead arched a high ceiling, painted in a style reminiscent of Michelangelo. It took a moment, sick and dizzy as she was, to recognize that this artist's winged creatures were not angels and demons but vividly depicted long-necked beasts. She forced herself up onto her elbows to see better.

The room spun faster and then went dark. When next she opened her eyes, a woman stood beside the bed, a cool hand on her forehead.

"Easy, child."

A sweet face, thin and deeply lined. Gray hair plaited into a long, thick braid. "I've fed your bird. He had a long soak in the bath and then insisted in perching there on your feet and staring you awake. I told him you needed more time to rest, but he doesn't listen well."

Words still felt far away, and Vivian didn't answer.

The woman walked away, then returned with a little

wooden cart on wheels. Arrayed neatly on a clean cloth was some sort of green paste in an earthenware bowl, bandages, scissors, a basin of water.

"Who are you?"

"I am Nonette, and I am a healer. You must rest—I thought you dead."

"My head hurts."

"I'm sure. I'll give you a tea for that and the nausea in a minute. It was the dragon poison I thought had done for you. I've never seen anybody survive that. The Warlord insisted that I try."

The Warlord. He had come back for her when she fell, had carried her to safety at risk of his own life. Had arranged for a healer. To what purpose? Surely not because he valued her as a woman; he'd made that clear enough. Duncan had said something about sacrifices.

The healer's capable hands removed bloody bandages from both of Vivian's shoulders and applied a green paste that cooled the fiery pain on contact.

"Pierced both shoulders with his claws. I can't imagine why he didn't just carry you away. Hurts, I imagine, but they're healing at an unusual rate."

"The dragon?"

"I'd forgotten—you're not from here. The dragons have poison spurs on their talons. Once they pierce your flesh, you die. Well, most people die. You seem to have some sort of immunity. Now—I'm going to help you to sit up, and then you're going to drink the tea I've made for you. That will ease the headache and the nausea. Ready?"

It wasn't what she'd tried to ask. She wanted to know what had happened to the dragons, the one that Duncan had wounded, the one that attacked her. It would wait. She bit her lip and endured as the healer pulled her upright. Pain sparked through her body—the scrape down her back, the muscles of thighs and arms, but this was nothing to the pounding and commotion in her head. The whispering of distant voices went on, and she grew increasingly worried that they were a product of her own deranged mind.

"Keep breathing; it will pass," Nonette said.

In a moment the pain eased to a tolerable level, although the voices continued. Nonette propped her up with pillows and handed her a cup of something hot and steaming.

"There are things you will want to ask," the woman said. "Drink. Ask. I will answer as I'm able."

Vivian sipped at the tea. It was both fragrant and bitter, laced with sweetness. Her stomach settled nearly at once. She thought she might ask about the voices, took another look at the sweet, sincere face, and changed her mind.

"Are the others all right? The Warlord, and Barson, and Duncan?"

Nonette turned her back and busied herself folding bandages. "The dragon attacked only you."

"What will happen now? To Duncan?" *And to me.*

"That will be up to the Queen. She's returned, they say. One hundred years gone, and as young as the day she took the throne. You will meet her, and she will decree your future."

"What is she like?"

Again, the healer avoided her eyes, turned her face away as she answered. "I have never seen her, child—I'm old, but not that old. There are legends—you will see them woven into the tapestries if you care to look."

"Tell me." She desperately needed information. The panic was held somewhat at bay by the pain, by the illusion of safety offered by this room. But the calm wouldn't last, and she knew it.

The woman tidied up all of her implements and wheeled the little cart off into a corner. "I must go. I will leave the salve for you here—you can dress those wounds again, if they pain you."

"Why can't you answer my question?"

"I'm a busy woman, my dear, I have others to attend to." Nonette paused with her hand on the door. "There are some herbs in a pouch in the bath chamber—sprinkle those in the water when you bathe, and it will ease your other hurts."

With that, she left Vivian in an empty room, staring at a

closed door, with nothing for company but the voices in her head and a silent but omnipresent penguin. The voices were getting louder; she caught herself listening for words.

A dull ache began again at the base of her skull.

A robe hung neatly over a chair nearby. Pushing back the covers, Vivian swung her legs over the edge of the bed. There was no part of her that didn't ache or burn or hurt. She took a few shaky breaths, waiting for the dizziness to pass again, shivering in the chill of a room that would never be warm despite the sunlight flooding in through a bank of windows that lined the outer half of the curved chamber.

Her head was still spinning when a knock startled her. Poe hopped off the bed and waddled over to stand in front of the door. He hissed and fluffed up his feathers. Again the knock—imperative, insistent. Vivian dragged her battered body to the chair that held the gown, each step sending a spike of pain into her shoulders and down her back.

The dressing gown was flimsy, silken, and she wished for something more substantial. At least the smooth fabric felt soothing on her wounds, but it wasn't much for either warmth or modesty. The knocking had begun to sound like someone was about to burst through the door. Feeling half-dressed and half-conscious, knowing for certain that open doors allowed in the improbable and the unknown, Vivian lifted the latch.

Two guards flanked the door, clad in chain mail, hands resting on their sword hilts in a way that meant business. A girl, no more than sixteen, with a cascade of fiery hair and a simple, floor-length gown, stood well back, eyes wide and watchful.

The knocker was the center of attention. Male, well built and tall, with a face designed for big-screen fame and eyes the color of jade. Thick dark hair fell loose just to his shoulders, which were covered by a cape woven in scarlet and gold. Scarlet hose ending in pointy-toed shoes emerged from green velvet breeches, fastened at the knee with golden buckles. A scabbard encrusted with gems hung from a belt at his waist.

Poe hissed.

Vivian blinked. "Jared—what the hell are you doing here?"

"My Lady, you mistake me—I am called Gareth, Chancellor of Castle Surmise. I have been sent by Her Majesty to welcome you." His eyes swept over her from head to toe, lingering along the way. She crossed her arms over her breasts and then cursed herself for doing it, as a knowing smile curved his lips.

"We would speak more comfortably in your chambers, I think."

He took a step forward.

"I've got a headache," she managed. "Maybe you could come back later—"

"I fear that is impossible."

"As is entertaining you just now." She lifted her chin, braced her legs to compensate for the weakness in her knees, and blocked the door as well as she could with her body. Maybe he wouldn't notice the shaking that she couldn't get under control.

She must not, could not, be alone with him.

He bent his head and brushed her forehead with his lips. She shuddered at the touch; Jared's familiar kiss delivered by a stranger. Desperately she jerked her mind back from that abyss. She must not, must not, think of Jared and what he had done in dream.

"Perhaps you are right," he was saying. "There is not time now for pleasure. Later, then."

Enduring the feel of his breath on her face, his body so close to hers, was a slow torture. Anger coruscated through the fear. Her fingers tingled with the urge to slap his self-satisfied face. She forced herself to stand quiet, not looking at him, every muscle flooded with adrenaline and ready to fight or run.

A clattering sound drew her eyes toward the corridor, curving to the right at a gentle downward slant. A wheeled contraption appeared, on which a bewildering array of gowns hung suspended from a wooden rod.

"Ah, here comes your wardrobe," Gareth said.

"My what?"

"There is a feast tonight, in honor of the return of the Queen. You will need appropriate clothing."

The wardrobe arrived at her door, propelled by a boy who looked to be no more than ten, who had to peer around the rack of clothing to see anything as he certainly couldn't see over.

"A feast? I—look, Jared—Gareth—maybe you didn't hear, but I've been clawed by a dragon, I think I've got a concussion, and the last thing I want to do is play dress-up and go to some feast—"

"The Queen commands your appearance. Prince Landon himself will escort you. He will come for you at seven."

"Pardon me—Your Lordship—but I can't see how the Queen would care whether I attend."

"Oh, she is most interested, I assure you. As am I." She shivered as his gaze pointedly lowered to her breasts, and she pulled her arms tighter around her body.

He snapped his fingers. "Esme, come."

The redhead stepped forward and curtsied, first to Gareth, then to Vivian. "Esme will help you dress. Step aside and let the page enter."

Vivian glanced from Esme to Gareth, and then to the wheeled wardrobe, loaded with gowns. This was not a battle she was going to win. Wordless, she stepped away from the door. The boy rolled the wardrobe cart into the room, Esme right on his heels.

Gareth reached for her hand, and she let him take it rather than create a scene. He turned it over and kissed the palm, his lips lingering. When he released her, the back of his hand grazed the silken fabric over her breast. Not an accident. Deliberately, watching his face as she did so, Vivian wiped her hand on the robe.

An insolent smile rewarded her act of defiance. "We will continue this—conversation—later, My Lady." He bowed and strode off down the corridor. The guards remained in place, stationed one on each side of the door.

Vivian watched him go with a sigh of relief. Maybe she'd think of something before he came back. If she was a prisoner here, she was certainly being treated with a high level of regard. Turning back into the chamber she saw Esme selecting gowns from the rack, laying them out on a satin-covered bench.

The boy stared, hands behind his back, legs spread wide. "Are you a princess?"

"No, I am not."

"Can I touch your bird?"

"That's up to him."

He took a tentative step toward Poe, holding out his hand. Poe stared, unblinking, a statue of a penguin, and the child lost his nerve. "Can I go, My Lady?"

"Of course."

Esme nodded her agreement. "Leave the rack. You can fetch it later."

The page walked gravely through the door, but as she was closing it behind him Vivian heard his feet break into a run and half-smiled. Boys. Dress them up as much as you like; some things stay the same.

When she turned back, Esme was draping a selection of gowns over the backs of chairs to show them off, caressing a frill here, smoothing a bit of lace there.

"Don't bother with all that," Vivian said. "I'm not going." Her body was one weary, quivering mass of pain, and playing dress-up wasn't an activity she enjoyed at the best of times. Besides, according to her grandfather's note, she could also expect to find Jehenna here somewhere. The very idea of this meeting turned her cold with dread. How, in all the worlds, was she supposed to fight a woman who had defeated her grandfather? At the very least she needed time to heal before she sought out such a battle.

Esme gasped, clutching a gown trimmed in peacock feathers to her breast. "But I've been instructed to help you dress, My Lady. It's expected that you attend. You must. While you are selecting your gown, I will prepare your bath."

"I know they expect it. I don't care."

"My Lady!" Esme's face was tight with anxiety. Her hands clenched in the fabric of the gown. "You are tired, My Lady, and sore, I'm sure. I heard about the dragon. That must have been terrifying. It's a miracle that you survived. Lord Zee is frightening all by himself; he's so harsh and has all those scars. I don't see how you survived both him and a dragon all at once. I'll run a bath for you, shall I? You'll feel ever so much better, and then we'll see about the feast when you've had a nice long soak."

"That is his name, then? Zee?"

Esme lowered her voice. "They call him Warlord, but they do say Zee is the name he was born with. I'm sorry, My Lady, you are weary and I am nattering. I'll go draw the bath at once." She released the gown with a little start and began smoothing the feathers. "Oh, no, I've gone and crumpled it. I'm ever so sorry—" Her voice sounded on the verge of tears.

"Never mind," Vivian said. "I wouldn't wear that gown in any case."

Esme drew a quavering breath. "As you say, My Lady. But it would be lovely on you. I could have it fixed—"

Vivian tried to picture herself in turquoise silk with peacock feathers and failed utterly. "A bath would be lovely."

"Yes, My Lady. At once." The girl bustled across the room and drew aside a tapestry hung on a rod with silver rings. Behind it was a bath chamber, complete with a toilet and a large round tub. At the sound of running water Poe looked up, then waddled straight for the bath.

Esme flapped at him with a towel, brow creased in fear, but bravely standing her ground. "My Lady, the water must be clean—"

Poe stopped, cocked his head to one side. He waddled one step forward; the girl took one step back. Vivian laughed. It felt good, normal, and some of the tension went out of her. "He won't hurt you," she said. "Penguins are aquatic. Of course he wants in there. In fact, he's already had a bath earlier. I suspect he thinks you're running that for him."

Poe stopped his advance and turned his head to look at Vivian. She shook her head at him. "It's my turn." He waddled away to the edge of the door, as though he'd understood, and took up a position there, watching.

The bath chamber, like the room, was round, with a stone floor and a marble tub. Tiles, hand painted in vibrant, primary colors, covered the wall. Esme, with a watchful eye on Poe, leaned over the tub, stirring the water with her hand. "I've put the herbs in that were sitting here—they smell nice," she said, straightening up and pushing back a lock of hair. "All ready for you."

"I hadn't expected—"

"What, My Lady?"

"Running water."

"They don't have that in your world? I don't think I should like to live there, then." Esme gestured at another fixture next to the tub. "If you need to, um, relieve yourself—"

"We do actually have those," Vivian said. Why there shouldn't be plumbing here, she didn't know. This was Surmise. There might be any manner of oddities that had found their way in; anything from a dream would be fair game. Like a penguin, for example.

Esme held out her hand. "Give me the robe, My Lady, and I'll help you into the tub."

Vivian had no intention, in any reality, of standing naked under the eyes of a stranger and a penguin. "I don't need any help. Maybe you could wait in the other room—"

"My instructions, My Lady, are to help you bathe."

"Look—no offense, but I know how to wash myself. And my name is Vivian. Enough with the My Lady, all right?"

Esme's brow rumpled. "I know not how these matters are where you come from, My Lady, but it is not so simple. There are rituals to be observed."

"You've got to be kidding me. It's a freaking dinner. Not

a wedding or a sacrifice or something." She said these words lightly, but feared the sacrifice as a genuine possibility.

Esme's lips set in a stubborn line. "A feast. And I'm to help you, My Lady. The Chancellor said."

"Nobody will ever know. Let's not, and say we did."

"I'll be whipped, I'll be cast out, I'll be given over to the dragons . . ." Esme fell on her knees, hands clasped, tears dripping down her cheeks. "My Lady, Vivian, please . . ."

"Oh, hell. Do you know what *histrionic* means?" But the girl's fear seemed genuine, and Vivian couldn't deny that not only were there dragons here, they were revered and protected and it was highly possible that unruly servants might be fed to them. With a vast and gusty sigh, she unfastened the robe and handed it over, refusing offers of assistance climbing into the tub. The herbs stung a little as she lowered herself into the steaming hot water, and then settled into a gentle tingling that was comforting and invigorating all at once.

Esme hovered, making clucking noises. Poe came over and stood at her feet, peering down into the water as though looking for something. Fish, maybe.

Vivian tried to ignore them, letting her stiff muscles relax into the soothing warmth. There were bruises on her arms, her breasts. Oval shaped, like fingers. It made her feel sick to look at them, remembering Jared and the dream, so she resolutely took in her surroundings instead. The bathroom tiles didn't make her feel any better. Long-necked winged creatures—dragons, no matter which way you looked at them—depicted in jeweled tones. Women in white drapery. Women in white drapery chained to rocks. Dragons eyeing women in white drapery chained to rocks. Dragons and bloodstained, empty white drapery lying on the ground beside rocks.

Closing her eyes to shut it all out, Vivian saw instead the dream memory of her own dismembered hand in a pile of autumn leaves, smelled the overpowering scent of dragon, felt the beating of the great wings.

Felt her own wings, spread wide to catch the updraft of

wind, soaring ever higher, the earth below a brightly col-ored patchwork of field and town and river . . .

Alarmed, she opened her eyes and took a deep breath of the here and now, letting the scent of the herbs fill her head, driving away the smell of the dragon, and with it the fear.

Esme's voice floated through the room like a vapor of steam. "My Lady? Please sit up. You must be washed."

Vivian didn't answer. The herbs seemed to be drawing the pain out of her shoulders; she imagined that if she could look behind her she would see swirls of black poison being sucked from her flesh and washed away.

The voice was insistent. "My Lady, the time is short."

"All right, all right." Vivian sat up, feeling exposed and embarrassed as Esme's competent hands picked up a sponge and began to wash her back, easing around the long gash. "Tell me about the dragons," she said. Partly because she needed to know, partly for distraction from the pain.

Esme's hands faltered, stopped, then began moving again. "What did you wish to know?"

"I'm curious. Everything here is dragons—painted on the ceiling, woven into the tapestries. And they fly around attacking people, and the man who defended me got in trouble for it."

"I don't understand your question, My Lady."

"They're frightening, marauding, evil, and yet—"

Again the sponge faltered, and Vivian heard a sharp intake of breath. "Do not say such things, My Lady, I beg you. The dragons are—sacred."

"That's what Duncan said. How are they sacred?"

"It is best, My Lady, not to speak of these things. Lie back—we need to wash your hair."

Again the wall of silence, first from the healer, now from the maid. The fear took on a three-dimensional quality, filling up the room.

Esme began pouring water through her hair, and Vivian brought her mind back to the business at hand, calmed her breath with an effort of will. Esme washed and rinsed her hair three times with three different solutions. The final herbal cycle clogged her sinuses with a perfume that set her coughing and made it difficult to breathe. Rebellious, she ducked her head under the water and rinsed out as much of the scent as she could, enough to allow her to breathe freely at least, and refused to allow any further ministrations.

"That's it," she declared, climbing out of the tub. "We're done." Testing her muscles, she realized that she could move more freely. The herbs had done their work.

Poe, with a sidelong glance at her, climbed into the tub with a splash of his flippers. "You'll be sorry," Vivian told him. "You'll stink for a year and a day. No other penguin will speak to you."

A moment later, still damp and shivering in the thin robe, she confronted a rainbow of velvet and satin gowns, all low cut and tight waisted, all beribboned and befrilled. She tried on one after another, finally flinging the last aside and turning her mounting frustration on the hovering Esme.

"They're impossible."

"What do you mean, My Lady? They look beautiful to me." Envious hands smoothed the wispy blue silk trimmed with peacock feathers, obviously her favorite.

Vivian looked at her reflection in the oval mirror, taller than she was, framed in dark polished wood, carved with images of the inevitable dragons.

"Why don't *you* wear it, then?" Vivian snapped. The girl flinched at her tone, and she was immediately contrite. "Look—too much cleavage, and it shows the scars on my shoulders. Plus it's so tight I can't breathe—"

"But it's the fashion, My Lady. And . . ." She stopped, looked down at her hands.

"And?"

"The Chancellor picked them out."

"He did, did he?" Vivian remembered the scornful eyes and the insolent touch. A flush of anger moved through her, from toes to forehead. Jared or Gareth or whoever, she'd seen that look before; her casual style never measured up to his idealized vision of what she ought to be.

She turned to the rack and sorted through the gowns that remained. "If this is what I have to wear, then I won't go."

Esme looked like she'd proposed cutting off her own head with a dull sword. "But—you have to go."

"Then find me something reasonable to wear." Seeing that the tears were about to begin again, Vivian sighed and tried to summon up a modicum of patience. "Look, Esme, things may be different in your world, but no man is going to tell me what to wear. If I must go to this feast, can you find me a gown that hasn't more than three frills and isn't so goddamned tight in the waist that I can't breathe?"

"You'll be out of fashion," Esme wailed.

"I don't give a damn about fashion. Bring me sensible shoes while you're at it. I can't walk in these things."

"I'll try, My Lady. But he won't like it." Esme scuttled out the door like a frightened crab. Vivian nearly laughed but quickly sobered at the thought of the girl's genuine terror.

After the door closed, she used the waiting time to look over the tapestries as the healer had suggested. There was one of a man, a maiden, and a dragon, arranged in a stylized triangle. Above their heads, dragons flew across the sky. The next tapestry depicted a larger version of one of the tiles—a maiden in white chained to a rock, with a predatory dragon ready to strike. A man in a crimson robe with a raised staff stood off to the side.

One tapestry held her attention longer than the others. Another dark-haired woman, this time wearing a sober black gown. A dragon flew overhead, and in what was meant to be the sky, a number of doors stood open, some round, some rectangular, and through them reached things best not seen. A tentacle, a claw, an amorphous mass that looked like swollen, skinless flesh.

A wafting of scent and a bump against her knee signaled the arrival of Poe. He stood beside her, contemplating the picture as though deeply interested, and then waddled over and poked his head around behind it, pecking at the wall. There was a sliding sound, stone on stone, and he vanished.

"Poe!"

Silence. Vivian peered around the tapestry to see Poe standing at the center of a large walk-in closet, his white patches ghostly in the near-dark. When her eyes adjusted, she could make out two garments hung on elaborate hangers. One was a trailing white gown, the other jet black, plain.

Familiar.

Dream memory flooded through her; the voices in her head surged in volume. Vivian let them carry her into the closet. She slid the black gown from its hanger. The fabric was silky, cool to the touch. A moment's pause, and then she shrugged out of the dressing robe and slipped the gown over her head. It fit so perfectly it might have been tailored for her.

When she stepped back out into the chamber, she thought for an instant that someone else was in the room. It took the space of several breaths to realize she was looking into the mirror.

This mirror self was not familiar, not ordinary Vivian in jeans and T-shirt. Her skin against the black of the dress was ghostly pale, except for the purplish swelling on her left cheek, a mark left by a blow struck in dream. And then, even as she stared, the gray eyes shifted to green and then to gold.

Vivian moved closer to the mirror, turning her head from side to side to change the light, but there was no mistaking. Her eyes were a dark golden amber, flecked with threads of green. Worse, the scars on her shoulders had healed into black circles, surrounded by what looked like an intricate tattoo of overlapping scales in shimmering gold, purple, and green.

The buzzing of voices in her head intensified to a dizzying crescendo.

Experimentally, she rotated her shoulders, one way, and then the other. No more pain. When she brushed over one of the marks with her fingers the skin was smooth and even; no thickening, no scarring.

Standing there, staring at this self that she no longer

knew, with the alien room behind her made doubly so by virtue of being a reflection, she felt disconnected and wraith-like, with nothing solid to cling to. She stretched out one hand to the mirror, half-expecting to pass through into something beyond.

Her fingers touched glass. Cool, slightly dusty, and decidedly solid. And looking into it, an ordinary woman with scarred shoulders, a crazy woman with voices in her head.

A woman with golden eyes that once were gray.

Nineteen

⚜

Vivian was still looking in the mirror when the door opened and the Warlord stepped into the room. His reflected eyes met hers with a look that was anger and hunger and something else that defied naming. His long dark hair was neatly braided, and he wore a well-cut gray tunic, plain and serviceable.

If she didn't turn around, if she kept him like this, as an image in the mirror, he would be only a fantasy, not a part of this absurd world that was re-creating her as some freak from a picture-book tale that could not be true.

One word sorted itself out from the babble and rang clear in her mind like a bell.

Destiny.

Vivian turned and made him real.

"What are you playing at?" He crossed the distance between them in a few long strides, his eyes raking over her. Vivian lifted her chin a little higher and held his gaze without flinching.

"I don't know what you mean."

"Let me be more clear. What exactly are you doing here? Why did you come?"

"I can't see what business it is of yours."

"It's my job to protect the kingdom. You have brought

trouble with you." There was no mistaking the fury in his voice. He towered over her, and she took a step back but found her own anger rising to meet his.

"You brought me here. I don't recall having a choice in the matter."

"Your eyes have changed. What manner of woman are you?"

She chose not to answer.

He stretched one hand toward her shoulder, and she flinched, half-expecting a blow.

"I don't hit women," he said. His eyes flicked pointedly to her cheek, and her own hand lifted to cover the bruise.

"Explain," he said. "Nobody survives the dragon poison."

"Except me, apparently."

"Tell me who you are and what you are doing here."

She sighed. "My name is Vivian Maylor. I came—through a dream. Don't all dreams lead to Surmise?"

His face remained implacable, eyes shuttered and cold. "What does it matter to you? What do you want with me?"

"Because of you, a dragon is dead."

"Your turn to explain. How is this a bad thing? They are vile creatures—"

His hands clenched and his voice softened, low and dangerous. "There is a law in Surmise. When a dragon dies, so, too, must somebody else."

A flash of intuition turned her cold. "Who?"

He laughed, a harsh, strangled sound. "Whoever killed it."

The pieces fell into place. "Oh, God. Duncan. You have to help him—"

"Nobody can help him."

"Not that it matters to you—"

"Don't speak of what you do not know, My Lady." He swung away, pacing across the room to the windows.

"In case you're wondering, I don't understand about the scars," she said to his back. "Or why I survived the dragon poison, or why my eyes changed color. It just happened."

"Just like that. No rhyme or reason. And the gown? Was

that an accident also? I hardly think that's what was laid out for you to wear to dinner."

"How could you possibly know what I was expected to wear to dinner?"

"I know the Chancellor, and the evidence is hardly difficult to spot." He nodded toward the litter of gowns, and Vivian felt herself flush.

"I had no interest in wearing frills and lace and tripping over my own skirts. This gown suits me. It's much more practical."

"Practical? Is that what you call it?" He kept his back to her; she couldn't read the tone of his voice, but he no longer sounded angry.

"What's wrong with it?"

Poe picked that moment to make his presence known. He squawked and waddled close to the Warlord. The two inspected each other in silence for a moment.

"Will there be more of these—birds?"

"Penguins? I rather doubt it." Even as she said it, Vivian realized that she had no idea. One penguin was so unlikely as to be impossible, and yet indubitably here one was.

The Warlord shook his head. "Forget the birds. Answer me—are you creating this look on purpose?"

"What look?"

"Don't play stupid with me, My Lady. I'm not buying."

"I like this gown. It suits me."

"The gown, the eyes, the marks of scales on your shoulders. Are you a sorceress, My Lady?" His voice sounded weary, maybe even sad, but his face revealed nothing.

"A sorceress?" She laughed bitterly. "Sadly, no. Things would be so much easier if I were."

"I don't know what to do with you."

"Why don't you forget about me and go do something about the man who's going to die because he tried to protect me?"

The words hung in the air between them. Something lethal flashed in the agate eyes. *Stop, Vivian. Back away.* But she was possessed by a mad rage, equal parts hurt, fear, and outrage, and she couldn't seem to stop. She stepped forward, spread her arms wide. "Go ahead. Kill an unarmed woman in cold blood. That would make you a real man."

His face blanched white, the scars livid slashes across his cheeks. He took a step toward her, then stopped. Held up a hand for silence. "Hush. Someone is coming." He drew his sword and crossed to the door, silent and quick as a cat.

Vivian's eyes followed the naked sword blade, resolving to guard her tongue in the future. She was in way over her head here without eliciting any extra and personalized hatred from a dangerous, sword-carrying Warlord.

"I don't hear anything," she said, after a few interminable breaths of waiting.

"Shh."

It was not reassuring that footsteps in the hallway put him on instant high alert, but she didn't dare to ask him what or whom he feared.

Then she heard muffled voices. The door swung open. One of the guards stood at full attention in the entrance and announced, "Prince Landon, My Lady."

A man entered and stood blinking at her. Gray hair hung over his shoulders, clean but untended. His face was deeply lined and far too pale, as though he never saw the sun. His tunic, a dull bruised color that might once have been purple, was torn and tattered, the pale flesh of his belly visible through a hole the size of her fist. His feet were bare, and black with dirt. He bowed and smiled, but the smile was grief and loss, laid over an unbearable weariness that cut her to the heart.

As if he didn't wish to presume, he stayed close to the door. "Good evening, My Lady. I've come to take you down to the feast." He nodded at the Warlord. "Lord Zee."

"You're—the Prince?" Vivian struggled with her voice, unsteady despite her best attempts.

"Appearances are deceiving," the Warlord said. "You would be wise to note that, My Lady." He bowed to the ragged man at the door, a deep bow, made with evident respect, and made his exit.

Vivian's eyes followed him. The Prince coughed, gently, drawing her attention back. "Shall we go, then?" He held out his hand.

"I would prefer not to."

"That makes two of us. However, I fear we have been summoned. Refusing is not an option."

Vivian opened her mouth to make a caustic remark, then shut it. This man was so obviously in pain. She didn't want to add to it. "But you're the Prince," she said finally.

"And you are—" His eyes ran over her again. She'd underestimated him. The gaze was intelligent and sharp, and she knew he was absorbing the color of her eyes, the marks on her shoulders. A spasm of pain crossed his face. "I'm not sure what you are, My Lady. You look rather like *her* in that gown, and yet not like *her* at all."

His was not an evil face—many of the lines were those of kindness—but a chill went over her at what she saw in his eyes in that moment. Death. She'd seen it in the Warlord's eyes, too, but despite his aura of violence, the Warlord would think twice about killing a woman. This man, if he felt it warranted, would not hesitate.

She took a step back and away from him. Nervous, her hands smoothed over the hips of the black gown, and her right encountered something unexpected: a hard object, long and narrow, trapped between the fabric and her skin.

Holding his eyes, hoping he wouldn't notice, she explored the object with her hand. "If I were to ask you what you mean by *her*, you will tell me you can't talk about it, right?"

She found a pocket, set seamlessly into the fabric. Her fingers curled around what she found there.

"I ask you straight out—are you a sorceress, My Lady?"

"Why do you people keep asking me that? I have no magical powers and I certainly don't plan to hurt anybody."

"Then why have you dressed as one?"

Vivian stared at him. "I found the gown—it was in the closet."

"You found it. Just like that."

Her hand clenched around the thing in her pocket, familiar and comforting, fitting perfectly into her palm. "The Warlord was just asking the same questions. I give you the same answer. I found the dress. I like it. It fits."

"It fits, yes." He sighed. "You have the look of magic about you, but not like her. Perhaps the difference is an absence of evil. We will hope."

He squared his shoulders, apparently having come to a decision, and held out a hand. "Shall we go? The Queen is not tolerant of tardiness."

Vivian breathed a sigh of relief. She was inclined to like this prince and had enough enemies already. But when she took the hand he held out to her, she saw something that stopped her cold. Circling the fourth finger of his left hand was a fine gold band set with tiny bloodred stones.

"What the hell are you doing with my mother's ring?"

His face went white to the lips, his eyes stricken.

She advanced on him, shouting. "You bastard! What have you done with her?"

"I? Nothing—"

He'd totally fooled her with that beaten-down act. She had the stiletto out, the blade flicked open, before he could finish the sentence. "Don't lie to me! She's here somewhere. You know where she is. Tell me now or I'll—"

"You'll what?"

He had drawn his sword. No longer a ragged, beaten lunatic. His face was alight, every line of his body awake and at the ready. "Put the knife away before one of us gets hurt, and listen to me."

"You're a liar, and I will not listen to a word you say."

"You will." His voice was pitched low and intense. "You will listen now, and stop this idiocy before the guards come in here."

He advanced and she retreated. Her only option was to throw the knife, too small to be of any defense against a sword. If she was lucky and killed him, she'd have the guards to contend with. And if she killed him she'd never find out what he'd done with her mother.

And then Poe abandoned her. She'd been aware of him in her peripheral vision, watching from the sidelines. With a little squawk, he waddled across the room and stood in front of the Prince, facing her, flippers spread in a defensive posture.

"The last thing in the world I want is to hurt your mother," the Prince said. "The ring is mine. Think. Hers would never fit my hand."

"You could have resized it."

"Please—I beg you not to make this mistake."

Vivian looked from him to the penguin, who had managed to get a disapproving look onto his face. "You're threatening me with a sword."

"I thought I was protecting myself." The Prince took a step back, sheathed the sword, and held both hands up in a gesture of peace. "No world exists in which I could harm Isobel's child. Do with me what you will, but I beg you— give me time to explain."

"I'm listening." Her hands were shaking. Every breath hurt.

"Your mother and I exchanged rings, long, long ago. Please. If you can save her, I will do anything in my power to help you. But if we are to do that, first we must go to the feast. And the guards must not hear any of this."

He glanced at the door and then back at Vivian.

Trust nobody.

And yet she found herself wanting to tell him everything. Maybe he could help her find Jehenna. Maybe he would know something about the key. Hell, Poe had sided with him.

Caution prevailed. Not now. Not yet.

She closed the knife and dropped it into her pocket. "All right," she said. "Let's go."

The Prince nodded and offered her his arm. She took it.

"Shoes."

"What?"

He glanced pointedly at her feet. "You'll need shoes."

"Oh, shit." Esme had never returned with the sensible shoes. Which meant the only thing available to her was a ridiculous pair of high-heeled sandals concocted out of velvet and lace. They lay on the floor where she had discarded them.

"Can't I go barefoot?"

"No, My Lady."

"But you—"

"It's not possible."

"But I can't walk in those." Her voice came out plaintive and fragile, and she felt herself on the verge of tears. Over a pair of freaking shoes.

"I'll help you."

Nothing else for it, then. Plopping down on the floor, gown and all, she picked up the instruments of torture and shoved them onto her feet.

"What of your bird? Will he stay here?"

"Don't ask me. He apparently does whatever he pleases." Poe looked at her, all innocence, and then hopped ahead of them to the door.

Swallowing all of the questions still clamoring to be asked, Vivian reached up her hand to allow the Prince to pull her to her feet, then wobbled beside him out into the corridor, Poe following at their heels.

Twenty

✣

The corridor wound around and around, ever downward, making walking in the high-heeled slippers a progressively more precarious and painful problem. Prince Landon had reverted to his ragged, shambling persona, apparently lost in his own thoughts. At intervals they passed servants headed in the opposite direction—a page, a girl carrying bedding, a couple of swaggering guards. All looked at Vivian askance, keeping a distance. Not one of them acknowledged the Prince.

Vivian let Landon lead her and tried to focus on one step after the other—*don't trip, don't stumble, don't limp, don't pay too much attention to the voices in your head.* The voices were so loud and distracting that the sound of wailing had gone on for some time before she registered it. She slowed her steps, listening, and turned her head to look back over her shoulder. Nothing but the empty corridor curving upward and out of sight.

The Prince tugged her forward. "We're late, My Lady. There is nothing we can do."

"What is it?"

The wail escalated into a high, wrenching shriek. Vivian twisted away from Landon's restraining hand and turned back. She kicked off the slippers, gathered up her skirt, and broke into a run. Isobel cried like that sometimes, when she was restrained and begging for knives.

She followed the sound down a passage that branched off the main corridor and then into a hallway narrower and colder. Stone floor, stone walls. No attempt here to create any warmth or comfort with tapestries or carpets.

Another curve, and then another, and Vivian almost crashed into a girl struggling in the grip of two of the castle guards. Her gown was torn and hung in shreds over one shoulder, revealing one naked breast. A livid red swelling disfigured her left cheek, beginning to turn black and purple around the edges. Strands of hair plastered across a face streaked with tears.

"Esme!"

"My Lady, help me! Please help me, don't let them—"

Without missing a step or changing expression, one of the guards lifted his arm and landed a backhanded blow. Esme's head jerked sideways. She went limp, hanging like a rag doll between their hands. Bright blood dribbled from her broken lip and down over her chin. The guards kept moving, dragging her along with her feet trailing useless on the floor.

"Let her go!" Vivian shouted, standing in their way.

One of the guards shoved her aside and they strode on, dragging their senseless burden between them.

Vivian turned to the Prince, standing just behind her. "Do something! Tell them to let her go."

"They answer to the Chancellor," he said. "There is nothing I can do." He wiped his mouth on his sleeve.

"That's stupid. You're the Prince! They have to listen to you."

He shook his head, not meeting her eyes.

"But this is outrageous—we have to stop them—"

The Prince gripped her upper arms and shook her a little, speaking in a low, urgent voice. "I cannot save her. You cannot save her. If you betray yourself, you will help no one. Do you understand?" The guards vanished out of sight with their unconscious prisoner. "Come," Landon said, his voice gentle now. The lines of pain in his face had deepened. "We must go at once."

He held out the slippers, and because there was nothing else she could think of to do in the moment, Vivian put them on and walked with him. "What will happen to her?"

"They will take her to the dungeons."

"But it's my fault—"

"Hush now—we must make a grand entrance."

They were approaching a circular staircase, wide enough for ten to walk easily abreast. Poe stood waiting at the top. Relief at the sight of his now-familiar form vanished as she spied the sea of courtiers below, all eyes turned upward to stare. A whole new cause of anxiety, all of those eyes. Landon's hand was steady on her arm, and he guided her forward without hesitation.

A footman in white satin breeches, pointy-toed golden slippers, and a green doublet announced in a loud voice: "His Highly Eminent Landon, Royal Highness, Heir Apparent of Surmise, and the Lady Vivian."

Four trumpets played a fanfare, nearly deafening in intensity, followed by little gasps and flutters of applause from the guests.

For the time it took to make it down the stairs, Vivian's entire focus was on one step after another, making sure that she didn't fall off the ridiculous shoes and make a spectacle of herself tumbling down in front of everybody.

Once at the bottom, she breathed a sigh of relief and looked around. The room gleamed with light from a hundred chandeliers. High above, the cathedral ceiling depicted dragons, maidens, and warriors in brilliant hues. Courtiers moved into their places at rows of tables set with golden platters and crystal goblets. One larger table at the far end of the room, elevated on a dais, remained empty.

Another fanfare, longer this time, complex.

"Her Majesty—Empress of Dragons, Queen of the Dreamworld, Weaver of Surmise."

All voices stilled. All eyes turned as one toward the commanding presence standing at the top of the staircase. An audible sound of indrawn breath, and then all knees bent and the entire throng, including the Prince, collapsed onto the floor in prostrate heaps of bright silk and satin.

The Queen was tall for a woman, with thick auburn hair falling unrestrained over her shoulders and past her waist. A crown of crystal flashed sparks of scarlet, purple, and vermillion wherever it was touched by the light from the chandeliers. Her gown fit her slender form like a second skin, shimmering in rainbow colors, shifting every time she moved in an ever-varying play of light and color.

Jehenna.

Vivian felt her heart stammer in her chest, her knees go weak. She should have guessed, should have prepared for this moment somehow. George had given her all the clues she needed, but her mind had been so muddled by the changes in her body and the voices in her head that she'd missed the obvious. And so she'd walked right into a trap without a plan or an ally or a hope of escape.

She managed to stay on her feet in the middle of the kneeling crowd, braced for what was surely coming. Out of the corner of her eye she caught a movement in black and white, picking its way over and around the courtiers toward the staircase.

Poe.

She knew him by now, knew exactly where he was going, and that this couldn't mean anything but disaster. "Poe! Come back!" Her whisper was as loud as a shout in the silent room, but the penguin ignored her. Vivian wobbled after him, realizing several breaths later that his arrival time at the foot of the staircase would coincide precisely with the end of Jehenna's royal progress. She picked up her speed to set an interception course, but the slippers and the prostrate courtiers slowed her down.

Poe beat her and Jehenna both by a matter of seconds, taking up a watch-penguin pose that blocked Jehenna from descending the final step unless she altered her course to move around him.

Vivian staggered to a stop right behind him, out of breath.

She met Jehenna's gaze, unflinching, until at last it was the Queen whose eyes fell. "Dreamshifter," she proclaimed in a voice meant to carry across the room. "We welcome you to Surmise."

Several possible responses presented themselves, but Vivian discarded them all, still reeling from the discovery that before Jehenna looked away there had been a flicker of fear in her eyes.

Footsteps approached from behind, and a hand grasped her shoulder, none too gently. "All bow before the Queen of Surmise," Jared's voice said, in the authoritative tone of Gareth the Chancellor.

"I don't."

A murmur and a rustle spread throughout the hall.

"Don't be a fool," Gareth hissed in her ear. "Bow to the Queen."

"If she insists, I'm sure Her Majesty can make me do the chicken dance. I will do nothing because *you* ask it." She let her voice carry, instilling as much disdain into her tone as she could manage.

Jehenna's lips barely moved, her voice pitched for Vivian's ears alone. "Kneel."

The voice echoed in her head, louder than the others. A tug at her knees, a pressure on her thoughts, followed. An impulse, no more. Her mind remained free, her body under her own control.

Interesting.

With a show of reluctance, which wasn't too difficult to summon up, she sank down to the floor and pressed her forehead against the marble tile. Best if nobody knew she had the power to resist.

Jehenna's voice rang out again, rich, magnanimous. "This is a time of rejoicing—let the wine flow, let all stomachs be filled. Let there be celebration and laughter. Chancellor—let my people be fed."

Gareth's voice followed. "You may all rise. The Queen in her abundance invites you all to feast. Take your places, and let the food be served."

A rustle of clothing, footsteps, a subdued hum of voices followed. Vivian remained on her knees, waiting for the command.

"Get up," Jehenna said.

Vivian obeyed with some difficulty, wobbling on the unaccustomed heels.

Jehenna leaned toward her and brushed her lips against first one cheek and then the other, whispering. "You think to humiliate me. Never doubt I will extract vengeance magnified a thousand times."

"I have no doubts at all."

"Where is the key?"

"Where are the dreamspheres?"

The hazel eyes passed over her from head to toe, not missing the smallest detail, lingering on her scarred shoulders. "I will have the key, soon or late."

Again that tug on her mind, easily brushed aside. "I don't know where it is."

Jehenna took a step toward her. Poe waddled between the two of them, hissed, spread out his wings.

"Remove that creature," Jehenna ordered.

Before Vivian or any of the guards could respond to this command, Poe darted his head forward and fastened his beak in the fabric of the Queen's multihued gown. Jehenna gasped and pulled away, dragging the penguin with her. A tearing sound, followed by the chiming of crystal on crystal. Poe stood with a fragment of the gown hanging from his beak, as a cascade of crystal globes hit the floor and rolled in all directions.

Everybody in the room froze.

"Gareth!" Jehenna ordered.

He dropped to his knees and began to gather the dreamspheres.

Vivian braced herself for a bolt of magical lightning, for the soldiers to come and drag her away. But apart from one murderous look, Jehenna ignored her. She swept away to the dais, head held high, as though nothing had happened. One of the courtiers assisted her up the steps and into an elaborately carved chair at the center of the high table.

Standing alone at the center of the hall, Poe at her side, Vivian felt herself go cold and quiet. She was the central focus for too many eyes, seen and unseen. Voices in and out of her head suggested various strategies that ranged from stabbing Jehenna in the heart to making a run for it. None of these were valid responses, and she had no idea where to go. Besides, her knees shook so hard that if she took a single step on her own, she feared she would fall off these stupid shoes and twist her ankle.

The Queen sat at the table, inclining her head toward the gentleman seated next to her, uttering some sort of pleasantry that Vivian couldn't hear. He smiled in response. Chatter gradually resumed at the other tables. Gareth crawled about on hands and knees around her feet, gathering the last of the globes and storing them in his pockets.

At last he stood and faced her. His jaw was set, his eyes hard. She recognized the rage. But he spoke politely and in courtly tones, as though nothing was amiss.

"My Lady, you must be seated. The guests await you before they begin."

He put his hand on her arm, urged her forward. She let him, leaning on him a little and keeping her pace as dignified as possible. He steered her toward the dais and the high table. Up the steps. Past the Prince who sat with eyes downcast, past men and women old and young.

Hungry, she realized, looking at the blur of faces. Waiting.

By the time Jared pulled out the chair next to Jehenna and indicated she should sit in it, Vivian felt like a sheep invited to dinner with wolves. Something more than food was on the table tonight. Gareth settled into the place beside her. His knee pressed against hers; his hand slid onto her thigh. On the other side, Jehenna's elbow dug into her arm. Vivian made herself as small as possible, went still and quiet. Waiting. Gareth's hand slid upward, caressing. She dug her fingernails into his skin. He retaliated with a brutal squeeze, fingers bruising deep into the muscle. The breath hissed out between her teeth at the pain.

"Are you well?" Gareth asked, his face a mask of concern.

"Fine."

"I thought perhaps your wounds were bothering you." His smile promised many things, none of them good.

Vivian felt the brush of feathers against her legs.

The next instant Gareth jerked his hand away, rocking backward in his chair. Bright blood welled up from the broken skin on the back of his hand, and he stared at it in disbelief.

"Are you well?" Vivian asked.

"Goddamn bird bit me." Gareth pressed a white napkin against his wounded hand, lips compressed in a cold rage.

Vivian shivered, one hand stroking soft feathers under cover of the table. She should placate him, somehow, but before she could think of a thing to say, a fanfare blew. Massive double doors at the end of the hall slowly opened, held by two young pages resplendent in crimson tunics and feathered hats. A procession of servers paraded in, bearing steaming platters above their heads. They wended their way past all of the other tables and directly toward the dais. Behind them, another procession of servers fanned out through the hall.

The Queen was served first. Then Vivian, then Gareth, and on down the table. Soup for starters, some sort of broth with fleshy lumps bobbing in it. A fishy steam wafted up into her nostrils, and her stomach rolled in rebellion. Voices hammered at her skull, both inside and outside.

Below her vantage point, a bewildering array of humanity talked and ate, the clink of silver and the buzz of voices a constant hum that mingled with the noise in her head to create a nearly intolerable volume. Prince Landon, seated farther down the table, spoke not a word to her or anybody else, eating silently and mechanically. He seemed to have aged since he'd picked her up in her room. New lines on his face, more gray in his hair. Jehenna and Gareth discussed the state of Surmise with a silver-haired, Vandyke-bearded aristocrat.

Vivian had plenty of time to wonder what game Jehenna was playing, that she should be seated here as guest of honor at this feast rather than locked up in a dungeon somewhere. Or dead.

A server appeared at her shoulder, leaning over to whisper in her ear. "Is the food not to your liking, My Lady? If not, we can bring you something else." He stank of sweat and fear, and Vivian thought suddenly of Esme. Chances were good that if she didn't eat, somebody else would be punished.

"Oh, no, it's fine," she said, "I was just—it's great."

She poked with her spoon at the flotilla of lumpy, flesh-colored objects floating in her soup bowl, looked left and right to note that the Queen and Gareth were engaged in conversation, then fished a lump out and held it under the table for Poe.

When he didn't take it, she leaned down to see if he was okay and caught a glimpse of something shiny in his beak. She cupped her palm and he dropped an item, round and smooth, and delicately took the lump of seafood.

Vivian tucked the dreamsphere into the pocket of the gown next to the stiletto. Then she spooned up some broth, closed her eyes, and forced it down. Not so bad, after all. The flavor was briny and good, the lumps just tasted like fish, and as she ate she began to realize that she was hungry.

She also began to notice things. A winged creature, more bat than dragon but as big as a cat, fluttered into the shadows and vanished. A slithering reptile shape appeared and disappeared under Gareth's chair. A naked gray tail twitched from behind a platter of bread. For an instant she was certain that a penguin stood by her chair, bearing a platter of fish, but when she turned her head it was only a fat, middle-aged server, hovering behind her with a goblet of wine. New rooms flickered into being at the edges of the great hall, then disappeared.

The globes, she thought. All were dreams. *All dreams lead to Surmise.*

Every person in this room—the Warlord, Gareth and Prince Landon, Esme, the servants and the courtiers—all were here because some dream portal brought them. And with them, why should there not be other elements of dream?

Poe nudged at her knee, rousing her out of her thoughts. She passed the last seafood lump to him under the table and started in on the second course, relieved to note that it looked and smelled very much like chicken.

The silence started at the center of the hall and spread in ripples until the only sound remaining came from the voices in her head. Vivian looked up from her plate, knife and fork in hand, her heart contracting in a spasm of fear.

A man in a scarlet robe stood at the top of the stairs, leaning on a carved wooden staff. His head was shaved bald. Motionless, he waited until every eye was trained on him, every voice hushed, and then he raised his arms above his head, flourishing the staff. His voice rang out in oratorical tones.

"People of Surmise."

Pause for effect. All eyes had already been directed his way. Nobody moved. In all that vast hall no sound other than that of breath. Gareth's slightly quickened. Jehenna's even and regular.

Vivian clamped her hands around the edges of her chair, waiting for the cruel jaws of the trap to spring.

"A dragon has been slain. In the face of this abomination there must be retribution. The usual penalty will be exacted. A death for a death."

Image after image flashed across Vivian's memory. Maidens and dragons and death. Her heart battered at the walls of her chest. Instinct screamed at her to flee. Gareth's arm circled her shoulders; his hand gripped her upper arm.

She was trapped.

Nowhere to run.

Twenty-one

✤

·

Zee, Warlord of Surmise, knowing he would be punished for his absence, was nevertheless far from the feast, deep in the dark and festering belly of the castle dungeons.

In total darkness, by sense of touch alone, he fitted a key into a rusty lock and shoved open a heavy stone door.

"Who's there?"

"Be easy, it's just me." Pulling the door closed behind him, the Warlord lit the lantern he carried and hung it on a peg set high in the wall.

Duncan scrambled up onto unsteady feet. Traces of tears smudged his cheeks. "Forgive me, Warlord—it's the light, making my eyes water—"

He had not been treated gently. His fair hair was dark with blood, his face swollen and distorted. The burn, untreated, oozed and had begun to fester.

"Darkness breeds fear—I felt you could use a little light."

"And the news?"

"The dragon died."

One ragged breath. Another. When he spoke, the young man's voice was very nearly steady. "When is it to be?"

"Tonight, I'd guess. Soon. I am sorry. The Queen has returned—I can do nothing to stop this."

"I understand."

"You did right, Duncan."

"It seemed like a good idea at the time. The woman?"

"I have no word on that."

Duncan turned his back, and his shoulders shook. Only for a moment, though, and when he turned, his face was set and hardened. "How is it to be? Can you tell me?"

"There will be another—Flynt, the farmer. Stabbed the dragon with a pitchfork when it went for his daughter. The fact that the dragon was flying around apparently well and healthy when it left the farm and came to you has no bearing—the investigator says he drew blood and the dragon is dead. He will share your death."

"Gladiators, you think? Me against the poor old sod?"

"Yes. I will see to it that both swords are sharp, understand?"

"You do us no good if you risk your own life."

The Warlord sharpened his voice. "The swords will both be sharp—it's already arranged. I've been to see Flynt. He understands."

For the first time the boy's voice broke. "I don't know that I can do this thing, to kill in cold blood—"

"A kindness. There are worse things than death at the hands of a friend."

The Warlord wanted to shake the boy's hand, to offer comfort, but it was a cruelty to offer comfort where there was none. Too much kindness and the control might break. He couldn't even leave the light, as somebody else would be blamed and punished and there was enough blood on his hands already.

"Good-bye, Duncan."

"Warlord—"

He turned. The boy held his eyes. "I will die well."

"I do not doubt it."

He closed the door as softly as possible, then turned the key in the lock. One step at a time, running a hand along the wall for balance, he continued down the dark passage that he knew by heart, turned right, opened a door, and closed it behind him.

Here he again lit the lantern and hung it on a hook.

A small room, with little more than a narrow bed and hooks for his few articles of clothing. A mirror hung on the far wall, with a washbasin on a wooden stand. Crossing the room, he confronted his scarred face in the mirror. Even to him, it looked deformed and frightening. Women cringed away from him; men feared him.

He had no problem with this—he deserved nothing more. He was the Warlord of the kingdom; it was his sworn duty to guard the populace from the dragons, to train and protect the men who served under him. In this task, he failed. Again and again he failed. In the past he'd managed to save a few men like Duncan, despite the rigid edicts of the law. A severe punishment—whipping, the loss of a hand—had sufficed. But when this Queen returned and demanded an accounting of the kingdom, he'd known at once there would be no mercy. For anybody. Ever.

As for the woman he'd found in the forest—her coming might be blessing or curse and he could not tell which. He knew her from dream; had walked beside her, sword in hand, and protected her, slaying all that threatened to touch her. In his dreams he loved her beyond any honor or duty or sense of right and wrong.

But this was not dream, and he was sick to death already of injustice.

When he'd seen her in the woods, bruised, frightened, and still defiant, he'd had a problem with his breath, as though some magic had sucked away all the air. A weakness had come over him, a softness, inexplicable and strange. He had wanted to scoop her up in his arms, to gentle her fear, to bury his face in her hair and breathe in the scent of her. Racing back to the castle under the dragon shadow without raising a sword to protect her had taken every ounce of willpower he possessed.

He'd thought she would die in his arms, bleeding from the dragon's talons, had waited for the inevitable spasms to twist her body, the burning heat. These things had not come to pass. The woman had power and was keeping secrets. She had survived the dragon poison. Her eyes had changed color; her skin bore a pattern of scales. She'd dressed herself in the gown of a full-blood sorceress.

Tales from the mists of time past told of dragons with the power to take on human form, dragons that had taken human women for themselves. Rumor, myth, or so he had always believed. How could dragon blood, corroding and toxic, possibly run in the veins of a human?

Seeing what he had seen this day, he feared that truth lay hidden in the tales.

One sorceress was enough in a kingdom. They did not need another.

For now, he would watch and wait. His duty was clearly to the kingdom. If the woman had power, then perhaps she and the Queen would destroy each other, and the kingdom would be free. He would wait, let things take their course. If need be, he would kill her himself, no matter how his heart might beat against it.

But today carried enough heartbreak without allowing himself feelings about a woman loved in dream. Another dragon dead. No matter how well he trained his men, how diligently he sought to repel the dragons and keep them in their own territory—providing food sources in the mountains when game was scarce, beating the bushes to scare them off when they encroached on civilization—still accidents happened. Either people died because they did not offer resistance, or they died because they dared to defend themselves, or more commonly someone they loved.

For this, for his inability to prevent the deaths of good men who had committed no sin other than that of self-preservation or the protection of their loved ones, he exacted penance, marking the memory of each death on his own body. Staring down his scarred face in the mirror, he drew the blade of his knife down his right cheek, from just below the eye to the jaw. Blood welled, flowed over his face and down his neck, staining his tunic. He repeated the motion on the left. One cut for each of the men who would die to-night. A small gesture: All the penance in the world was not enough.

As he faced himself in the mirror, it seemed in that moment that his image shifted, bent, until he looked into another face. The eyes were his own, but this face bore only a single fresh wound, horizontal across the cheek. As the Warlord leaned forward to look more closely, the other face did likewise. The mirrored eyes widened in surprise.

And in that moment the Warlord felt a shift, as though his dream self stepped out of the shadows and stood beside him—himself, but with a different set of memories, thoughts, and emotions. Only a moment, and then the sensation faded.

Only his own face, scarred and bloody, looked at him out of the mirror.

He turned away, blotting at the blood with a towel. He owed it to Duncan to witness his death.

After that he would do whatever needed to be done.

Twenty-two

✣

The priest's words echoed through the silence in the hall. No one spoke or moved.

At last Jehenna pushed back her chair and rose to her feet. "Nahl—you who serve as High Priest to the Dragon. Tell us, what shall be done to appease the gods, that no further harm shall come to the kingdom?"

"There must be a death."

"But my people are at feast—"

"It must happen now, My Queen."

Jehenna inclined her head, the personification of a deep and heavy sorrow. "The gods have spoken. You will all proceed to the arena at once."

The words were too rehearsed, too planned.

A tumult of voices arose. Chairs pushed back. Courtiers jostled and pushed in a frenzied rush toward the door, abandoning their plates and the food spread untouched on the tables. Vivian stayed in her chair, Gareth still holding her arm. She was overwhelmed by the chaos, by the prospect of violence and the eagerness of the crowd to embrace it. Landon had disappeared, but she thought she caught a glimpse of fluttering rags vanishing through a doorway. Poe was nowhere to be seen.

Gareth got to his feet, closing one hand around her wrist. "Come."

Vivian tried to twist away, but the hand clamped tighter. Her head throbbed. Cold sweat trickled down her back while her heart beat a rapid and uncomfortable rhythm. Her feet ached in the stupid shoes as she took a few running steps to catch up and ease the pressure on her wrist.

"Gareth, please. Let me go."

He didn't slow, or stop. Didn't even look at her. "You are the guest of honor. We must not be late."

Fear shafted into her belly. Being the guest of honor was not a good thing. Images of all of the tapestries and paintings flashed through her mind: maidens sacrificed to dragons, again and again and again.

She dropped to her knees, twisting her arm against the weak spot between Gareth's fingers and thumb. She managed to break his grip, but before she could get back on her feet and flee through the crowd, his hands were tangled in her hair. A sharp yank brought her staggering up onto her feet.

"Every time you struggle," he said, leaning close so she could hear him through the noise, "every insult you cast my way, somebody will pay. You. Esme. That abomination of a bird. Understood?"

She nodded, wishing she hadn't eaten the soup after all as her stomach churned.

"Not far now," he said, his voice pleasant and ordinary, as though they were taking a stroll in the country, as though he hadn't just threatened her and those around her with violence.

He picked up the pace until she was forced to cling to him in order to keep her balance. They passed out of the castle through wide-open doors and walked under unfamiliar stars. Ahead lights blazed into the night sky, the mass of moving humanity pouring toward them and vanishing through a gate.

The gate opened into a giant oval, half football stadium, half coliseum. The entire structure was built out of stone.

Narrow stairs led down through row upon row of seats, many of them already filled. At the bottom, a twenty-foot sheer wall separated the playing field from the spectators. At one end of the field a red stone thrust up out of the earth. Fragments of chain hung from it, and in a wide circumference no grass grew, the earth burned black.

At sight of the stone, the voices in her head leaped to a crescendo, warning of danger.

As if she'd needed any warning.

She stumbled after Gareth, keeping on her feet with difficulty. The shoes had been difficult before; now they were dangerous. She was going to sprain an ankle, going to fall. People drew back as she passed, as if they feared contamination by a casual touch.

To her right, about halfway down, a banner and pennons waved—scarlet dragons on a purple background. Jehenna sat within an ornate private box, surrounded by courtiers and guards. Gareth led her on past, all the way down to the front row.

Ahead of them gaped the maw of a black pit. One last time Vivian thought about fighting. A swift kick to the groin, then run like hell.

Right. In impossible slippers, directly into a stadium full of loyal subjects who would never let her go. Besides, she had no doubt that Gareth would keep his promise of retaliation. If she was able to get clear, someone else would suffer.

And so she followed him down a dark and narrow staircase. A smoky torch sputtered at the bottom, dimly lighting a small box of a room that held a chair and a battered wooden table. The guard leaned over a nearly empty plate. At sight of Vivian and Gareth he sprang to his feet, wiping his mouth with one hand and saluting with the other.

"Open the gate," Gareth commanded.

The guard nodded, lifted a wooden latch, and pushed open a panel exposing an expanse of grass bounded by a high stone wall. Above it rose row on row of seats filled with shouting faces. A hard shove against Vivian's lower back thrust her reeling forward. She fell heavily onto her knees in the damp sod. Heard the gate slam shut behind her.

The noise from the crowd intensified; flags waved, feet stomped.

Kicking off the stupid shoes, Vivian scrambled up onto her feet, dug her toes into the grass, seeking courage in the solidity of the earth beneath her. Only it wasn't solid, not at all. The voices muttered about a vast network of tunnels beneath her, connecting chambers large and small. She could sense them, as she could sense the doors that closed and opened.

Esme must be down there somewhere. Duncan. Maybe Isobel.

If she survived, she would know where to look.

Not if, she told herself. She must survive. She was the last of the Dreamshifters; there was work to be done. Calmer now, she scrutinized the doors opening out of the arena. Counting the one behind her, there were six small ones, three on each long side of the oval. Two larger doors at each end of the stadium. Each could be a possible escape route.

But each could also allow something to enter the arena.

One of the doors on the end was big enough to drive a semi through. This one worried her the most; it was also large enough for a dragon.

A fanfare played.

The crowd screamed.

Whatever was coming, it was coming now.

Run for one of the small doors, she told herself. *Only one guard each. Half a chance to get past. Run for it now, while you can.* Her muscles buzzed with adrenaline, but she lingered, the huge door holding her gaze with a sick fascination, certain that the age-old story of the dragon and the maiden was about to be played out for all eyes to see.

She was wrong.

Two small doors opened, instead. From each emerged a man, costumed in a white kilt, chest bared. One was old, his hair rough and gray, a thick beard cascading down over his breast. The other couldn't have been more than twenty-five, muscular and tanned with long blond hair.

The young man stopped at the center of the arena, looked directly toward her, and raised his sword in a salute. His face was too broken to grin, but he made an attempt, the muscles on one side contracting into a grimace.

Duncan.

One of the large doors—not the largest one, not yet—opened, and the priest trailed out in his scarlet robe. From here she could see the dragons embroidered on it in gold. As before, he raised his arms for silence, and the crowd hushed.

"A death for a death," he said. "The dragon gods must be appeased." No long speech for the occasion. He turned and stalked back through the door. It clanged behind him, steel on steel.

A trumpet sounded a single tone.

Duncan turned to face the gnarled old man at the center of the oval. The two saluted each other, then advanced into combat range and began circling, swords at the ready. The old man held his sword awkwardly in both hands. He slashed. Duncan parried. The blows were halfhearted even to her untrained eyes, slow, easily blocked. For what seemed like hours, although she knew it couldn't really have been more than minutes, they circled each other.

Above in the stands, feet stomped, hands clapped. The roar of the crowd took on an ugly tone. "Kill, kill, kill!"

As if on signal, the two men stopped their sparring. They stood about five paces apart, breathing hard. Duncan inclined his head in a gesture of respect, and the old man followed suit. Then, simultaneously, they brought their sword points out straight and level ahead of them, holding the hilts steady with both hands. Their eyes locked. Duncan made a small gesture with his head. A signal.

Vivian felt herself screaming, soundless beneath the roar of the crowd, as the two men flung themselves toward each other, using the momentum to thrust their bodies onto the blades. One freeze-frame moment they stood motionless, mouths open in shock and agony. And then they released their grip on the swords, flung their arms around each other's shoulders and clung, pulling closer and closer together until they were locked in a death embrace with the bloody blades thrusting through and through. They sank to the ground joined like lovers, blood staining the whiteness of their clothing, pooling on the grass. Duncan cradled the old man's head with his hand, keeping it from the sod.

A murmur of disappointment ran through the crowd.

This was Vivian's last chance to run, to get away through a door, but her legs carried her the wrong way, across the grass toward the bloody tangle of limbs and bodies.

Duncan was still breathing, although his face had taken on the pallor of death and blood gushed from his mouth. The old man was already dead.

Vivian's brain took her through the drill she knew so well. His airway was obstructed by blood; every shallow breath gurgled in his throat. He was bleeding externally and internally, pulse shallow, fluttering, far too rapid. Already he was white with shock.

"Hang on," she said. "We need to stop the bleeding . . ." Even as she said it she knew this was stupid. Too much blood, too much damage; even with immediate access to an operating room, with IV fluids and blood transfusions and a team of skilled responders, she could never save him.

Still, she rested her hand on his brow, smoothed back the hair. She was grabbed from behind and pulled away, not roughly. Two men in red tunics leaned over the bodies, pulled them off the swords and apart. A wet sucking sound, a gush of blood and fluid. Duncan's eyes widened; he gasped. It was his last breath. His head lolled to the side. More men appeared, gripping the bodies by the feet and dragging them across the grass, heads on limp necks rolling and bouncing.

"That was singularly unsatisfying," Gareth's voice said in her ear. "They'll be cursed for that."

"They are beyond cursing." Vivian's lips felt like stone.

She was surprised that her voice still worked, still sounded like her own.

"Cursed in the world to come," Gareth said. "If they had followed the commandments of the High Priest, they would receive expiation and pass into a better place. As it stands—they are condemned to a series of hells."

"It's barbaric," Vivian said. "As was making me watch from here. Bastard."

Gareth grinned, white teeth gleaming. "You haven't seen anything yet." She sensed his heightened excitement, knew that the bloodshed had roused him in every possible way. She wanted to claw the grin from his face with her fingernails.

"Come," he said. "I have something to show you."

"Fuck you. I'm not going anywhere with you."

He lifted her bodily to her feet, grabbed her arm, and towed her along, following the grisly procession ahead of them. Vivian's bare feet squished in grass wet with blood. She twisted and struggled but Gareth didn't deign to slow, to turn to look at her, or even to slap her. Just kept walking, her arm pinioned by his hand.

Recognizing futility, half in shock, she went with him. Up the stairs, his arm tight around her shoulders, forcing her against his side. An enormous swollen moon hung over the castle, dull red, brooding. The crowd flowed left toward castle and moon, a turgid river of humanity. The men dragging the dead turned right, and Gareth and Vivian followed behind.

A few more steps and they came upon a small black-and-white figure, waiting. The penguin lengthened his neck, hissing. It must have been the moonlight that made his eyes flare red.

Gareth's hand moved to his sword hilt. "That creature is an abomination."

Poe hissed again, then waddled off to the side and into shadow. Vivian followed him with her eyes, trying to pick him out of the darkness, but nothing moved. As far as she could see, the grass, the bushes, the castle, all were lit by that unearthly reddish light.

Ahead of them, at the center of a small space of flowers, towered an oak tree with wide and spreading branches. A tire swing twirled gently from a wide bough, a swing that a child might sit in to commune with sky and grass and tree for a long afternoon of dream. A wail of grief and loss rose in Vivian's throat, half-choking her as she held it back.

The men they had followed stopped beneath the tree. Sick and dizzy, Vivian could only watch as they wrapped rope around the dead men's necks and hoisted their bodies up to hang beside the swing, the wind making their loose limbs dance and sway.

"Why?" Vivian turned to face Gareth. "Why did you bring me here?"

"Her Majesty wishes for you to know what she can do with dreams."

Vivian closed her eyes to shut out the travesty, but the bodies swung behind her eyelids as though on a screen. "Please," she said. "If you have any decency, take me away from this place."

"Of course." His voice was unexpectedly gentle.

He released her arm and took her hand, twining his fingers with hers as though they were lovers and she were not his captive. She went with him willingly when he began to walk, not caring where they went, so long as it took her elsewhere. Only when the fragrance of roses reached her did she realize her mistake.

The dead were not a threat to her; she should have stayed with them. Should have run, run like hell into the darkness and the hope of an escape. Not this, not a rose garden and a fountain by the light of this red moon. Not in the company of this man.

The scent of roses was overpowering, heavy, too sweet. A breeze blew spray against her face from the fountain in a pool behind her. Weary, heartsick, and afraid, she sank down on a stone bench, cool against her thighs through the fabric of the gown.

Gareth dropped to his knees in the grass and kissed her.

Fighting back a shudder of revulsion she held herself quiescent, neither responding nor resisting. His lips burned, too hot, too much pressure. She did not respond, did not try to pull away. Waited.

Lips still fastened on hers, he circled her throat with both hands, pressing lightly on the arteries with his thumbs. Black spots danced before her eyes. If he applied strong pressure, in seconds she would slip into unconsciousness and it would all be over.

But the hands released her, slid down to cup her breasts.

It was not to be borne. She turned her head to break the kiss, shoved at him with all her strength. He was too heavy, too strong. He squeezed her nipples, hard, in retaliation.

"Gareth, please . . ."

His voice was husky, caressing. "I knew I could make you beg. Say it again."

She slapped him. An angry red patch appeared on his cheek. He slapped her back, a blow that jolted her head to one side, turned her cheek to fire.

Still, he had released her breasts; his lips were no longer on hers. Gasping for breath, she asked, "What did she promise you?"

"Who?"

"The Queen—she gave you something, promised you something—"

An instant of hesitation told her the guess was right. Maybe she could move him, turn him. He was a stranger, but not entirely. The worst of Jared, but Jared still; she knew him.

A pulse beat in his throat; the muscle in his jaw clenched and released.

"She doesn't care about you, Gareth, not really. Not you or anybody. This—place—Surmise. It isn't real. All built of stolen, twisted dreams. In another place, another world, you are a decent man. You don't have to do this."

"You know nothing about what I have to do."

"I know what she is, what she does. She's using you—"

Wrong words. His eyes went flat. "You think I am some

stupid pawn. Think again. She has given me more power than you can imagine."

"Right. She sees that you are valuable, but she—"

"You say this place isn't real."

"Well, it is, but it is not—"

"If it's a dream, why get so upset about a death or two?"

Esme limp and unconscious between the guards. Bodies hanging from a spreading oak tree. Vivian swallowed. "It's complicated."

"Explain."

"Jehenna, she can enter dreams, change them, trap the dreamer—"

She could see by his face that she wouldn't sway him. Even if he wasn't under Jehenna's control, he was already set on a course. In her pocket, she remembered, was a dreamsphere. The one that Poe had picked up off the floor. Surely it would end this, would take her somewhere away, give her time to think, to plan.

Her hand reached into the pocket of the gown even as Gareth's lips claimed hers again. She let him kiss her while she fumbled for the globe, pulled it out, and then broke away and held it up to the light.

Gareth reached for it. "What—"

A splash turned them both toward the fountain at once.

Poe was swimming in the pool. Diving and surfacing, part fish, part bird, pure essence of sublime joy. A dive beneath the surface and out of view, and then he shot up out of the water onto the rocks, only to dive back in and traverse the pool in a series of leaps like a dolphin.

"Get that creature out, at once!"

Even in the moonlight Vivian could see that Gareth's face had gone white, a note of fear edging beneath his command.

"You don't understand. The fountain is off-limits. If she finds out—"

"I guess you shouldn't have brought us here then." Her own voice surprised her, level and calm. The crystal hadn't taken her away, but it had changed something. She had felt the shift, and then Poe had been in the fountain. In her mind the voices kept a waiting silence, as though they were holding their collective breath.

"Get him out."

Vivian spread her hands in a gesture of helplessness. "You're talking about a bird, not a dog. He doesn't understand commands." In reality, she was pretty sure Poe understood a lot more than she'd given him credit for, but she wasn't about to admit it.

Gareth ran the few steps to the fountain, making shooing gestures with his hands, but never quite touching the water. "Get out of there, you stupid bird!"

Poe did come out, to Vivian's surprise, although he never seemed to notice Gareth's flapping hands, or his shouts. In his beak he carried something that wriggled and flopped and sparkled in the moonlight. Waddling across the grass, he dropped it carefully at Vivian's feet.

A fish, only not like any fish she had ever seen. Luminous and shining, rainbow colors shifting over its body in waves. Its fins were winglike, diaphanous, emerald green and cobalt blue.

A shout went up from the voices in her head and they all began talking loudly and at once, a babble of excitement with overtones of awe and wonder.

Gareth stood silent beside her, staring.

The wondrous creature was dying. It flopped in the grass, gasping, gills distended. The brilliant colors were beginning to fade. Vivian bent to pick it up. She must return it to the pool at once; surely in the water it would revive and go on swimming. But the instant her fingers made contact there was a chiming sound and a flash of light. The fish vanished. In the grass lay a gleaming black object.

Vivian picked it up. A chord of music sounded, all of the voices in complex harmony, and then silence. The object felt and looked like stone but seemed to her more solid, more real, than any substance she had ever touched. It was roughly cylindrical, the length of her palm and middle finger, unexpectedly heavy for its size. One end was thicker and etched with rough dragon symbols. The other end was carved into a complex shape, familiar, but before she had time to sort out what it represented, Gareth's voice said, "I'll take that."

The voices shouted objections with a volume that nearly split her skull.

"No."

Perhaps her grandfather's last note had made sense after all: *Beyond the living rainbow the dragons guard Forever.* Could this be the key? She didn't know what she'd expected, but it wasn't this.

Gareth drew his sword. "You will give it to me."

"I will not."

Nightmare slow, Vivian backed toward the fountain.

Out of the darkness beside her, a small figure ran toward the Chancellor, wings spread wide, neck stretched long, beak open in a hiss.

Gareth spun on his heel and thrust with the sword.

Before Vivian could release the scream rising in her throat, the sharp blade pierced the penguin's white breast. In that moment, it seemed that time stood still. She saw Jared's face, twisted with hate, Poe's beak gaping open, the red stain growing around the steel that spiked his breast. And then, in all of the agonizing detail of slow motion, Jared lifted both sword and penguin, gave his wrists a contemptuous flick, and the body slid off the sword and hit the ground, limp and unmoving.

Vivian's legs refused to hold her. She dropped to the cool grass beside Poe's body, searching for signs of life. "Oh, dear God, what have you done—"

Gareth stood over her. "It's only a bird. Get up."

"You killed him—"

"What does it matter, if none of this is real?"

She just stared at him, and under her scrutiny something in his face shifted a little. "You'll see, when I give her the key." Bloody sword still in hand, he reached for the black cylinder with the other and wrenched it out of her clutching fingers.

"Come now. It's a lovely night. Kiss me—"

"Are you insane? You just killed my penguin in cold blood."

He smiled. "Come—the garden is beautiful by moon-light."

"Over my dead body."

His face changed, hardened. "I said get up."

"No."

He grabbed a fistful of her hair and yanked.

Her feet caught in the hem of the gown as she staggered upright, and she hung for an instant from her hair before she could catch her balance. "Let me go—"

Twisting his hand so that she cried out with the pain, he forced her head back and pressed his mouth over hers, thrusting his tongue between her lips.

She bit down hard, tasting the rush of salt as her teeth pierced soft flesh. He released her, stumbling backward.

"Fucking bitch." He drew the back of his hand across a trickle of blood on his chin and wiped it on his silken dou-blet, leaving a rusty smear.

Taking advantage of the moment, she tried to knee him in the groin but was hampered by the gown. He pinioned her by both arms in a grip she couldn't break, and dragged her back to the bench.

She braced her feet, put all her weight against him.

Releasing his right hand he hit her again, closed fist this time. The world shattered into darkness and fire. He flung her down onto the bench, jolting her bones against the stone, her head striking hard enough to make a flash of stars.

"You are mine—mine—you understand? The Queen herself promised me this. If you fight me, I will hurt you. If you scream, I will hurt you more."

She struggled, tried to free herself, but he straddled her, pinning her down. Her arms were trapped, her legs tangled in the gown. His weight compressed her ribs. She couldn't breathe. In her peripheral vision she could still catch a glimpse of black and red.

His breath was hot on her face. As his lips again closed over hers, she remembered for the first time what was in her pocket. One of the voices separated itself from the others, made itself easily heard.

Calm down. There is a way, but not if you panic.

She stopped struggling, focused on trying to catch her breath. If there was a way, she would find it. He had done this to her once. Twice she would not allow.

But he must not have the key. No matter what it costs you.

"I'm sorry," she whispered aloud. "I'll be good. I swear. Just don't hurt me anymore."

"I'm not stupid. I don't trust you for a minute."

But the iron grasp on her wrists eased, just a little. When he kissed her again, she kissed him back. At the dark side of Jared was a man who needed to believe that every woman wanted him. Wanted to believe. All she had to do was help him with that.

She moaned softly, returned his kisses with lips and tongue.

He loosed one of her hands so he could reach down and free himself from the confinement of his breeches, and she slid her freed hand down between his legs in a slow caress, cupping the heavy, hot weight of him, stroking.

In response, he moved his lips down her neck toward her breast, and freed her other hand.

Pleasuring him with one hand, she slid the other down over her own hip, feeling for the pocket. At first all she felt was an expanse of unbroken fabric and her heart constricted in fear. Maybe the pocket was tucked up underneath her hips; maybe she couldn't reach it. But then her fingers caught the edge of an opening and she managed to work them inside.

Jared knelt over her, preparing to take her by force as he had done once already in dream.

He didn't hear the click of an extending blade. Vivian cupped his balls and then squeezed and twisted with all her strength. His body jerked and stiffened on a gasp of pain, and in that instant she sank the blade of the knife deep into his buttock.

With a shriek of pain and outrage, Gareth rolled off the

edge of the bench and onto the grass, doubled over on his knees, both hands pressed to his wound.

Vivian sprang to unsteady feet and bent to retrieve his sword from where it lay in the grass. It was heavy, but two-handed she was able to lift it.

"Why?" he asked, in the tone of a child who has been beaten for no reason.

"Seriously? You killed Poe. You tried to rape me—"

His eyes looked unfocused, his forehead creased in thought. "Vivian, I would never—"

In that moment he sounded like Jared in one of his softer moments. She steeled herself.

"Look, Gareth. For all anybody else knows, you had your way with me and are leaving here a sated and dominant man, although you might want someone to bandage those wounds."

"Please," he said. "I'm bleeding."

"You won't bleed to death. No major arteries to worry about. First, you are going to help me."

"What do you want?"

"Information. Tell me what Jehenna wants with the key."

He swallowed hard, kept silent.

Vivian moved toward him, holding the sword. "Tell me."

He crawled backward. "Don't hurt me."

His confusion appeared genuine. She tried to think what to do, but the voices had increased again in intensity, were a siren song, pulling her away from the here, promising, always promising. *Listen, listen, listen.*

Vivian clenched her jaw, drove the energy of her full attention onto the man in front of her. And as she opened her mouth to speak, she felt it all, like a towering wave, like the climax of a symphony, all of the energy of all of those words coalescing into her voice at once. "Tell me."

As they emerged from her lips, the words felt more solid than anything else in this place, more real than her grief or the blood on the grass.

His eyes widened and focused. "I was to—kill the bird. Give her the key, if I ever found it."

"In exchange for what?"

"You. She promised me that if I gave her the key, you would love me."

"And you believed her? Tell me when this happened."

"I . . ." He swallowed; his eyes drifted far away. "I—it was a strange place. Many houses, all in a row. The street was hard and black. I do not know this place. A dream, perhaps . . ." Vivian remembered Jared standing at her doorway with his hands full of roses, Jared who'd arrived only moments after Jehenna left, who had mentioned a key before she knew that there was one to be found.

"What does she want with the key, Gareth?"

"I don't know. She spoke of the Forever, said she wouldn't need the dragon anymore. I don't know what she meant." His face was slick with a cold sweat; his voice broke on the words.

More gently now, she said, "Give me the key, Gareth."

"She'll kill me—"

"She doesn't need to know."

"She knows everything."

His face was so white she thought he might pass out. He wiped one hand across his forehead, leaving a smear of blood. There was no place here for mercy. She used the Voice again. "The key, Gareth."

Without further hesitation he drew it out from inside his tunic and handed it to her.

"Now, get out of here."

No need for the Voice with this command; Gareth was more than happy to be gone. He moaned as he got to his feet and hobbled across the grass and away into shadow.

Which left Vivian alone with her dead. Kneeling beside Poe, she laid her hands over his bloodstained breast, tried to summon some magic that would heal this wound, make his heart begin to beat again. If she had the power to make Gareth talk, maybe she could reverse a death.

You couldn't save one boy poisoned by a dragon, not with a crew and modern technology to help you.

Her breath was a difficulty in her throat, a sharp pain that wouldn't ease, but her eyes remained dry.

"Good-bye, Poe," she whispered.

A whisper of sound, steel against leather, drew her eyes upward. Standing before her, the blade of his sword naked in his hand and death in his eyes, stood the Warlord of Surmise.

Twenty-three

✤

"Y ou, too?" Vivian asked. She felt inexpressibly weary, and it took all of her waning energy to drag herself up onto her feet and face him.

"What happened here?"

"What does it matter to you?"

"All bloodshed in Surmise is my concern."

"I suppose Gareth sent you to finish what he'd left undone."

"I do not answer to the Chancellor."

"Jehenna sent you, then."

"Nobody sent me." His scarred face was in shadow, the naked sword red in the light of the terrible moon. "I asked you before. Now I ask you again. What are you?"

"I am a Dreamshifter."

"What more?" His hand tightened on the sword hilt. He took a step toward her.

"I don't know," she whispered.

"Are you a shape-shifter as well? Answer me!"

"I don't know what that is."

He paused, the sword half-lifted. "Don't lie to me! You survived the dragon poison. You are marked with scales; your eyes have changed. Tell me what you are doing in Surmise."

There were no words for this, for the pain at her heart that made it so hard to breathe. If he forced her she would use the Voice on him, but it felt wrong, had felt wrong even to command a man like Gareth. Jehenna controlled people. Maybe she, Vivian, was becoming the evil that she hated.

"I should have killed you when I found you," the Warlord said.

"Maybe. I couldn't have stopped you then."

"And now?"

"I think I could. If I must. Please don't test me. I swear to you I mean no harm to anyone except her. Jehenna."

She saw his face go still. "You can speak her name."

"Jehenna?"

His sword arm trembled, and his voice was tight with contained emotion. "Nobody in Surmise can speak her name. Either you are her creature, or you are stronger than she is."

There were fresh cuts across his cheeks, still bleeding; the pain in his eyes went soul deep. So much here that she didn't understand, but one thing she was sure of: Whatever this man was, it wasn't evil.

"Maybe it's because I'm not from Surmise."

"Nobody is from Surmise. Our paths cross here, end here. Beginnings all happen elsewhere."

"You asked me what I am. I'm trying to figure that out. Again, I swear it—I mean no harm to anybody here. I'm sick about what happened to Duncan. It was wrong."

"And yet there is blood here—on the grass, the bench."

Vivian held out the stiletto, flicked the switch to release the blade. "The Chancellor—he wasn't expecting this."

A long pause, and then the Warlord's scarred face contorted into what might have been a smile. "I'm surprised he didn't kill you on the spot."

"He was shamed, I think."

No doubting the smile now, but it faded almost at once. "He will seek revenge. Go back, My Lady, to whatever place you came from. You may be strong, but you cannot win against *her.*"

"I can't go back." Before she could stop herself she blurted it all out. "I am the last of the Dreamshifters. Je-henna has stolen the dreamspheres and is using them for evil. I believe she holds my mother captive here, somewhere. If I walk away, then . . ." She held her hands out, palms up, out of words and hoping he might understand. Deliber-ately she avoided mention of the key, hoping he wouldn't notice.

"A mission, then," he said. "A sacred trust."

"Yes."

"A thing you are prepared to die for?"

She nodded, not trusting her voice.

"I can't protect you from her. I will help you where I can, but I cannot act against her."

"I understand."

She flinched as his voice lashed out. "How could you possibly understand? I hate the dragons with every drop of my life's blood but can't raise my sword against them. Atroc-ities of injustice day after day. My men, brave men like Duncan, dying for doing what is right. And I stand by and can do nothing." He was breathing hard, his face twisted with emotion. "I lack the courage to die, to end my role in this once and for all—"

Vivian forgot that he was the Warlord. Forgot the scars and the sword and the power he wielded here. She placed her hands on either side of his face, looking up into the eyes that belonged to him, but also to Zee.

"You are an honorable man. A good man."

A tremor ran through him and he pulled away from her touch as though it burned him. His chest heaved. "No woman has touched me in years. They shudder and run when they see me. They fear me. Even you—"

"Because your eyes are the eyes of a man I know, but your face is so changed."

"I don't disgust you, then?"

"You have the most beautiful eyes in all the worlds," she whispered. "I believe you have the soul to match."

He shook his head. "It's a dark thing, my soul."

"I don't believe that is true." They stood, not quite touching. His big hand grazed her bruised cheek, ever so gently, and then cupped her chin, lifting it so he could scrutinize her face.

Vivian's heart hammered so loudly she was certain he could hear it; her knees trembled.

"I have dreamed you," he said at last. "Night after night, for as long as I can remember."

Vivian tried to find the words to tell him that she had not only dreamed him, that she had met him in another world, another time, but her lips refused to move.

His head bent toward her, his eyes on her lips, and she closed her own eyes in expectation. A slight pressure warm against her hair, and then cool air where the warmth of his hand had been. She opened her eyes to see him walking away.

He bent and lifted Poe's body in his arms. "Come."

"Where?"

"Back to your room. In the castle."

"I—"

"There's nowhere safe for you in this kingdom," he said. "But I believe the safest place will be in that room, with two of my guards at the door."

No grabbing, clutching hands; no demanding. He only stood looking at her, the dead penguin cradled in his arms. Vivian went with him. In silence, they walked toward the castle. When they reached the oak tree, Zee stopped and laid Poe gently down in the grass.

"Wait," he said.

She watched as he sliced through the ropes that held the swinging bodies; they hit the earth with a heavy thud, first one, then the other. Vivian shuddered and swallowed back a wave of nausea. Zee bent and straightened the crumpled limbs, folded their hands over their breasts. It was too late to close the eyes, and they stared blankly up at the merciless moon.

The Warlord placed the penguin beside the fallen men. "I will see that he is buried, with honor."

"Thank you." Tears tracked her cheeks for the first time in this long and difficult day.

"Now," he said, "about the key."

Vivian had been beginning to relax a little, to feel safer, sheltered, in his presence. She sucked in a breath, backed away from him, flicked open the blade of what now seemed a pitiful little knife.

His expression was unreadable, but he stood still, did not reach for his sword or come after her. "I'm not going to take it from you," he said. "But she has enlisted many to look for it. It is dangerous for you to carry it so."

"Do you have a better idea?"

"I could carry it for you."

"I don't—" She heard the tremble in her voice, stopped and steadied herself before going on. "I don't even know what it's for."

"Nothing good," was all he said. "Do you wish me to carry it?"

The temptation was great, but it came down to this—all Jehenna need do to take the key from the Warlord was to command it. Vivian could, at least, resist the Voice. Reluctant, feeling the weight of responsibility heavy on her shoulders, she shook her head. "I need to carry it myself. To destroy it if I can."

He nodded, as though this answer came as no surprise. "Come—you are cold and weary. Let me take you back to your room. And then I will come back and tend to these."

Twenty-four

✤

With a growing sense of unreality Zee stood beside the open trapdoor. The cat scampered past him, descending rough wooden stairs, little more than a ladder. Zee followed. A cramped earthen crawl space led into a tunnel with a floor of packed dirt. Wooden timbers supported a rough ceiling too low for him to stand upright. Dim lightbulbs swung from naked wires.

Bent nearly double, Zee followed the cat. She scampered playfully ahead, pausing to crouch and then leap at unseen objects. Zee's back ached with the constant stooping; the sword bumped awkwardly against his thigh.

All told, the tunnel ran for what he guessed was a good half mile before ending with another rough wooden ladder. When he reached it, the cat sat on the top rung, waiting. Above her head, another trapdoor. Zee gave it a hard shove and it opened into a spotless, well-lit garage. A workbench ran across all of one wall, holding toolboxes and a telephone. An old radio broadcasted country music.

Most of the interior was occupied by a vintage VW hippie van, painted in technicolor flowers and peace signs. A familiar van—George Maylor had been driving this identical rig ten years ago, on the day he bailed Zee out of jail.

The keys were in the ignition. A case of bottled water, a

box of energy bars, sealed packages of dried fruit and real jerky were neatly stored in the back, along with blankets, pillows, and other emergency items.

The van offered an escape. He couldn't go back to the cabin, not with the cops there, and they might be watching it for a good long while. As far as he could figure, he had two choices: find a place to hide out or keep looking for Vivian, and between those two options the choice was clear.

Not that this was simple in any way. He had no idea where or how to find her. Plus, if he pulled out of the garage now the cops might see him and follow. Maybe he'd do better, after all, to just stay put right here for a day or two.

Schrödinger stared up at him out of scornful, unblinking green eyes. *Coward.*

"Hypocrite," Zee muttered. "I don't see you taking any risks."

The cat meowed and coiled around his ankle, purring, then stalked over to empty food and water bowls under the workbench. Zee found a five-gallon jug of water and a bag of cat food. He filled the bowls and bent to pat the cat. "What if I don't get back? I don't want you trapped in here and starving to death."

There were no windows in the garage he could crack open, but a brief search revealed a cat door leading outdoors. That was that, then. At least she would be able to get outside to fend for herself.

Zee turned off the light switch, plunging the garage into darkness. It would be dark outside by now. A glow of light when he opened the garage door would be equivalent to standing on the roof and shouting through a loudspeaker. He fumbled his way to the door and lifted the latch. He'd half-expected it to creak and groan with disuse, but the action was smooth and noiseless.

More darkness, lit enough by moonlight to let him see a narrow track, screened by trees. In the distance, red and blue lights strobed, rhythmic, persistent. Leaving the vehicle lights off, Zee backed out of the garage, between the tree sentinels, and onto the road. For a mile or two he drove without headlights, watching the rearview mirror for signs of pursuit, but nothing moved, other than the occasional deer and a careless skunk, and he was soon deep into uncharted territory.

Without any logical progression of thought, he found himself heading for Finger Beach. As a plan it wasn't much, but it beat driving aimlessly without a destination point. And if he was looking for some sort of paranormal activity, the beach was the most likely place to find it.

About an hour into the drive he was wishing the old man had stocked a case of cola along with the water; a little caffeine would have been more than welcome. In an effort to stay awake, he drove with the windows down, shivering in the cold wind. Music would have been good, but there was no reception over the pass and there was no CD player in the ancient van.

Hours later, Zee rolled into the parking lot at Finger Beach, bone weary and anxious. A harebrained scheme, coming here. He had no contingency plan, no purpose to his life beyond finding Vivian and saving her if he could.

The moon rode high in the sky. Constellations arched overhead in the old familiar configurations. They comforted him—the sheer vastness of them, the knowledge that they had been there when life first began on this planet and would still be there when it ended. That when his small life was over, something beautiful would still shine in the sky above him.

The pungent scent of pine filled his nostrils as he stepped out of the van and breathed in deeply of the cool night air. His footsteps crunched on the gravel of the parking area, rustled through dry grass before the gritting of sand alerted him that he was on the beach.

The Finger glowed with a dull red light of its own, and he paused for a moment as he always did when he ventured down here, to acclimatize to the sensation of raw power that flooded the place.

One of the thin places, he thought, where the fabric of reality might be breached. If science fiction stories had any truth, if there were doors from one world into another, this would certainly be one of them. Whatever had happened to Vivian, whoever the witch woman was, it involved some explanation beyond what physics and science could tell him. If there was such a thing as a Dreamshifter, then it made sense that there were gates leading to other realities.

He shivered a little at the idea of things crossing boundaries from dream into reality. People spoke of dreams coming true as if this would be a good and wonderful thing. They tended to forget that nightmares were dreams as well.

Tonight the stone felt portentous, threatening. Zee approached with caution, opening himself to the currents of energy, letting them find their way through his body and then ground back into the earth. Most people fought it, but he'd always figured that if the old tales were true, fighting the power was what made people crazy. Treat it like a dream, let it flow through you but not touch you, and you'll be okay.

He hoped sincerely that his theory was right.

In a sudden flare of red light, an enormous white bear materialized beside the stone.

Zee was not prepared. An instant of hesitation and disbelief almost cost him his life. In the nick of time he ducked and rolled, a massive paw whistling past his scalp.

Surging back onto his feet, Zee drew the sword.

The bear reared up onto its back legs, mouth open in a spine-chilling roar to reveal teeth far too long and sharp. Swinging its deadly paws, it lunged.

Zee ducked, sidestepped, just out of reach of the lethal blows. At first the sword felt awkward, as if his mind remembered the way of it but his body did not. But as he danced away from certain death, his muscles began to remember and he drew first blood, a bloom of crimson against the whiteness of one of the paws.

Bellowing pain and rage, the bear crashed down onto three legs, swinging its head with jaws wide open. Zee feinted sideways, not quite fast enough. Something burned like fire down the side of his face, caught his shoulder. The blow flung him backward and he fell hard, his head bouncing against a rock.

Half-blinded by blood, dizzy and dazed, he slashed upward on instinct, felt the blade connect with flesh. Another bellow of rage and the creature retreated.

The world rocked and spun as he got to his feet. Pain hammered in his head with an intensity that twisted his stomach. His limbs felt loose and only half under his control. His left arm hung limp and useless from the damaged shoulder. There was a lot of blood.

The bear was not unscathed. One side of its face was laid open to the bone, a flap of flesh and fur dangling down over the jaw. It shook its head from side to side, spraying blood, roaring its agony and rage.

And then it came for him. Swift, lethal, huge. A death machine of muscle and teeth and claws.

Zee braced himself. He tightened his grip on the sword. Waited, timing the stroke. An instant before the bear struck, he swung with all the strength he had left. A fountain of hot blood burst over him as he was borne to the ground, crushed beneath the creature's weight. He couldn't move, couldn't breathe. Blood, his own or the bear's, ran into his mouth, blinded his eyes. He braced himself for jaws on his throat, but the bulk on top of him lay still.

The bear was too heavy. He couldn't move. It crushed his chest; he couldn't draw a full breath. His face burned like fire.

Pain and lack of oxygen took their toll, and he slid away into blackness.

Twenty-five

✤

Vivian scrubbed away blood and dirt in a hot bath, hoping to warm the bone-deep chill that set her teeth to chattering. But the cold had little to do with temperature, and being naked in the tub only increased her feeling of vulnerability and exposure and didn't help her relax at all. Besides, it made her think of Poe splashing happily in the bathwater, which reminded her of the limp body sliding off Gareth's sword and onto the moonlit grass.

This memory drove her out of the water and onto her feet, pacing, wrapped in a quilt pulled off the bed for warmth. So many other scenes that she did not want to see played over and over in the theater of her mind. Duncan's eyes as he died. The bodies swinging from the tree, *her* tree. Esme begging her for help. As long as Vivian kept moving, she could hold these pictures back, but she could not suppress the voices. They went on and on, an incessant annoyance that would not be stilled.

In her hand she carried the stone key, or what she had assumed was the key, although it bore no resemblance to any item by that name that she had seen in life or on the movie screen. Destroy it, George had said. Very funny. His directions all along had been less than helpful, and this one topped the charts.

The thing was too real to be destroyed. This she knew to be true, even while she struggled to make sense of what this meant. It wasn't just the unusual weight of it, or how it was black in a way that made obsidian look faded gray. The true strangeness of the key was in the way it seemed indefinably *more*, as though it possessed an extra dimension, a substance and weight unknown in any of Vivian's realities.

How could one destroy such a thing? Where could it be hidden?

Briefly, she'd thought of throwing it back into the fountain. Maybe she should have done so, but Gareth would tell Jehenna all, sooner or later, either of his own will or under duress. And she would search the fountain, surely, just as she would search Vivian. Which meant getting out of here, now, and running—

Where? Where in all the worlds could she go that the Sorceress would not find and follow her?

The only hope, if there was any, was to end this. To find a way to destroy Jehenna, to stay alive long enough to make this happen. Or to figure out what the key was for and use it herself. It must lead to some kind of power or Jehenna wouldn't be so interested. If only George had been able to teach her things.

So hard to think with the clamor in her head, but it seemed clear to her that she must act. Retribution would come in the morning, of this she was certain, and so she must not be here in the morning.

All that remained to be decided was where she would go.

She thought longingly of Wakeworld. George's cabin was there—he might have books or papers that would give her information about the key and what it was for. Zee would help her—she had a feeling he might possibly even accept the tale she had to tell about Surmise and all that had happened here.

It would be safe, if anywhere was safe.

Until Jehenna came looking for her. Wakeworld was no refuge, and how much further harm would be inflicted on innocent people if the Sorceress turned her attention in that direction? Besides, Isobel must be here somewhere. Esme was in the dungeons because Vivian had been too stubborn to dress for the banquet. Already people had died in Surmise on her account.

And there was only one place in Surmise that she knew to go.

The decision made, Vivian felt a space of calm at her center. It spread through body and mind, ending the shivering, calming the voices, allowing her to sense the doors both seen and unseen that surrounded her.

She unwrapped the quilt from around her shoulders and spread it on the bed, taking time to lay it smooth. Put the gown back on. Checked that the stiletto was safe in the pocket. The key posed another problem. It was too big and heavy to carry safely in the pocket. After pondering this problem for a little while, she tore two long strips from the bedsheets and used them to fasten the key to her thigh. It felt heavy and awkward, but it was hidden by the long skirt of the gown, and a few experimental leaps and twists assured her it would stay in place.

All preparations made, she crossed the room to the tapestry that concealed the walk-in closet, picking up a candle along the way. In the faint, flickering light, the back wall appeared solid, but the voices told her otherwise.

"Open," she commanded, and the outline of a door appeared.

She shoved the door open, the candle illuminating a spiral staircase curving down and out of sight in total darkness. It was carved of stone, gleaming black in the flickering light. No railing, nothing between her and a plunge into impenetrable blackness.

One hand against the clammy wall for support, she took the first step down, and then another. Beneath her bare feet the stone was damp and slick, treacherous.

Outside the small circle of light shed by her wavering candle, she could see nothing. Each slow footstep echoed, from above, from below, creating the sounds of a phantom army that seemed at times to pursue her, at others to ascend toward her.

She felt suspended in space, with nothing in all the worlds but stairs and the darkness and the wordless murmuring of the voices. With every step the fear expanded, growing into a terror of darkness and of falling. But always she took one more step. And then another.

A fluttering sound, a small gust of wind. Something brushed against her hair. She ducked, lost her balance on the slippery stone and barely caught herself from falling. Hot wax spilled over her fingers and she dropped the candle. It plummeted downward, a tiny glimmer of light in unfathomable blackness, and went out.

Again the brush against her hair. She crouched, shielding her head with her arms, waging war against her fear. Little by little her heart rate slowed, her breathing eased. Whatever was flying around hadn't hurt her yet. As for this stairway, there was nothing magical about it. It was a real and solid thing; it led somewhere.

Downward. Where the dungeons were.

Tentative at first, she straightened, put one hand against the wall and felt her way, first one step, and then the next. Down and down she went, one slow step at a time, until at long last her searching foot found not another stair, but level floor. Three cautious paces brought her up against a solid wall.

Her hands fumbled for a door, but found none. No handle, no frame, not so much as a crack in the stone. She reminded herself that she was a Dreamshifter, that this was not the first time she'd needed to open a door. But just as she opened her senses to search for a way through, listening to the voices to see if they would offer a clue, she heard the rustle and flutter of a multitude of wings.

Vivian spun around, her back flattened against the wall, to see green eyes glowing in the dark. Not just one pair, but many, hovering high and low. Shrill screeches filled the air. And then one pair of eyes arrowed directly toward her.

Throwing herself sideways, Vivian staggered into empty

space and fell heavily on hands and knees. Scrabbling forward on a cold earth floor, fighting the long skirt that bound
her legs, she cracked her head against something solid. A
flash of stars spun before her eyes. One of the creatures
screeched close to her ear and Vivian dragged herself onto
her feet, fumbling for the stiletto.

Green eyes dove. She waited, waited, until the thing was
almost upon her, and then stabbed at the eyes in the dark.

A scream of pain and anger, and the green lights blinked
out, but there were more, too many to count, coming fast.
Her hand bumped against a wooden latch, clung to it. It
shifted beneath her weight, and she heard a grinding sound.
Empty space now where the wall had been. A door. She
flung herself through. A wing buffeted the side of her face.
Claws raked her arm, tearing through the fabric of the gown
and into her flesh.

She slammed the door closed with her shoulder and
leaned her weight against it, holding her breath, straining her
eyes and ears for anything that moved. Nothing happened.
No more sounds, no more green eyes. Only a darkness that
seemed deeper if possible, laced with a sharp, fetid stink.

Dragon.

Of course there would be dragons here. Maybe they were
locked away; maybe they roamed freely through the network
of tunnels and dungeons. Maybe they were waiting for her.
This, at least, was a familiar fear. Vivian laughed a little,
there alone in the dark, and began to walk in the only direction open to her, one shuffling step at a time.

How far she walked she couldn't tell. The voices gave no
more direction, had receded into a distant buzz. Time and
distance were measured by her hesitant footsteps, the beating of her heart, the rhythm of her breath. Her feet and legs
began to ache.

When she felt the touch on her face it was no more than
a wisp of sensation at first, a thin strand across one cheek,
no more alarming than an unruly hair. But it clung, and as
she stepped ahead there was another, and another, sticky
strands of something across her nose, her mouth, catching

in her hair. She tried to scrub them away, but they clung to hands and arms, and she realized there was only one thing they could be.

Webs. Giant webs. Somebody's nightmare made real.

The sound of her own breathing swelled to fill the darkness. Not just any spiders, then. Dark-dwelling spiders who shunned the light of day. Black widow. Brown recluse. Funnel web. No boundary of reality, either, not here. Why stop at the spiders she knew, not when there were creatures like Shelob and Aragog—giant spiders, with hairy legs and mandibles and multiple eyes that all could see in this dark. Eyes that were watching her now, right this minute, waiting to grab their prey.

Something was surely crawling on her scalp and she swatted at it, shaking her head, running both hands through her hair and bringing them away sticky with webbing too strong to break.

"What kept you?" a voice said, about six inches from her left ear.

Vivian's heart lurched sideways. "Who's there?" she demanded. "I'm armed."

"I'll be sure to keep my distance." The voice was vaguely familiar, but she couldn't put a face to it. "If you'll promise not to attack, I can give us some light."

There was a grating sound, followed by a spark that brightened into a steady glow. At first she shielded her eyes, even from this small brightness, but in a moment she was able to see and recognized the face of the Prince, holding up a lantern in one hand.

The light illuminated countless webs strung across a corridor that led off into the darkness. Behind the Prince was an open door. Vivian caught a glimpse of a narrow bed, bare stone floors and walls. He held the lantern to his advantage, keeping his own face in shadow and illuminating hers.

She blinked. "Where the hell were you? What are you doing down here?"

"Sleeping. Or at least I was until I heard you stumbling about in the dark."

Vivian looked over his shoulder to the bare chamber, trying to make sense of his presence here. She wanted to shout at him for abandoning her to the ugliness in the arena, and what came later. Instead she heard herself saying, "But you're the Prince—"

"So why am I sleeping in a cell in the dungeon? Astute question. You may also have noticed I don't exactly dress in the latest fashion."

"Jehenna is responsible for this."

"Actually, no. In fact, if she knew exactly where it is I lay my head, I'm not sure she would approve."

"Then, what?"

"The old shifter. Your grandfather. He told me you would come, and he left something for you. Come in, and I'll show you."

She hesitated, and his face softened. Very gently, he grazed her bruised cheek with his fingertips. "Whatever happened tonight, I truly regret. I—" He sighed. "Please, come in and I will try to explain."

Trust no one.

But there wasn't a choice, not anymore. There was absolutely no way she was going to survive unless she enlisted some help. And so she entered, recognizing a whisper of dream as she crossed the threshold.

Landon followed, hanging the lantern on a hook where it illuminated a painting, the only thing that hung on four bare stone walls.

It was life-size, done in oils. Another dragon, serpentine neck, clawed feet, dragging tail, every scale rendered in exquisite detail, wings spread. But the face was yet the face of a woman, just lengthening into a dragon snout, auburn hair blowing back in a tangle of curls. Golden eyes that Vivian had recently seen in a mirror.

Involuntarily, her right hand went to her shoulder, stroking the skin there. Still soft, still smooth. Still human, thank God, no matter what sort of pattern had been tattooed upon it.

"Where did he get this?"

"He didn't say. Not real talkative, the old one. He also said to give you this."

This was a notebook with pages pasted into it and a few handwritten notes. Vivian scanned the headings: *Dragon Goddess of Borneo*, *Dragon Queens*, *Mother of Dragons*, *The Dragon Ladies*. Drawings accompanied some of them, images of creatures part woman, part dragon. Scaly wings and breasts and long human hair.

"Maybe you need to sit down." Landon's voice sounded far away, and she barely felt his hands on her elbows as he maneuvered her across the room. When something touched the backs of her knees she collapsed onto a wooden chair, numb, disbelieving.

Fairy tales and myths. Women who had dragon blood in their veins, who transformed at will into dragons. Fine for a fairy tale. Not so fine for a woman named Vivian looking at an image of herself transforming into a monster. She pressed the heels of both hands against her eyes to shut out both painting and notebook. "I fucking hate dragons," she muttered.

"That," said the Prince, "is likely to be a problem."

"It's not possible," Vivian said. "I don't know what the hell kind of game he was playing at, but this is ridiculous. Where did he get that freaky painting done, I wonder?"

Dream images, long suppressed, spilled over into consciousness. Always there had been the dreams of the dragon pursuing her, but side by side there had been the others—the dreams in which she soared through star-studded night skies on giant wings, the dreams in which fire flamed from her throat.

Getting up from the chair, she moved closer to the painting, scanning all four corners for the artist's signature. She found it at last, half-hidden by the spiny tip of the dragon's tail. One angular, stylized letter. Z.

The same hands that had painted the cover of the *Dragon Princess* book. Had caressed her skin through dream after dream, slain dragons on her behalf, carried the crumpled body of a bird. *The same hands, and yet not the same.*

Landon stood behind her. "It is said that—she—the Queen—has dragon blood in her veins."

"What the hell does that have to do with me?"

"You don't know." His face registered something part shock, part sympathy. "This complicates things."

"I don't know what?"

His eyes were grave. "Je—*she* is Isobel's mother."

Vivian stared at him. He waited. And the last fragments of her own carefully created reality dissolved. "My grandfather and Jehenna—" The Dragon Princess fairy tale suddenly made perfect sense—not a fairy tale at all. A knot of pain lodged in her solar plexus. She thought she might disintegrate, the cells that made up her body like so many dandelion seeds drifting through uncountable doors into uncountable dreams.

"Seduction, magic," Landon said. "She ensnared him. Much harm was done, and in the end he locked her away."

He taught Jehenna the Dreamshifter lore. He was only allowed to teach it once, and when he tried to give it to Isobel, her mind broke. Fighting for breath, for something solid to hold on to, Vivian managed to ask, "And then what?"

He shrugged. "Apparently she got free. Some years ago he felt her growing stronger, his own power weakening. That's when he brought these things here and asked me to tell you all of this if you found your way to me."

In all the worlds, the Wanderer was alone. He'd tried to tell her about what he'd done in a story. An attempt to break her in gently, perhaps. But how could you possibly come gently into the knowledge that your grandmother was an evil sorceress, that your destiny was to transform into a dragon?

"I hate dragons," she said again, tasting bile in the back of her throat, remembering the body of a teenage boy blackened and smoking on an emergency room treatment table. Duncan and the old man skewered on each other's swords in the stadium. The hideous *thing* that had hunted her through all of her dreams.

Herself.

Breathing around the knot of pain that drew tighter with every beat of her heart, she turned her attention back to the Prince. "What happened—between you and my mother?"

Landon's voice sounded old and weary. "She dreamed me into life, your mother. That's how it began. She had the Dreamshifter's blood in her veins, and some dragon blood as well, and with that the power to make her dreams real. She dreamed me a prince, my kingdom only a garden—roses, and a bench, and a fountain. A small kingdom, but more than enough as long as she was there."

Vivian closed her eyes against this, fisted her hands until her nails dug into her palms, thinking about just such a fountain, and what had happened to her that night. Knowing that her mother's dream, like her own with the tree, had been twisted and woven into the fabric of Surmise.

"And then?"

"Your grandfather took your mother away to teach her."

"And Jehenna dragged you and your fountain into Surmise, made you Prince but never King . . ."

He shook his head. "Hate her for many things, child, but not for that. It was your grandfather brought me here."

"That makes him as bad as she is—"

But the Prince shook his head. "No. Jehenna was locked away. Your mother's mind—broke—with the dream sickness and she could not come back to me. My choices were bleak: spend the rest of my life alone by the fountain or be wiped out of existence as if I had never been. He offered a third—that we bring your mother's dream, and me, into Surmise. He said I would be needed here. And he opened a way into this room for me—that I might live long enough to do what is needed."

"I—don't understand."

"Child—I have lived for more than a century. Without a special room, I would have been dead years ago."

She just stared at him.

"But my mother—Jehenna—"

He shrugged. "Nobody knows how old Jehenna is. There

is some magic that keeps her alive. As for your mother—the Dreamshifters are long lived, and she has Jehenna's blood as well."

Vivian struggled to accommodate so many new beliefs, thought about Zee, waiting in the bookstore for her to show up so he could hand over the messages George left with him. Zee, who had painted her transforming into a dragon and had still looked at her as though she were desirable. "So you've existed here—all these years—so that you could help me when the time came."

"That, and hoping against hope that Isobel would find her way back to me. She did, one night, come to me in a dream . . ."

"And my grandfather knew all of this, planned all of this. He knew Jehenna would kill him."

"He hoped to find a way to destroy her. He didn't want to involve you, but he said he feared it was your destiny."

"I don't believe in destiny—"

The Prince cut her off with a short laugh. "You, of all people, had better believe."

Vivian was thinking, and not liking what came into her mind. "Why?" she asked, finally. An inadequate question, she realized, even as it left her lips.

"Because of what you are."

"And what am I?"

"A powerful woman—one with the blood of Dream-shifter, Sorceress—"

"And dragon." Vivian's eyes went to the picture. She shuddered, reached for the comfort of the pendant, and then remembered that this room was in Dreamworld.

If anybody had earned her trust, it was Landon. She hoisted up the skirt to reveal the black cylinder strapped to her thigh. "This was in your fountain," she said. "Inside a fish."

He drew an audible breath. His hand reached out as though to touch, then drew back. "I don't know what it is, but I am certain it should be hidden."

"He said if I were to find it, I must destroy it. I don't know how."

Both were silent for a space of several breaths. At last Landon asked, "What will you do now?"

"Whatever I can. I was—directed—to come here. I believe Isobel might be held here in the dungeons."

"I'm coming with you." His face had hardened, no longer vague or even good-natured. He looked dangerous, the fairy-tale prince about to confront the dragon in order to save the princess. "My promise to the Wanderer is fulfilled. I would welcome death with open arms, if it meant that Isobel was safe."

Vivian nodded, feeling a small warmth at her heart to know that she need not be completely alone.

Landon blew out the lantern, plunging the room into darkness. She felt his hand on her arm, let him guide her back into the tunnel.

Twenty-six

✦

Strands of spider silk clung to Vivian's face, wrapped around her wrists and neck. She thought she could feel spiders in her hair, crawling down her back, over her arms. She heard herself whimpering a little with every breath, wanted to break into a full-out run but it was too dark.

"Three hundred fifty-six paces," Landon whispered, "and you'll be clear of them."

Vivian counted each step in her head. Left, one. Right, two. Left, three. On and on. As the Prince had promised, when she reached three hundred fifty-six, the webs stopped. She stopped, too, scrubbing spiderwebs away with her hands, searching out the spiders she was certain were crawling all over her. She found three, the largest the size of her fist, and flung them away into the darkness. She began to walk again, but still her flesh quivered with the sensation of legs and feet, always crawling, weaving phantom webs into her hair.

Even with company, the darkness pressed in, overwhelming. She began to feel it would never be light again, that she had entered hell and would walk through this darkness for eternity. Her eyes ached with the relentless search for a gleam of light. Her bare feet hurt, heels and toes rubbed raw from constant friction with stone. The voices in her head muttered endlessly, close to comprehensible but never quite understood.

Once or twice she thought she heard footsteps but could never be sure.

As they moved deeper into the dungeons, the voices began to grow distinct once more. She understood a word here, a phrase there. Strange sensations began to plague her. An itching of her skin, as though it were too tight. A heat in her belly. Her senses sharpened; she became aware of subtle scents—clean sweat from Landon, the earthy smell of the stone, a distant dripping of water.

And definitely now, footsteps somewhere behind them. She looked back but could see nothing in the darkness. Landon seemed unaware.

She kept on walking.

At last they rounded a curve and saw a gleam of light ahead. Vivian's nostrils flared with a scent of unwashed bodies, a faint contagion of fear. Beneath it the rich, salty heat of blood. Appalled, she felt her mouth flood with saliva, her stomach stir with sudden hunger.

The darkness lightened to a dim gloom, and her eyes began to pick out details. She could make out jagged stone above her head, a widening of the passage. And then, all at once, the corridor opened out into a massive cavern. Roughly carved pillars supported a vaulted stone roof. Hanging lanterns illuminated a path that spiraled downward and inward.

The cavern was enormous and awe-inspiring.

The prisoners were something else entirely.

Barbed-wire fences ten feet high lined the path, and between them and the stone wall behind them, hundreds of people sat, stood, or lay. They didn't speak, didn't look up at the sound of approaching footsteps; no curiosity dawned in their faces. They simply watched, or not, with nothing—neither fear nor hope—behind their eyes.

Vivian stopped. Moving forward against the weight of all of that humanity seemed to her in that moment impossible. Her eyes scanned over the throng of faces in horror.

Men, women, children. And even the children sat silent. No cries, no speech, no games.

"What has been done to them?" Vivian's breath felt harsh and ragged.

Landon's voice broke when he tried to answer. He swallowed hard, drew a deep breath. "She says it is a kindness to take away all will from them when they come here."

"Sedated and penned like cattle." Rage simmered in her belly.

"Cattle is precisely what they are."

After a moment, without another word spoken, the two of them began to move forward once again. Out of the sea of humanity, a young woman caught Vivian's eye. She sat cross-legged next to the fence, one hand curled loosely around a strand of wire. Her hair hung in a tangled mass over her shoulders, once flame bright, now dulled by dirt. A bruise purpled her right eye, and her upper lip was puffy and flecked with dried blood. Her left cheek was disfigured and swollen.

Vivian exhaled sharply between her teeth. "Esme." Pulling away from Landon's restraining hands, she darted over to the fence. The girl's eyes remained focused on nothing, empty, not so much as a flicker of recognition. The fingers twitched once and were still.

"Esme. Wake up!" Vivian squeezed the limp hand, trying to pull the girl's mind back. The bloody lips parted, revealing broken front teeth, and Vivian leaned forward to catch any whispered word, but they closed again, without a sound.

An old woman clicked toothless gums together in a meaningless, arrhythmic sound. A small boy, maybe five years old, dirty and thin, twisted a strip of rag between his fingers, endlessly winding and rewinding. He looked at Vivian but didn't seem to see her. A woman held a baby in her arms, without affection, and the small creature did not even whimper, its eyes moving without interest or focus in a pinched and dirty face.

"There is nothing we can do here." Landon tugged at her arm. "Come."

Vivian heard his words layered over the multitudinous voices, as something far away and without meaning.

"We have to get her out."

And then, in her mind she felt the dragon stir and wake. Felt the creature's suppressed rage, her hunger. A new voice spoke directly into her head, this time clear, articulate.

Come, hunt with me.

An answering hunger stirred in her own belly, and with it a startling and unwelcome thirst for blood. A heavy dragging sound reverberated through the cavern, louder and louder.

"Dragon," Landon warned.

This time, Vivian felt no desire to run.

The creature emerged through a great arch at the back of the fenced-in area. Beyond old, once diamond-bright scales dulled by uncounted years in the dark. A webbing of fine silver mesh circled the scabrous belly and bound the wings.

Unexpectedly, Vivian felt a pang of loss, born of a yearning for the sky and the keen, bracing winds over the mountains. Something in her vibrated in response, and she pressed closer to the fence, feeling awkward and strangely heavy, as though her shadow had weight. They faced each other over the witless victims, the woman and the dragon, for time out of mind.

Change, the creature said into her mind. *Be Dragon.*

No.

Is this not why you have come?

Vivian shuddered, feeling her flesh respond to the dragon's words. The coal of rage in her belly glowed white hot. Her skin tightened over muscle primed to fight.

"Never," she said aloud.

A cry issued from the dragon's throat, a sound that would have once dropped Vivian to her knees. She felt the Prince stagger off balance, but she felt no fear. The dragon lumbered toward her, crushing bodies beneath her great feet. Bones snapped with a sound like dry branches breaking. Crimson wounds opened where sharp talons caught an arm, a chest, a thigh.

The horned head darted out snakelike on a long neck. A crunch of bone, a wet splattering of blood and viscera, and nothing was left of a man but his legs. Blood and tissue drenched the woman next to him, but she continued gazing into the distance, absently wiping the wetness from her face with her hands. The dragon trampled more inert bodies.

Vivian lusted for blood. It was a deep and primal desire that sprang up from a darkness she had always kept buried in the unplumbed depths of her soul. These were human beings, she tried to remind herself, but the voice of rationality was obscured by a furnace in her belly. Something about her shoulder blades felt wrong. She twitched them restlessly, feeling the fabric slide cool over her skin, half-expecting the catch of something sprouting, growing into wings.

Esme's finger traced idly through the dirt, her tangled hair screening her face.

The dragon's eyes focused in her direction.

Vivian reached for the Voice, the command that must be obeyed, but had somehow lost the capacity for words. Her tongue felt thick and too large for her mouth. Instead, she spoke directly into the dragon's mind.

Leave that one alone.

The dragon raised its head and looked at her. *That won't work on me, human. I go deeper than your sorcery.*

Vivian's body was too large for her skin; in a moment she would burst through it, take on a different form and shape. Her hearing had sharpened. She could hear her own heartbeat, Landon's, Esme's, the suss and flow of blood through arteries and veins. Again she found she could almost taste the hot salt of flesh and blood, with a growing desire to rend and tear. Flesh was only flesh. Food. These were cattle, penned for the taking.

She pushed against the fence, felt it begin to give against a body grown awkward and clumsy, impervious to the prick of the barbed wire.

Awareness of the door exploded on her consciousness an instant before it appeared in the middle of nothing, a black door, stone. It opened, and Jehenna stood there, no longer robed as a queen but wearing a black gown identical to Vivian's.

"Mellisande, hold." Jehenna's voice lashed through the cavern.

Vivian felt the command strike the dragon's silver bonds, cringed away in sympathy from the web of pain that immobilized the creature in her tracks.

Negligent, Jehenna waved her hand. "Esme, awake."

The girl blinked and looked around her. Fear distorted her face and she cowered back against the fence at the same time as she began to scream in absolute terror.

"Come here," Jehenna commanded.

Esme got to her feet and staggered over to the Sorceress, who pressed a stone knife against her pale throat.

"Now, Dreamshifter. Get yourself under control, or I will kill her."

Vivian struggled to hold on to herself in the middle of overwhelming and warring sensations.

Kill. Eat. Burn.

Save the girl.

She was aware of her identity sliding away, of the dragon self growing stronger, all compassion dissolving. The world was hard edged, brilliant hued. Somewhere above these dungeons a vast night sky promised the exhilaration of flight.

No, I have to do—something. Something small, insignificant . . .

"Vivian."

A familiar voice that caught and held her rapidly fading memory.

Again the name that held her, spoken by a tall man bearing a bright sword. He strode toward her and laid a hand against her face. Cool. It stirred memories, faint and distant, of pleasures other than blood and flight.

His eyes burned into hers, and he spoke the name for the third time. "Vivian. I name you."

She breathed in, deep, felt the coolness of the air ease the fire within her.

The man bent his head and pressed his lips against hers.

He tasted of something precious, remembered and lost, a sweetness that drew everything she was and ever had been, in all the worlds, into one long, lingering kiss.

When at last they parted, Vivian's knees buckled and she clung to the Warlord, breathless and trembling, her cheek resting against his chest, letting his strong arms support her.

His voice low and intimate, whispered in her ear. "Are you yourself again?"

"I—think so." She felt small and frail. "How did you find me?"

"I thought you would come here. I followed you."

"Perfect," Jehenna said, applauding. "Well done, Warlord. Had you allowed her to change, she could have killed me—now she is mine."

Vivian turned out of the Warlord's arms to face her enemy.

Jehenna still held Esme in front of her, the knife pressed against the girl's throat. Whimpering noises escaped from between lips blanched almost white.

"Now, Dreamshifter. The key."

Still disoriented and shaken, Vivian shook her head. "I—it isn't here."

Jehenna's eyes narrowed; her nostrils flared. Vivian felt a touch on the surface of her thoughts, light, persistent. "Of course. Tell me where it is."

"Let Esme go."

"You dare give orders to me? Let me teach you your place. Come here and kill her yourself."

Vivian felt that slight tug as the Sorceress used the Voice, but it was a small matter to shrug it off. "No."

"You cannot refuse me. Now. Kill the girl."

"Your sorcery doesn't work on me, Jehenna." Then, speaking from that place of power newly discovered, Vivian used the Voice herself. "Let her go."

The hand holding the knife began to shake. Jehenna's jaw tightened; a spasm traveled across her face. Her arms dropped to her sides and the frightened girl scuttled away, sobbing, toward the fence and the promise of protection.

Vivian felt a brief bright flare of victory that faded at once. Jehenna's face was pale with fury, but it held an expression far from defeat. She smiled. "Child, you are so young. Power you may have, but you know nothing. This servant girl, that you claim to care for so much. Here she is, living. And yet you refuse the one thing that will keep her alive. All I ask is a thing. A small object. A key. So little in exchange for a life."

"I won't let you hurt her. I've just proven I'm stronger than you."

"Are you, truly? I wonder."

Vivian knew, knew in her gut and her soul before the voices could shout a warning, that a blow was coming. But she didn't know from where, or how to counter the unknown.

The Sorceress walked over to the dragon and laid a hand on the scaly skin, just above the creature's knee.

Through the unspoken bond with the dragon, Vivian felt a flash of hatred in reaction to the touch, but Mellisande stood unmoving, docile, controlled by the silver web that bound her wings.

Esme had scrabbled over to the fence and pressed against it, heedless of the barbs tearing into her clothing and skin. "Help me," she pleaded, reaching her hands through.

"It's cruel to keep the poor thing suffering," Jehenna continued. "Don't you think? So much kinder to allow her the dullness, that she might not know what is going on."

"Leave her alone," Vivian said. She took Esme's hands in hers, clasped them tightly.

"My Lady, help me."

"Hang on, Esme. We'll get you out."

"One way or another," Jehenna said. She smiled. "Mellisande. Dinner."

Before Vivian could even draw a breath, the dragon's head shot forward and Esme disappeared into her gaping jaws. Hot blood sprayed over Vivian's face, blinding her, mercifully, to the rest of what followed. She felt the crunch of teeth on bone reverberate through her own body. Her hands still gripped Esme's, but when she managed to blink the blood from her eyes, she saw that the hands ended in bloody stumps of protruding bone.

Doubled over, vomiting up a bitterness that burned her throat, her nose, Vivian heard a warning shout from the Warlord. Heard Jehenna's voice, right behind her, far too close, commanding, "Warlord, sheathe your sword."

Something cold snapped around first one wrist and then the other.

An instant weariness came over her, as though she'd been ill and bedridden for days, as though she'd run for miles through desert heat. Breathing hard, wiping blood and vomit from her face with the backs of her hands, Vivian straightened, swaying, but still upright.

The Warlord's hand was clenched, white knuckled, around the hilt of the sword he had been forced to sheathe. The Prince stood beside him, his breathing as ragged and raw as Vivian's own. She refused to look at what lay just through the fence, at either the dragon or whatever remained of Esme. Each of her wrists was encircled with a bracelet of silver.

"Ah, Dreamshifter." Jehenna shook her head. "If only you had given me the key. I asked you courteously. And now we have come to this. Look at what you have done."

The compulsion burned through the bracelets and into her wrists. She could not close her eyes or turn away but was forced to turn her head, to see the wreckage of what had been Esme. Mellisande stood listless, head hanging low to the ground, bloodstained and hideous. One human leg, shattered femur bone protruding, lay in a pool of gore, half under the fence. At Vivian's feet, where she had dropped them, Esme's severed hands reproached her, fingers still curled and clinging now to empty air.

Vivian's stomach heaved and she swallowed, hard. Her breath came in small, sobbing gasps.

"Now, about that key."

"I can't," Vivian said. To her horror, she found that she was sobbing and could not stop. Now, when she most needed to be strong, she was falling apart like a small and frightened child.

Zee stepped forward and circled her with his arm. She felt his solid strength, inhaled it into her body. Landon stood on the other side, taking her hand in his.

Jehenna's face darkened.

She stepped forward, stroked the Warlord's cheek with her fingertips. Beads of sweat stood out on his forehead, the muscles corded in his neck as the fingers traced the network of scars. "You have betrayed me," she said. "What shall I do with you now?"

"I betrayed my men. My self. You never had my loyalty to begin with."

Jehenna jabbed her fingers into an unhealed wound, dug deep. Blood welled, making a trail down his cheek like crimson tears. He stood expressionless and impassive. She slapped him.

"Leave him alone." Vivian's voice sounded fragile to her own ears, powerless and small.

"He is mine, little Dreamshifter, to do with as I wish. Shall I show you?"

"No. Please." She hated herself for pleading, but it was all she could do.

"Kiss me, Warlord." The voice of command, with a purring undertone of seduction.

Vivian felt a jolt go through him, as though he'd been struck by a current of electricity. The arm around her waist went rigid and then fell away. Slowly, he bent his head and pressed his lips, brief and dry, against Jehenna's.

Again the Sorceress slapped him, raking her fingernails over his bleeding cheek. "Kiss me like you kissed her. Show her how you want me."

Sickened, Vivian watched helplessly as he followed the command, crushing his lips against Jehenna's, passionate, demanding. His hands caressed her, stroked the length of her back, pulled her body hard against his. The Sorceress molded herself around him.

There was nothing Vivian could do except close her eyes. Anybody she loved, anybody she cared about, Jehenna would torture. Would kill in the end. She felt Landon's hand squeeze hers, warm and steadying.

"A casual observer might think you jealous, My Queen," he said. His tone was casual, conversational. "Desperate, even. A kiss given under duress will never equal one given in love."

Jehenna stiffened and broke the embrace. Her eyes flashed with fury.

"You. Poor little prince. Hiding in the dark and mourning his lost love. Are you challenging me at last?"

Landon sank onto one knee. "No. I am offering myself. Let these two go."

Jehenna's laughter was a cold and evil thing, winding its way through Vivian's brain and making a darkness of every memory where there had ever been light and love. "Ah, my little lordling. I have a surprise especially for you."

Vivian fought the sickness and the weakness, searching for some way to fight back. Jehenna began to mutter under her breath, words rhythmic and incomprehensible. The air thickened until it was difficult to draw a breath. A door appeared, its edges shimmering with green light.

It opened on a bare room, scarcely larger than a cell. White walls, white floor, harsh white light. Isobel sat in a corner, curled over her knees, rocking. Her hair fell tangled over a tear-streaked face. Lost in torment, she did not even look up.

"Isobel!" Landon cried. He flung himself forward. Green light flared as he struck the open door, bounced him backward to lie dazed on the cold stone. Vivian stepped forward cautiously, put her head close to the barrier, not quite touching.

"Isobel!"

"She can't hear you," Jehenna said. "No sound in there. Nothing to see, or touch, or feel. No passage of time. Not a thing but what is already in her head."

Vivian, knowing something of what was in her mother's

head, swept her hand across the invisible barrier. A shock of pain, a flash of green light. Her hand and wrist went numb; her arm ached.

Landon moaned and pushed himself back up onto his feet. "Isobel." All the long years of separation were in his voice.

Almost she seemed to hear him, pausing in the rocking and raising her head to look around. Then she made a small sound of despair, like an exhausted child, and began rocking again.

"Let's make this more interesting," Jehenna said. She tossed something through the doorway, a thing that clattered and skidded across the floor, bumping up against Isobel's bare foot.

A knife.

Again Vivian tried to press her way through to her mother. Green flame from the edge of the doorway grounded into the silver bracelets. Her muscles convulsed in an agony of fire that dropped her to the ground where she lay, twitching and helpless, able only to watch and do nothing.

Isobel stopped rocking. She picked up the knife, turned it in her hands. One finger tested the blade. She smiled, ran it delicately the length of her forearm, laying open the flesh with surgical precision. Again she ran a finger along the blood-wet edge, testing, then set it against her skin once more.

Jehenna laughed, releasing them all from the force of her will as she focused on the suffering woman.

"Now, Landon!" the Warlord shouted. He thrust the blade of his sword into the force field. Green light arced and writhed around his hands, his arms. His entire body went rigid and convulsed as the force field grounded itself through him and into the cavern floor. The Prince flung himself forward. For the length of one long breath he hung motionless in the air, his body outlined in green, flickering light. But then he was through, clasping Isobel tightly, tightly, removing the knife from her hands. She buried her face in his shoulder and clung to him.

Jehenna hissed through her teeth, her beautiful face distorted by rage.

Vivian drove her shoulder into the Warlord's chest, pushing him backward and away from the current that held him. Released, he sagged onto the floor, unconscious, the sword clattering to the stone beside him.

Down on her knees, Vivian checked his vital signs. There was a pulse, faint and thready, but he wasn't breathing. Tilting his head, she sealed her lips around his and breathed into him. Once, twice, three times.

He drew a deep shuddering breath on his own. And then another.

When she looked up, the door was gone, and Isobel and Landon with it.

"They'll be sick of each other soon enough," Jehenna said. "The knife will come in handy, years and years from now, when they've had nothing but each other and the love turns to hate. I couldn't have planned a fate so perfect."

"Why?" Vivian asked. "Why do you hate your own daughter so?"

"She was always her father's more than mine. I bore her to please him, but it wasn't enough. He turned against me, locked me away into that room. Do you understand what that means? One hundred years of nothing but my own thoughts and memories. Every long empty minute I worked to build my power. So much time to plan revenge. It was perfect. And when I broke free—"

"You killed him."

Jehenna kicked the unconscious Warlord in the ribs, a sharp and vicious blow. "I weary of this game," she said. "Perhaps I will kill him with his own blade." She bent and picked up the sword from where it lay beside him. "Bare his chest."

And Vivian felt her own hands moving, unable now to resist the Voice. She unfastened the chain mail shirt, lifted the tunic beneath it. Gasped at the network of scars marring the skin of his chest.

"Such a foolish man to punish himself so." Jehenna

positioned the tip of the sword in the space between two ribs, directly over the heart. "Shall I?"

Vivian's own heart keened in her breast. "Stop," she croaked. "Please."

The Warlord's eyes flickered open, those beautiful agate eyes.

"Where is the key?" Jehenna demanded.

"No," the Warlord said, "My Lady, no—"

Bound with silver, her will not her own, Vivian could no longer refuse. "I have it."

"Give it to me."

Knowing that great evil would follow, Vivian unbound the fabric strips that strapped the key to her thigh. It felt extraordinarily heavy in her hand, almost as though it was sentient and resistant to the exchange.

"No," the Warlord whispered.

But the thing was already done. With a cry of exultation, Jehenna took the key from Vivian's hand and pressed it to her lips.

Twenty-seven

✤

Vivian opened her eyes to complete and utter darkness. Someone seemed to be pounding her head with a hammer, in perfect time with the beating of her heart. Her throat felt bruised, her mouth so parched she could barely swallow. The air was cold, musty, heavy with the stink of human waste, sweat, and despair.

Memory showed up a few heartbeats later, reminding her that she was locked in a cell in the dungeons, that she wasn't going to find a way out. Cold silver circled both wrists, controlling her, blocking her ability to create a door, to use the Voice on a guard, to do anything to help herself.

Alive, but not for long.

With a groan, she pushed herself up to sitting, waited for the storm of agony in her head to settle, then tried to make sense of her surroundings.

She sat on a pile of damp, rank-smelling straw. Her bare feet reached out and found clammy stone. It took three attempts for her to get onto hands and knees, and from there to stagger up onto her feet and stand, swaying. When the pain in her head eased back to what she was coming to think of as normal, she limped cautiously forward on her bruised and aching feet.

Five tottering steps brought her to a stone wall. She felt

along it for maybe ten paces before it intersected with another wall.

Definitely a cell. She went over it again and again, exploring every reachable inch with her hands for anything that
could be used to help her escape, but there was nothing. No
cracks, no loose stones. At last she sank back down on her
pile of straw, remaining perfectly still except for the necessary act of breathing.

There would be no rescue attempt.

Prince Landon might have tried, but he was locked away
with Isobel. The Warlord, if he was still alive, would not be
free to come for her. Last she'd seen him, when the guards
dragged her away, he'd been lying on the floor with Jehenna
still standing over him pressing the tip of her sword against
his bared breast.

Tears threatened, but Vivian blinked them back.

Her thoughts flickered in and out, short-circuited by cold,
hunger, and fear of the unknown. Would she be sacrificed
to the dragon? Or would she be left here to molder away,
slowly decaying in the dark? It would take ten days, more
or less, to die of dehydration. A month or more to die of
starvation if they decided to bring her water. She feared this
more than the dragon, she realized. It was too much like
Isobel's fate, locked away with her guilt and failures with
no hope of setting them right.

Footsteps sounded in the hallway, slow and halting. She
had time to picture a deformed monster come to torment
her before there was a soft grating sound, and a flickering
yellow light illuminated the line of a half-open door. Above
it, distorted by the shadows, Jared's face. No, not Jared, she
reminded herself. Gareth.

"Come to gloat, or to finish what you started?" she asked.
Automatically she reached for the knife, but her pocket was
empty. Of course, Jehenna would never have left her something that could be either defense or a means of self-
destruction in the face of torture or starvation.

Gareth flinched as though she had struck him. He entered
the cell, a lantern in one hand, pushing the door not quite

closed behind him. "I never wanted this." His voice sounded, just for the moment, young and a little bit lost. He bent his knees as though he would sit beside her in the straw, then changed his mind with a little gasp of pain.

Vivian kept silent, waiting for him to declare his purpose.

"Is there anything I can do to ease you?"

Water, food. She bit her lip rather than ask him for anything. "I didn't expect you to be up and around quite yet."

One of his hands twitched protectively to rest on his buttocks. "No permanent damage, the healer said. But it makes sitting difficult."

"Why are you really here, Gareth?"

"I came to tell you you'll be sacrificed to the dragon at dawn."

"Always the bearer of good news."

"Not just you—the Warlord as well, if he's not already dead."

Her heart skipped a beat in mingled hope and dismay. "What?"

"One rumor says he's in the dungeon awaiting punishment. The other that she's killed him already."

Vivian found that she couldn't speak.

"My Lady?"

"You've delivered the message. You can go and tell her I'm quivering in terror."

A strangled sound escaped him, somewhere between a laugh and a sob, and then he did lower himself, very slowly, to sit beside her in the straw. "That's not why I came."

"So why are you here?"

"To explain. The thing that happened with your bird. She ordered me to do that. Said the creature must be removed."

Vivian's temper flared, but she kept her voice even. "And now—what? You want my forgiveness before I die?"

"Yes. I mean no—I don't want for you to die, at all. She said the key was dangerous for you, that once it was safely in her hands you would be safe. I heard that she had found the key. That you had been locked in the dungeon. I went to her; I asked that she would keep her promise. She—laughed. She said that now she has the key she has no need of you . . ."

"If you're so sorry, get me out of here. Free me."

He moaned, buried his face in his hands. "I can't. There are guards everywhere."

"People are dead because of you. Esme was eaten by the dragon last night. Did you know? She spattered. A great deal of her is now stains on my gown. And now it's my turn."

"You have power. Can't you do something?"

Vivian stretched out her wrists, the silver bracelets glinting in the lantern light. "She has bound me."

Gareth took one of her hands and ran his fingers over the silver. A familiar touch. In the darkness she could almost imagine that he was Jared, that perhaps he loved her. Almost. But Jared's hands had also turned against her. She shuddered but would not give him the satisfaction of pulling away.

He turned one of her wrists, held it closer to the candle, and bent his head to examine the clasp.

"Look. You've said what you came to say. Go back to your chambers. Get some sleep. Tomorrow morning comes early. You won't want to miss the show."

Turning aside, he set the lantern down, well away from the straw, and then took her right wrist in his hands again. Pressure. A click. And the bracelet fell away. He took her left hand and repeated the action.

Vitality flooded back into her body. Voices shouted in her head, as though a switch had been turned on. The weight of responsibility settled back onto her shoulders; the harsh flicker of hope beset her heart.

"Why would you free me?" she asked.

"You were right—what you said about the dreams."

Vivian closed her eyes to shut out his face, walling off a cyclone of emotions that she had no time to sort out. Too many lives hung in the balance for her to indulge in vengeance in this moment. Clenching her fists, she steadied her breathing and her voice.

"What did I say?"

"That I was a better man in my dreams. I—have loved you, I think."

"Whatever it was, it wasn't love."

"She made me, you have to believe that. I had orders . . ."

Vivian wanted to believe him. But he hadn't acted like a man under duress. She thought about the Warlord, the way he'd fought the compulsion. The cold sweat, the way his face had twisted in hate and resistance when he'd been forced to obey.

She shook her head. "No, Gareth. You acted as you wished to act. She gave you the opportunity to live your own dreams. You took it."

"My Lady—"

"Go back to your bed." Half-unconscious, she used the Voice.

He stiffened as the command jolted into him. Picked up the lantern and took a step toward the door. "But I freed you."

"Did you expect a reward? Get out, before I make you hurt yourself."

Her own words echoed with the other voices in her head as the door closed with him, shutting out the last glimmer of light.

You acted as you wished to act.

There was truth in these words. Surmise was not entirely of Jehenna's making. Each dreamer here bore some responsibility for the way things played out. They made choices, even in dream, and Surmise shifted and changed because of them. Things could be altered; nothing was set.

Perhaps it was not necessary to die.

Curling back into the straw, she tucked the bracelets into her pocket. Her brain spun in circles, trying to make sense out of Surmise and the Between. At last the voices carried her off into a fitful sleep, in which she dreamed of Poe, and the key, and of soaring through a cold night sky on wide strong wings.

She woke to the sound of boots echoing in the corridor. Time, then. She fumbled for the bracelets and slipped them onto her wrists, where they dangled loosely. Her body went weak at the touch of the silver.

When the door opened, it revealed a withered crone standing in front of three guards. Off to the side and a few safe paces back, a young girl waited, something white and diaphanous draped across her outstretched arms.

Two guards took up positions on either side of the open door; the other entered the cell, followed by the old woman. Her face was sun weathered, creased into lines so sharp they looked like they could cut.

"I'm guessing it must be almost dawn," Vivian croaked. She swallowed, trying to moisten a throat parched with thirst.

The crone grinned, revealing a mouthful of brown and broken teeth. She gestured for Vivian to get up.

No reason not to comply, except that her first effort failed, her legs giving away and dropping her into a heap. The guard seized her by the wrists and hauled her bodily onto her feet. She braced herself, her aching head making the room spin.

A gesture from the old woman, and the guard pulled a canteen from his belt and handed it to Vivian. Water. Warm and stale, but gloriously wet. She drank long and deep.

The dizziness receded and the pain eased to a tolerable throbbing.

Another gesture, and the guard stepped behind her. She flinched at the touch of his fingers as she realized he was unfastening the gown. But even when he bent to lift the skirt and pulled the gown up and over her head, she offered no resistance, only taking care that the loosened bracelets didn't catch on the sleeves and slide off with the torn and bloodstained garment. The guard's eyes, even his hands, on her naked body were a small thing, meaningless in the face of what lay ahead.

But he didn't touch her, only stepped back. A page appeared in the hallway with a basin of water, and the old woman's gnarled hands bathed Vivian from head to toe and then raked a comb through the tangles in her hair.

Another gesture, this time to the maiden waiting in the corridor who entered the cell, carrying a white, trailing gown.

Every tapestry, every painting, in the castle depicted a maiden wearing a white gown such as this. And every maiden wearing a white gown stood face to face with a dragon. As Vivian donned the gown she felt the first cracks in her unnatural calm. Her insides trembled as though a small and private earthquake were taking place within her.

Clawed old hands smoothed the dress, fluffed her hair, turned her from side to side to see that all was in order. And then the old woman nodded once at her handiwork and, without ever speaking a word, turned and hobbled away down the corridor, leaning on the arm of the maiden.

This left Vivian alone with the guards.

They watched her closely but kept a respectful distance.

Again she heard footsteps, and a moment later the priest stood framed in the doorway, clad in his scarlet robes. The lantern light reflected in his eyes. He thumped his staff onto the stone with a sharp return like a gunshot. Vivian flinched in spite of her best intentions.

"Is the sacrifice ready?"

He was apparently speaking to her. She didn't answer.

"Maiden, do you give yourself willingly as a sacrifice to the Dragon, that the people of this land may walk in safety, that the doors may be safely closed between this world and the others that may do us harm?"

"Fuck you," Vivian said.

The priest's narrow face paled. A faint sheen of perspiration appeared on his forehead. "I ask you again—do you give yourself willingly as a sacrifice?"

"No. And whatever sort of twisted game this is, I'm not playing. Do you hear me? I am not a volunteer."

"But it's traditional—"

"Oh come on. Are you going to call off the sacrifice because I haven't said the right words? What do you suppose *she* will do to you then?"

"This is a rite. A holy ceremony, conducted for the good of the people . . ."

He faltered under her steady gaze, shuffling his feet a little in the silence that followed. "Bring her," he said. Without further debate, he spun on his heel and led the way down a long, dark passage. Level, not sloping either up or down.

Vivian followed, pacing between the guards. Still they did not touch her. Behind them followed a procession that had arrived with the priest—maidens in white, long hair loose on their shoulders, all bearing candles.

The maidens began a slow, heavy chant. Vivian found herself thinking that a dragon chant should be sharp and so clear it can cut. It should soar high and dip low in the spirit of freedom, not bondage in the darkness. A reluctant empathy for the old dragon stirred in her, pity for the change wrought by the long years in the dark. She, too, had been twisted by Jehenna's meddling.

It wasn't a long walk, not long enough given what waited at the end. A door opened, framing a rectangle of bright daylight. Thunderous noise swept into the passageway through the open door—voices shouting, hands clapping, feet stomping. It sounded for all the world like the crowd at a football game.

Twenty-eight

⚜

Consciousness was a fragile thing, frayed around the edges, constantly trying to slip away. The weight of the bear pressed down on him, making it impossible to draw a full breath. Air hunger was a pressing need, a black panic edged with crimson. Zee forced himself to take shallow breaths, to stay calm, to think, despite the pulse of pain over his cheek and jaw. Somewhere inside he was laughing at the bitter irony of this death, picturing in his mind's eye the newspaper headline: *Fugitive Felon Dies, Crushed by Dead Bear.*

Sheer force of will kept him conscious, pushed the panic away. He discovered that it was possible to move, one infinitesimal bit at a time. Foot, leg, finger, wrist. Shift, wriggle, turn, bend. Shallow breaths, each one smelling of blood and fur and the rank, wild scent of the bear. Hopeless, maybe, but as long as he could manage to breathe he would continue to fight.

At last he felt a shift, got an arm and a leg free, and slithered out into a night just edging into dawn. Air was a miracle. He sucked it deep into his lungs. It smelled of frost and coming winter, clean and life-giving. For a space of time it was all he could do to lie flat on the sand and breathe.

His body was a welter of aching bruises, but careful

exploration revealed that everything was in working order. His shoulder was stiff but functional. No bones broken, no tendons damaged. He touched his fingers to his cheek, relieved to find that though the lacerations were deep, he still had a face, that the blood was beginning to clot. He'd pictured the whole cheek torn away down to the exposed bone. It would scar, but it would heal.

Cold, though; he needed to move. At length he mustered the strength to stagger to his feet. He found the sword, fallen clear of the bear's carcass, and cleaned it as best he could in the sand. Holding it unsheathed and ready, he took a cautious step toward the place where the bear had appeared out of thin air.

Jehenna was responsible for this. He had been trying to get to Vivian. Now he understood that there was only one way to find her.

As he approached the stone he heard a buzzing, faint at first and then louder. A softening of everything in his line of vision. His heart beat faster. A thin place; a crossing. He had no idea of what lay on the other side.

Blood calls to blood, she had said. *Just call my name if you want me.* "Jehenna," he breathed like an invocation, took another step.

And stood in a dark cavern, lit by flickering torches. A massive column of red stone rose before him, thrusting up and away into the darkness. Compared to its raw power, the Finger was a child's toy.

"Magnificent, isn't it?" a voice said behind him. "It rises through the roof and into a chamber above—through that again, until it reaches the open air. That's where you'd find your Dreamshifter—if you could get to her."

He swung around, ready to strike, but the sword stopped against his will, hanging in the air, immobile.

"You," he said.

"You called me. I admire your perseverance, but you will not be able to save her."

Vivian was still alive, then. Whatever the witch said, there must be a way. He looked around him, taking in the high stone altar, the carved pillars, registering the reek of blood.

"Don't be too sure," he managed.

She laughed at that, fondly, as though he were an adorable child. "You would be just in the nick of time if you were not down here in the temple. She's right above you, you know. Your Dreamshifter. And the dragon."

"What dragon?"

"Oh, come now. It's an old tale, that of the maiden and the dragon. Played out through so many worlds over so many years. You might as well put that sword away. You can't kill me, and it would be a shame for you to hurt yourself."

Before the sword was fully sheathed he was halfway to an open door, driving his weary body to reach it before, before—

"Stop right there, hero. You're not going anywhere."

An invisible barrier bounced him back. Again and again he threw himself against it while Jehenna's laughter echoed around him. His brain kicked in at last and he stood, breathing hard, within arm's reach of an open door that posed more of a barrier than prison bars. "Why?" he said. "What do you stand to gain?"

In answer to that, she only smiled. "You might as well sit down; you'll be here for a while."

"Please—you can do whatever you want with me. Just let her go."

"I can do whatever I want with you, anyway. All I need do is speak, and you will dance for me, a puppet on a string. At the moment your vicarious suffering is sufficient. Let me tell you what is happening up there. Your beloved, dressed in a gown of white, is chained to the tip-top of this Blood Stone. The dragon isn't in a hurry—it's too well fed. It will toy with her at first, but soon, very soon, it will devour her. There may be leavings—a hand, a foot, a fragment of clothing. I'd love to have you watch, but it's so much safer if you stay here."

She walked over to him and ran her hand over his mangled face. He sucked in his breath at the pain but managed to hold his head steady, not to flinch away. "Oh, the scars.

Priceless. I must say I thought the bear would win when I sent it through—I underestimated your abilities. This has been an interesting visit, but I'm afraid I must leave you now."

"Off to watch her die?"

"Oh, no. Fascinating as that would be, I have a more important thing to do." She reached into a pocket and extended her hand toward him. On her open palm lay a black stone object, intricately carved.

"You see, I was able to find this without your help. The Old One thought he could outwit me. It took the girl and the flightless bird, both, to find the key. But it is mine now. And I have no more need of Dreamshifters or dragons, spells or potions or incantations." She pressed her lips against the gleaming thing. "This will grant me life everlasting and unrivaled power."

There was nothing he could do. All of George's warnings in his head, his driving passion to save Vivian, to destroy the witch before she could make good on her plans—were as a child's whim, and with as little power.

Jehenna smiled, slow and seductive, then leaned toward him and kissed him. He closed his eyes to shut out the sight of her face, and when he opened them, she was gone.

His mind sprang free, his body once again his own to command. He leaped for the door, closed now. It had no lever, no handle. Pushing against it had no effect. He ran at it, struck with his injured shoulder, and landed in a heap on the floor, biting his lip until it bled to keep himself from whimpering with the shock of pain.

There must be another way out.

Searching the room, he found a metal grate, big enough to drive a semi through, but it was also locked. No other doors. He circled the chamber seeking an exit, unwilling to believe that he could not get to Vivian, could not stop the witch, after all he had done to get this far.

Steps led up onto a stone dais. He climbed them. Clotted blood in a basin, mixed with something black that had etched away stone where it splashed out onto the dais. Zee shivered, a sense of something evil and dark coming over him, and he retreated, sick at heart, to sit down and press his back against the wall next to the door.

The best plan he could come up with was that if anybody came in, he'd make a dive for freedom while the door was still open. If he was too late to save her, he could avenge her. And for that he would need to spare his waning strength.

Remembering, he put his hand into his pocket and brought out the cloth-wrapped object. *Open only at the end.*

Not quite yet. Not the end so long as there remained the smallest fragment of hope.

Resting his head back against the wall, he closed his eyes and focused on his breath, waiting.

Twenty-nine

✣

Vivian looked out across the closely trimmed and carefully tended grass, emerald green and weed free, to where the stadium walls rose sheer on all sides, the seats beyond that, tier after tier, filled with shouting humans. Above, blue sky, without the shadow of a single cloud.

Across the field she saw the red upthrust of stone. She could feel its power flickering at the edges of her reality, despite the blunting effect of the silver. Her guards, still careful not to touch her, signaled that she should walk the length of the field to the stone. Steadying herself, she stepped out onto the grass.

The vox humana crescendoed into a roar. A fanfare floated out of the stands.

Last night, she had been a spectator. Tonight, she was the show. Head held high, not willing to let the maddened crowd see her fear, she crossed the stadium. The longest walk of her life, but not long enough, a duality of time expanding and contracting, both eternity and an ephemeral breath.

She pressed her back against the stone, feeling its power pulsing against her skin. The guards fastened a heavy chain around her waist and left her there. The silver bracelets were loose around her wrists; she could slip them off at any time and—do what? Hope withered under the gaze of thousands of hostile eyes, thousands of voices shouting for her death.

Jehenna had the key.

She, Vivian Maylor, the last of the Dreamshifters, had failed in every possible way.

Trumpets blared. The priest paraded to the center of the field. He raised his staff and waited for the crowd to quiet so that his voice could be heard:

"In the last night and day, portents have been written across the sky. Strange creatures have appeared and disappeared. Reality twists and bends in on itself. Is it coincidence that these things should come to pass at the same time this sorceress appeared in Surmise?"

The crowd moaned, pressing forward against the barrier. "Death, death to the sorceress," a single voice shouted. The crowd took it up as a chant.

The priest raised his hands for silence. It took longer this time for the ebb of sound, but he waited, master of the drama, until all tongues were stilled, all ears listening. "We hereby give this woman in sacred ceremony to the Dragon, that the portals may be closed and the evil be driven from our kingdom."

A deafening response from the crowd.

"Let it be so!" He turned and joined his entourage, crossing the grass to a small postern gate that opened to let them through to safety.

A grinding of gears and pulleys, and the great door at the far end of the stadium began to rise.

The noise of the crowd intensified into a solid wall of hatred that beat against Vivian with a physical force. Mellisande's massive head emerged from the dark doorway, swinging side to side at the end of her long, scaly neck. Amber eyes blinked in the sudden light. She didn't hurry. One slow step at a time she half-crept, half-slithered into the arena, improbably big and unspeakably ugly. A barbed tail furrowed a long dark scar in the grass. Batlike wings lay furled along the long, sinuous spine, fastened in place by the silver mesh fastened around her belly.

A retinue of white-clad maidens followed, half-fainting with fear, driven forward by men with swords, then abandoned to press screaming against the unyielding stone barrier in frantic efforts to escape.

The dragon paused, turning her head to the side and surveying the selection of maidens. A small flame jetted from her nostrils. She opened a mouth full of bloodstained teeth, flickering a thick black tongue as though tasting the air.

Then, unhurried, Mellisande turned back toward Vivian, dragging her ungainly body across the arena, emitting little puffs of smoke from her nostrils.

I am about to be eaten by a dragon. About to become a spray of blood on the wind, a stray bone, a fragment of flesh. It was the old nightmare, finally come to claim her. Vivian watched, quiescent, mesmerized, as though the eyes in her head and the brain that processed the images belonged to some casual bystander. As in every nightmare, she was unable to run, to scream, to offer up any defense.

Take off the bracelets, the voices all shouted, but she continued to stand passive, shocked and beaten by the enormity of her failure and the hatred of the crowd.

And then another door opened and a man burst into the arena. His black hair hung loose on his bare shoulders. He wore nothing but a pair of cotton breeches. Scars slashed across the muscles of back and chest. In his right hand he carried a hunting knife; a ridiculous weapon, a toy, compared to the size and ferocity of a dragon.

The crowd fell silent for a moment, and then a cacophony of sound went up—cheers and shouts and sounds of dismay.

The Warlord's eyes met Vivian's, unflinching. Improbably, a smile lit his scarred face. He inclined his head toward her, ever so slightly, then moved to stand between her and the dragon.

Spewing fire that blackened a wide swath of grass, Mellisande lunged forward. Her long neck stretched and snaked, jaws opening over razor-sharp teeth. The Warlord dropped and rolled between her clawed feet, leaping into the air as he slashed upward at the exposed belly with the knife. A gash followed the blade, black blood steaming onto the earth, pouring over his naked arm.

A gasp rose from the crowd as the arm dropped limp and the knife fell to the earth. The Warlord bent and picked it up with his left hand. Bellowing, the dragon twisted into a circle, reaching for him, her head weaving from side to side.

Another gout of flame, a roar of rage and pain as again the knife drew blood. The dragon's neck bent into a deep curve, bringing her head low to peer between front legs as wide as tree trunks.

The Warlord threw the knife, end over end on a direct trajectory toward one of the enormous eyes. But already the head was moving and the blade struck against the skull, inflicting nothing more than a shallow cut before bouncing off and to the side. He was undefended now—there was no way he could reach the blade.

Vivian wanted to close her eyes and shut out the inevitable outcome. What had happened to Esme was bad enough; she didn't think she could bear to see Zee ripped apart before her eyes. The voices surged in her head, but she couldn't make out words—they were dulled by the silver bracelets.

The dragon lunged forward, flaming. The Warlord dived to the left just ahead of the gaping jaws, but the flames caught his breeches and he rolled in the grass, extinguishing the fire. For an agonizing moment he lay still. Then he rolled onto hands and knees, got one foot under him, and staggered upright, swaying.

Vivian had to do something, take some action to help him. She slipped off the bracelets. At once, a deeper awareness flooded in. The power of the stone at her back. The excitement and fear of each separate person in the crowd. Above all, the consciousness of the dragon—the pain of her wounds, her long, deep anger, and behind everything a yearning beyond words for the clear cold mountain air and empty sky.

Free me, Mellisande said into her mind.

The dragon swung her head low for the killing blow. *Free me or he will die, and you after him.*

Vivian flung herself against her chains, shouting, "Break the binding!" She could scarcely hear herself above the roar of the crowd and screamed the words again, tearing her throat with the effort to make him hear.

The Warlord leaped up from the earth, both arms raised above his head, and caught his fingers in the bindings that held the wings. Clinging with his left hand, he fumbled at the silver harness with the burned fingers of his right. Mellisande reared upward onto her back legs, the man dangling high above the earth.

His hold on the silver slipped, and his body lurched and swung.

The crowd went silent.

And then the Warlord plummeted earthward, lost to sight when he struck the ground between spiked claws. Behind him fell the silver mesh, striking out sparks of light.

The great wings of the dragon expanded twenty feet into the air.

Withdrawing as one body from the sudden menace in the ring, the crowd shrieked in terror.

No longer slow or cumbersome, with one flap of her wings Mellisande lifted into the air and circled the stadium. Then she dove, blasting flame as she flew low over the crowd. A pall of smoke rose, stinking of brimstone and burning flesh.

Screaming, the crowd stampeded in all directions—tripping over each other, trampling the fallen and leaving them where they lay.

Mellisande flapped harder, driving her heavy body high above the stadium in a smooth circle. Then she spiraled downward to land, unexpectedly graceful, in the grassy field. Close up, lighted by the sun, the dragon's scales were not black but dark purple, veined with green and gold, more beautiful and rich than any gem Vivian had ever seen.

Mellisande lowered her head, turning it to one side so she could look directly at Vivian out of one huge eye.

She is coming, the dragon's voice spoke into her mind. *You must kill me now.*

What? Why? You are free to go back to your mountains, to fly with the stars.

It is fated. You must kill me.

Vivian tried to back away, but the stone at her back blocked her. She shook her head in denial.

This is the only way.

I have no weapon. I wouldn't know how to begin to—

Slay the dragon? You must change, Little One. I have lived too long—it would be a gift. Quickly. She comes.

Vivian's eyes flickered away to the mass exodus out of the stadium, a stream of humanity trampling the fallen, some few shielding their loved ones or trying to drag them to safety. The priest had vanished. Somewhere in the midst of that crush of bodies and feet, the Warlord lay where he had fallen. Vivian tried not to picture his trampled, battered body.

Right through the center of the crowd, against the flow, came Jehenna. Not stalking with her usual proud gait, but running, a wicked-looking blade in her right hand, black, carved from stone. She used it like a machete to clear a path, felling anyone who didn't get out of her way. Her lips moved as though she were shouting, but the noise of the crowd drowned her out. At her heels ran Gareth.

As she approached, Vivian finally understood the words. "Mellisande! Do not kill her. I have need of her yet!"

Now, the dragon said. *Before the chance is lost forever.*

Still, Vivian stood, stupid and dull. Jehenna slowed as she approached and placed a hand on the dragon's front leg, possessive. "Mellisande. Hold."

Gareth stood a little back, and behind. No time for more than a glimpse to see a green fire of desire burning in his eyes.

"Dreamshifter," Jehenna panted. "An amusing little spectacle you and your Warlord arranged. Pointless, but amusing. Did it please you to watch him die?"

Vivian felt her blood heating, rage burning hot in her belly. She bit her tongue and did not answer.

Jehenna's eyes narrowed, scanning Vivian's bare wrists. Her nostrils flared. "Who freed you?"

Vivian held her silence, kept her eyes from flicking toward Gareth. She owed him that much. It seemed to her that there was fear in the hazel eyes, along with a wild desperation. "I thought you wanted me dead."

"Pah." The Sorceress spit on the ground at her feet and then flung the stone key down to lie in the muck. "This key is not the one; it doesn't work. He tricked me, yet again. And until the one is found, I need you alive. You and your mother. Mellisande, go back to your den."

The dragon, no longer bound by silver, didn't move.

Power surged into Vivian from the rock at her back. Voices filled her head. The rage in her belly flared, burning, heating her blood. Her skin began to itch and stretch.

Smells burgeoned into color. Mellisande appeared with a breathtaking clarity—every scale a prism, emitting a vibration not felt before. Off in the distance Vivian perceived other systems of vibration, other beings of wings and light and fire. Each of them responding to this awakening. Each altering the path of flight to fly in her direction.

The chains snapped as her body grew too large and powerful for the links to hold. Jehenna appeared far away and oh so small.

Mellisande clapped vermillion wings together over her back—once, twice, three times—a thunderclap of sound that rolled through the stadium. A challenge.

You must kill me.

No.

Swift as thought, Mellisande struck, her teeth raking a line of fire down Vivian's neck. Acting on instinct, she struck back, slinging her head toward the dragon, her own neck grown long and powerful.

The blow left a trail of black down her opponent's shoulder. Mellisande roared with pain, shifting her weight to relieve pressure from the damaged limb. Awkward and ponderous, Vivian dragged her unfamiliar body to the right, slowed by the need to move four feet at once, distracted by the unexpected weight of her tail.

Mellisande's teeth tore into her side.

With the onslaught of pain, Vivian was seized by a battle frenzy, a thirst for the dark blood of her foe.

Beating her wings, Mellisande thrust her body upward, taking all the weight on her back legs. Front claws extended, she spurted flame from her open mouth with a blast of heat that seared Vivian's eyeballs, half-blinding her.

Heat roiled in her belly in response; her body became a furnace, building to an agony of pressure that had to be released. Taking aim, she spat out a gout of fire that enveloped the other dragon's head in flame.

Mellisande's body recoiled, twisted, the scales of head and neck blackened. Her wings beat an uneven rhythm, rapid and desperate, lifting into the sky. Vivian followed, buffeting her foe with her wings, engulfing her with blasts of fire, driving her higher and higher.

The wounded dragon breathed hard, her wings laboring. Black blood ran from her wounds. Vivian rolled onto her back and raked the underside of the pale belly above her with all of her talons.

Mellisande twisted away, evading, but she was slow and Vivian was strong. She repeated the maneuver, drawing her talons through the wounds she'd already made, through skin and muscle and deep into the belly. Waiting her chance, she watched Mellisande blunder through the air like a bat in daylight. Opportunity presented, and Vivian darted in, jaws wide, and crunched down at the base of one wing, biting, tearing. The damaged wing collapsed, twitched, refused to stroke. The other wing continued flapping, throwing the gigantic body into a lopsided spiral. For a moment it hung in the sky, a huge whirligig, moving neither up nor down but careening in a drunken spin. And then the good wing tucked into the body, blackened and distorted and broken, and Mellisande tumbled and spun like a giant meteor toward the earth. Her body struck with a concussion that shook the stadium. Dust billowed up amid smoke and a sudden burst of flame.

Vivian swooped downward to land on the body of her fallen foe.

Thirty

⚜

The apocalypse began without warning.

Zee was on his feet before his eyes were open. The chamber shook in the grip of a giant spasm. Chunks of stone rained down from the high carven ceiling and shattered on the stone below. The earth groaned and creaked. A crevice opened in front of his feet.

Pressing his body back against the wall to avoid the falling debris and keep his balance, Zee waited for the earthquake to settle.

It didn't.

A chunk of stone the size of a small car plummeted down onto the dais in the center of the chamber with a deafening crash, sending a cloud of dust and debris into the air that set him coughing.

And then the locked door burst open and a man dashed through it, rending long crimson robes and wailing, "The dragon is dead. The end of all things is at hand!" He scrambled up the stone steps to the ruined altar, a flaming torch in one hand, a long staff in the other.

The earth shook with new intensity, flinging Zee sideways. With both hands pressed against the still-solid wall at his back, he kept his feet, but the man on the stairs stumbled and fell. The staff rolled away from him, clattering down the stairs, but he managed to hold on to the torch.

Zee edged toward the open door.

The man clambered up the rest of the stairs on hands and knees, hampered by his long scarlet robe and the torch he continued to clutch in one hand. He picked his way to the top of the fallen rubble, spread his arms wide in a gesture of invocation, then held the torch to the flowing sleeve of his robe. The fabric combusted, instantly turning him into a pillar of flame. The earth shook once more, and a wide crack opened in the stone floor. The priest dove, flaming and screaming, down into the chasm.

Zee reached the door. He was through, scrambling up a steep stone staircase that gaped and cracked beneath his feet. Chunks of stone fell around him. Flying shards struck his face, stinging, drawing blood. The step directly beneath his feet cracked and fell away. A sickening moment of nothingness, and then his upflung hands caught on the step above. He clung there by his fingers, refusing to fall. Hope drove him on and he found the strength to swing himself up to safety.

Just a few more steps. Almost there. And then a dead end—a solid obstruction at the top of the stairs.

It must be a door, but there was no handle and it was locked, or blocked. Beneath him, what was left of the staircase swayed like a rope ladder in the wind. Steps cracked and broke in chain reaction, stone fragments bouncing and rattling into the killing drop. Zee pressed his back against the wall as though he could stick to it, like Velcro, eyes scanning for a way out, one last escape.

As the step beneath him broke in three places, he unwrapped the thing that George had given him, because he couldn't see any way that this was not the end. Then, falling, he whispered one last word.

"Vivian."

Thirty-one

⚜

Disoriented and cold, save for the heat burning up through the soles of her naked feet, Vivian stood in her own human form atop a massive wreck of scales and broken wings. She was naked, but it didn't seem to matter.

Grief choked her. No victory, this.

The Warlord dead. Mellisande slain, and for what? She, Vivian, had allowed herself to turn into a dragon, and in that form had killed not Jehenna, not her true enemy, but instead this pitiful creature long enslaved in the dark and so newly freed.

From somewhere below, a shriek of rage and grief reached her ears, distant and nearly irrelevant.

Through a heavy torpor that enveloped both limbs and brain, Vivian walked over the dead dragon's side, careful not to cut her feet on the sharp edges of scales, and looked down to see Jehenna kneeling in the blackened grass, both hands on Mellisande's head as though she could somehow restore life with her touch.

Something was wrong about those hands. Bony, blue veined, the skin spotted with age. The face that had been young and so dangerously beautiful was withered and wrinkled; the hair hung lank and gray over a bent and crooked spine.

Jehenna looked up at Vivian and shrieked, "Look what you have done!"

Words were still far away, and Vivian could only stare as Jehenna held out her hands, turned them one way and then the other, and shrieked again, "Look what you have done!"

The Sorceress got to her feet and hobbled up the dead dragon's neck, reaching out with bony fingers to scratch at Vivian's face.

"You've grown old," Vivian said in wonder. "And weak."

An easy thing now to trap those wrists, thin and frail, and hold Jehenna off like a fractious child. To shove her backward and away. The Sorceress stumbled, collapsed to her hands and knees. Clumps of hair drifted from her scalp. A dry racking cough shook her, and she spat teeth out into the palm of her hand.

"You've killed me," she gasped. "So close to the Forever, and now it's lost, all lost."

A deep rumbling groan rose out of the depths beneath them, and the earth shook. Vivian kept her feet with difficulty. Jehenna fell onto her belly and began to slide backward over the sharp-edged scales, feet first, hands scrabbling for a hold. When she hit the ground she rolled, labored onto her hands and knees, remaining crouched in the black ashes. Her face was a grinning skull, wrinkled skin stretched over bone, gums toothless, her eyes filming with the white of cataracts. The royal robes hung loose and shredded over a skeletal frame. Her hands bled, cut by dragon scales during the long slide down.

Vivian walked carefully across the swell of Mellisande's belly, down the slope of the shoulder and onto the neck, and from there down onto the ground. She looked around for Gareth, but he seemed to have vanished.

"You were connected to Mellisande somehow. Tell me." She used the Voice, saw Jehenna stiffen against it, then shrug and acquiesce.

"An ancient blood rite. We share a death, Mellisande and I." Her mouth stretched into a toothless grin. "And Surmise. You have killed everybody in this kingdom."

The earth rumbled and shook. A section of the stadium wall cracked and collapsed into the arena with a crash and rattle of cascading fragments of stone. The seats warped and buckled as though they had grown liquid, then began to break under the stress, sharp retorts ringing out like machine-gun fire.

The few remaining people screamed and struggled toward the stairs. Some of the wounded crawled on their bellies. Vivian had been staring blankly into the chaos for several minutes before she noticed the bloody figure swaying on its feet at the center of the field. It lurched toward her, dragging its right leg. One arm hung limp. The body was blackened with dragon fire, the face covered in blood. It seemed impossible that he should be moving, but moving he was, one slow step after another. He wavered and almost fell, then caught himself and took another step.

The Warlord.

Vivian realized she was stretching her arms out toward him, uselessly, willing him on. She got her feet moving in his direction, saw his face change and heard his warning shout. "Behind you!"

Vivian spun to see Jehenna still crouched, but with the stone knife clutched in her hand. Her arm was drawn back, her face twisted with malice.

"It is too late for me, now, Dreamshifter. Even if you had the key I would be dead before we reached the Way. If I must die, so must you."

Vivian thought to run, but the dead dragon blocked her. Legs as big as tree trunks fenced her in on either side. She could scrabble up and over, but it would take too long.

The knife left Jehenna's hand in a slow and lethal arc.

All the world slowed.

Vivian had more than enough time to watch the blade fly arrow-straight toward her heart, but not enough time to duck. Her scream stuck in her throat.

And then, with an impossible leap that carried him into the air, arms spread wide, the Warlord flung his broken body between her and the knife.

A small, wet sound as the blade entered his body. A grunt as he struck the earth.

Time returned to normal and he lay at Vivian's feet, the hilt protruding from his chest.

With a wordless wail of grief and denial, Vivian sank to her knees by his side, eyes locked on his, so beautiful still in a face burned black by dragon fire. His lips moved, as if to speak, but he only sighed and did not breathe again.

Vivian placed both hands on his face, gentle on the damaged skin. Even as her medical training kicked in, as she listened for breath, felt for a pulse, denial ran through her, like a litany of grief.

This is the part of the story where the fallen hero appears to be dead, but really isn't. This is the part where he looks at the heroine and proclaims his love for her at last, where she saves him from the wound that is not quite fatal. This is the part where unsuspecting magical powers kick in and the hero is snatched from the jaws of death.

But he lay as he had fallen and did not move. The strong heart no longer beat. No breath moved in and out of his lungs. His open eyes stared straight upward at the sun.

The power that Vivian had, to open and close doors, to shift into a dragon, could do nothing to save him.

Jehenna's cackling laughter coiled around her like bitter, choking smoke. "Enjoy your life, little one. May it be long, and lonely."

Vivian withdrew the knife from the Warlord's chest. Closed his eyes. Stroked the blood-matted hair back from his burned forehead.

"It all ends with me," Jehenna said. "You are the Dreamshifter. Walk through one of your doors, and live to remember that you killed thousands in order to get to me."

Vivian felt like she was choking. She shook her head, unable to find her voice.

"Think, little girl. Surmise is my weaving. It dies with me. And with it, every single soul who has found their way here."

Her heart felt flat and cold inside her chest. A small thing, beating out the rhythm of a small life.

Jehenna's voice was faint, little more than a breath of wind. "You amuse me. Deny as you will; you will see the truth." She was still laughing when her body began to disintegrate. Feet first, fraying into particles of dust so that she fell to her knees. And all the while the laughter spewed from her throat until she had no throat to laugh with, and even then her mouth remained open in soundless, evil mirth, her white-filmed eyes bulging in a face coming apart at the seams.

And then it was over, a gust of wind scattering a heap of dust across the stadium floor. A new shock wave, greater than the last, shook the arena, throwing Vivian to the ground. Another section of the wall caved in. Seats dissolved into a cloud of dust. Voices screamed.

As Vivian stared, numb with horror and grief, half of the field simply vanished.

It wasn't due to something comprehensible like a giant sinkhole or a crater sucking matter down into the earth. Instead, grass, soil, and a huge section of the restraining wall disappeared. No sound, no fury. No wind rushing into the vacuum.

Just Nothing.

Vivian shook her head and blinked, attempting to grasp the concept of matter that did not follow the laws of physics. But dreams were another story, and Surmise had been built Between. All of the people of Surmise would not only die, they would just Not Be.

She bent to kiss the Warlord's lips, already cold, soulless, and then the lips vanished along with everything else.

One heartbeat.

Then nothing.

no air
  no sound
  no light
  no dark
  no body.

A faint memory of arms and legs, hands and feet. An echo of breath and heartbeat, cold and warmth, pleasure and pain.

All that existed now was mind and spirit. Memories. Ideas.

And emotions. A deep and encompassing regret. Grief. Despair. So many dead because of her failures, and now she was beyond hope of putting things right.

Fear came next. An eternity of existence only as consciousness. Memories and thoughts—guilt, loss, regret— and nothing else. No future. No escape. Only the unquiet mind, forever and ever and always, and it was amazing how sharp the pain of this could be.

And then even the pain began to fade, the last thing, slipping away no matter how she tried to hold on.

An odd tug, a little jerk, and . . .

Vivian lay flat on her back. Something soft was beneath her, and the scent of fresh grass and flowers filled her nostrils. Opening her eyes she saw, high and far away, three dragons dancing on the wind.

She pushed herself up on her elbows and her head throbbed with the change of position, a familiar and oddly comforting thing in a world altered beyond comprehension.

Across a wide field of grass and flowers towered a pure-white castle, as unlike Surmise as a castle could ever be. Slender turrets sprang upward toward the sky, graceful and light.

No fallen Warlord lay at her feet. No dead dragon, no little heap of ashes.

An emptiness of grief and loss took her breath and doubled her over with both arms clasped around her belly. Alone in all the worlds.

Tears would have been a mercy, but her eyes were dry and there was no way to ease the relentless pain at her center. Unless she were to change, to fly with the dragons.

Not now, not yet. She still had work to do. Massive failure on her part didn't justify sitting around bemoaning her fate. Doors still stood open into Wakeworld, dragons running loose. Her mother and the Prince were still trapped. She needed to find the dreams that Jehenna had stolen. Recover the key.

Something soft brushed against her arm. She jerked away, startled, turning to see the most penguiny-looking penguin she had ever seen. Too big for an Adélie, too small for a King, with a breast a little too white and a beak a little too yellow and obsidian eyes that glittered with unnatural intelligence.

"Poe?"

The penguin squawked and flopped into her lap.

She flung her arms around him, pressed her cheek against his head, even as she murmured, "You're not real, you can't be." Her hand went to the chain at her throat and found the pendant. Not a dream, then. Still somewhere in the vastness of Between.

One tear escaped her and fell on the penguin's head, a small crystal drop repelled by waterproof feathers, gleaming diamond bright in the sun. Poe was dead, and this couldn't really be him.

A line of crimson feathers on his white breast caught her attention. She ran her fingers over them, feeling a scar marring the skin beneath. There was another scar, smaller, on his back.

"It can't be," she whispered.

Poe *quawrked*, then hopped down and waddled off to explore.

Following him with her eyes, Vivian noticed for the first time the people clustered across the meadow in groups of two and three. Something about their behavior was—not wrong, exactly, but different. Old people and young, disheveled and ragged, some of them bloodstained, all speaking in hushed voices and looking around them as if waiting for something. A woman sobbed softly against the shoulder of a man whose own shoulders were shaking, his face buried in her matted hair. Children stood or sat in the grass, eyes vivid and taking in everything, but too serious, too quiet.

Refugees, Vivian thought. Unsure what is expected of them, waiting for instruction. One of the faces looked familiar, and then another. Prisoners, faces she had last seen blank and aimless in the dungeons.

As she scanned the scene again, things made more sense. Where there was now this field of grass and flowers, there had once been a stadium. The castle had changed in form but stood in the same relative location. This was still Surmise, only drastically changed.

A guard stood at a cautious distance, trying to maintain his dignity while evading Poe's investigation of his bootlaces. When her eyes fell on him, he sank to his knees and bowed his forehead to the grass. "My Lady, I meant no insolence by standing in your presence . . ."

"Get up," she said.

"Yes, My Lady." He got to his feet but kept his eyes averted. A muscle bunched and twitched in his jaw. As she searched for words to put him at ease, he removed his belt and sword and laid them in the grass before pulling his tunic off over his head.

Vivian took a step backward, thinking he had lost his sanity. "You need to put your clothes back on."

His face turned ashen, but his jaw tightened stubbornly. Keeping his eyes on the ground, he held the tunic out toward her in a trembling hand. "My Lady, you are naked."

A profound act of courage, she realized, as she took the garment from his hands. It was roughly woven and smelled of sweat, but she pulled it on, accepting both gift and giver. As far as she knew, the man had risked his life in concern for her comfort. She could trust him.

"Thank you," she said. "Can you tell me what happened just now?"

He blinked rapidly, then opened and closed his mouth before answering, "Forgive me, My Lady, but surely you are the one who knows the answer to that question."

"Humor me."

Again the rapid blinking. He swallowed hard. "Well—Surmise was here, and then it wasn't, My Lady. After you destroyed the dragon and the Queen." If possible, he paled even further, dropping back to his knees. "Of course, she is—was—not the Queen. You are, My Queen, I meant to say. Please forgive me, My Queen, it all happened so suddenly, I lost track of the protocols."

"Don't be ridiculous. I'm not a queen, and I mean to find Prince Landon and put him in charge straightaway. Seriously—get up. No more bowing to me."

Again he scrambled to his feet. He stood a little straighter, shoulders square, and met her eyes.

Vivian managed a brief smile. "You served the Warlord—I remember. Tell me your name."

"Tellar, My Lady."

"All right, Tellar. I owe the Warlord a debt. You have my word that I mean no harm to you. Now—take me to the Chancellor."

"I—don't know where to look for him, My Lady. The castle is gone."

The man had a point. "All right, then. Do a couple of things for me, will you? Find some of the men you trust. Have them hunt for the Chancellor, and find out what has happened to all of the prisoners. Make sure nobody is trapped in the dungeons, all right? And have your men keep their eyes out for an object—this size—carved from black stone."

His face brightened, hope flaring in his eyes. A quick salute of genuine respect, and he headed off with a steady, measured tread.

Vivian turned her back to him. She drew a deep breath, and then another. Grounded herself, and then thought her way through a tangle of doors and dreams without moving her body at all. When at last she found the door she sought, it opened at her command.

In an empty white room, the Prince sat in the corner, stroking Isobel's hair. She lay motionless with her head in his lap, eyes closed, her face smooth and unlined, flushed a little in sleep. Vivian had never seen her look so serene. Landon did not look up, did not stop stroking Isobel's hair.

"Jehenna is dead. You need to come out here and be the King," Vivian said. "Do you hear me, Landon? You're needed."

His eyes turned toward the door. He saw her but didn't move, and Vivian remembered that he couldn't hear her, that there was no sound in that chamber.

Isobel stirred and opened her eyes. For a moment they were confused, far away, and then they cleared and focused. She smiled, then sat up and turned to Landon. Placing a hand on his cheek, she looked long into his eyes, and at last he nodded. He kissed her, very gently, and the two of them got up and walked to the door, hand in hand. Both hesitated, then stepped through the doorway together.

"You've killed Jehenna," Isobel said. It was a calm statement of fact without a hint of question.

Vivian nodded. "And Mellisande."

"Poor old dragon," Isobel said. "But you couldn't have killed Jehenna if you hadn't."

"You knew?"

"I remember—bits. The ceremony, when I was a child. She made me watch. Made me drink—" Her face twisted.

Landon put an arm around her shoulder, drew her against him, a protective gesture. As though the two of them were under threat. His eyes were bleak, his face drawn.

Vivian looked at him, bewildered, and then began to understand. Another grief, another loss.

"I didn't really kill Jehenna," she said, hearing her own voice speak what she didn't want to acknowledge. "After the dragon died, she just—disintegrated."

Isobel nodded. Vivian thought already her mother's face looked older, that there were lines under her eyes that hadn't been there a moment ago. Threads of silver in her dark hair.

"I'm over a hundred years old, darling. She bound me

to Mellisande's life, as well. My age will catch up with me now."

"We could stay in the room of nothingness," Landon said. "There is no time there."

Isobel smiled at him, shook her head. "No, my love. All my life I have been locked up one way or another. I'm free—Mellisande has given me back my sanity. And the people of Surmise need you."

Vivian couldn't catch her breath. She would watch these two age and die, just when she had found them. The mother she had never truly known. This man she believed might be her father. They needed time to be together. It was one more wrong that Jehenna had done, another evil.

And one that maybe didn't need to be.

"Wait," Vivian said. "I have an idea. There are other places outside time. Like Landon's room in the dungeon. I know a certain fountain . . ."

Isobel's face brightened. "We couldn't stay there always, but it would slow the process."

"Are you certain?" Landon asked her.

She smiled. "We need to live, Landon, not just exist. And the kingdom has suffered enough."

Landon drew her into his arms and buried his face in her hair. "My love."

"Stay here until it's set," Vivian said. "I'll come back for you."

Isobel smiled, and the two of them stepped back across a threshold no longer spitting green fire. Vivian left the door open, that they should never be imprisoned again.

For a moment she found herself disoriented and lost, unable to remember how to get back through the maze. But then she felt the faint tug, the tide of dream that always pulled toward Surmise. Even as she followed this, she added it to her list of things she needed to put right. Nobody lost in dream should be drawn into Surmise unless that was where they wanted to be.

Standing again in the field of flowers, she blinked,

grounding herself with her bare feet planted in the grass and one hand on the pendant. Poe presented himself, standing at military attention with his best penguin stare. Time had passed. The sun hung low on the horizon.

Tellar stood waiting. When her gaze turned to him, he stepped forward and saluted sharply. No more bowing and cowering. He spoke with confidence.

"We have searched the castle, My Lady. No sign of the Chancellor. But we found this where his chambers should have been." He held in his hands a box, big enough for secrets, small enough to carry with you. Carved on the lid, two dragons intertwined.

Vivian took it from his hands, opened it.

It was empty.

"My Lady?"

She realized she had been staring at the empty box for far too long. Well. Time was one thing she had plenty of. She would find Gareth; she would find the dreamspheres.

"You found nothing else in his chambers?" she asked, thinking of the key. Perhaps it had simply vanished with the old Surmise, but she didn't think it could be that simple. She remembered the glow in Gareth's eyes and that he had been standing behind Jehenna when she threw the key to the ground.

"Nothing, My Lady."

"All right. And are there prisoners in the dungeons still?"

"The dungeons are missing, My Lady. We can find no doors, no tunnels, no trace of anything leading below the earth, either here or in the castle."

Vivian blinked. "And the prisoners?"

His jaw hardened. "They were all standing about in the field. We've released them, My Lady. Told them they were free to go wherever they please."

Watching him, she saw that he feared her anger, had anticipated it, but had done this thing anyway.

Which pleased her immensely. "One thing wrong with that plan, Tellar. They will have nowhere to go. Make sure they are all safe in the castle by dark. Fed, bathed, and clothed."

"Yes, My Lady. There's one other thing."

"Yes?"

He shuffled his feet and she saw his jaw tighten again. Still, he met her eyes and spoke in a clear and steady voice. "We discovered a man among the prisoners . . ." His eyes flickered away. "He is . . ." Again he broke off. "Perhaps you should just see him, My Lady?"

"Fine. Where is he?"

"We've been watching him." He raised his arm in a beckoning gesture, and a small group across the meadow began to move in Vivian's direction with purpose and military precision. Chain mail clinked. A tall man walked at the center, not in step with the rest. Instead of chain mail and breeches he wore blue jeans and a T-shirt. Long dark hair fell to his shoulders. His face was bloodstained, but familiar.

Vivian was on her feet and running before they'd taken more than a few steps. Over the grass, never feeling the stones on her bare feet, focused on one goal and one only. The guards parted before she collided with them, and she flung herself against Zee's broad chest. His arms circled her, tight, tight, so that she could barely catch her breath. She could hear his heart beating, feel his cheek pressed against her hair.

"Vivian," he gasped. "Thank God."

Behind her, somebody cleared his throat. "My Lady, I'm not sure this is wise. We all watched the Warlord die. This appearance of a double can mean nothing good—"

Vivian looked back up at Zee and her heart lurched. "You're hurt." The right side of his face was caked with dried blood; his hair was matted, his clothes torn. But his eyes were the same clear agate, light filled, and his lips curved into a crooked smile, half mischief.

"Bear attack," he said. "Not quite the same scope as a dragon, but it was a big bear."

"Your wounds need attention."

"My Lady—"

"What?" She whirled around to face the speaker, annoyed now. One look at the expression on her face and every one of the guards dropped into a deep obeisance.

Vivian took a deep breath, forced herself to speak calmly. "I am not going to hurt anybody, and you don't have to bow. Get up; tell me what you need to say."

"My Lady, he had this on him."

Tellar held out a crystal sphere. It was larger than the others, the size of a golf ball, swirling with a play of color and emitting an audible vibration. Vivian touched the shining thing with the tip of one finger. Then she looked up at the changed landscape and began to understand.

"Where did you get this?"

"George left it. With a note that said, 'Open only at the end.'"

"I think—it's like he created his own version of Surmise. But I don't understand how that is possible with the intersection of all of the other dreams . . ."

"I wasn't sure when the end would be. So I waited. And then I thought I was too late." His voice was raw, his breath uneven. He didn't take his eyes from hers, those beautiful eyes.

She swallowed hard, steeling herself against another loss, the hardest of them all. "Zee . . . Things have happened."

"I can see that." His lips quirked in a half smile, but his eyes burned, and the way they looked at her, the way he breathed—

Hope, that most dangerous of emotions, flared within her as his hand, strong and warm, closed around hers. She pushed the hope away, remembering a thirst for blood, an enormous clumsy body, all scales and claws and wings.

"You don't know what I have become."

"Tell me."

She shuddered. "A thing. Part sorceress, part Dreamshifter. Part dragon."

"You're still Vivian."

The words undid her fragile control and she buried her

face in her hands to hide the rush of tears. The Warlord had named her so when she was first transforming into the dragon, had called her back from the edge with a kiss.

Zee cupped her chin in both hands and turned her face up to his. "I know what you are, Vivian Maylor. A closer of doors, a dreamer of dreams. And yes, a dragon shifter. I knew before I met you. I've been there with you, in every Dreamworld . . ."

"Don't," she said, placing one hand over his lips. "I can't go back, Zee. I can't be with you . . ."

He kissed her palm and moved her hand so that it rested against his chest, over his heart. "My sword and my soul belong to the Dreamshifter, and my heart was yours before I met you. Where else should I be, if not beside you?"

"But, Zee—"

"You have been the focus of my life. Would you truly send me away?"

And she steeled herself, then, to do what must be done. Put aside the possibility of joy. Took a step back and away from him and made her voice ring clear and certain, so there would be no mistake. "I am not free to follow my heart," she said, watching the light fade from his eyes. "I must find the key and destroy it. Recover the spheres and restore the balance between Dreamworld and Wakeworld."

Zee dropped to his knees at her feet. "Then permit me to go with you. To protect, to serve."

Looking down into his upturned face, Vivian knew two things.

First, that granting this request would bring great heartache to them both. And second, that this was the one thing she could not deny him.

They came through the doorway onto Finger Beach just as the sun was setting. All the sky to the west burned red, and the river reflected it back. A dead bear lay not far away, white fur stained black with drying blood, twice as big as a grizzly.

Vivian held her breath, letting it out in a slow sigh. "You killed that?"

"It was a near thing."

His ravaged face was proof enough of that. He was already changed, Vivian saw with some grief. More warrior than artist. Scarred and hardened by what he had been through, and they were only at the beginning of this journey.

Still, he laughed with pure glee as Poe waddled across the beach and flung himself headfirst into the river and began to play.

Above, somewhere in the sky, a dragon flew. Vivian couldn't see him, but she could feel his thoughts like a distant wordless hum. Another task, to coax the creature back through the doorway and into the Between, away from this world where he did not belong.

"Where will we go?" Zee asked. "I'm wanted—the cops will pick me up on sight."

"The cabin, I think. There is a room there—"

"I know."

"How—"

He grinned. "A long story, but we will have time enough for tales. Now we should go, before the authorities show up. I drove his van here—still up in the parking lot, I'd guess. Shall we?"

Vivian looked at the hand he held out to her—the hand of a warrior, cuticles still stained with paint, defining all the contradictions of who this man was and could be. This much, at least, was permitted. She put her own hand in his, so small in comparison, and let him lead her away from the beach toward whatever would come next.

ABOUT THE AUTHOR

Kerry Schafer lives in the town of Colville, Washington, with her family, which includes two cats, a rescue fish, and a preternaturally large black dog. A self-styled perpetual student, she earned an RN from Royal Alexandra Hospital in Edmonton, Alberta; an Honours BA in English from York University in Toronto, Ontario; and an M.Ed. in counseling psychology from Washington State University. Visit her online at www.kerryschafer.com.

*A romantic urban fantasy novella set
in the world of Kate Daniels!*

From *New York Times* Bestselling Author
ILONA ANDREWS

MAGIC DREAMS
A companion novella to *Gunmetal Magic*

Shapeshifting tigress Dali Harimau finds herself
in deep waters when she must challenge a dark
being to a battle of wits—or risk losing the man
for whom she secretly longs.

Magic Dreams previously appeared
in the anthology *Hexed*
and is now available as an eSpecial.

✦

facebook.com/Ilona.Andrews
facebook.com/ProjectParanormalBooks
penguin.com

M1100T0412